SUMMER ACCOMMODATIONS

A Novel

SIDNEY HART

Copyright © 2005 by Sidney Hart

ISBN: 0-9764340-0-8

LCCN: 2004116664

Cover photo by Sidney Hart

Printed in the United States of America

For Madeline Jared and Alexandra

Author's Note

I have been asked if this book is a memoir or a work of fiction. Most writers will tell you they use elements of their lives and experience to create their stories and characters. Saul Bellow, Philip Roth, John Updike and John Irving, for example, have had to address this question frequently, Mr. Roth endlessly.

This book is primarily a work of fiction. It conflates the six summers of my experiences working and living in a variety of resort settings into a single summer. If you are left wondering what becomes of certain characters it is because the lack of resolution of individual stories is a phenomenon of that summer experience. One arrives at a hotel and meets other staff members who will share living quarters and work space. Gradually owners, social staff, tennis pros, lifeguards, bellhops and even housekeepers become part of your world. And then the guests come and go. Some relationships are intensely positive, some unhappily negative, but almost all of them end with the same parting words: "Have a good life."

This interruption of the relationship to others is much more common in real life than in the neatly resolved plots of a fictionalized world. It is also very like the experience of the practice of psychiatry; people come for assistance, reveal the intimate details of their personal lives and emotions, and then leave, their life stories still unfinished. Such is life as it is actually lived.

Prologue

In those days the bumper stickers read "Visit Howe Caverns" or "Santa's Workshop," not—"Shit Happens." Back then men wore jackets and ties to baseball games and hats almost everywhere; in recollection it seems an idyllic time. The Korean War had ended, Joseph Stalin was dead and the other evil Joe, Senator McCarthy, was in disrepute. Jonas Salk had devised a polio vaccine, air raid drills had become a thing of the past, America's economy was booming and economic growth seemed as natural and good for us as spring water. We were filled with excitement and hope about the future. We were in love with Lucy and mesmerized by the images the skeletal forest of rooftop antennae plucked from the sky and deposited in our living rooms—family rooms didn't exist in the Bronx. There was a parking space available curbside for your family's two-toned, whitewall tired, chrome encrusted American car. There were no Japanese cars and "Made in Japan" was a euphemism for "cheap junk." In that summer of 1956 Ike was in the White House, the Dodgers were in Brooklyn, Marilyn Monroe was in Hollywood, and I was in the Catskills.

The Catskills. The worn and tired hills of lower New York State west of the Hudson, south of Albany, a few meager hours from the city that never sleeps and the shores where most of Europe's wretched refuse yearning to be free washed up in hopeful, frightened bewilderment. It was for them that these unmajestic hills became "the mountains," the "Jewish Alps." By the time I arrived, most of those wandering Jews had died and their offspring peopled the resorts. And many of the people I worked with in that hotel dining room, the children of the immigrants' children, swore they would as soon have returned to the ghettos of Europe as register as guests in these palaces of excess and ethnic insularity. In our arrogance we believed ourselves better than all of them, the guests, the owners, the regular staff. Our embarrassment at their coarseness, their gluttony, their buffoonery, their garish taste in clothes was transmuted into mocking humor amongst our selves and well disguised condescension toward the others. We could not assimilate into mainstream America fast enough and the money we would earn those summers in the mountains would buy our tickets of admission to the American dream.

Chapter One

I am the youngest of three brothers. My older brothers, Jerry and Steve, were born a year apart and I came along seven years later. This gap had been discussed with me in so many different ways by each of the four other members of my family I am convinced my birth was an accident or, to put it more bluntly, a mistake but I'm very glad to be here and bear my parents no resentment for their romantic folly. Steve took particular pleasure in taunting me with his "you are a mistake" interpretation but Jerry, in soft reassuring tones, would say Steve's jealousy of my father's affection for me made him unkind. That will give you a sense of how different they are, or were when I was growing up. While Jerry had a dreamy, kind, almost romantic nature, Steve was an edgy, street-smart fast talker who was always on the look out for an angle. My mother called him "an operator" but she said it with affection and a hint of admiration.

In my last year of high school as I was preparing my college applications, Steve sat me down to give me a lecture about life. I remember little of that talk, most of it being about girls and sex in a crude and smirking style, but one thing he said has always remained clear in my memory because it seems to have been proven true over and over again: "The good things in life you have to seek out and reach for; the shit will always find you."

That message was still fresh in my mind when I applied to the Hotel Braverman for a job that summer of 1956. I was just eighteen years old, younger than the usual age hired as dining room staff but, because my older brothers had been so popular and reliable, an exception had been made allowing me to work there. I had already been waiting tables for two years, one year in a summer camp, and one year in the outer Catskills, the German section of Fleischmanns New York, so I was in no way a novice; this was to be big time, borscht belt, dining room money; this was to be the golden opportunity to bring home the gold.

Arriving that first day at The Hotel Braverman, known simply as Braverman's, I was met by my headwaiter, Sammy, the man I was to work for. He was always just "Sammy" like a rock star with only one name. Being Sammy's busboy was to be an honor of a sort but, more important, it meant I was likely to make more money than any other busboy in the dining room and as much as some waiters set off in the rear corners near the windowless walls.

"Melvin!" he shouted in greeting while I stood right in front of him. He was an ebullient man of around fifty, trim and covered with hair, hair everywhere except on the top of his head; wiry, curly body hair peeking out of his ears, raining from his nose, creeping up his back to his neck, on every digit of every finger. "How's the boy? How're Jerry and Steve? How're your folks?" He didn't wait for my answers. "Come on, I'll show you to the waiters' quarters."

I knew where the waiters' quarters were because my parents had vacationed at the hotel part of every summer to be closer to my brothers when they worked there.

"So what are Jerry and Steve up to?" They were always referred to as Jerry and Steve, like Martin and Lewis or Abbott and Costello, and I was glad to be so much younger and to have an identity all to myself.

"Jerry is graduating medical school this month, and Steve has another year to go at NYU dental school." I was pretty sure Sammy knew this already, but I was a polite and accommodating boy.

"And you, Melvin, what are you going to be?"

"I'm just waiting to hear from the college I want to go to. First things first."

"Don't tell that to the guests at my station. They'll tip you better for wanting to be a doctor. Tell them you want to be a doctor like your brother Jerry because some of them will remember who he is and tip you just for being his brother."

We had passed most of the main hotel building and had reached the kitchen area in the rear. The smells that emanate from a resort kitchen are always recognizable if unidentifiable, the smell of something baking the prevailing odor, but always intermingled with that of other foods cooking.

"You'll be bunking with Ron Alter, a junior at City College, and Harlan Hawthorne, a senior at Harvard." Knowing Sammy, I assumed that Harlan Hawthorne was a comic invention meant to trap me. The notion that any Harvard man would be working in the Catskills was completely preposterous to me.

"Aren't you going to ask me anything about them?"

"What do you think I should know?" Having two older brothers had made me cagey and not easily led into traps.

"For Chrissakes Melvin, doesn't Harlan of Harvard pique your curiosity, stimulate your stilted imagination, engender interrogatories?"

"What's that smell, Sammy? Everywhere I've been where there's a large kitchen—camp, hotels—I smell that smell but I don't know what it is."

"Melvin, if you are going to work for me you are going to have to listen to me. I ask you a question about Harlan of Harvard and you ask me about smells?" His voice became loud from his confusion and frustration. I affected a well rehearsed look of contrition and muttered some self-effacing banalities. Sammy rejected my effort to reconcile with an impatient wave of dismissal signaling that I had missed my chance.

"Here we are," he said as we reached the long barracks-like waiters' quarters. "You're in room G." We entered through the screened door into a narrow corridor with just enough room to stretch out your arms from your sides.

"Single file," I said mordantly trying to ingratiate myself with Sammy, but he would have none of it. He was teaching me a lesson. I was to give him what he wanted when he wanted it, not on my timetable.

"You have to be in the dining room at five-thirty to eat and set up for dinner which is at seven. In the morning I expect you in at six. Breakfast is served from seven-fifteen until ten and then you have to be back in again at eleven-thirty. Some days you won't get to leave the dining room from the time you come on until three-thirty, but usually you're out by two, two-thirty." I must have looked sick because his manner softened and he said, very reassuringly, "Don't worry, we have a good time, it isn't all scut work."

When we came to room G Sammy knocked once and pushed the door open before his knock was answered.

"Thanks for coming," a sarcastic voice said from the lower level of a double decker bed. I couldn't see the speaker because he had pulled his sheet completely over his head.

"Alter, meet Melvin White, your new roommate. Where's Hawthorne?"

"Hello Mel," the voice said. Ron Alter had not moved a muscle. He lay flat on his back, his arms at his sides, the covering sheet pulled tight from his head to his toes, like an interred Egyptian king. Against the wall opposite the double decker was a single cot, its linens stretched tightly across the mattress, the blanket folded into a neat square and laid carefully at the foot of the bed.

"Nice to meet you," I said, and looking at Sammy I added "hope this is a good summer for us." Sammy looked away.

"Which is Harlan's bed?" Sammy demanded.

"The one that gets an A in geometry. Yours is up here on top Mel," Ron said, and his left hand came out from under the sheet and tapped the frame of the bunk above him.

Sammy sighed. "Where the hell is Hawthorne anyway?"

"Probably over at Heidi Braverman's getting laid."

"Everybody's a comedian, goddamn bunch of wise guys I have working for me."

"I thought I was working for me, Sammy, and Harlan is shtupping Heidi Braverman, take my word for it, it's no goddamn joke." With that Ron Alter pulled the sheet from his face and sat up in his bed. He was solidly built with muscular arms and a thick chest. His dirty blond hair was tightly curled and clung to his head like a wool watch cap. In his right hand was a

pair of wire rimmed glasses he balanced by resting the nose
pieces on either side of his thumb. He put his glasses on and
looked at me. "Young."

"Ron, are you really serious about Harlan and Heidi, because if you are you'd better get him the hell away from her before Ben finds out and . . ."

"Hey! I'm not Harlan's bodyguard, big brother, bosom
buddy or anything else. You've got a problem with him screwing
Heidi, you do something about it. Leave me out of it." Then looking at me he said, "Big bad Ben is believed to have gotten pissed
off at one of the wino dishwashers once and kicked him to death
in the parking lot behind the kitchen. Sammy is afraid that if Ben
finds out about Harlan he'll be a waiter short this weekend."

"Button it Alter. Ronald over here has a problem with working and playing with others," Sammy said to me in the language
of an elementary school report card. I smiled weakly and kept
still. The last thing I wanted was to be sandwiched in the quarrel between my waiter and roommate on my first day.

"Do you need any help with your stuff?" Ron asked, changing the subject and abandoning Sammy's agenda.

"Yeah, go get your things. The parking lot for the staff is
over there," Sammy said, waving in the direction of the single
window between the beds. "See you at five-thirty."

My brother Jerry had let me borrow his car, a '51 Studebaker, to bring my things up to Braverman's; Steve would drive
him up during the week to retrieve it. They had both encouraged
me to work at Braverman's because I would earn a lot of money.
My two previous waiting jobs had been more instructive than lu-
crative. Waiting tables in a summer camp had taught me about
the workings of a large kitchen and, more importantly, how to be
nimble toting a heavy tray load of dishes. The next summer I
took a job in Fleischmanns, New York at a hotel that in later
years would be struck by Jewish Lightning, the insurance industry's term for the abundant arsons that took place in the bank-
rupt resort hotels. The Royale was the dumpiest of the dumps
catering to a clientele of poor German Jews who, despite the hor-
rors of the holocaust, still spoke the cacophonous tongue of

their former homeland. "You cum to Fleischmanz und you don speak Cherman?" they would inquire. I quickly learned to just smile and shrug. It would not have enhanced my economic outlook to berate them for their misguided sentimentality. The job was an apprenticeship in which I learned to pour soup from metal cups without splashing it over the rim of the flat soup dish and to take verbal insult stoically. I made $1200 that summer and counted the days until I could flee back to New York City. Now I was ready for the big time, even if it meant being downgraded to the position of busboy.

"So, where will you be going to school next year?" Ron asked as we headed out of the waiters' quarters to my car.

"Well, I've been accepted at a few places, but I'm waiting to hear from Columbia. That's where I really want to go."

"A few places. You mean City and NYU, don't you?" he said with undisguised annoyance. "Let me set you straight right now. Don't be coy and secretive in this place. You eat, sleep, shit and jerk-off with everybody else in the waiters' quarters. If you don't burn your mail after you read it its contents will be common knowledge within 24 hours. That's just the way it is here. So, am I right about NYU and City?"

"Yes." Ron smiled at my answer, somewhat smugly I thought.

"It isn't hard to figure out Melvin. If you were going to go away to an out of town college you'd be working in a summer camp or your father's office. The only guys here who aren't at school in the city are the basketball players and the tennis pros."

From what my brothers had told me I knew this was true. Most of the waiter corps in the mountains was made up of boys from the outer boroughs of New York City on the make for money for college and then graduate school and the prestige and income of a professional career. And that was why the notion of a Harvard man, a Harlan Hawthorne, waiting tables at Braverman's was so perplexing and so deliciously tantalizing. What was he doing in the borscht belt? Was it just the money he'd come for, like the rest of us, or was there something else he was looking for. And what could that be? Sex with Jews? Sociological research for Harvard? I was immediately fascinated by the possibilities, the mystery.

"That's my car over there," I said when the Studebaker came into view. My wash and wear Dacron shirts were hanging in the window and I had clipped bow ties to the collars of two of them.

"How many shirts did you bring?"

"Four. For the dining room I mean. My brothers said that would be enough." I knew from past experience what I needed, but I always thought Steve and Jerry's authority to be more compelling. One brought four shirts to be prepared for an accident or an unpleasant body odor that would limit a shirt's usage to a single meal. That meant you could use up three shirts in one day, and with the extra one, you could wash the soiled shirts at bedtime and still have a clean shirt for breakfast. The wash and wear shirts would be ready to use by lunch, and so it went. "And three pairs of black slacks. And one pair of black Navy surplus shoes." He hadn't asked me, but I felt it necessary to describe the inventory of work clothes I had brought with me. His irritation had made me defensive. In a matter of hours it seemed as if I was on the wrong side of Sammy and Ron and I hadn't even worked my first meal yet. "So what's this guy Harlan like?" I asked, hoping to deflect Ron's bad mood.

"You'll find out soon enough. Take the shirts, I'll carry the suitcases."

"How long have you been up here?" I asked, looking for another entry into civility. I had just graduated from high school, but the vacationers had started arriving at the hotels in the area in mid-June so some staffers had to be there ready to serve them.

"Couple of weeks. Sammy's been talking about you the whole time like you were his long lost son. Do you know him?"

"Not really. Well, I know who he is, I've met him before, but I was just a kid then and we didn't talk to each other or anything." I felt it best to minimize my knowledge of Sammy and let Ron tell me what he thought I should know. Actually, I knew a great deal about Sammy from my brothers. I knew that Sammy had never been married, that he worked the resorts in Miami Beach in the winter and the Catskills in the summer, though Braverman's was

the draw not the other Catskill hotels, that he had a loyal following of guests who would only sit at his station and be served by
him, and that he was extremely self-conscious about his lack of
formal education and diligently studied dictionaries in an effort
to compensate.

"Well, he's a prick as far as I'm concerned, a case of arrested development. He's old enough to be the father of everyone working in the dining room but he's still flicking his towel at
your ass after you come out of the shower."

"Well, he sounds like someone to feel sorry for. My brothers say he's very self-conscious about not having an education.
Here he is working with all these college boys and . . ."

"Don't break my heart. My father didn't go to college either
but he educated himself, started a business, and made a life for
his family. Don't feel sorry for Sammy, Melvin. One summer here
and you won't feel sorry for anybody. Except maybe judge Crater,
if you can find him."

"We'd all like to find the judge, I'm sure, but why here?"

"Don't you know he's our resident ghost?"

"Come on, you're not serious."

"You bet I am, you'll see."

Now, everyone loves a good ghost story and the further
you go from New York City the greater the number of ghosts you
will encounter. We're raised with the story of the headless horse-
man in Sleepy Hollow near Tarrytown and his horrifying decapi-
tations but as you proceed north up the Hudson River the
number of lesser known spooks swells. For example, in Hudson,
New York it is said Mabel Parker can be heard on the second
floor of her former home now called Dietz House; Albany's Rus-
sell Sage College uses buildings that were once part of a children's sanitarium (Parson's home for children) and they say
numerous ghosts there still can be heard; and at Belhurst Cas-
tle in Geneva, New York amid the Finger Lakes, the ghost of the
beautiful Italian opera singer killed in the collapse of a secret
tunnel she and her lover employed can be seen—a woman in
white standing silently on the hotel's front lawn in the middle of
the night. There are dozens more reported all over the state but

the ghost that I was to become intimately involved with was the ghost of Braverman's, the ghost of judge Crater.

Unless you were born in the days when radio was the major source of home entertainment, judge Joseph Force Crater's name may be unfamiliar to you. The judge was a New York City lawyer who, four months before his disappearance on August 6, 1930, was appointed to the New York State Supreme Court by the then governor, Franklin Delano Roosevelt. The stories about Crater's character ranged from that of a teetotaling Methodist to a womanizing gambler with connections to the unseemly. His was the most notorious missing person case of the century up to that time, similar to that of Jimmy Hoffa's in the 1970's, and his name was used and abused by radio comedians in order to tease laughter from their audiences. His mysterious disappearance had reduced him and his name to the status of a reliable punchline. But you'll hear more about the judge later.

"Anyway, even if you don't meet the judge you'll meet an annoying assembly of irritating and bad tipping complainers and gluttons, so get ready for a typical Catskill summer."

This seemed a grim forecast and it troubled me to hear it from Ron. This wasn't summer school at a university but it wasn't a prison work farm either. I was on the verge of calling him a cynic but thought it the better course to just let this forecast pass. He had been in a bad mood when I arrived so it clearly wasn't my fault. His grousing was really not much more than the petulant whining of an over-tired child and I took note of that for future reference. We returned to the bunkhouse in silence, Ron kicking stones down the path as we went.

2.

At 5:00 Ron said that we should go to the kitchen so he could orient me to the system and introduce me to the chefs. I slipped into my white Dacron shirt, clipped my bow tie to the left collar point, neatly folded my side towel into a narrow oblong and, tucking it under the right side of my belt, stepped into my black lace-ups. We entered through the screen door at the rear of the kitchen. The dishwashers were lolling about, smoking and distracted, seemingly indifferent to one another. Looking like the supernumerary street people of "The Beggar's Opera" these shabbily dressed men of indeterminate ages with several days' growth of beard, red and rheumy looking eyes, some trembling on the brink of D.T.'s, looked at us impassively with the dead-eyed stares of water buffaloes as Ron led me to the dish racks and rows of plates, bowls, glasses and goblets.

"It's pretty straight forward, bowls and monkey dishes here, salad plates, dessert plates, dinner plates there, glasses and goblets over there," he said, while gesturing limply with his right hand, like Leonard Bernstein cuing the violas. "You bring your silver back to your station for drying and sorting in the side stand." The side stand was a serving table at each station that the waiter used to set down and unload his tray. In the shelf beneath that top was the bin for the busboy's dirty dishes, and in the drawers beneath the bin were compartments for the cutlery. Braverman's did not have a kosher dining room so we used the same dishes and silver for every meal, both meat and dairy. "The water pitchers are over there, one per table. They're heavy when they're full so don't try to carry more than four at a time, two in each hand," he said, motioning at the pitchers that looked like brightly colored bowling balls with spouts and handles. Against the wall, between the double doors to the dining room and the shelves where the dishes were stored, were deep sinks, amalgamations of iron and zinc, where the dirty dishes were washed, and in front of them wooden tables for the busboys to drop their loaded bus boxes and retrieve clean ones for the bins in their stands. Across the kitchen, on the wall farthest from the dining room so their heat would not radiate into the eating area, were the ovens and stoves, huge metal structures looking like fugitives from an iron foundry. In the middle of the floor, occupying the space between the sinks and the ovens were rows of butcher block tables where most of the cleaning, cutting, chopping and preparing of food was done.

"You'll catch on after a few meals. If you have a problem one of the guys will help you out. C'mon, I'll show you the dining room."

"I know it," I said too loudly and insistently, trying to establish some semblance of competence. "I've eaten in there with my family many times," I added more softly. "But you can show me the waiters' stations."

"C'mon, I'll show you where I work. If you've eaten in here you know where Sammy's station is," he said as we passed through the double doors. Sammy's station was diagonally across from the kitchen, up towards the entrance to the dining room, nestled in the arc of an oversized bay window. It was called "the Gold Coast" because it was situated near the front of the dining room, close to the entrance, but not so close as to disturb those seated there with the commotion and tumult of the hungry horde stampeding by to the less important tables at the side and rear of the room. The bay was the largest window in the dining room and overlooked the hotel's "Famous Olympic-Sized [sic] Pool" that was featured in all its advertisements and promotional literature. To be seated there was to be twice blessed: to display one's self while simultaneously appraising all who passed before you, and to be able to do that from the coveted tables of the hotel's legendary headwaiter, from Sammy's station. In the tiny culture of Braverman's at the time, this would have been tantamount to sitting with Sherman Billingsley at the old Stork Club in New York City. And one paid handsomely, and gladly, for the honor so it was expected that as his busboy I would be rewarded as well.

"I'm right across from you over here," Ron said, standing in the broad center aisle that divided the room in half and pointing to the tables opposite Sammy's. "The waiter just above me is Ivan Goldman. He's an All American basketball player from the University of Kentucky. Just below you is Abe Melman, the lawyer. You'll meet the others as we go along," he said, weariness in his voice. Ron seemed to get frustrated and irritated easily when discussing things that held no special interest or meaning for him. "Let's go back in the kitchen and I'll introduce you to the chef."

The head chef, Rudy, was a crazy Hungarian whose temper tantrums were well known to me from my brothers' dinner time antics and stories, each in turn acting out one of Rudy's outrageous eruptions. Rudy, they said, brandished meat cleavers and carving knives whenever he felt his authority challenged. Deft and strong, he could divide a side of beef into steaks, rib roasts, and chops while muttering expletives in Hungarian, punctuating the occasionally vehement whack of the cleaver cutting through animal flesh and crashing into the wooden work table beneath, with the bloodcurdling shriek of the name of the waiter or busboy who recently had most irritated him.

Rudy's voice was loud enough to hear even before we pushed through the swinging door to the kitchen but once inside, it was booming.

"Vhat you mean you don know?" he raged at the busboy cowering in front of him. "Is missing, maybe stolen. Maybe you took." He grabbed a meat cleaver from the work table and to punctuate his point, swung it in the air and brought it down on the table with a crash.

"I didn't do it Rudy, you gotta believe me, I didn't do it," the busboy said, his voice quavering, his legs going rubbery beneath him.

"Dot's it. I hate liars. Dot's it!" and brandishing his cleaver in his right hand, he engulfed the quaking boy with his left arm and began dragging him across the room.

"Shit, he's taking him into the meat locker."

"What?" I said, my own knees turning to rubber.

"Who's talking?" Rudy bellowed. "Shot op or I come get you too!"

"Help me, please help me, somebody please," the boy pleaded.

"Can't we do something?" I whispered to Ron, but he grabbed my arm and pulling me close to him hissed at me through clenched teeth,

"Stand still and shut up."

Rudy dragged the limp, simpering boy to the wooden door of the meat locker and still grasping his cleaver in his right hand, pulled the refrigerator door open and then hurled the busboy inside. Looking back at me and Ron and several others of the dining room staff who had assembled in the kitchen, Rudy glowered, shook the cleaver in the air, and then entered the meat locker slamming the door behind him and closing in the feeble cries of his victim.

"Who was that? What the hell is going on? Isn't anybody going to do something?" I was terrified, but the others just seemed morose and resigned.

"It's Rudy's sick sense of humor. He won't hurt him but it's his way of initiating a new busboy. He won't be satisfied until the kid shits in his pants. Consider yourself lucky it wasn't you. Since you've seen the act he'll have to wait for another new guy to do it to next time."

"Jesus, that's sick," I said, relieved there would be no bloodshed, and especially relieved he hadn't selected me for his charade.

"Yeah, Rudy's a good guy, just a little sick is all," said one of the waiters. "By the way, my name's Ivan, Ivan Goldman," he said extending his right hand. "You're Melvin, right?" Before I could answer the door to the meat locker flew open and the hapless busboy came stumbling out screaming. His hands were clutched over his groin and blood was gushing out from under them soaking his pants and leaking on to the floor. He collapsed into the pool of blood at his feet sobbing and moaning with the most agonized and pathetic cry I had ever heard. I was still holding Ivan Goldman's hand in an arrested handshake, and my breathing had stopped at the sight of the blood. Everyone in the kitchen was frozen in place, as if in a tableau vivant, when Rudy appeared in the doorway of the refrigerator the bloody cleaver in one hand, and in the other, a piece of flesh smeared with blood, a cylinder-like piece of flesh several inches long, dripping blood.

"Dis von vhas vell hung! Look at dis!"

"Oh God!" several of the waiters cried out "You've gone too far Rudy, too far. What have you done?! My God! What have you done??!!" Ron shouted. Chaos. Pandemonium. Waiters, dish-washers, kitchen helpers all running and shouting at once while Rudy stood in the doorway of the meat cooler laughing. I stared at the bloody object in his hand with total disbelief. It was a penis. He was waving the busboy's penis in his clutched fist. And then he began to dance around the writhing busboy, a brutish jig of contempt, while the mutilated and emasculated victim screamed and writhed along the floor. Never in my life had I known such horror, such terror and disgust. Then, all at once, I felt very light, almost as if floating, and yet I couldn't move. It was as though my legs were stone, inert, too heavy for such a light body, but still I was determined to go to the boy on the floor. Struggling against gravity, trying to reach him, I felt the room suddenly begin to spin, turn upside down, and then right itself, while the floor rose up and hit me on the head. It was a most pe-culiar feeling. I was sure I had not fainted, merely stumbled, ex-ecuted a somersault of a kind that had caused me to strike my head, and then landed in a seated position. As my mind cleared I realized everyone in the kitchen was standing above me laugh-ing, the kitchen staff, the dishwashers, Ron, and the other wait-ers and busboys. The busboy who had been writhing in his own blood just minutes before, now stood with his arm over the mad Hungarian's shoulder, while Rudy, enormously pleased with himself, grinned down at me. "Vhas funny joke, no?"

"No!" I said emphatically.

"I was great, wasn't I Rudy? Did you hear that scream? I was fuckin' great," the busboy-victim said, provoking me to scan the area for Rudy's meat cleaver.

"Is turkey neck and cow's blood. Funny. Don be imbarrass. Dey all faint."

When we sat down for dinner Ron nudged me with his elbow and then pointed across the room to a sandy-blonde haired fellow who was laughing quietly with Rudy. "That's Har-lan," Ron said. "He's a real charmer." I already had gotten the feeling that Ron disliked Harlan when Sammy was asking about him but, after our little face-off in the parking lot, I couldn't tell if Ron was just a guy with a chip on his shoulder, or someone who was selective in his dislikes.

"Uh-huh," I said, being as neutral as I could. "Which one is Abe?" Abe was another professional waiter in his fifties that my brothers had told me about. A man with a law degree who eschewed the practice of law to wait on tables. In describing him to me my brother Steve had said of Abe, "He's a man who loves humanity; it's people that he hates." When I took the job at Braverman's I thought Abe would be the puzzle I might attempt to solve, but suddenly there was Harlan Hawthorne to be considered and everything about him, from his appearance and manner to his attendance at Harvard, made him immediately more interesting.

"Abe doesn't eat with the staff. The Braverman's have him eat at their house. I think he's a relative of theirs but nobody knows for sure."

"Is he really a lawyer?"

"That's what they say. It drives Sammy crazy that Abe has a college degree and a law degree and is still waiting tables just like him. Sammy thinks that if you have degrees you should have it made. Listen to the two of them go at each other, well, I should really say listen to Sammy go at Abe. He carries a dictionary in his pocket and studies it whenever he can. He uses the ten dollar words like some people use stilettos. You'll see." He broke off abruptly and suddenly sat there stiffly.

"Hi! I hear you're my new roommate, hi Ronald." Harlan Hawthorne was standing over us wearing a congenial smile. I started to stand up to shake his hand, but pressing his hand down on my shoulder he said, "Hey, you don't have to get up for me Mel, I'm just another one of the shleppers like you." God he was something. Soft spoken, handsome, possessing what my mother called "presence," his was a poised and relaxed confidence contained in a lithe, athletic physique. He had the look of someone who had never been introduced to failure, the look that implied acceptance wherever he found himself, the look of princely dominion.

"Is there room for me here?" he said to Ron who shifted to his right on the bench allowing Harlan to sit down between us. "So Mel, I hear you're going to be Sammy's busboy. That's a great deal for you, Mel. You should make some good money doing that." It crossed my mind to say, "So, I hear you're fucking Heidi Braverman. That's a great deal for you," but I was too unfamiliar and too impressed with Harlan to play that Bronx schoolyard game with him. I smiled and nodded.

"Do you play tennis Mel? We could play a couple of sets tomorrow if you like."

I'd never played tennis. I'd played paddle ball with wooden racquets and pink, Spalding rubber balls on cement courts in the city playground but not tennis. I was becoming aware that Harlan addressed me by name in almost every sentence he spoke to me. My salesman father once had explained that he did that whenever he met someone new to engrave the person's name on his memory. Those were my father's exact words, "engrave his name on my memory," and it was such an unusual and literary turn of phrase for him to use I never forgot it.

"I didn't bring . . . I forgot to bring my racquet, Harlan, but maybe we could shoot some baskets if you like." I was a pretty good outside shooter, two-handed set shot, one-handed push shot, an occasional jump shot from the key.

"I don't know Mel, you're taller than I am and basketball was never my best sport. We'll see."

"Anytime you're looking for a game of horse let me know," Ron interjected. Suddenly my time was in demand and the feeling of acceptance that brought to me made me happy for the first time since my arrival at Braverman's.

3.

When it was time to serve dinner Sammy took me by the elbow and moved me from the kitchen to the side stand at our station.

"The first thing I want you to understand Melvin is that this is my station. I have been working at Braverman's for more than twenty years. Usually most of the people sitting at these tables have requested to be at my tables. That means they will expect me to give them my attention. You will be doing more work than the other busboys, but you'll be better paid than any of them for that work. You'll set up, you'll break down, you'll bring out my trays and bring in your bus boxes. I do all the serving, you get to pour the water and the coffee. Even the soup I do. Keep the bread baskets full, keep the butter dishes full, keep the water glasses full, be nice, smile, have a good time, make lots of money."

Sammy had been firm, but friendly. These were his basic ground rules. What he was telling me was that I would be doing most of the physical labor for the two of us. All the other waiters would be carrying their own trays for the various courses, appetizers, soup, salads, entrees, and dessert, while Sammy would merely schmooze the tables. Then he'd lay out their plates and schmooze some more. I knew to expect this and was not surprised. I would do whatever it took to make the money.

"So, do you have any questions?" Eager to demonstrate my eagerness I had already prepared questions before coming to the dining room.

"Is the split still five and three?" This meant is the tipping practice still five dollars per person per week for the waiter, three dollars per person per week for the busboy.

"Yeah, that's how it is usually. Of course my regulars do better than that, and I hope they'll do the same for you. Sammy winked. "But this weekend no one knows what to expect. Harold Braverman has rented out the hotel to a Lions Convention from Utica. The whole place." Sammy seemed to be sinking under the weight of this information even as he conveyed it to me. "He looks at your generation of Jews and sees no business for the mountains so he's decided to attract some other kinds of vacationers. Goyim." Indeed, Harold had been prescient. Recognizing in the sometimes surly, sometimes contemptuous attitudes of the dining room staff the likely loss of a whole generation of Jewish vacationers, cleverly he had begun to market the resort to the upstate gentiles. If he were to succeed with this venture he could secure his fortunes for another twenty years. Then he could sell out and the hell with the rest. Sammy narrowed his eyes and shook his head from side to side, agitating it minimally, his nose moving no more than one inch from center in either direction. "Goyim in the Catskills. Go know. Yeah, the Irish have a resort north of here, and they say there are even schvartzes in some part of the woods, but goyim? From Utica? It's the end for me if that happens. I squeezed his shoulder, gave him a pat on the back, and mentally discarded my other questions.

While I filled my water pitchers for dinner my brother Jerry's old busboy, Bob Gelman, came up behind me and gave me an affectionate goose which caused me to lurch and splash myself with the water.

"Hey!" I shouted.

"Hi ya Mel, how're all the famous White brothers." Bob was an annoying wise guy but I was glad to see a familiar face, and gladder still that he had missed my acrobatics over the turkey neck.

"Hey, wait 'til you see this crowd of Lions. You've never seen anything like it. Terminal pastels, man, terminal."

"Hi Bob, how come you're still working here? I thought you were in law school."

"Just waiting tables some weekends to help out and to grab some cash. Come July I have a job with a law firm for the summer. Hey, if you need a day off over the summer, you know a weekend day or something, I'll come up and help you out. Two meals, fifty bucks." Some bargain. Stuart Stein, the maitre d'hotel came into the kitchen fussily.

"Come, come, come. Let's get out there and set up. The dining room opens in less than five minutes. I want everyone looking crisp and smart. Hal B wants to make a good impression on these folks so if you want to be here again tomorrow you'd better look smart tonight. And no funny business." Stuart was a science teacher in South Fallsburg who could not leave his teacherly ways in the classroom. Steve used to say he always expected to see a pocket protector in Stuart's short-sleeved white shirt, or chalk dust on his hands and in his hair. He was the kind of teacher who probably had to pull thumbtacks out of his ass ten times a term.

When the guests began filing in for dinner it was immediately obvious we were dealing with a different population, almost a different species of animal. An assortment of pale faces poised above pale pastel colored clothing entered tentatively, cocktails in hand, and advanced cautiously down the center aisle of the dining room. Bob and I exchanged smiles across several tables, the kind of smile that can be like a fuse on a bomb of hysterical laughter, and sensing the precariousness implicit in this smile I turned away and busied myself with the remaining napkins, folded like Bishop's miters, to be placed in each guest's empty water goblet. Bob coughed and cleared his throat loudly. I knew he wanted me to look up but I wouldn't permit myself that indulgence because I could feel the laughter gathering in my stomach, roiling there, waiting for the opportunity to burst out of me in explosive, convulsive waves. My first night and I was determined to make my debut unmemorable, better still, invisible. I would not look at Bob.

"Ahem, good evening ladies and gentlemen, nice to see you all this evening. Welcome." From the corner of my eye I saw Bob remove his side-towel from under his belt, wave it ostentatiously through the air, and then make a low, foppish bow, the towel extended at arm's length from the tips of his left thumb and index finger. The members of the Lions Club, Utica Chapter, fidgeted nervously, the ice in their drinks tinkling musically, while they searched one another's faces for some ruling of protocol. It was as though they suddenly had come upon an aboriginal who, if treated improperly, might slice them into steak tartare and devour them, pastels and all. "Gelman!" shouted Stuart Stein, fuming at the lectern he used for writing the table assignments. He glowered in Bob's direction, but Gelman wouldn't meet his gaze. "Gelman!"

"Gelman!" echoed Bob, bowing low to the parade of guests now tip-toeing past him, as if fearful that a loud noise might provoke pandemonium from the madman with the lunatic grin bent over in their path.

"Gelman to you too," ventured a brave guest who then scanned the room for an approving face. When his eyes met mine I winked and gave a short, brisk nod as if to say, "right!"

With that he hurried back along the line of Lions and their wives, whispering and gesticulating, an ardent interpreter of the new ritual he had just discovered. And as the line began to move again each person passing in front of Bob greeted him with a spritely, "Gelman!" and made way for the next visitor. Stuart Stein, scowling at his post, had a wise guy on his staff and that was not to be tolerated, but that night at least, there was nothing to be done. For the remainder of the meal the members of the Lions Club, Utica Chapter, exchanged "Gelmans" with the dining room staff as if they were "shaloms," and after the clean up Bob Gelman was told to be gone. Working my first meal had been easier than I'd expected. The guests were polite and agreeable and I dutifully, if pointlessly, assured them that I was hoping to be a doctor when they inquired about my career plans. Sammy tried to make jokes with his new patrons but was distinctly uncomfortable with this non-Jewish crowd and eventually gave up his ambition to charm them. The other waiters and busboys had been friendly and the ridicule I anticipated for my nose dive following Rudy's performance hadn't occurred. I had finished bussing the dishes and glasses, in that order, and was drying the silverware and sorting the pieces into their compartments in the drawer of the serving stand when Sammy began to hold forth.

"The dignity of hard physical labor does not extend to waiters and busboys, Melvin, so let this job be a lesson to you. Stay in school, get your degree, and become a doctor. If you become a lawyer, you may never get out of the mountains." He was starting. I knew this was for Abe Melman's benefit, not mine. "Did you know that Abe over here has a law degree? A lawyer and still he waits tables. Go figure. Why would an educated man, a man with a graduate degree from New York University want to wait tables, can you tell me? Please Melvin, I'd appreciate any help you can give." Though groomed to answer questions, to be the bright boy, I had no idea and couldn't even begin to improvise convincingly on the issue, nor did I have any desire to try.

"You can't can you? Well, neither can I." Turning in the other direction he said, "Ivan, wouldn't you say that Abe is a parsimonious, penurious, pusillanimous putz?" Abe, setting his tables for breakfast, abided Sammy's abuse with indifference, the way a Masai herdsman abides flies.

"Whatever you say Sammy," Ivan said, sorting through his cutlery. I sat quietly at the serving stand counting my spoons. I didn't like this kind of meanness but knew there was nothing that I could do. While each hotel dining room might have its own subculture, certain rules were transcultural. If you are new you must keep a low profile until you've had your place in the ordinacy defined. Were I to come in too quickly on Sammy's side, despite his intense disdain for Abe he would suddenly recognize in him a friend worthy of my respect and admiration, and he'd call me an ass-kisser for trying to suck up to him at Abe's expense. For the rest of the summer I'd be known as "Ass-Kisser" and summoned by that name in the kitchen, the dining room, the waiter's quarters, and in the company of any girl I might try to link up with or impress. But come to Abe's defense and the ignorance of that position would inflame Sammy, and then my name would become "Shit-head" in the aforementioned venues.

"I have to take a leak," I said, trying to exit the scene. "You should wash your hands first," Sammy called out. "What?" Disbelieving, I stopped walking. "What did you say?"

"You should wash your hands before you go to take a leak," Sammy said approaching me. "People always get that backwards. Consider this. You took a shower before you came to the dining room tonight, am I right?" I nodded. "Then you handled food, plates, your dirty side-towel, the broom that's been knocked over on the floor, all kinds of dirty things, but your washed and rinsed schmekele has stayed in your pants all night, right?" I nodded again. "So why would you wash your hands after you touch the one clean piece of your anatomy? Do you pee on your hands when you go to take a leak? Of course not! So go wash your hands first. Simple logic."

I was flabbergasted. Sammy sounded completely insane to me.

"Keep your eyes straight ahead," he called out to me again, "and remember, life is a one-way street."

Back in the waiters' quarters we took turns in the shower, the usual nervous jokes about bending over for the dropped bar of soap being made each time one waiter or busboy left and a new one came. The male dread of the possibility of homosexuality was at its peak because we were mostly new to each other and still young enough to worry that we might be secretly queer. "Gay" was not in fashion then and the derogatory names used to separate us real guys from those of the other kind were homo, pansy, fairy, limpwrist, queer, fag, and faggot, the latter two having broader usage to also define mama's boys and those who could not reach the backboard from the foul line on a basketball court, or slide into third base on a diamond.

Ordinarily, after dinner the dining room staff was expected to show up at the casino or recreation hall and to dance with the daughters of the guests, but these guests had not brought their families with them. I hadn't given much thought to the evening and was just grabbing my towel and drying off when I saw that Bob Gelman had been in one of the other shower stalls. We waved to each other.

"These guys have no sense of humor," Gelman complained coming out of the shower. "Do they actually believe the Lions are going to make Braverman's their vacation paradise? Haven't they ever heard about oil and water not mixing?" By then we were standing in the middle of the corridor that divided the waiters' quarters in half and Bob was declaiming to anyone who might listen to him.

"You always were a pain in the ass Gelman," Sammy said, poking his head through his doorway. "Personally, I'm glad to be rid of you. Good riddance."

"Fuck you, Sammy, who the hell wants to listen to anything you have to say. In five years everybody here, EVERYBODY, will be doing something useful, but you'll still be right here telling your stupid anecdotes to college boys who don't give a flying fuck about your stale old good times." At that moment I felt a surge of guilt that demanded I accept some of the responsibility for this situation. After all, it had been my wink that triggered the Gelmanizing amongst the Lions.

"Cut it out Bob, calm down." I pulled him into my room. "Why do you want to hurt Sammy? This is his whole life." Ron snickered but Harlan, who was clipping his fingernails, looked up and smiled at me.

"Melvin, save the White righteousness for Yom Kippur. I don't like being lectured to by a kid." Stung, but undeterred I persisted.

"C'mon Bob, forget about it, there are plenty of other places where you can get weekend work when you want it. It's just a job schlepping matzoh balls. No big deal."

I spent the rest of that night keeping Bob company. We went down to see the show at the casino, an all purpose recreation hall where the entertainers performed and then the guests danced to the hotel band's music. We had a few drinks, Tom Collinses, gin mixed with what must have been the precursor of unsweetened Fresca, and then headed back to the waiters' quarters. As we passed by the main building we saw the Ford station wagon with the large rectangular signboard mounted along its roof. The message in bright blue letters said, "Jack Whitman for Better Lionism."

"Oh boy, look at that. Do you see what I see?"

By that time of night my guilt had dissolved in the gin. I was feeling that Bob Gelman had been treated unfairly and that Stuart Stein was to blame for the debacle, not Bob, not me.

"Looky, looky," I said. I was drunk.

"Come with me," Bob said walking up the steps to the main entrance of the hotel. Normally timid, I fell in behind him and marched fearlessly into the lobby of the hotel like an apostle of temperance raiding a gin mill. Bob went directly to the registration desk where a woman, with hair of a red color so peculiar and unnatural as to make me wonder if she might be rotting from the inside out, was sorting through index cards. "Excuse me Belle, can you help me out?" The woman raised her head slowly and stared at him dully from under her heavy eyelids like a giant tortoise.

"Whaddaya want?" she asked in a raspy baritone.

"Some note paper, a blue pen, ballpoint is fine, and some Scotch tape please."

"Whaddaya need it for?"

"I'm making a list. And checking it twice." Leaning forward into the woman's face he asked in seductive tones, "Have you been naughty or nice?" and he chucked her under the chin with the side of his index finger. She blushed, pushed some paper and a pen at him, and then, with a smile whose sleaziness was a match for Gelrnan's voice, tore off two strips of tape and pasted them across Bob's mouth saying, "Don't be fresh," but clearly meaning the opposite.

"Thanks Belle baby, you're a doll." I thought I'd choke. Outside, Gelman scribbled boldly on the paper and then ripped the page in half. He tore each strip of tape into two pieces and affixed a piece to the top and bottom of each one of the papers. "Take this," he said handing me one of the papers. "When I say 'Go' slap this here," he said pointing to a site on the signboard.

The next morning Ron woke me before my alarm clock had gone off. Standing in the middle of the room, right arm akimbo, left hand extended palm out in the direction of Harlan's cot, like Betty Furness bringing her audience's attention to the refrigerator of their dreams, he said, "Your buddy never made it home last night, Heidi, Heidi, Heidi, Ho." I rubbed my eyes and squinted at the alarm clock for the time. "The question is this—did he spend the night under Heidi's covers, or was he planting his seed under someone else's bush?"

"What time is it?" The Tom Collinses of the previous night felt like they were sponsoring a Mambo festival in my head.

"It's Howdy Doody time of course, time to say howdy doody to Harlan and his cutie. Get up. We're going to Heidi's room." The dim, early morning light of dawn was visible in the sky through the room's single window.

"Harlan is hardly my friend and I'm not going to look for him. And if it bothers you so much that he might be with Heidi take Sammy with you. I just want to sleep. I've got a headache."

"Up, up!" he said, pulling my covers from me. "Let's go. We can be at the main house in a minute if we hurry. Come on!"

"What is the matter with you?" I was as much startled by his bold intrusion as I was irritated by his aggressive removal of my bedclothes. It had been less than twenty-four hours since my arrival and it seemed that Ron was behaving as though he were my brother Steve, and I resented his presumptuousness.

"What's the matter Melvin, you scared?" This taunt, one that was time-honored on the city streets of my childhood, stirred the familiar stew of fear and anger in me. I was just about to respond when a loud noise in the corridor interrupted us. I looked at the clock again and with the blurriness cleared from my eyes saw it was only 5:10.

"Gelman you little shit where the fuck are you?" It was Moe Braverman, son of Ben, brother of Harold and Heidi, the family's enforcer. "Gelman, get the fuck out here!" he railed. I was pretty sure this was about the signboard Bob and I had tampered with, but did anyone else know that I had been a conspirator in that escapade? Moe continued to stomp through the corridor shouting for Gelman, occasionally banging open the door to one of the dormitory rooms and demanding to know if Gelman was in there.

"He's gone." Abe Melman's deep and sorrowful voice carried the message to all listening. "I saw him carry his suitcase out early this morning."

"Sonofabitch. If I ever get my hands on him there won't be enough left to mail home in an envelope with a three cent stamp on it." Harlan entered our room wearing a pair of blue boxer shorts, a towel draped over his head, his dop kit under one arm. Droplets of water glistened on his torso. He went straight to the dresser under the window and set the kit down, then sat on his cot and began drying his hair with the towel. Ron looked at him and sneered.

"Where've you been?"

"Looks like I've been in the shower Ronald, wouldn't you say?" Harlan said good naturedly without a trace of defensiveness or irritation in his voice. Before Ron could speak Moe Braverman lurched into the room.

"White, weren't you with Gelman last night?" he asked suspiciously. My heart leapt up into my throat.

"I had some drinks with him," I said struggling to keep my voice below the strangled falsetto range, "that's all."

"Do you know what he did after that? Do you?" His voice swelled with outrage and he glowered at me from the side of my bed, his face level with mine. Dear God, I prayed, strike Belle dead, please.

"The little shit, he pasted Z's over the L's in Lionism. Now the sign says 'Jack Whitman for Better Zionism.' Putz! Shmuck! Trumbenik! Bastard! They'll never come back here now." He reeled over to Harlan's side of the room and turned back towards me. "Are you sure you don't know nothing about this?" He had just given me my freedom. I hadn't even been asked but knowing I was one of the upstanding White brothers Moe had granted me amnesty.

"No, honestly," I lied, "I didn't know." I had lied honestly only once before, in grade school. My friend Malcolm and I had been belching to The Star Spangled Banner while our sixth grade classmates earnestly sang it when Mrs.Castleman, our music teacher, located our eructations and confronted us. Malcolm had a reputation as a trouble maker and a wise guy but I was the class spelling champion and all around goody-goody. "No, it wasn't me, honest," I had lied, turning a deep crimson, and Malcolm, accustomed to making the trip to the principal's office, didn't rat me out. "It was my fault," he said. Later that day, the war in Korea in progress and the recently ended world war shaping our play and our language, he said, "Forget it. When the grenade landed in our foxhole I jumped on it. Why should you die too?"

"If any of you ever see him around I want to know, got that?" Moe commanded, and he stormed out of the room. As soon as the door to the waiters' quarters slammed shut Ron burst into laughter. I exhaled with relief and couldn't wait to tell Malcolm, who was working on the social staff at Brown's Hotel, about my participation in the joke, but he'd be the only one in the Catskill mountains that I'd tell.

"So, Melvin, you have some balls after all," Ron said, but I just rolled over and faced the wall.

"And as for you, Hawthorne, I'm not fooled by you for one minute. Shower my ass." But Harlan kept his towel in motion across his body and said nothing in response. When Ron left the room for the shower I jumped down from my bed and collected my towel and dop kit.

"You were up pretty early Harlan," I said.

"Early is the best time of day," he said. "Just before daylight it's very peaceful. The crickets have quieted down and the birds have yet to begin chirping and the sky has the palest pale blue color, almost like slate. There are some stars still visible in the sky and the dew on the grass glistens and twinkles like little jewels spilled at your feet. It's a magical fairyland. I like that quiet time. I walk the grounds, I stare into the lake and begin the day in a state of calm." His voice was indeed very calm, almost dreamy, nothing at all like Ron's, and it struck me then how odd this living arrangement was. We'd been lumped together without rhyme or reason like discards in a thrift shop. While there were commonalities I shared with each of them, there seemed to be nothing Ron and Harlan could call common ground. It was at that point on that morning I decided I was going to apprentice myself to Harlan and learn how to be in the world in his way.

"You should try it some time," he said abruptly, as if coming back to the reality of Braverman's.

"Sure, I'll do that," I said, politely. I'd have said yes to almost anything he might have asked of me just then; I was enthralled by his physical grace and verbal elegance. He was everything I had always wished to be.

Breakfast was quiet and easy. Harold had not attempted to introduce the Lions to the dietary delights of urban Jewry so there were no appetizing appetizers: no smoked white fish, no smoked Nova Scotia salmon, no pickled herring or lox. No Matjes herring, no herring in wine sauce, no herring with onions in cream sauce, no baked or fried herring. No Scotch kippers, no pickled salmon, no sardines, no anchovies. This would have been fine except there was also no bacon, no sausages, no ham. Bagels, like toy truck tires, sat piled in the bread baskets while busboys kept the bakers busy making white toast by the loaf. A grim silence took possession of the dining room. It was like study hail, only the occasional cough or shifting of chairs assured you that there was life there. The rest of Saturday's meals passed in similar waves of awkward unfamiliarity and painfully felt politeness. We knew there would be a thin crowd for Sunday breakfast and wondered what kind of tips we'd harvest. Since it was an experiment of sorts no one was too hopeful that the Lions would shower us with generosity. We were more or less resigned, too, to being the scapegoats for Harold's misguided efforts to attract the upstate gentiles, and for Bob Gelman's (and my) assault on Jack Whitman's signboard.

Still, by noon I had collected $12 in singles, two plastic ballpoint pens, a clip-on tie with a Lion's insignia, and a brief note wishing me success with my college quest. One man, it may even have been Jack Whitman himself, winked, pumped my hand while slipping me two dollars, and said, "Good luck with the distaff physiognomy." I borrowed a dictionary from Sammy to translate the message and was surprised to learn that it was about the female anatomy. Jack Whitman was definitely my candidate for the Lions' presidency, but was Utica up to his vision?

4.

Steve and Jerry drove up to Braverman's Tuesday of that first week. Neither had called to tell me they were coming and I'd begun to imagine the Studebaker really was to be a surprise graduation gift from them and my parents. It was already five years old and not especially sleek as cars went in the mid-nineteen fifties so it didn't seem unreasonable to dream that I might be the beneficiary of the consumerism that was promoting cachet over utility to the new generation of prosperous Americans, but that Studebaker was not destined to be mine.

My brothers had gone directly to the kitchen upon their arrival and were talking to Rudy and Sammy when I appeared for lunch. My injured surprise was an opportunity for them to make jokes with their former compatriots.

"Look who's here, always the late comer."

"Still haven't gotten your timing down right I see." Private laughter was then shared among the four of them.

"Stop it, Jerry, you know how sensitive Melvin is about being late. So, little brother, did Rudy drag you into the meat locker yet?" They all laughed again in a knowing, insider way, like fraternity brothers with a newly recruited pledge.

"Why didn't you tell me you were coming up?" I asked, trying not to sound hurt and whiny.

"We wanted to surprise you. Sammy got us seats at his station and we were hoping that you wouldn't know we were here until you came into the dining room for lunch. We were going to tip you Mel, I swear, the whole three dollars for just one meal," Jerry said. Laughter again, and back slapping as well among the initiated.

"Well, it's good to see you anyway," I said grudgingly.

"Never start a sentence with 'well' Melvin, don't you remember anything Mrs. Friedman taught you?" Steve chimed in.

"You know, I'm glad you two surprised me because sometimes I forget what a pain in the ass you can be," I said, grabbing a plate from the pile in front of the sous chef.

"Come on Melvin you haven't got all day to stand around here and chit chat. Eat your lunch and get set up." Sammy said. "If you waste my time I'll see to it that the only person you'll be fit to be working for is judge Crater, and ghosts are lousy tippers."

While filling my plate on the food line I heard their laughter and the sound of their voices at play with Sammy's and once again experienced the vast space separating us, whatever it was comprised of; years, tastes, temperament, it had always been there, this vast chasm of differences. Often I thought it would always be there but, then, I'd assure myself I was being overly sensitive and revert to the hopeful admiration of my big brothers. As much as I liked watching them in action and admired and looked up to them, their remoteness always seemed like some kind of reproach, one I could not comprehend. It felt like something other than the big difference in our ages. But right then and there I knew I could no longer deny that the unbridgeable gap was real, and their sarcasm and insults, like the casual cruelty of some children, were meant as much to distance as to tease. Immediately, without effort, like a reflex, I thought of Harlan's friendliness, a welcoming full of promise. I could learn a great deal from him, his manner and style, his comfort and ease, his self-containment. He didn't seem to need anything from anybody.

That would be just perfect, I thought, the antidote to my hero worship, unmindful I was simply replacing one idol with another.

At lunch some old timers among the staff welcomed Steve and Jerry with enthusiastic shoulder punches and handshakes (hugs had yet to become fashionable among men) some feinting, dodging, and dancing as if in a boxing ring, and a torrent of questions about how they were doing in school and what they were doing for ass. Steve did most of the talking, always the more voluble of the two, while Jerry looked wistfully around the dining room, the dreamy smile of reverie on his face.

"Heard any good jokes, Jerry?" Sammy asked, always looking to extend his repertoire.

"As a matter of fact I heard a great one just yesterday but I don't know if you'd be able to understand it."

"Oy veh! Listen to this wise guy. So where's your drummer?" We all laughed because we knew the drummer was the comic's audible punctuation mark following a punchline. They ate lunch and did indeed insist upon my accepting a five dollar bill from them. Before they left Steve walked around the Studebaker with great ceremony, inspecting the fenders and doors, kicking the tires, peering at specks on the hood and running his fingers over the sideview mirror before smiling and nodding at me.

"You did very well. It'll only cost you five dollars for the wear and tear on the car," he said, smiling and lifting the five Jerry had tucked into my shirt pocket. I thought it was just a joke, but he drove away without giving me back the money. That was my brother Steve for you.

When I went back into the dining room I asked Sammy why there was so much joking about judge Crater. I'd never heard him mentioned in relation to Braverman's by anyone in my family and my brothers hadn't prepared me for the constant reference so it was a surprise his name kept coming up.

"It's an inside joke, Melvin. We keep it amongst ourselves."

"But why judge Crater, why not Kilroy or Harvey, the giant invisible rabbit?"

"The judge did like to come here during prohibition, they say, but that was before my time so I don't know if it's true or not, but what difference does it make? He's gone and we're not causing him any harm it's just a joke. Look, if we want to choose him as our ghost that's our business and that's all there is to it. Why are you so upset about the judge anyway?"

"Our ghost? Do we need a ghost? Who decided we need a ghost at Braverman's?"

"Melvin, it's just a joke, relax. You know what I think, I think you are much too serious for a young man. Why get so upset by a silly joke? Why take it so much to heart? This is going to be a long summer with plenty of heat and plenty of hard work and everybody needs a good joke to make the time pass in good spirits. It's something like a mascot just amongst our selves. Judge Crater is our mascot, our joke. Why, you believe in ghosts? You're afraid maybe he'll come after you in your bed at night? What is the problem, what is wrong with a little fooling around?" He was getting edgy.

"Sammy it's a question, not a problem. Jesus, talk about getting carried away."

"Let's have some respect here, Melvin, remember you're working for me."

"Understood, " I said, with a smile and touching the finger tips of my right hand to my forehead, lips and chest in sequence I bowed a low bow topped off with a flourish, relieved when Sammy laughed heartily.

Chapter Two

The summer season's regular guests began arriving towards the end of that first week, vacationers hopeful of avoiding the usual crush that took place on Sundays. Traveling up route 17, the long arduous path from New York City, most made their way into the country on Sunday afternoon each car a link in a steel chain that dragged slowly towards liberty, and Liberty, the last of the many towns they were headed for, the birthplace of the Jewish vacation resorts.

The road was a two lane affair that passed through the Shawangunk mountains before reaching the Catskills. The most daunting part of the ride involved negotiating the long and steep hill at Wurtshoro, a hill that was the vacationer's equivalent of the dragon that had to be slain in order to rescue a distressed damsel imprisoned in a tower. Radiators boiled over, geysers of steam erupted into the air, traffic stalled, horns blared, tempers exploded in competition with the radiators, cars were pushed on to the road's narrow shoulders, but the chain continued its slow, steady crawl languid as a snake in the sun. And when they arrived, the sodden vacationers, dripping with a hot perspiration, entered the broad drive and reception area of Braverman's with the exhausted relief of a desert caravan reaching an oasis.

Bernie Abramowitz, the resident tummler and social director, organizer of volley ball games and Simple Simon Says calesthenics, caromed from one newly arrived family to the next in a frenzy of welcoming.

"Bernie Abramowitz," he shouted, while slapping backs, pumping hands and pinching cheeks, "Abramowitz, everything from A to Z!" The returning old timers knew the joke, but the perplexed newcomers had to have it explained.

"A—bramowit.—Z. get it?" Bernie had made a stab at being a comic in the manner of Danny Kaye but he lacked Kaye's good looks, intelligence, charm and comic brilliance. That aside, he couldn't comprehend why he'd had a problem establishing himself in the firmament of comedy. In the first weeks of the summer season each of us in the dining room would be taken aside individually to hear how antisemitism had destroyed his career in show business. That Kaye, Eddie Cantor, Milton Berle, Jack Benny. Sid Caesar, Alan King and dozens of others had succeeded, because of or in spite of their Jewishness, was of no concern to Bernie. "It must have been my material," he'd lament, "but who knew someone could hate gabardine that much. No, but seriously, and like all comics I'm basically a serious person, it was my Holy Family routine that was too much ahead of its time. Have I ever told you the routine?" I smiled and shook my head no for what would prove to be only the first of a thousand tellings. He was so pathetic in his eagerness to charm and amuse it was painful to be with him for any length of time.

"Hey! Look at me! I'm Joseph the forgotten man. What's with this 'Jesus, Mary *and* Joseph.' I'm the goddamn Zeppo Marx of the Holy Family! Try to put yourself in my place. You marry this good looking girl, Mary, a kid but great tits, and the next thing you know, every time you try to lay a hand on her you get a headache like you wouldn't believe. What's this, I say to myself, am I the husband or am I the wife? Nobody told me what I was getting myself into. Nobody said, Hey Joe, God needs a beard, you want the job? Nobody said that. Look, I was a good lookin' fella, a punim like a movie star. I'd had more women than the Egyptians had locusts. Did I need this?" His monologue always ended there. I never knew if it was because he hadn't written more or if it was at that point he had to run for his life to get away from an irate mob. Lenny Bruce himself wouldn't have dared that routine in the 1950's.

After unloading their luggage, the bellhops escorted the families to the registration desk, chatting up the wives and children, assessing the nubility of the teenaged daughters and the flirtatiousness of the married women in the process. Tired and bedraggled as they were, it heartened the bellhops to see these women revive with a little flattery and attention. Their whiny brats were always the cutest, their teenagers were assured of the great athletic program, and their husbands were completely ignored. While some of the bellhops were college students, most were hustlers who were looking for a buck anyway they could make it. They hung around the card room and fetched drinks and cigars for the gin rummy, pinochle and poker players compensating for crummy tips by short-changing the obviously timid and snaring any bills or change that landed accidentally on the carpeted floor. The women canasta players got little attention because women were lousy tippers. "Thank you dolling, and a pinch on the cheek is nothing to take to the bank," they'd complain.

Table assignments in the dining room followed room assignments at the hotel. Stuart Stein, the Maitre d' who called himself "Sandy" in the summers, dispersed the guests according to a plan he had designed years before. The young singles were clustered to the rear of the dining room but dispersed among three different teams of waiters and busboys. The singles were notoriously cheap and often skipped out without tipping. The "young marrieds", as they were called, couples without children, sat towards the front across the aisle from Sammy's station. The waiter assigned to them was usually a basketball player, often an All-American like Ivan Goldman, who was admired by the husbands and swooned over by the wives. Sammy, who was tolerant but cool towards these jocks, his celebrity being confined by place while theirs extended far beyond such local borders, was assigned the Braverman regulars, repeat vacationers who requested Sammy's station and were rewarded for their generous tips with seats by the windows overlooking the pool. The less generous or more querulous were given to Abe who rarely complained and accepted his lot stoically. Abe's tables abutted ours along the wall just down from the windows. Stuart took pride in his distributions, rewarding the more compliant and cooperative waiters with new guests who drove fancy cars, information the bell boys supplied, and punishing the trouble makers by assigning them the families that arrived in old wrecks loaded with children and grandparents, large families with little likelihood of proferring munificent gestures of appreciation. I wondered what kind of group Harlan would harvest. His station was located at the rear of the dining room diagonally across from me and from all the windows. Most likely he'd get the newer and less aggressive vacationers, perhaps newlyweds who only had eyes for each other anyway and couldn't care less about views.

Then there were the guests, especially the women guests. They came in all shapes and sizes, in all tones of the flesh from milk white to olive bronze. They had blonde hair, red hair, black hair, chestnut brown and champagne pink hair. They were obese and slovenly with tubular rolls of fat hanging like aprons over the waistbands of their pedal pushers and toreador pants, their bulging buttocks straining the seams of these too-tight garments. Or there were the friendly but plain ladies who looked like the mothers and sisters of my friends in the Bronx, non-descript, hardly worthy of a young man's notice, eliciting neither critical abuse nor lustful fantasies from the dining room staff. But then there were the shapely and gorgeous ones who seemed to find one another quickly and clustered together at poolside like members of an exotic harem; women with fiery red talon-like nails, luscious lips bathed in a creamy, cherry- red wet and glistening lipstick which they licked and caressed with the tips of their tongues; deep tans on their bodies which they oiled and basted by the hour as they lounged on their chaise lounges—the Catskill translation of chaise longue—and discussed their lives, their dreams, and what to do to keep a man reined in and grateful for any attention bestowed upon him. It was not as though they were as thoroughly cynical as this may sound. They truly believed in the virtues of their values and their experiences had rewarded them for staying close to that system which had guided their fortunes. Their husbands were always referred to as "decent and hard working" when they spoke of these men to the other women. But, occasionally, one of the beauties would tell of the dull accountant who was seen in a nightclub with a young showgirl, unmindful of his family's fight with the mosquitoes of Monticello, and they all the while feeling sorry for him for being trapped in the smoky, humid heat of New York City in the dog days of summer. Then the women would cluck their tongues and wag their heads in disapproval and the silent lamentation that seemed to say "Men" rippled through their assembly until another story was told.

The men also came in all shapes and sizes, if they came at all. Many were happy to toil in the city all week long and settle for weekend visits. Some families stayed for the whole season in the cottages located along the small lake across the state road from the hotel's main buildings. They were entitled access to the hotel's facilities, the swimming pool, tennis courts, shows and dances at the recreation hall, but they cooked their own meals and did their own laundry. Husbands might spend a week or two on holiday and then come for weekends, but the wives and children were there by themselves most of the time. It was always rumored that many of those women were lonely, horny and available. And many of their husbands looked as though they weren't particularly happy to be in the company of their wives and children when they were together which seemed to lend credence to the tales of the women's sexual availability. I fantasized about some of them but guiltily because it was as though I was invading someone else's domain. It's not as though I thought of women as property, it was just that they belonged to someone else. Wasn't that the way the songs of those days expressed love? "You belong to me, I belong to you." Whether single or married I had been instructed women were either seduced or misled but never voluntarily pursued illicit relationships. This victimology was my mother's teaching which stemmed from the experience of her sister, my aunt Ceil, who had a long series of broken hearted romances with married men, "the using bastards" as they were called by my father. But, since losing my virginity had been one of my goals for that summer, that there were sexually experienced, horny women potentially available for pleasure was both exciting and daunting.

2.

   The first meal served to the full complement of newly arrived vacationers was Sunday supper and it bore very little of the burden of the hotel's reputation as an eat-all-you-can-eat, stuff-it-in, wrap-the-rest-in-a-napkin-and-take-it-back-to-your-room, medium sized hotel with a kitchen reputed to be worthy of the Concord or Grossinger's. Whether or not it deserved this reputation was never something the dining room staff concerned itself with. We were fed leftovers buried in a brown gravy sauce that overpowered the flavor of any meat immersed in it. Even garlic couldn't defeat it and this unappetizing fare fostered something called "scoffing" a term meaning eating on the sneak. It originated with the British Merchant Marine in the 1800's and some romantic must have felt it suited the crew manning the dining rooms of the Catskills because it took root there quickly and was understood by everyone who ever set foot in a hotel kitchen. Scoffing was elevated to an art form by the quick handed basketball players brought up to play in the hotel basketball league. Ben and the other owners might have wanted to field good teams in the Friday night basketball circuit but they weren't about to serve then prime ribs for their efforts. So an extra steak might come out for a guest who did not appear for dinner, or one who was delegated the reputation of consummate glutton by the waiter who then brought extra portions out to his side stand where they were partaken of quickly and furtively, as if by hyenas, between trips to the kitchen. More commonly, breakfast lox and dinner desserts were consumed in a single swallow on the fly with one's back to Stuart Stein who was responsible to intercept and interdict such activity. I can't remember his ever succeeding but his conviction that it was happening all around him all the time made him testy and wary with the waiters and busboys. And this finicky punctiliousness served, in turn, to make it a contest within the staff to scoff in full view of everyone in your area without being seen by Sandy Stein. Sammy, who expressed no opinion about the practice, actually demonstrated a remarkable facility with it on occasion just to show he was still one of the boys, which left Stuart Stein alone in a position of miserable isolation in his own dining room. To me he was little more than an usher showing people to their seats. As Sammy's busboy I was under his protection and therefore relatively immune to the maitre d's nit picking.

Sammy's station was full that first Sunday. Most of his guests were returning veterans of Braverman's and there was an aura of reunion complete with handshakes, hugs, reminiscences, and the recounting of personal news. People were curious about me and when Sammy told them I was the younger brother of Jerry and Steve White he also added that I was planning to be a doctor just like Jerry. I was so busy carting out tray loads of food that I hardly spoke to anyone. As he had explained, Sammy took the diners' orders, communicated them to the kitchen and then sent me to fetch them. It required two trips to deliver the load of juices, sliced melons, orange and grapefruit sections, and grapefruit halves for our thirty two guests. I had no sooner deposited the second tray on the side stand when Sammy whispered to me that it was time to refill the bread baskets and water goblets, check the glass boats of olives, radishes, celery sticks, and carrot slices, and top up the pickle dish. That accomplished I then began to bring out tray loads of hot soup, cold soup, salads, dishes of salad dressing, and more baskets of bread and rolls while Sammy passed out the food and regaled his clients with anecdotes, jokes, personal vignettes, and bits of gossip.

"Sally, did I tell you that Esther Gaussman got married?"

"NO!" expostulated Sally, obviously stunned by this news.

"In Miami Beach. A widower. Murray Fiedelman. A jeweler," he said in a peculiar telegraphic staccato.

"Mazel tov," said Sally in a tone that made it sound to me more as though she meant, "that's life" or "go figure."

The pace of the meal accelerated into the main course. It being Sunday night the choice of supper entrees was somewhat limited. The noon meal on Sunday was the big sirloin steak dinner, a dinner that people anticipated all week long as though meat was still being rationed and was hard to come by in 1956. Steak was in fact quite plentiful, if costly, but being served a steak dinner by a waiter in black tie and on tables spread with white linen did seem to make it taste better and engender a more luxurious experience. For the Braverman family it was a way to send off their guests with the feeling that they had been treated lavishly, feasted and indulged, and it was hoped that the memory of this extravagance would serve to lure them back again the following summer. With that goal set in motion, Sunday night, while the new crowd was still recovering from the trip through the Shawangunks and likely to be too exhausted to be focused on that meal, the usual fare included flanken, or boiled beef, a meal destined in large measure for the sous chef's brown sauce, stuffed chicken breasts, broiled halibut, and garden vegetable dinner. The meals would then work their way towards more elaborate and expensive fare as the week progressed achieving a heightened excitement with prime ribs au jus on Saturday night and climaxing with the sirloin steak for Sunday dinner. It was the convention in the smaller hotels to set up daily menus Sunday to Saturday and to repeat them in rotation without variation. Sunday supper and clean-up ended for me at 9:45.

Back in my room I turned the radio on and climbed up into my bed. I was exhausted. Doris Day was singing "Que Sera, Sera" and I was wondering if what would "sera" for me would be an endless summer of doing all of Sammy's lifting and porting as well as my own cleaning up and bussing. That would lengthen my day at the expense of the little leisure time a busboy had, and I began feeling sorry for myself. Maybe Sammy's regulars would be no more generous than anyone else? Who had worked with Sammy before and why wasn't he eager for the job again? None of the other waiters in the dining room suggested he had worked his way up from that position; no one had said the money's great, hang in. Maybe they all died of exhaustion before the end of the summer season. I was working my way towards teary eyes when Harlan came in and grimaced.

"Would you mind if I changed that music, Mel?"

"That's okay," I said, happy to have his company. The radio whined and rasped as Harlan steered the dial across a path of weak signals and then halted in the middle of an Elvis Presley song, "Heartbreak Hotel". "Ugh" I groaned.

"You don't like Elvis? Learn to like him Melvin if you want the girls to like you. They love him. Loo-oove him," he crooned. Then, positioning his hands on an imaginary guitar held in front of him at hip level, he curled his lips into a sneer, waggled his hips, and said "Bayba."

"I don't like him and I don't like that music. I like jazz." I also liked the more conventional sounding ballads and themes: "Love is a Many Splendored Thing," "Moonglow," "The Poor People of Paris," songs that seemed earnest and sincere about love. Elvis was about lust and that was something for darkness and secrecy, I believed, not bright lights and sound stages.

"Jazz is good, but Elvis is better. All the little Miss Prissys melt their circle pins when they hear Elvis. He's the bad boy every good girl would die to give herself to. You can't say that for Count Basie or Stan Kenton, Melvin."

"There are some girls who wouldn't waste a wink on him. He's a goddamn truck driver."

"Pretty snotty stuff for a busboy, Mel. You watch, Elvis is going to bring about some big changes. It's going to be motor-cycle boots, not white bucks, leather jackets, not tweed sport coats and chesterfield overcoats, and lots of black." Harlan looked very serious.

"What makes you so sure that's going to sweep the country? I know lots of guys who were wearing motorcycle boots and leather jackets three or four years ago. They didn't start any trend."

"Those same guys were probably still filling up condoms with water and dropping them out of their bathroom windows." We both laughed at that image—and its accuracy. "Elvis is the real thing. Elvis is animal magnetism, he's passion, he's a mutineer of the sexual order. Join him, don't fight him. You might just as well fight the changing of the seasons." Harlan said all of this in the calm and even voice of absolute conviction.

"I suppose they really love him at Harvard." I was fishing. I hadn't seen anything with the Harvard name or colors among Harlan's personal things so this made me a little suspicious of his attendance there. Had it been me, at the least I'd have worn a t-shirt with the school name or logo showing.

"Depends on who you talk to. Some of the Cliffees are wild for him. Some of the Wellsley girls too I can assure you of that," and he winked at me, a single, brisk wink without a leer or an elbow in my side to emphasize his point.

"You really go to Harvard Harlan?"

"You sound like you don't believe I do."

This was unexpected and disarming. I had imagined if he did attend Harvard he gladly would have acknowledged that, and if he didn't he might have become defensive, maybe even a little aggressive. That was how it worked where I grew up. "It's not that I don't believe you, it's . . . well, how come you don't have any sweat shirts or t-shirts that say Harvard on them?"

"That would really help my income, wouldn't it. Do you think people would feel more or less generous tipping a waiter who happens to attend Harvard? You might be impressed, but many more would feel jealous or resentful. Somehow in their minds it's the same as being rich, or privileged."

"Then what do you tell them when they ask you about school?"

"I tell them I go to a little school outside of Boston and change the subject. Cambridge is outside of Boston so I'm not lying, and I deflect their attention with other ploys."

"Oh."

"Of course I've also considered saying I don't go to college because I can't afford it. That I'm here to save up the tuition for at least two years of school before I apply, but that may sound a bit too pathetic. I have to give it more thought."

"I would be so excited I would boast about it all the time," I confessed. "You know, I'm trying to get into Columbia and I would tell everybody except I'm afraid that if I don't get in I'll look like a fool, you know, not good enough."

"It's never wrong to try, to reach for something, to take a chance, and the people who would laugh at you for making that stretch don't deserve to have your attention. Learn that one early, kiddo." The radio was now playing "Why Do Fools Fall in Love". I decided to repay Harlan for his advice on the spot, cued by the lyrics of love. "Harlan, you're dating Heidi Braverman, right?" He nodded and a smirk appeared on his face. "What?"

"Dating is not exactly the way I'd put it, but go on."

"The day I arrived here Sammy made a point of telling Ron to try to get you to stop seeing her. I thought you should know about it."

"Thanks. Ron hasn't tried to do that yet but I know that he would if he thought it his business." He frowned then and narrowed his eyes. "Ron doesn't like me, that's obvious. I don't really know why, he doesn't come right out with it, but it's very clear how he feels. Frankly, Scarlet, I don't give a damn. What's between Heidi and me is between Heidi and me. She's a big girl. Do you have a girl Melvin?"

"Nobody special if that's what you mean."

"Well then, maybe I can get Heidi to fix you up with one of the camp counselors." Ron entered just as Harlan suggested that and he picked up immediately.

"Looking for a girl Melvin? There are a few regulars up here that I can put you on to." He looked at the radio and frowned. "Mind if I turn that off?" he asked, turning the radio off before either of us could answer. "I feel like reading." He flopped onto his bunk and pulled a paperback out from under his pillow. "Rosie's always ready and willing, and then there's Diana. She's quite a number." He broke the spine of the book, flexing the pages back and forth a few times, and then fell silent. Harlan looked at me and shrugged. I raised my eyebrows and smiled sardonically. Neither of us was prepared to take Ron on.

"Tell me about Diana," I ventured.

"You can't get to Diana unless you start with Rosie. Those are the house rules." He had kept the book in front of him when he spoke so I couldn't tell if he was serious.

"Okay, then tell me about Rosie."

Exasperated, Ron pulled the book away from his face and rested it on end against his chest. "There's very little to tell. Rosie was put on earth to give virgins like you their first fuck. She has big tits and small brains. Her brassiere size is bigger than her I.Q. She's probably nineteen years old now but she's been doing the deed since she was twelve and is happy to oblige. Buy her a flower and she'll blow you too. Anything else?"

"Where is she?" I was both excited and disgusted by Ron's offering. I desperately wanted to lose my virginity but I didn't want it to be in a degrading way. It sounded like if Rosie was indeed real there would he no way to accomplish that goal. But on the other hand, I was determined to have the initiating sexual liaison and quickly. It would be like having my tonsils out, just something to get through and be done with, a once in a lifetime experience this being de-virginalized. "Where do I find Rosie?"

"Melvin." Harlan said in reproach.

"Stay out of this Harlan. You really want Rosie? Seriously? I'll introduce you to her, but don't ever say that I didn't warn you."

"Warn me about what?"

"About the possibility of venereal diseases, the clap, the syph, who knows what else she might be carrying, and the most miserable affliction of them all—the afters."

"What are the afters?" I knew about gonorrhea and syphilis but I had never heard of "the afters." Ron had made it sound like something terribly ominous.

"I can't tell you that. You'll have to find out for yourself."

I turned to Harlan but he just shrugged.

3.

When I arrived in the Catskills that summer I had one clear goal: to earn about fifteen hundred dollars to pay my college tuition and to provide pocket money. My other aspirations were clouded by uncertainty because I truly believed I had no control over them. I'll call them the prizes. First and foremost was whether I'd be accepted to the freshman class at Columbia but a very close second was whether I'd lose my virginity, or in the language of the time, perhaps of all times, score; get in; get laid. My anxieties about these two intentions brought me into the Catskill mountains with a discomfiting sense of powerlessness. It was a mystery to me if I'd get either prize.

So, while there were these two mysteries—would my brain and my body both be rewarded that summer—it had taken almost no time at all for there to be yet another mystery waiting for me in the Catskills, Harlan Hawthorne. What the hell was he doing there? I have already described him briefly to you but you must understand the effect his demeanor and carriage had on me was profound. His was a very different style, one that relied on a withholding of his opinions and a general quality of self-containment and restraint. This was in stark contrast to the relentless babbling of opinions and gibes that characterized the generic mountain rat. Morning until night, from the showers to the dance floor, a snide recitative droned all around me but Harlan, wearing a bemused smile, hummed quietly to himself. The target of many taunts and jeers he'd simply cock an eyebrow, smile tolerantly, and shake his head gently from side to side in a gesture of muted disbelief. He was somewhere else.

While he was an enigma to many of us working in the dining room, Sammy had an especially difficult time understanding Harlan's style.

"Who does he think he is? What does he want here? What is he looking for?" These questions were posed rhetorically, Sammy's way of thinking out loud. No one believed that Harlan was working as a waiter because he needed the money, not the Jewish boys from the city, not the basketball players from the south, and certainly not Sammy. Abe was mute on the subject. The puzzle so frustrated Sammy it made his usually artful jibes cruel and clumsy.

"Harlan, come to my room later so I can circumcise you. I can't stand the idea of a putz working in my dining room." Seeing his perplexity Abe explained to Harlan that while a "shmuck" was the entire male member, a "putz" was just the foreskin.

"What is it Harlan, you're schmekele is cold? It needs to wear a turtleneck? Do you think a Jewish girl wants to have to deal with that? She'd probably faint when she sees it." Harlan countenanced this barrage with composure and equanimity saying nothing. Girls didn't seem at all put off by him, quite the contrary, whether or not they had seen his anatomical anomaly, the foreskin being anomalous only among Jews. Indeed, mothers and daughters could sometimes be seen elbowing one another out of the way to get in front of him, the mother's being more seductive than their pouting daughters had ever imagined possible. It was something amazing to observe.

"They don't really know what to make of me, do they?" he asked me as we lay in our bunks staring at the ceiling one afternoon after lunch in mid-July.

"You are very different, Harlan. They can't understand why a Harvard man is waiting tables here. At the Concord or at Grossinger's there might be an Ivy but at Braverman's?" I was hanging "they" as a curtain in front of my own curiosity.

"I didn't have enough experience to work in those hotels. They're more demanding in their hiring practices than the Bravermans. I'm here for the same reasons all of the rest of you are, to make money."

I heard "all the rest of you" as "JEWS" and bridled inside, but then saw an opportunity in that statement. "That may be so Harlan, but all the rest of us are also Jewish and you're not."

"And the basketball players from Mississippi and Kansas?"

"They're basketball players. They're different."

"And I'm different too, Melvin."

Whenever people called me Melvin instead of Mel I always felt that they were angry at me, an imprinting by my parents who used my full proper name to alert me to their imminent castigations. I didn't want Harlan to be angry with me and I didn't want him to call me Melvin. I didn't want anybody to call me Melvin. "I wish you wouldn't call me Melvin. Mel is fine."

"You don't like your name, do you. I've seen you grimace when Sammy or Ron call you Melvin. What's wrong with it?"

"Haven't you ever seen Jerry Lewis do his Melvin routines? Do you have any idea what it felt like to be a Melvin when that was the name that meant hopeless moron, shmuck?"

"I understand. It's not the most square-jawed of names, is it? I bet people tell you, 'Hey, there's Mel Torme and Mel Ferrer and they're great,' right?"

"Were you hiding under the bed? That's exactly what they tell me. And don't forget Melvyn Douglas, who just happens to look like my father's twin brother so how can I complain? Yeah, that's exactly what they tell me when they're not yelling at me to stop feeling sorry for myself."

"Then, why don't you change it? You can call yourself anything you like. You can call yourself–Jack. I like that. Jack. That's a good name. Jack and Jill, Jack and the Beanstalk, Jack Armstrong, the All-American Boy! You are now Jack."

"There are Jakes where I come from, Harlan, but no Jacks," I objected.

"Great, then you will be the first, that's even better. C'mon Jack, do it." I looked over at him lying on his cot. His hands were clasped behind his neck, his arms forming triangles on either side of his head, and he was smiling a smile of genuine pleasure and satisfaction. "C'mon."

"I don't think I can do it, I really don't think so."

"Jack, I'm going to tell you something and I don't want you to repeat it to anyone. Can I trust you to do that? Because if I can't trust you, Jack, I'll be terribly disappointed."

"I swear." I almost promised to cross my heart.

"Once, at Harvard, when I was trying to impress a TA, that's a graduate student who is teaching a class for a professor, I told her my name was Packard Studebaker because I didn't want her to look me up in the student directory and find out I was only a sophomore. The name just fell out of my mouth, and she just fell into my arms. With the right name in the right place you can reach for the things you dream about from the shelter and safety of a new identity. Jack will be like your suit of armor."

"People will laugh. Sammy and Ron and the others will be merciless, they'll ride me day and night, they'll . . ."

"Forget them. Just let it roll off your back. What do you care what they say. Are they the rest of your life, or is Jack Armstrong, the All-American boy, the rest of your summer?"

"I could never do that . . ." It was such a recklessly bold and exhilarating proposition I began to laugh, as if intoxicated, silly, giddy laughter.

"You can and you must. Listen to me. This could be a critical crossroads, Melvin,—your moment of truth. You can live the life you want to live, or you can be a spectator to it, a resentful, unhappy spectator. Take a risk, take a chance, take the name Jack." His tone was fierce.

"How will I explain it to everyone?"

"It's your middle name and you've decided to use it. You don't like Melvin or Mel and so from now on it's Jack. Say it. Say 'Jack.'" He was staring up at me with an intensity that informed me I had no choice but to do as he said.

"Jack. JACK! Jack, Jack, Jack. I am Jack White, pleased to meet you. My name is Jack White, what's yours? Hi, I'm Jack."

"Keep saying it until you believe it. You have to feel you are Jack, feel it inside you. Say 'Jack'."

It was becoming frightening to me. It was beginning to seem more important to Harlan that I be Jack than it was to me.

"Cut it out, Harlan, I'm Jack, okay? Let's not get carried away with this. I promise, from now on I'm going to be known as Jack White."

"Okay. I was just trying to help you out, don't get so tense."

Perhaps a more experienced and less credulous person would have become suspicious of Harlan at that point. It had been so easy for him to solve my problem by breaking through the conventions framing ordinary existence, such an effortless rupture of propriety, that I was both thrilled and appalled. But to have balked would have seemed hopelessly middle class, the single most searing epithet amongst my brilliant high school friends, and accepting his advice did feel thrilling and liberating, over the edge.

Later, walking to dinner, I told Ron what I had decided to do with my name.

"Jack? You really like that? Jack?"

"Well, like Harlan says, it is a simple, square jawed All-American name, as in Jack Armstrong, All-American . . ."

"The only All-American you know is Ivan Goldman, the All-American basketball player from the Bronx. Jesus Mel, I thought you were sharper than that. I told you Harlan isn't somebody you should trust."

"But Jack is a great name, the hero of most nursery rhymes, a name that has deep, safe associations in our minds, Jack and Jill, Jack and the Beanstalk . . ."

"Jackass, Jack off, Jack shit, Jack the Ripper. Jack." He was sneering as the name came out of his mouth. "And while we're at it, Mr. Whatsinaname, where did White come from, Weiss? Weissberg? Weissman? You know it was never just plain old Mr. White." I knew he was right, but that was information hard won and I was not about to give it away to him just for the asking.

"You won't guess, so don't even waste your time trying. Anyway, White is the name I was born with, I didn't change it." In spite of my efforts not to I was sounding very defensive, and totally oblivious of the irony that I could trade Melvin for Jack readily, while cringing at my grandfather's decision to swap Zwartzoffski for White.

"C'mon, what was it, some thing really grotesque like Baumbergsteinwitz ?"

"No, actually it was Sheenykikemockyjew. We changed it because it was such a bitch to spell."

"Just asking, Mel, no offense intended. But we both know there were never any Whites, Blacks, Greystones, or Taylors in the ghettos. I could alter my name, but . . ." That was one of Ron's jokes, alter Alter.

"There are alternatives I'm sure," I said, hoping we were done with the genealogical survey of my family. To try to insure that I added, "Boy I'm hungry, I hope some of that roast beef is left over from Saturday night."

"You want to know what's left over from last Saturday night? Rosie is left over from last Saturday night. Are you ready for her yet?"

"Sure." I felt myself blush and my heart flipped in my chest like a fish in a net.

"Then I'll take you to meet her after dinner. I'm sick and tired of listening to that goddamned cha-cha music in the recreation hall anyway. Do you think the Cubans ever play Klezmer music at their resorts?" Seeing my perplexity Ron waved his hand and said, "Forget it."

I was distracted all through dinner and Sammy was irritated with me for not schmoozing the guests more enthusiastically. He cornered me in the kitchen as I collected the salads and various dressings.

"What's the matter with you Melvin, aren't you interested in making any money this week? Why aren't your pecuniary proclivities in a pulsatile pandemonium?" Sammy had been studying P words.

"It's Monday night, for godsakes, get started and be friendly already. You want that I should earn you your tips?"

I kept looking over at Ron's station but he paid me no mind whatsoever. Ron was being very polite and charming to his guests and totally oblivious of my eager glances. After clean up and the ritual wiping and sorting of the silver he came to my station and asked if I was ready to go.

"Is there really a Rosie?" I asked trying to sound wary and shrewd. "And how come you haven't pointed her out if she really exists." I was hoping that she was a fabrication of his, not real, not flesh and blood.

"When you're done whining we can get washed up and I'll take you to meet her. She's waiting for us."

At nine o'clock we left the waiters' quarters and cut through the line of trees that separated us from the dormitory housing some of the other hotel employees. Trying to be cool I kicked at a stone as we passed through the weeds, but the stone was embedded in the ground and didn't budge causing me to stumble and abrade my hands when I fell. "Gee, I'm bleeding. Maybe we should go back so I can wash up."

"Rosie would welcome you if you were wrapped in a plaster cast from head to toe. Chickening out Melvin? Podus frostus? Feetus coldus?" he rode me gleefully.

I pulled out my handkerchief and dabbed at my palms. "Lets go then."

Rosie's room was in the rear section of the building where some of the chambermaids lived. The older ones drove in each morning from the nearby towns but the younger ones, like Rosie, lived on the grounds and their room and board made up a big part of their pay, just like the waiters and busboys.

"Do you have a girl up here Ron?" I asked as we climbed the back stairs.

"Vivian works in a summer camp near Liberty. We don't see that much of each other up here. We're going to get married after we finish school. This way." he said leading me through the rear door.

"Ron." I stopped and stood my ground until he came back to me. "Please introduce me as Jack. Please." He rolled his eyes and then nodded his assent.

"Rosie are you here?" he called out. A girlish voice said "Who's that? Is that Ron? Ronnie is that you?"

"The one and only," he called out. "Is Rosie here Martha?" A plain looking girl in shorts and a halter top with a terrific figure and a moderately bad case of acne came out of one of the rooms along the hall and leaned herself languidly against the wall. She raised up her right arm, configured her fingers in the shape of a gun and, squinting her left eye, sighted Ron down the barrel of her index finger.

"Ronnie's looking for Rosie but he's found Martha," she said in a petulant voice. Then, as if noticing me for the first time she asked, "Who's he?"

"This is Jack. Jack, Martha. Martha, Jack." he said, nodding at us each in turn. "Actually, Martha, I thought you and I and Jack and Rosie could go out for a few drinks, have a little fun, you know." Martha still had him in her sights. "Rosie has the rag on, Jack, still interested?" I swallowed hard and looked at Ron.

"Of course he is," Ron said as he walked up to Martha and ran his hand gently along her extended arm over her shoulder and down her neck to her breast. Martha pressed herself against him, took his face in both her hands and kissed him fiercely. So much for Vivian, I thought. They stood there grinding and groaning for I don't remember how long and I was about to leave them when a pudgy, round faced girl with long black hair still wet from the shower, came out of the bathroom.

"Looks like Ronnie and Martha have got something straight between them," she said, tugging at the bath towel wrapped around her body. "Who're you?" she said motioning at me with her chin.

"That's Jack," Ron said before I could speak. "I brought him around to meet you. What say we all go to Freddy's and have some drinks?" Rosie studied me disinterestedly and shrugged. "Come on, we'll have some fun. Jack's buying." Rosie looked back at me and I smiled and nodded. I felt like I might throw up, but I smiled.

"Wait downstairs," Rosie said. We did as we were told. On the back steps I took out a pack of Old Gold Filters and, with shaky hands, lit a cigarette.

"What's that you're smoking?" Ron said. I showed him the pack. He shook his head and frowned. "Can you get this one right? This is not the rest of your life. This is an initiation ceremony. Put a flag over her face if you have to. Just remember, Diana is out there waiting but you have to go through Rosie first."

"I don't know if I can go through with this, and what about Vivian," I said irately, as if she were my sister. "How can you do this to Vivian?"

"Did you see that body on Martha? Don't be a prick."

When the girls came downstairs Ron said he'd drive. He wrapped an arm around Martha's shoulders and walked ahead while Rosie and I followed behind.

"So, you live around here all year round?" I said, trying to break the ice.

"Yeah." she said.

"That must be nice." The clicking of her chewing gum was her only response and it was obvious that Rosie was not adept in the art of making conversation.

"You're cute," she said, sliding her hand down the inside of my arm. "What's your name again?"

"Meh, Jack!" I fumbled, almost bleating my real name as we arrived at Ron's car. Once inside Martha was all over Ron and it looked as though she was going to sit in his lap for the ride.

"Don't be so bashful," Rosie said, rubbing my thigh and crowding me in my seat. "I like that name, Jack."

"Me too," I said, like an idiot.

Freddy's was a townie bar, one that I had walked past when in town for toiletries and such, but I'd never been inside. Even on warm sunny days you could see men hunched over the formica bar when you looked through the windows and there was something uncomfortable and a little ominous to me in that sight. I had been raised to be wary of gentiles drinking alcohol. Visions of Cossacks besotted with vodka had been conjured for me every Passover but others too, whether Irish, Polish or Italian, were always defined as dangerous when associated with alcohol. Throughout high school I argued against these stereotypes citing the friends I had made with members of those groups, but here on unfamiliar ground that early indoctrination triumphed and prevailed. We parked just down the street from the entrance and as we approached the place Martha was hanging all over Ron, kissing him on the neck and laughing loudly. Rosie seemed a little disappointed with me and walked ahead. I couldn't tell which was making me more nervous, the prospect of a bar brawl or the prospect of sex with Rosie. Either way, my nerves were so jangled I thought they'd sound like a pocket full of loose change if they could be heard. Two men in their twenties came out of the entrance to Freddy's and stopped on the sidewalk.

"Hey Martha, got yourself a rich Jewboy?" None of us spoke. I felt the fear creep up my neck and my mouth went dry. My muscles became rubbery like they'd been detached from my bones.

"Hey Jewboy, Martha is my girlfriend. What are you doing with my girlfriend?"

"I'm not your girl, Joe. Don't listen to him, Ronnie, lets just go inside and have some fun." Ron had stopped walking and stood facing the two men. They were of average height and build. They were both wearing jeans and boots and smoking cigarettes. The slightly taller one had his cigarette pack rolled up in one sleeve of his T-shirt, an affectation of some street toughs I knew. They wore cocky, leering smiles on their faces.

"I think you owe me an apology for calling me Jewboy," Ron said in a cold and flat voice.

"An apology! Did you hear that Joe? He thinks that you owe him an apology. Why don't you give him one," he said stepping forward, "or should I."

"Why that's very kind of you Johnny," Joe said.

Ron pulled off his glasses and handed them to Martha. He started to open the clasp on the expansion band of his wristwatch when the one called Johnny leapt at him and took a roundhouse swing. Leaning back as the punch arrived, the man's fist grazing his chin, Ron just continued removing his watch. He flipped it to me quickly, caught the off balance Johnny from behind, lifted him off the ground as if he were no heavier than a feather pillow, and threw him through the air to the brick wall framing the plate glass window of Freddy's.

"Joe, you asshole, I said I think you owe me an apology," Ron said. Joe looked over at Johnny who lay moaning on the ground. "I never use the same wall twice. That means I'll have to heave you through the window. Ever fly through a plate glass window Joe? It really hurts. Very bloody." He took a step forward and Joe's arms flew up in the air, his empty palms framing his face.

"Hey, it was just a joke, only kidding around. Martha will tell you I'm a real kidder, right Martha?" Martha turned away silently.

"I guess you just told me a lie too," Ron said. Then the one named Joe turned and ran away. Johnny rolled over and sat up.

"Let's go, Ron, this place is too crowded," I said with bravado.

"Your pal really takes good care of you, Johnny, doesn't he. But understand that's what Jews do for each other, we take good care." Ron stood over the one he had flung through the air and looked down at the blood oozing out of a gash on his elbow. "I still haven't heard you say you're sorry for what Joe said to me." Johnny snickered. "Ohh, I wish you hadn't done that." Ron bent down and placed his face close to Johnny's. "You can say 'I'm sorry' or you can go home with your nose pointing at your ear, it's your choice. No? I guess you want me to hurt you." But as he closed his fist and cocked his arm Johnny said, "Sorry."

"Let's just go," I said. Ron glared at me.

"You're lucky that Jack is feeling sorry for you. His head is as soft as his heart. Martha, Rosie, I want you to tell all of your friends about what happened to Johnny and as for you Johnny, the next time that you're feeling tough remember that it was a Jew who kicked your ass. And learn to show some respect for your betters," he said over his shoulder as he walked away. He motioned to us to go with him and we all got back into the car. "Well, I guess Freddy's is out of the question," he said starting the engine, and we all laughed.

4.

When we got back to the hotel Martha wanted to go to the recreation hall to dance but Ron said he wasn't in the mood. I wasn't in the mood either. All I could think about was when Joe and Johnny would find their way to Braverman's and get even. Rosie came up to me, slipped her arm around my waist and said, "I have a portable radio in my room. Why don't we get that, go down to the storage shed and dance there?" The shed was where the pool furniture was stored during the winter. In the summer it was empty save for some broken chairs and umbrellas. "Great! Come on Ron lets do that," Martha said.

Ron looked at me and cocked an eyebrow. "Jack? Are you in?"

"Sure," I said. My mind had been dwelling on how long it would take Joe and Johnny to round up their gang of thug friends and descend on the waiters' quarters to kill us all. A thought like that can have a definite dampening effect on one's libido. What the hell, I thought, if I was going to die I might just as well have a crack at Rosie first.

Rosie and Martha went for the radio, a clumsy hunk of plastic that ran on four large flashlight batteries, while Ron and I went back to our room to get some blankets.

"You never give those fuckers an inch, understand?"

"Who?"

"You shmuck, the Joes and Johnnys of the world. The only thing that they understand is power. Once you have it over them you exercise it to the limit. There'll always be some Yahoo ass-holes waiting to get their hands on you and you must show them that you will crush their hands." He was angrier than I'd ever seen him. "They feel no pity for you, don't waste your pity on them." He was breathing very hard and I saw tears in his eyes. I stared at him but said nothing feeling frightened by his display of rage, afraid that if I reacted in the wrong way he might turn it on me. He pulled the blanket from his bed and squeezed it into a ball. Then he seemed to relax all at once.

"My father saw all of his friends and two of his brothers die in the Warsaw Ghetto uprising. He escaped just before the Nazis completely destroyed it. I will never walk away from a bully. I will lift him off the ground and fling him against a wall, and I will do the same for you or any other Jew if you are too afraid to do it for yourself. As for Martha she's just another one of them. Fucking her takes nothing away from Vivian."

We met at the shed. Ron and I had spread our wool blankets in opposite corners of the space piling some of the broken umbrellas and chaises in the center to create a blind and to provide each of us an illusion of privacy. Rosie and Martha had put on perfume and brought a bottle of Seagram's Seven and one of Seven-Up with them. Rosie turned on the radio. "The Great Pretender" was playing.

"I love this song!" she said passionately, joining in with the lyric at "pretending that I'm not afraid". That makes two of us, pretending, I thought to myself. Ron and Martha began to dance, holding each other tightly, staring intently into one anothers'eyes, rubbing their groins together.

"So, Rosie, you wanna dance?" She clicked her chewing gum a few times and nodded.

"You're cute," she said when I put my arms in place, and she closed the space between us as the song ended. I started to move away but Rosie held on. "Wait, there'll be another song soon," she said, and the words were barely out of her mouth when the radio began to play Elvis Presley's "Love Me Tender" and I thought of what Harlan had said about Elvis, that he was a mutineer of the sexual order. With Elvis crooning and Rosie hanging on to me pressing her pelvis hard against mine, I began to think about sexual mutiny and wondering what exactly that would entail; at times of stress I had a tendency to intellectualize. Understand that it was not all that sexually exciting to be with Rosie. She was not attractive, not even remotely pretty, and up close the sulphuric smell of her anti-acne medicine was too strong for the perfume she wore in an attempt to disguise it. She was pudgy, very pudgy, bordering on fat not simply overweight. Her body felt soft, but like something that is overripe not vital, and with the engulfing, enclosing quality of a giant amoeba. Nonetheless, we continued to grind our way across the makeshift dance floor exciting ourselves with the warmth and pressure of the other's body and the sight of Ron and Martha doing the same. Ron had pulled Martha's blouse out of her shorts and had his hands under it on her breasts. Martha grasped his buttocks and held him tightly against her while they kissed, their tongues licking languidly at each other's mouths. Unquestionably, it was more exciting watching them than being with Rosie but, being a quick learner, I pulled her shirt out of her toreador pants and slid my hands underneath its cover to her breasts. They were nothing like the breasts of other girls I had fondled. These breasts seemed curiously lifeless, without buoyancy or resilience or smoothness. Her breasts felt like plastic baggies filled with tap water.

"Kiss me," Rosie moaned. Ron and Martha must have heard her because they both groaned "go on" to me before disappearing behind the blind Ron and I had laid out earlier. "Don't be shy, kiss me," Rosie said more insistently, and she bit me on the lip and then licked it with her tongue. "Love me tender, I'm the pecker bender," she said nipping my ear lobe and grabbing at my crotch. We sank slowly to the floor, Rosie coming to rest underneath me on her back, and suddenly I was sure that I didn't want any part of this initiation. I was disgusted and ashamed and without any sexual desire for her whatsoever.

Another tonsillectomy would have been better than this. With these thoughts and feelings, my erection began to disappear as surely as if it had been dipped in ice water and Rosie, experiencing it shrivel in her hand, tried to pump some life back into it further forcing its retreat.

"Hey," she said, a look of surprise and annoyance on her face. The radio was now playing a commercial in which a singing group was insisting that we would "wonder where the yellow went" when we brushed our teeth with Pepsodent, but it certainly wasn't the disappearing yellow that Rosie was wondering about. Then Martha screamed out Ron's name three times, "Ron! Ron! Ron!" and ended her set with a long and satisfied groan that glided slowly across the room towards Rosie and me like a complacent cat.

"What's the matter Jack, don't you like me?" Her voice was tense and she was clearly feeling challenged.

"No, that's not it at all," I dissembled while struggling to fabricate another excuse, "it's just that I like to have a little party first, you know, a seven and seven or two. Didn't you bring seven and seven?" I asked, stroking her face. Her lips puckered with the effort of her concentration and she stared intently into my eyes.

"Are you telling me the truth, Jack?"

"Of course I am, Rosie, I swear." It amazed me that one could lie so often and so easily without incurring an immediate penalty. "C'mon, let's pour our drinks."

Rosie opened the whiskey and took out the paper cups and soda she and Martha had brought down in a beach bag. Across the room Ron and Martha, who were now playfully relaxed in their postcoital satiety, slapped at each other with light love taps that made them giggle and purr. They seemed totally oblivious of us, but Rosie and I began listening more closely to the two of them. The smell of their excited effort wafted across the shed towards us and their giggling became muffled in a new embrace. When the drinks were mixed Rosie and I lifted our cups to each other, nodded a silent toast, and then drank. Rosie shifted herself closer to me and, taking another large swallow of the whiskey, I placed my hand on her thigh and began stroking her.

The breathing across the shed deepened and quickened and the sound of their bodies undulating on the floor began to revive my erection. Touching Rosie's thigh was pleasant but imagining that maybe Martha would crawl over already wet with excitement and begin to lick my neck aroused me almost instantaneously. Ron was right, she had a hell of a body. Then she and Ron were at it again. I closed my eyes and embraced Rosie wondering all the while what the one word aural equivalent of voyeur was. By keeping an image of Martha's body in my mind I was able to stir some passion with Rosie and proceeded to undress her. She began to moan. The whiskey on her breath and the sulfuric smell of her anti-acne cream challenged my ardor and I took another swig of my seven and seven. The thought of making love to her held no excitement and Martha's image was fading fast.

"Do you love me Jack?"

"What!!?"

"Say you love me Jack." Knowingly, Rosie took my hand and pressed it against the moist and furry cleft between her legs, while grabbing my member with her other hand. "Say it."

"I . . ." The door to the shed creaked open and the beam of a flashlight caught me full in the face before circling left to Rosie and darting to the opposite corner and capturing the full moon of Ron's buttocks. A girl's tittering preceded Harlan's clear and emphatic "Sorry!" and then the door creaked shut. "Shit!" Rosie said. I had come in her hand.

When we got back to our room I was feeling wretched, disgusted with myself and with Rosie. As usual, Harlan was not there. Ron looked at Harlan's cot and snickered.

"I guess he doesn't get to see enough of my ass in here so he had to chase me down in the storage shed. I wonder what Heidi thought about what she saw. Who knows, maybe she'll start playing up to me. A Jew is much sexier than a smooth skinned, pale toned bland goy. Rye bread versus white bread. What's the matter with you?" he said, noticing my dejection.

"Nothing." I was feeling a terrible sadness, the ache of a reproving conscience which, like a black hole, had sucked in all my hope and hollowed me out in the pit of my stomach.

"Why do people always say 'nothing' when they don't mean nothing." He took off his shirt, threw it on his bed and went to the mirror on the back of the door to our room. He studied his face and then took a deep breath. Expanding his chest and sucking in his stomach he admired his muscular build. "So how was Rosie?" he asked, turning sideways to get a look at his body in profile.

"All right, I guess." I didn't think for a minute that I could tell him how thoroughly sordid and shabby I felt about myself and the entire experience.

"Why don't you just say 'nothing' again?" He turned around and stood facing me. "Admit it, you feel like shit."

"No, it's just. . . .

"Don't bullshit me Melvin. You looked like you were going to cry when we left the shed." I started to protest but Ron raised his hand to stop me. "I told you, you'd have to risk a variety of venereal infections but the worst would be the afters. Looks to me like you have a classic case of the afters." He grinned. "Classic."

"I thought you were going to be a lawyer, not a doctor."

"Why can't you admit that I'm right? It's nothing to be ashamed of. Everyone goes through it at one time or another. Just hope that you didn't make her pregnant."

"Well, I couldn't have done that. I never got inside her."

"Uh oh. Feeling this bad and still a virgin? This may be worse than I thought." He scratched his head, grabbed a book from under his bed and riffled through its pages as if in search of something that he knew would be in there. "Ahh, yes, here it is. 'Coitus Failurus Afterus: The subject is feeling degraded and disgusted as much for the failure to penetrate as for the choice of object with whom he has struck out. The remedy for this requires that the subject quickly identify and acquire access to a more attractive and desirable object.' Well Mel, I guess it's time for Diana."

I grabbed the book out of Ron's hand and then laughed when I saw what it was, "Love Without Fear" by Dr. Eustace Chesser, the marital sex manual of its day.

"Do you really think this Diana will go out with me?" All at once I was feeling much better.

"Oh yes. Leave it to me. She's a number, but I think she'll go for you."

"What do you mean by a number?"

"Patience Melvin. Recover from Rosie first. Don't get greedy on me."

5.

The tapping woke us before the alarm clocks went off in the quarters. Ron groaned but Harlan sat bolt upright and stared at the door. The metallic tapping, as if with a coin not a knuckle, resumed and was accompanied by the muffled sound of Harlan's name being uttered against the panel of the door. Harlan pulled his covers aside and jumped out of bed. I heard Ron sit up in the bunk below me. Moving quickly and quietly Harlan went to the door, opened it a crack then slipped through the doorway into the hall pulling the door closed behind him as he talked to his visitor.

"What the fuck is that?" Ron said. We could hear their voices and though I couldn't make out what they were saying the visitor sounded more distressed and seemed to be pressing Harlan for something. When the door opened again Harlan backed into the room saying, "I'll take care of it, don't worry, I'll make good on it."

"Yeah, but I want it on Sunday when you get your tips, not later than Sunday, Harlan, I need it."

The door closed and Harlan, sighing, a frown on his face, walked back to his bed and flopped down. I recognized the voice as Artie Stein's, Ivan Goldman's busboy, and so did Ron.

"What did you do now, Hawthorne, rob poor little pimply Artie?"

"What a pain. He won some money from me at cards and you'd think his life depended on getting that thirty dollars."

"No, maybe he just knows who it is that owes him the cash and how hard it will be to collect."

"On what basis do you say a thing like that, Ron, on what grounds?" He sat up tense and irate.

"You don't know about your reputation around here I suppose."

"What reputation?" I said.

"You don't have to defend Harlan, Melvin, he's a big boy and he can take care of himself."

"Yeah, but what reputation," I asked again.

"Ummm, great lover, charmer, intellectual snob?" Harlan offered with relaxed amusement.

"Charmer, yes, but also cheat, chick chaser, chicken-hearted, and charlatan," Ron said.

"Really? Well, try chivalrous and charismatic, you churlish chump."

"Hey, what did you two do, rob Sammy's dictionaries?"

"You can make all the jokes you like, Harlan, but people are on to you. You're not charming you're slick. People don't walk right behind you because they're afraid they'll slip and fall on the slime you leave in your tracks."

"Brilliant, Ron, really brilliant. I am cut to the quick." With the back of his hand at his brow Harlan sighed and swooned backwards on to his cot. "I am undone," he groaned.

"And I am going to the shower," I said, jumping down from my bunk trying to sound playful but upset by their exchange. From my first day Ron had made it obvious he had bad feelings about Harlan. Maybe he was jealous about something I didn't know of. You rarely know the real reasons for people's attitudes. I had already decided to study Harlan and learn from him and I'd seen no reason to mistrust him so I wouldn't allow myself to be influenced by Ron.

"Yeah, go to the showers, Jackass, you're out of the game. You're also out of your league but you're too green to know it." Ron's words bit at my pride.

Later that morning at breakfast, Sammy called for a meeting after the cleanup.

"This will take just a few minutes so don't grumble so much. Ben Braverman is concerned there's a thief around the hotel. He's not saying who, or where but he knows something's up. Guests have had their jewelry taken, some cash has disappeared, cigarette lighters, every kind of valuable. So, to calm his guests down a little bit he's having his daughter, Heidi, circulate in the dining room at lunch. And I don't want any of you playing any tricks or making any cracks to her. That's it. That's all I have to say. Except it better not be one of you boys who's the thief."

"What good will Heidi walking around the dining room do?" one of the waiters called out.

"It'll make the waiters and busboys happier," someone else called out.

"Maybe Judge Crater ran out of money and had to find a way to make ends meet?" someone else offered to the applause of a few waiters.

"Enough, enough. Comedians. It's his way of hearing the gossip, the stories, the rumors, the worries, you never know what you find out this way. Anyway, be nice to Heidi and, AAN-NDD," he shouted to quiet the chattering group, "if you hear anything that you think could help tell me first, not your buddies or your girlfriends. Personally I don't think it's one of you. You all make too much money to be so stupid to go stealing from the guests, but if it is one of you . . ." and he just shook his finger at the assembly.

I looked over at Ron. He was craning his neck trying to locate someone at the rear of the huddle of staff.

"Who're you looking for?"

"I want to see the look on Harlan's face."

"Why, because Heidi will be spending her lunch hour in here?"

"Because I think if there's one crook in the dining room it's him." I shook my head.

"Boy, when you have it in for someone he can't do anything right."

"No, not Harlan. I spotted it the minute he walked into my room, the way his eyes scanned my things while he put his hand out to shake mine. It felt like an insurance appraisal or something. He's not to be trusted, I've told you that but you're going to have to learn the hard way."

I shrugged. It made no sense to continue the conversation because it would only lead to the same dead end. There was no budging Ron once he took a stand. Well, at least Heidi's presence during lunch would be a pleasant distraction, I thought, and maybe she could get to know me and set me up with one of the counselors in the day camp. I looked around for Harlan to see if he was happy Heidi would be circulating at lunch. He was talking with Ivan and when he saw me approach he beckoned me into their conversation.

"Ivan and I were just saying that it's likely it's one of the bell hops who's doing the thievery because they get to size up the merchandise, so to speak, on arrival. You know, the kind of car the guest is driving, the quality of the luggage, the jewelry the women wear even when they're dressed casually for the trip up, a lot of little clues if you care to pay attention." Ivan was staring at Harlan with great concentration.

"You know, Harlan, that wasn't *we* who were saying that, it was all you. You seem pretty aware of what a thief looks for in a target."

"Ha, ha, yeah, well I read a lot of crime novels—Mickey Spillane, Raymond Chandler, they tell you how it's done. Why, you think I'm the thief, Ivan?" Once again Harlan's honesty was being challenged and I was angry about it. I was sure that Ron had led Ivan down this path.

"Why would Harlan . . . ?

"I can speak for myself, Jack, don't jump in here. Are you saying I'm the thief, Ivan?" Harlan suddenly stood straighter and taller as if readying himself to square off with Ivan Goldman who was easily three inches taller and thirty pounds heavier. But, as often happens when someone plants his feet and stands up for himself, his accuser backed down.

"No, no, Harlan, I was just saying that you should get all the credit for those ideas, that's all. I wasn't trying to accuse you of anything, okay? I'm going to shoot some foul shots before lunch." He gave me an affectionate punch in the shoulder and left.

"Jack, I appreciate your interest and concern but don't get involved in matters pertaining to me, all right? I can see it's going to be an uphill fight for respect in this place and I'll tell you if I need your help, okay?" Embarrassed, I nodded. "You know he wasn't trying to give me credit for figuring out who the thief might be, don't you? He was making an accusation. That really pisses me off. Mr. All American misjudging me really pisses me off." And then, as quickly as he had become angry, he was in a happy frame of mind. "So, I get to see my Heidi at lunch time every day, pretty good, right?"

"Yeah," I said, "pretty damn good."

By lunchtime that same day Heidi was in the dining room. She was totally unlike any other girl I had seen at the hotel and so unlike all the other Bravermans in looks and manner that I wondered whether she might have been adopted. She was very beautiful, looking uncannily like the actress Susan Strassberg, and as graceful and nimble as a dancer. She walked on the balls of her feet, like someone unaware that the high heels had come off her shoes, and her long, straight hair was pulled back in a magnificent ponytail that flowed out behind her and seemed to do a dance of its own as she walked. Her manner was soft and self-assured, her voice musical, her disposition cheerful. She bore her gifts gracefully and graciously as though oblivious to the effects of her allure. I was emptying my dirty dishes in the kitchen when she came up beside me and began to speak.

"Are you interested in meeting a nice girl, Jack?" she asked, adopting my adopted name.

"Sure," I said. Actually, I was more interested in meeting a not so nice girl, but there was always room in my life for love.

"Well, I think I may have someone for you but I'll have to feel her out. She's really cute. How do you like working for Sammy?"

"Great. The money's been terrific. How's camp going?" There was an awkwardness to these polite exchanges. I was also aware that Rudy was watching us from his worktable with an intense curiosity. He and Harlan had been very chummy and he probably was wondering why Heidi had come to talk to me.

"I love it. The kids are great, especially the littlest ones."

"How come you came into the kitchen to talk to me, what's wrong with the dining room?" I said, returning Rudy's stare and trying to reach Heidi on more direct terms.

"Oh, those guys in there are very immature. I don't appreciate their wisecracks and sexual innuendoes." I knew what she meant. Beautiful women tend to bring out the worst in most young men. Like small boys who have just learned to whistle, they are compulsively driven to prideful displays of themselves and their new talent even if for a totally disinterested audience. Then, too, it occurred to me I was being auditioned and she didn't want to be distracted by them.

"Well, if this girl is available I am too. Tell her I won't tell any dirty jokes if you think that will help." Heidi laughed her lilting laugh but I felt embarrassed because I had made such a pointless and stupid joke. That's what can happen when you try too hard to be witty and sophisticated, you sometimes end up sounding like an ass. "Harlan asked you to set me up didn't he," I said, trying to find a firmer footing with her.

"He mentioned that you were interested in meeting someone but I just thought that this might be a good match. I remember your brothers and if you're as nice as they are, well, we'll see."

"Actually, I'm much nicer than they are so don't hold back, you won't regret it."

"Really, well if you get cocky I just might regret it."

"Hey, I was only teasing, Heidi, I didn't mean to put you off." I was scrambling to recover my poise and her interest. "I've not met a nice girl in the weeks I've been here and really want to meet somebody I can date."

"Well, I think the girl I have in mind is someone you'll like but I don't know if she's available right now. Can you keep a secret?"

"Sure."

"I don't think the boy she's dating is right for her and I think she's on the verge of figuring that out for herself. Be patient, Jack, I'll let you know when it's time."

Chapter Three

The next day it rained. I worked breakfast as usual which is to say I worked and Sammy schmoozed. People arrived in dribs and drabs, one or two at a time so it was easy for Sammy to stand around telling stories and nodding at me whenever a guest asked for something to eat. A Catskill breakfast was a small banquet. There were three or four different fruit juices, melons, grapefruits, orange sections and of course stewed prunes, the latter often accompanied by a cup of hot water with a wedge of fresh lemon a concoction reputed to stir the slumbering bowel. Before the dining room opened I had already placed breads, rolls, bagels, pastries, jam and butter on each table. I kept a pot of coffee at my serving stand and periodically refilled it when I went to the kitchen to refill a water pitcher. All the various kinds of herring, lox served with sliced Bermuda onion and tomatoes and capers, and the sardines and white fish which the Lions had snubbed during their Catskill adventure were feasted upon by the Braverman regulars who, like a starving army, consumed them quickly and voluminously. There were three different hot cereals and cold cereals beyond counting which the guests could partake of with any fruit available, bananas and berries to tangelos and Valencia oranges. And partake they did, course after course, from juice to pastries. People could have eggs anyway they wanted from one minute soft-boiled eggs to poached eggs on toast and who was to say they couldn't have them both if that's what they wanted, thank you very much. Then, of course, there were the pancakes and the

French toast offered with "your choice" of maple syrup, jam, confectioner's sugar, honey, or what the hell, take them all you're paying for it. As if from a giant cornucopia breakfast seemed to spill endlessly from seven-fifteen until ten o'clock every morning but amidst all these toothsome choices, there were no meats. While the kitchen wasn't kosher there was an effort to recreate breakfast as it had been cooked by your old Jewish grandmother so there could be no "traif"—no bacon, ham or sausage. There had been a brief flirtation with a bacon substitute called "Beef Crisp" but it was cancelled from the menu when an actual Jewish grandmother who caught a whiff of its bacon-like scent fainted dead away over her Cream of Wheat.

Food wrapped in paper napkins left the dining room with every guest that morning. Rainy days seemed to make people do that. If they couldn't sun themselves or play Simon Says or shuffleboard they could at least have a snack. It seemed greedy and gluttonous to me until Ron pointed out that many of these vacationers had saved money week by week for their two weeks in the country and that was all the time off they'd get for the entire year. Rain, like a thief, was stealing their holiday so the food was taken as if in compensation. They would not be deprived.

As for us, the members of the dining room staff, we worked that summer the way people had worked for all the centuries before the twentieth, long hours, day after day, as if our very survival depended upon these efforts. We did not even merit a day off but worked all day everyday. The rhythm of the days expanded into a weekly rhythm but there was no numbing effect of this tedious repetition. The physical labor was not of the bone-wearying kind but it still could be tough. We were on our feet from the time the dining room opened until we returned to our quarters at breaks, and we were always lifting or carrying something somewhere. Most of the guests were decent enough but there was always that population of ball busters you could never please and to them we were no better than lazy wretches robbing them of their pleasure. This brought the staff together in a spirit of cameraderie; the outer-borough New York City Jewish boys, mid-western and southern gentile basketball players shared this plight, but the older professionals like Sammy and Abe seemed much less affected by the belittling disparagements of the malcontents. The decent kind and unpretentious people have vanished from memory, if ever there had been a place for them there. It is as though they left no mark in my mind, though the abrasive, the crass and demanding, linger. In that way our personal histories are like world history, more often populated with villains who seem swollen disproportionately large when compared to the others in our lives. "Bad impressions, alas! engrave themselves as deeply on the memory as the good, and often the latter even are effaced while the others still remain," wrote the American composer Louis Moreau Gottschalk comparing his reception in neighboring towns in Connecticut after a tour. As Sammy's busboy I met a good number of abrasive guests, people who, wherever they might vacation, would demand to be seated at one of the head waiter's tables. If they were not among his regulars and did not show him the proper deference he pushed them off on to me and this obvious snub caused them to distribute their sense of humiliation throughout the staff, but it was I who ended up getting most of it. No juice that I poured, no dish that I served to them could be eaten without complaint.

"You call this oatmeal!? It's like plaster for Godsakes." This critique was usually shouted rather than spoken and before I could respond Stuart Stein would be standing at my side. "Take this back and get Mr.Feifelman a fresh bowl of cereal." It felt demeaning to have Stuart Stein behaving that way but all the waiters and busboys at Braverman's knew that ingratiating himself with the guests at our expense was his way of cadging tips. Still, I didn't think it fair for his tips to be at my expense and materializing the way he did seemed to imply that I, not the kitchen -if indeed anyone at all- was to blame. This kind of officiousness was one of the reasons so many of us enjoyed the scoffing contests in the dining room. It was like giving the finger to a martinet.

But then of course there was Harlan, unique as always, gliding smoothly over the rough spots without so much as a bump. And the guests at Harlan's station were different too. Food was of no consequence to them because they had come in search of love; love was the staple they most eagerly craved.

"Doesn't anybody here ever get to you?" I asked him as we left the shower one evening after a particularly busy dinner meal.

"Get to me how? You mean irritate me? No." He shook his head for emphasis. "No, everyone is here for a reason. If my reason doesn't get in the way of yours there's no cause for conflict. I'm here to make as much money as I can in a short period of time and the guests, they're here to eat drink and be merry because tomorrow they have to go back to their boring, awful lives. Don't you see, Jack, they come here to dream. These Catskill resorts are basically a dreamland where many dreamers bring their hope to be living in a fairytale. The unmarried secretaries, bookkeepers and shop clerks come in search of love and romance. The salesmen and the accountants come with lust in their loins and fear in their hearts. What if they make someone pregnant? Worse still, what if they have to return to New York with no conquests to boast about to their cronies? So I encourage their dreams and they tip me for my considerateness." He smiled that open and friendly wonder-rapt smile of his and looked around so that anyone watching him would think he was just having the best time imaginable at whatever he was doing. "I am making a great deal of money, Jack. Don't say anything about this to anyone but I'm doing about $6.50 a head at my station." His smile never wavered as he recounted this to me, that affable smile that never betrayed the private motives and truths for his presence in the Catskills. "That's what we're here for, the money, isn't it?" I nodded, but I still couldn't, or more truthfully, wouldn't believe that was all he'd come for.

"Here for money, and for love. And how's your love life? Have you met anybody yet?" I didn't want to tell him the details of the Rosie debacle. He had seemed so disapproving of the very idea of Rosie and Diana I just said, "No."

"Maybe Heidi can fix you up with one of the counselors."

"Oh, that would be great if she would do that."

"Okay! That's the spirit, give me a little time. I'll work on it and let you know when things work out. Some of the girls are probably seeing what they've gotten themselves into with their new boyfriends about now and there'll be some break-ups coming. Be patient, things will work out, you'll see."

I finished dressing and was preparing to go down to the casino to see if there were any girls around when there was a knock on my door. When I opened it, standing in the doorway still dressed in his waiter's outfit was Abe Melman, his face stretched by a broad smile such as I had never seen on him before, and he began to speak immediately.

"So, Melvin, I haven't really taken the time to get to know you but you shouldn't take that personally. So tell me, how do you like working for the famous Sammy?" Taken so completely off guard I was speechless. "You've got nothing to say?" He stood on his tiptoes and peered into the room. "I can come in maybe for just a second?" It sounded like a question but before I could demur he had pushed past me and was already wiping the invisible dust from Harlan's blanket. "I'll just sit for a minute." He lifted and refolded Harlan's squared blanket and then sat on it. "Sammy is a real character, in case you didn't notice. He has a way with numbers. If he asks you something once he'll tell you it was twice. If he sees three people waiting on line he'll insist there were six. He's a putz. Harmless, but a putz. It's his insecurity that makes him do that. Those kind of exaggerations are his way of trying to make up for his lack of education." Having avoided being drawn into their feud in the dining room, Abe had brought the feud to me in my quarters. "Still speechless Melvin?"

"Well . . ."

"It's all right, you don't have to talk if you don't want." His face had relaxed into its usual state of gloominess. "I would like to get to know you better. You look like a nice boy, Melvin." His offer held no allure whatsoever for me and I resented being called a boy. I was not yet a man but no longer still a boy either.

"Well, thanks for stopping by Abe but I have to meet somebody down at the casino right now."

"Yeah, yeah, he said, waving his hand as if to shoo flies, "I'll get out of your way, but some time we should talk."

I followed him out of my room and left the building. His friendliness had seemed forced, something he was unaccustomed to offering, and the gloomy climate of failure that surrounded him was unnerving. Once you experienced it you treated

Abe like someone afflicted with a deadly contagion and fled from him as rapidly as you could. I would probably never know why he was as he was, what had happened to make him give up a decent life, but I knew I didn't want to be infected with Abe's failure. I lit up a Newport and went to the bar at the casino where the usual disappointment of my expectations with girls was likely to be waiting for me.

2.

On Wednesday afternoon I awoke with a start and leapt from my bed in a state of confusion. The room was disorientingly bright and Harlan and Ron were gone. What meal had I missed? I was positive that I was supposed to be in the dining room serving either breakfast or lunch but couldn't understand how I could have overslept. And where was all the light coming from? Powerful feelings of guilt and distress gripped me. I was nothing if not reliable, even if only for a silly and trivial busboy's job. My head was just beginning to clear when Ron barged into the room. "You're not going to believe this one," he said shaking his head and kneading the fingers of his right hand with his left. "Incredible story, just incredible." I could tell he was waiting for me to egg him on, but my head was still foggy and his excitement was more jarring than infectious.

"Interested? Hello, anybody home?"

"Sorry, I just woke up and I didn't know what time it was and thought that I had missed lunch or breakfast . . ."

"It's the middle of the afternoon," he said impatiently, frustrated with my lack of enthusiasm.

"So what's incredible?" Ron stared at me, frowning, considering whether or not I, having completely deflated him, was worthy of his story. Then he shrugged and began to speak.

"Lenny the handyman says he knows where judge Crater is buried here on the hotel grounds. He says the judge was dumped into a well that they don't use anymore out in back of the waiters' dormitory." With eyes wide and glowing he smiled and waited for a response.

"Do you think John Steinbeck had this Lenny in mind when he wrote 'Of Mice and Men' or do you think it's just a coincidence that both Lennys are morons."

"Hah, but you know they never found Crater. No one knows what happened to him or where he disappeared to, just that he disappeared. Why not here? Isn't he our resident ghost for a reason?"

"Why not in Mexico? Come on Ron, are you going to believe a moron like Lenny?"

"I didn't say that I believed him, but it is a fascinating and curious notion you have to admit, and it certainly makes me curious." I could tell that Ron was trying to enlist me in the service of satisfying his curiosity and I was reluctant to commit. I flopped down on Harlan's bunk and picked up the Life magazine that was on the floor, looked up at him and said,

"Guess what killed the cat."

"I was thinking that we could just spend some time talking to good old Lenny and find out where the body is buried. Maybe there's a reward." I didn't answer. "Just come with me and talk to him. Hear it for yourself and then we can both decide if it's worth taking seriously. C'mon Mel, it's just a crazy possibility that he did die here, and if it's true we'd be the ones to break the story, maybe get on TV who knows?"

"I'm too tired. You do it."

"Melvin, don't be a pain in the ass. It'll be fun. Come on. I pulled the pages of the magazine taut in determined resistance to his plying.

"The name's Jack."

"Come on, it'll be a kick," he crooned, "come on." I sensed at that moment that Ron's persistent coaxing, gentle but relentless, had probably gotten him where he wanted to go often, usually into some girl's brassiere, occasionally into her pants, and that he would continue to apply the pressure persuasively until my resistance was worn down. "Come on."

"Shit! You don't quit. Okay! Let's just get it over with."

"Whoa big fella, what kind of an attitude is that for fun? Relax. This is a small adventure, so treat it like one."

We cut through the weeds separating the back of the waiters' bunk house from the shed where the dishwashers and handymen were billeted. The warm, mid-afternoon air smelled of cheap muscatel and beer. A radio was playing "Sixteen Tons" but the music was being crowded by the boozy snores and grumbles of the dozing dishwashers, bums who had been lured into pick-up trucks with fifths of cheap whiskey and half gallons of muscatel and Thunderbird wine and then driven from the Bowery to the country. Like the sailors of another age these men had been hijacked and impressed into service. Their port of call was to be one of the Catskill resort hotels not some distant continent or exotic island and as long as they had a reliable supply of cigarettes and cheap wine, a cot to lie on and three meals a day they didn't cause trouble beyond the walls of their own quarters. But to me, they were derelicts, bums and drunkards, dangerous, unpredictable, embodiments of chaos and violence. There were always stories about their fights and their brutality and at least once a week someone would turn up in the kitchen with a black eye, a swollen nose or a split lip. They rarely talked to the waiters and busboys but they eyed us mistrustfully and swaggered around us as we loaded and unloaded our trays, occasionally leaning in too close as if to speak, and then withdrawing. I was more intimidated by this behavior than the others seemed to be and mistaking their bravado for menace, never made eye contact with them, behaving like I was riding the subway in New York City.

"Lenny?" Ron called out. "Come out here Lenny." With a shaking hand I pulled a Kent king size from its box and beat a tattoo on my lip with its filter trying to get it into my mouth.

"I thought you smoked L&M regulars, what are those?"

"Just wanted to try them." I'd left my Zippo lighter back in the room and had stashed a pack of matches in the cigarette hard pack. I pulled a match forward and closed the flap behind it. Then, bending the match into an arc so that the head was over the strike board on the back of the cover, and grasping the matchbook in my palm so that my thumb was over the match head, I pushed the head down and quickly across the black gritty surface. I cupped my other hand over the flame and brought my head down to light the cigarette. This one-handed light was meant to convey a tough and rugged persona and though it was at odds with my actual mien I nonetheless relied on it to daunt anyone watching me.

"LENNY! Hey, don't be nervous Mel," Ron said, watching the cigarette flutter in my mouth like a flag on a windy day, "they're harmless. It's all they can do to stand up at this time of day, relax." I grinned, but felt ashamed of the fear that accompanied me whenever I ventured out of the security of my safe and comfortable world.

"Hi ya Ron, how ya doin'?" Lenny came through the door in a sleeveless undershirt and torn, dirty, gray work pants. Looking into Lenny's face was looking into the face of chaos, evidence that God could make mistakes. His features were askew, the left side of his face shifted up almost an inch higher than the right, not quite Picassoesque, just misshapen, like a piece of wax left too close to a fire so that one side had partly melted. His lips were thicker and fuller on the right side, his cheek rounder, and his right eye, buried in a thick cushion of fat, wandered and searched around in its socket as if trying to make sense of these derangements. Ron cocked his head when he spoke to Lenny as if to align the features, and I was unsure if this was done unconsciously or deliberately to evoke laughter from me.

"Hi Lenny, you know Mel here," he said nodding in my direction and then he asked about the judge.

"Yeah, like I told you it was around this time of year, I don't remember exactly when but it was summer, very hot and muggy like now." He scanned our faces measuring our attention, his eyes pointing in different directions so that it was hard to know which one was looking at you. "He was wearing a brown suit and a white shirt. Very natty. He'd come to gamble like he always did. This used to be a roadhouse where people came to drink and gamble. It was very big during prohibition, before your time," he said proudly, owning something the two of us could not. "There was a fight. Fights broke out all the time because the liquor was very strong. Somebody accused the judge of cheating and he stood up and pushed the table over . . ."

"Who pushed the table, the judge?" Ron asked.

". . . I was gonna tell you. No, it was the guy from Chicago. I don't remember his name but Mr. Braverman, Ben, not one of his boys that you work for, he told me to make sure that the man from Chicago's ashtray was always empty and his glass was always full. He was a big guy. He pushed the table over and grabbed the judge by his tie and pulled him right up against himself. See, even though it was so hot and muggy the judge never took off his tie. He was a very natty guy. He really liked to dress up."

"So what happened then?" Ron was getting impatient and afraid that Lenny might wander off into the weed patch of his non sequiturs and be lost for the rest of the day.

"Somebody yelled 'Get Lenny out of here!' and I was dragged outside by the bartender. Then there were the shots. Three of them. Bang! Bang-Bang! Curly, that was the bartender, pulled me up to him and said 'I didn't here anything just then and you didn't neither.' I said no, that's not true there was gunshots, but he said you made a mistake, those was cicadas, they make a big racket and that's what you heard. Then, later that night they told me they needed me to work on the well, that it had gone dry from all the heat and they were going to fill it with stones to press the water down so it could come out from the new well they were going to dig. I never heard of anything like that before but I knew not to ask any questions because Curly told me don't ask anything, just do what they tell you. Besides, it had been the hottest summer I remembered so maybe that was why the well was dried up. While I was loading up stones in that field over there," he said, pointing to the field bordering his shack, "Ben came up to me and asked me if I'd heard any strange noises tonight after I left the casino and I said yeah, very loud cicadas." Ron and Lenny both laughed but I just smiled weakly. "Cicadas," Ron repeated, slapping his thigh and bowing with laughter, "Holy shit! Cicadas!" He and Lenny laughed some more and then Ron said, "So Crater's in the old well, is that what you think Len?"

"Gee Ron, I never said that. All I heard was cicadas," and then he slapped his thigh and doubled over with demonic laughter. I'd had enough and turned to leave but Ron grabbed my arm.

"Wait up. Let's at least see the well."

Not ready to relinquish his hold on us, Lenny said, "I can show you the well Mel,—Hey! I'm a poet and I don't know it! It's right near here, I can show you."

"C'mon," Ron said, "we've got nothing else to do right now anyway. Let's just see it." And then, gratuitously, he added, "Lenny won't push you in, will you Lenny?"

"I couldn't anyway because it's all filled up with rocks and dead cicadas," and Lenny fell to his knees, his body wracked by his diabolical laughter making me feel uncomfortably closer to the bottom of that well.

Lenny led us back towards the waiters' quarters and then to the dense thicket of fir trees that had been planted in the space separating the dining room staff from the housing for the band and the social staff, the tummler, the tennis pro, the life guards and the camp counselors. Behind their building was the one where the chambermaids and cooks lived. We all had assumed this thicket had been placed there to keep us from peeping on the girl staffers while they changed their clothes, but Lenny said that this was where the old well had been.

"Look over here," he said, parting some weeds in the middle of the thicket, "see the stones?" Ron and I pushed the weeds apart and leaned over the ground where some stones could be seen breaking through the dirt. It was here that I had stumbled and fallen the night Ron took me to meet Rosie Moldar. We swept the top layer of soil aside with our hands to reveal a circle of stones measuring about five feet in diameter. Weeds and vines were tangled across the site whose dimensions I would have missed had I not been searching for it. Ron knelt down at the periphery, separated the turf from the stones and smiled.

"Mortar," he said, holding up some pieces of cement. "This damn sure was probably a well." He stood up and came to me with a smile on his face. "Want to meet judge Crater Melvin?"

When we were changing for dinner I said to Ron, "That still doesn't prove anything. Okay, so there was another well once but that doesn't mean Crater's in it, for godsakes. And even if Lenny is telling the truth are you expecting me to dig up the well with you?"

"No, Melvin, I expect you to do it by yourself," he said sarcastically. "Actually Lenny was accurate about the location of the well and maybe the judge is inside it after all, who knows." "How come he chose to tell you of all people Ron, have you asked yourself that? How come for twenty five years he doesn't say a thing to anyone and all of a sudden today, of all the waiters and busboys and social staff that have passed through Braverman's, he decides to tell Ron Alter." Ron shrugged, looked away, put his hands in his pockets, took them out again and sighed.

"I lent Lenny money that's why. He said he had a sure thing in a horse race somewhere, I don't know where, but it was a long shot that was supposed to be a fix. He was so excited. The bookie in Monticello has been taking his money for years and if that horse were to come in it would be fantastic for him."

"How could you lend him money? I don't understand why you would do such a . . . reckless thing," I said, catching myself before I said "stupid thing".

"Lenny is a harmless guy. Look hard at him and maybe you can learn to be grateful for what you've got, a normal mind and a normal body. I have a cousin like Lenny, retarded, deformed. I used to be embarrassed to be seen with him. Now I'm embarrassed by the way other people behave when they're around him. It's probably no different for Lenny. Twenty bucks for him is a small fortune. When the horse came in it became a large fortune, a thousand dollars, a fifty to one winner. I took back my $20 but I wouldn't accept any more than that. This story about Judge Crater is his way of saying thanks. It's his way to take a risk for me." This was an aspect of Ron that took me by surprise. There had been no display of sensitivity or compassion to anyone other than himself in the entire month I'd known him, yet there was no disputing that Lenny had aroused tender feelings in him.

"So you think that makes his story more believable?" I ventured.

"It's certainly possible and that's what counts. What we do with it I don't know but I'll think of something. And don't go telling anybody about this. I probably shouldn't have told you either but it's too late to change that."

"Don't worry, I'll keep it just between us," I said, wondering if my first call would be to Malcolm or to one of my brothers. After all, there are always those others whom we rely upon to keep our confidences. The thought of telling Harlan tempted me but he was so angry with Ron I didn't think I could trust him to keep his knowledge of the secret from him. I'd never seen Harlan do anything to deliberately provoke another person but his dislike of Ron had become obvious. In the beginning of the summer when Ron began displaying his critical and rejecting attitude Harlan had remained cordial and polite, but lately Ron had worn through the veneer of civility and now they moved around each other silently and warily, like stray dogs in a vacant lot. I would have liked to repair their rift but knew it was well beyond my capacity for mediation and rather than make it worse than it already was I opted to keep the judge from Harlan for the time being. And the more I thought about what Lenny had said the more plausible it seemed, plausible though not likely. But why not? Strange things do occur; life resists our efforts to organize the world and all its pieces; life conforms only to nature's laws. So why was I obliged to conform to Ron's laws? I decided to submit to the impulse to call Malcolm and tell him about the judge.

"What??! Judge Crater? That's impossible! He was never in the mountains. He went to the clubs in the city or he went to . . . I don't know where he went, but not the Catskills."

"Just because you didn't know, it doesn't mean it didn't happen."

"I can't believe you'd be so naive, Mel, I can't imagine anyone buying such bullshit. Anyone but you I guess."

"That's really nice of you, Malcolm, thanks. I thought you were my friend."

"I *am* your friend that's why I won't lie to you. Come on, Mel, you know who you are, I'm not telling you anything that'd surprise you, you're a sitting duck for every scam artist there is."

"This guy Lenny is no scam artist, believe me, he's too dumb to try anything like that. I think he may have the true story on Crater." I was standing in a phone booth inside the canteen trying not to be too loud, but Malcolm's skepticism frustrated me and caused me to raise my voice. I looked around to see if anyone was watching. Harlan was buying a pack of Luckys at the counter and several guests were looking at the New York City newspapers but no one seemed to take notice of me. Lowering my voice I continued. "Why not, Mal, why not here. This was a gambling den hidden in the woods, a perfect place to be private and safe. The big hotels weren't even built then."

"Yeah, but has anybody ever said he was in the Catskills? I don't know the details but I've heard things like Yonkers or Chicago but never upstate. So how are you doing for ass?" He was finished with the judge.

"Aw, not very well what about you?" There was a rap on the glass door of the phone booth. Harlan waved at me on his way out of the canteen and was gone before I could stop him. Although Malcolm was my best friend I would have hung up on him to spend time with Harlan, that's how taken I was with him; my feelings bordered on hero worship. There might come a time when telling Harlan about the judge would be possible, if only just for a good laugh. At that time I had no idea how much Harlan and judge Crater would become involved in the course of the rest of my summer.

"Pretty good. You know the social staff always does better than the guys in the dining room do because we have the chance to meet everybody. I'll try to get you something here next summer."

"Yeah, but what's the money like, is it any good?"

"Hey, Melvin, you know there's no better money than the wait staff. Do you want money or do you want to get laid?"

"I'm greedy, Malcolm, I want both. I'll talk to you." I hung up without waiting for his goodbye, disappointed that he couldn't get more enthusiastic about the judge, but willing to stick with Ron in the search.

3.

After the luncheon cleanup, while the next wave of vacationers was arriving, I went to the pool for a swim. We had the use of all of the hotel's facilities with the understanding that we were never to compete with guests for any space they wanted to use. After all, they were the paying customers. Sunday afternoons the pool was less populated than usual because many vacationers were leaving and the new arrivals were unpacking and settling in. The bunk house was full of waiters and busboys who seemed to prefer spending the day complaining about the lousy tips they got to sitting in the sun. I can't remember ever hearing a group of busboys and waiters celebrating their take. Still, bad as it was said to be, they were on line at the bank every Monday morning between breakfast and lunch, depositing their hoards of crumpled one and five dollar bills into savings accounts. I didn't want to listen to them, I wanted to find a girl. I was determined to find a girl. Time and the summer were passing me by.

Women were the primary users of the pool. Actually, they used the lounge chairs more than they used the water and by the time I arrived most of the chaises were aligned in parallel facing south where the sun crossed the sky. I found one unoccupied and laid down my towel and Modern Library edition of Faulkner's "The Sound and the Fury" and "As I lay Dying" with the intention of reading after a swim. No nubile young things were stretched out within my line of vision so it would not be difficult to concentrate. I was bending over arranging my towel when I became aware that some kind of disturbance was occurring, a mild perturbation of the previously calm poolside atmosphere, and looking up I saw that Harlan was walking down the broad cement stairway to the pool. At the bottom of the stairs he paused, assessed the crowd and began to walk towards the diving board, his towel slung over his shoulder, his bathing suit and sandals the only other things on his body. As he proceeded along the row of sunbathers flanking the north side of the pool arms were raised in greeting and a muted commotion of salutations and teasing remarks coursed in succession through the group, like a wave in a crowded football stadium. Harlan, a close-lipped smile fixed on his face, nodded to each woman in silent acknowledgement until he reached the ladder to the diving board where he dropped his towel, kicked off his sandals and climbed confidently to the top. He walked the length of the board, rose on his toes, and dove knife-like into the glistening

aquamarine of Braverman's "Olympic-sized" pool. The sighs of
the onlookers, like a breeze through pines, seemed to rise above
the nattering of the gossips and pontificators and still the assembled. Harlan broke through the surface of the water, swam
back to the deep end, hoisted his dripping body from the water
with just the effort of his arms, and returned to the diving board.
Again he went up the ladder in brisk, regular steps until he was
at the top and on the board. Then he went to the edge, turned
around, backed up so that only the balls of his feet and his toes
held him in place, and then sprang up arching his back and diving in a beautiful arc that ended with his body again fully extended sending him into the water as straight as a knife blade.
It was a truly wondrous sight and when he broke the water's surface again I trotted over to the deep end to greet him when he
emerged from the pool. The sighs of the women had become enthusiastic cheers of admiration; applause were in order. The
women seemed stimulated, restless, squirming in their chairs to
see him as he wiped his hair with his towel and then draped it
over his shoulders like a cape.

"Your dives are fantastic, Harlan, really great," I raved.

"Thanks. Do you dive?"

"No, not me. But you dive like Johnny Weissmuller."

"Tarzan? Me?" He laughed, and changing his voice jokingly
said, "Me Tarzan," and we both laughed. I was aware that there
were those in the assembly of women who were watching us, or
more truthfully watching Harlan. Still, it felt good to be in his
company and share in the attention. I was too young to know
that the problem with reflected glory is that you are required to
be no more vital than the crust of the moon, a lifeless surface
mirroring another's fires.

"So where did you learn to dive like that, school? Camp?"

"My mother taught me, she was a champion." He cocked
his head and jumping up and down on his left foot he tapped at
his left ear to evacuate the water trapped there. "Come on. Get
out!" he chided the obstinate liquid.

"Harlan?" An attractive woman approaching from behind
me called his name tentatively, like a petitioner at a royal court.

"Could I talk to you for a minute?" He smiled, rubbed his head with his towel again and stood waiting for her to speak. "I saw you diving and I just wanted to tell you how thrilling it was for me to see someone as accomplished as you are right here at the hotel." She averted her eyes, as if embarrassed, and then looked up at him again. "What I wanted to ask you was would you be willing to give my little boy, David, diving lessons? I don't mean back flips and those kinds of high board athletics but simple 'in you go' kind of dives from the edge of the pool." She demonstrated the "in you go" method by poking her extended hand into the air with a brusque jerk. "He's afraid of jumping into the water and having someone like you spending time with him would be so good for his self-confidence." She was almost dithering.

"Maybe," he said with a shrug. "I don't have very much free time but maybe I could spend a half an hour with him a few times next week." I was aware that while talking he had somehow appraised the woman's figure and the level of interest in his voice had changed with his appreciation of her sexual attractiveness.

"Oh, would you?" she gushed, grabbing his arm at the wrist and stroking his shoulder with her other hand. "I can't thank you enough. You go back and practice your diving and I'll talk to you at dinner. Thank you so much!" And with a goodbye wiggle of her fingers she left. I had achieved a weed-like status with her, an unremarkable feature of the landscape so ordinary as to be virtually invisible.

"Well," I said, "looks like you have an admirer."

"It's not me she admires, it's my diving. The diver is not the dive, DiMaggio is not the homerun." I scrunched up my face in confusion. "One day you'll understand, don't worry." And he sped up the long metal ladder again and fell, arms and legs flailing wildly, into the pool, disappearing for a long time before rising to the surface with a broad smile illuminating his handsome face. I closed my eyes and shook my head in appreciation and when I looked again there was a beautiful girl leading a troop of children to the kiddy end of the pool. Though I had never seen her before she had a comfortably familiar air about her that permitted me to smile at her as though it was a perfectly natural thing to do. She returned my smile and then dashed to the pool's edge where a little girl was poised, waving wildly at Harlan and calling for his attention.

"No, no, no, Rosalie!" the pretty girl called out as she scooped the child up in her arms and made a playful game out of her rescue. Harlan waded to the shallow end of the pool where they exchanged some words and then he swam back to where I was standing.

"Who's that?" I asked, hopeful that it might occur to him to introduce me to her.

"You know, I'm embarrassed, I don't remember her name. I don't think she's free though. She's dating the tennis pro and they're pretty involved from what Heidi tells me."

"Oh, too bad. She looks really cute."

"Well if things break you'll be the first to know, I promise." Then he drenched me with handfuls of water he scooped from the pool in rapid succession. I was delighted with his horseplay.

Chapter Four

To this day it astounds me how strong and irrational is my capacity to make judgments about total strangers. Driving in my car, glimpsing a woman making a turn at a traffic light, I know instantly that there is no possibility of chemistry between the two of us and I know this within milliseconds. She might be young and comely or ripening into middle age, it doesn't matter. It is not about pretty or ugly, old or young, rich or poor, it is something else entirely, something closer in function to the human immune system which distinguishes familiar from foreign. This process extends to animals, to cities, to whole countries, this so-called gut reaction. Despite my years of education, my good intentions and my noble aspirations, I remain imprisoned inside this system of appraisal and, sometimes, it is only with great effort of will that I can subdue this primitive response when attempting to do business or break bread with a perfectly reasonable human being to whom my initial reaction had been one of rejection.

With Harlan Hawthorne my first impression had been confused. He was so different from anyone I had known, I felt lost and without reference points, yet I liked him and knew that I wanted him to like me and that ambition made me very uncomfortable with myself. I didn't understand why I even cared but I did. I don't think I ever saw him tense or harassed on the job, a job notorious for pressure and irritation. You might find him smiling or laughing softly at a table of young singles, men and women both, and each one of them in his thrall, or listening with effortless concentration to the lamentations of a teen aged girl, like a wise uncle, not a sexual predator. Yet, for all of his charm, outside of the dining room he had no special friendships. Even Heidi Braverman was rarely seen in his company, their private schedule separating them both from the rest of us at night. I would have been his friend happily but he seemed not to want one and I found that style to be attractive as well; Harlan as the urban Marlboro man, the strong silent type, the characteristic ideal American male of the time. You'd never find him sorting through the pile of mail in the waiters' quarters after breakfast like everyone else and he was never called to the pay telephone that hung on the wall next to the entrance to the bunkhouse. Rather than make him seem peculiar, these facts only served to reinforce his solitary and mysterious tone for me.

Why he had chosen to work as a waiter haunted me continually. Ordinarily, I thought, someone like Harlan would have been at a beach resort on Cape Cod or on the south shore of Long Island, or perhaps in Vermont or Maine or the Berkshires, but never the Catskills. Never. He said he'd come for the money just like the rest of us, but I didn't believe him and was reluctant to press him or challenge his position. My fascination, indeed my awe of him, discomfited me and made me too eager to please him or too often awkward in his presence without apparent cause. There were several sleepless nights spent debating with myself if the odd, intense feelings that I was experiencing could mean that I was a homosexual. I had never had any sexual thoughts about him or any male, never tried to imagine us in any circumstance of physical intimacy and the mere thought of someone else's erect naked cock within three feet of me aroused only disgust. Wrestling with this problem on one occasion I forced myself to picture us sucking each other off and my repulsion was so great there was no doubt in my mind that a sexual liaison with him was not my desire and while I was reassured my fear was unfounded, I was no more enlightened about the intensity of my interest. And there was little consolation in knowing that my curiosity was not unique. Several times I overheard other waiters and busboys puzzling over Harlan's presence in the

Catskills. A few days after the Rosie Moldar debacle, for example, returning to my room after lunch, I came upon Ron and another busboy, Gerry Goldstein, talking about him.

"He's here for the Jewish pussy, Ron, that's what he's all about, I just know it." Gerry was a short, homely, acne-ridden boy with the filthiest mind I had ever encountered. To even hear Harlan's name come from his lips seemed to be a contamination and I wanted him gone.

"Gerry, you know shit about Harlan, about women, and about sex, so why don't you go outside and fuck yourself for a while because Ron and I would like to talk about some things," I said entering my room. Accustomed to being abused, Gerry seemed not to take offense at this kind of mistreatment.

"What, do you two homos got to do something to each other or something, like play with your turkey necks Melvin?"

"Fuck you!" Rudy's ruse was common knowledge.

"Fuck off, asshole," Ron Barked.

"I'll go do my homework. Let's see, Goldstein's law states that the angle of the dangle is equal to the heat of the meat when the mass of the ass is constant." he singsonged as he left.

'So, what is it?" Ron asked.

"Nothing, I just wanted to get rid of him."

"Don't give me that shit, Melvin, I know when something is eating at you, what is it?" he insisted.

"I don't want to spend any more time speculating about Harlan, talking about him behind his back. I just don't want to. He's a friend, just like you, and it makes me feel disloyal."

"It's not disloyal to be interested in someone. Besides, I don't like him and I don't trust him. There's something just a little too smooth and easy in that goy, er, I mean guy," he snickered.

"Fuck you. I hate that Jewish stuff all the time. Anybody who isn't Jewish is the enemy and anyone that you admire or look up to has got to be a Jew, or at least an honorary Jew. I'm Jewish but I'm not so tribal I can't make friends with people who aren't Jews."

"Do you know who wrote 'God Bless America' and 'White Christmas?' Irving Berlin, a Jew. 'Rodeo' and 'Billy the Kid?' Aaron Copland, also a Jew. The opera 'Porgy and Bess?' George Gershwin, another Jew. Be proud. They're Jews and so are you, Melvin, and being Harlan's friend won't change that. You're so knocked out because you think that he goes to Harvard, aren't you."

"It's pretty impressive, you have to admit, but I know guys who are going to go there in the fall and," my voice trailed off as I heard myself think, "and I'm not falling all over them."

"Listen, I don't have to admit anything. There you go with your Ivy League bullshit again. It doesn't matter where you go to school, it only matters that you get a good education." He waved his hand at me in disgust and started to change out of his waiter's clothes. "This is not a rehearsal, Melvin, this is your life. If you keep looking only at the future your life will slip by and you won't even notice it."

"Hey! I'm just eighteen years old! What's slipping by? What are you talking about? Going to a good college is what I should be thinking about now. That and getting laid." My joke broke the tension and we both laughed.

"Speaking about getting laid, where is this Diana you're always talking about? I've never seen her around. Is she real or is she somebody that's made-up."

"Oh she's real," Ron said with a laugh.

"So, if this Diana is real when do I get to meet her?"

"Hey, you just struck out with Rosie, take a rest. There's not that much good material up here so take your time. Why don't you try out one of the teenaged daughters?

"Oh sure," I said, feigning contempt, though the truth was that almost every week or two it was as if the same raven-haired beauty arrived in the company of her parents causing me to fall secretly and hopelessly in love with her. Hopelessly because she never in any way acknowledged that I even existed. She'd spend her day poolside in a leopard print bathing suit and backless slippers with big, furry pompoms at the toes,—mules, though for the life of me I can't imagine why that lounge wear would be given the name of such a reliable drudge, they should have been called sloths—her suntan oil, her fashion magazine, her towel, but not so much as a glance for me. Sometimes I'd pull up a chair in her line of sight while she spread out on a chaise longue in the sun.

Then I'd open my book, a Faulkner novel or a Dostoyevsky tome, holding it so that the author and title were clearly facing her and hope that she would be so impressed by my taste and intellect she'd approach me to solicit a seminar. What a dreamer! A girl who looked like that was quickly in demand and usually petulant with all comers from the dining room. Her parents probably spent half of their vacation time reminding the band and the tennis pros about the statutory rape laws. The members of the harem would critique these younger lovelies and I even saw one of them deliberately spill her gin and tonic on the bare abdomen of a particularly gorgeous girl, though she swore it was an accident in her profuse apology. In the blinding sun and reflections at poolside I learned to content myself with a single intense examination imprinting her image on my retina as if it were a photographic plate. Then I could turn back to my book and with my eyes shut behind dark glasses ogle the curves and folds of her young, goddess-like sublimity.

"What do you care if they're beautiful or not. You have a better chance of scoring with someone who isn't everybody's dream girl."

"I just can't do that. That's why it didn't work with Rosie. I'm a fast learner, I don't have to try that again. It's bad enough having to go to the social hall to dance with one of those vertical piles of cottage cheese. The only good thing in that is at least someone will get a better tip because her mother and father are satisfied their precious girl was paid some attention."

"Well Diana is too much for you right now. I'll let you know when I think you've earned the right to her. Maybe you should wear a rubber all the time so you don't come in your pants when you do meet her." Wounded and deflated, I skulked around our little room.

"You're not going to let me forget that are you."

"It's for your own good. Don't overreach. Go buy a Playboy Magazine and play with yourself for a while. When I think the time is right you'll meet Diana and not one minute sooner." At that moment I hated Ron more than anyone in the world.

2.

July was a hot, almost rainless month that summer and the weather served to make the resorts busier than usual which was good for everyone. The hotel owners filled every bed and bungalow in turn filling every chair at every station in the dining rooms, and every chaise at poolside. The tipping was unusually generous as though, somehow, the staff was personally responsible for providing relief from the overheated city. By the night of July 22nd I had saved $550 and with almost seven weeks to go my goal of saving $1500 for the summer appeared to be within reach. My college goal seemed less secure; Columbia would close its freshman class during the course of that week and I had yet to hear from them. Throughout July, each day when the mail was dropped off in the waiters' quarters I had nonchalantly sorted through the pile of letters while my heart pounded so forcefully I feared it was audible to anyone nearby. My parents had been instructed to put any mail from the school into a manila envelope and forward it to Braverman's unopened. This experience, for better or for worse, belonged to me and I didn't want to get the news second hand from one of them. That Monday there was no letter either raising me to ecstatic heights or crashing me into hopeless despair; there could be no consequences other than those. Ron saw me slink away from the mail table and grabbed my arm.

"No news?"

"No news is good news, isn't that what they say?" I lied bravely.

"You should come to City College. Why spend all that money when you'll get as good an education for free?" I shrugged. "I get it. Columbia is 'Jack' to you; at City College or NYU you're just Melvin. Well, it doesn't look too good does it? But who knows, maybe you'll have a miracle happen. Do you believe in miracles?" Ron placed his hand on my shoulder.

"As a matter of fact I've already experienced one."

"Go on." We returned to our room and started to change out of our work clothes.

"I swear it was a miracle. It happened when I was just about to graduate from the eighth grade. I was a short, fat, and self-conscious kid who would be meeting a whole new bunch of kids in high school. The miracle was an accident that completely changed me in time for the changeover, changed me completely."

"Well, was it a miracle or was it an accident?" Ron was getting impatient for a change.

"Both. Either the accident was a miracle in disguise, or the miracle was an accident." I could see he was confused. "One day my friend Billy said he wanted to go for a bike ride, so I went with him." I fished an L&M filter tip regular from its pack, lit it with my Zippo, inhaled deeply and closed the lighter with a loud snap, its signature sound. I did not offer Ron one. He was always annoyed with me for not choosing one brand of cigarette and sticking with it but I had yet to find the brand that reproduced the sweet tobacco smell I associated with my earliest exposures to its allure. Harlan came in and sat down on his bed without greeting either one of us.

"We rode to Yonkers on a main street until we could cut across to the park that Billy said he wanted me to see. We found it and then rode through it on a dirt road for at least another three miles before we saw the huge swimming pool that Billy was looking for. Just as we approached the pool a little kid on my left threw his beach ball to a little kid on my right. I looked up just then, saw the ball near my head and braked and swerved to avoid it. My bicycle skidded and I lost control of it. The next thing I knew I was on the ground in terrible pain."

"Broken, right?" Ron said, urging me on towards the conclusion of the story.

"I thought so. I looked at my leg when I pulled myself out from under the bike and my foot was pointing in one direction, my knee in the other, and the leg in between was swelling up even as I watched. A park police officer showed up and said I should definitely not try to stand on it." "But it was broken. You knew that. You could see that. So what was the miracle? I don't see any miracles coming in this story," and he got up from his cot and started to change into his basketball shorts.

"Wait! The miracle is coming." I loved this story and was not about to abbreviate it for anyone. "They called an ambulance and took me to a nearby hospital. I had broken both the bones below the knee in my right leg in two places. I was kept in the hospital for a week and then sent home for two more weeks of bed rest. My leg was in a cast from the sole of my foot to my groin. Everyone was concerned that I'd become a record break-ing fat boy, too big even for the clothes at Barney's Huskytown, BUT!" I shouted, to hold Ron's attention, "and here is where the miracle comes in, when I finally gave up the bed for crutches and could stand up, I had grown four inches and slimmed down. The kids who came to visit me were shocked by my transformation. Some of them thought it wasn't me but some new kid my folks had traded me for at the hospital. And this change didn't stop there. On June 14th, the day I broke my leg, I was five foot three inches tall, short and tubby. On September the 8th I arrived at my co-ed high school, a lean and lanky five foot ten and still growing. Was that or was that not a miracle, you tell me."

"Sounds miraculous to me, Jack." Harlan had been listen-ing in the whole time.

"Almost as much of a miracle as spelling Melvin J-A-C-K," Ron said sarcastically. "So you grew seven inches in that sum-mer, is that what you're saying?" I nodded. "Impossible."

"Oh yeah, then it truly was a miracle because I have the photographs to prove it." I smiled, complacent with the evidence in my possession and the truth on my side.

"Well, I don't know that you can get another miracle. In fact, I'm positive that you've used up your quota of miracles, one to a customer one time. That's it. Get ready for NYU Melvin," Ron gloated.

"I don't know anything about a quota on miracles, Jack. Keep your hopes up and don't let Ron discourage you."

"Oh, Mr. Miracle himself is talking now. You know what I think? I think it would really be a miracle if you were actually a student at Harvard, that's what I think."

"Call them up and ask." Harlan said, extending his hand towards Ron as if offering him a telephone.

"I already have," Ron said. I was stunned.

"And?"

"They 'decline', I love the gentility of that word," Ron said with contempt, "they decline to give out information about their enrollees. That is to say they would neither admit nor deny that you have ever so much as broken a book's bindings, or a pencil, or bread or wind on their campus in Cambridge."

Harlan chuckled. "It's the summer and they don't know where any of us are, that's all it is, take my word for it."

"We'll see about that," Ron said, unwilling to admit defeat. He grabbed his towel and left for the basketball courts in a bad temper. The drama of my miracle, dramatic to me at least, had been totally eclipsed by their exchange. I didn't know if Ron was being honest about calling Harvard or if he was just bluffing, but I did know that, were I to ask, he would not tell me the truth.

"Well, at least Ron's mistrust is out in the open now. You know, Jack, he says that it's Harvard that he doesn't buy but I think it's me and everything about me that he doesn't believe." Harlan lit a cigarette and exhaled the smoke through his nose in two even columns. "What do we have, six weeks left 'til we're finished up here? Why does he care so much about me, about who I am?"

"I think it's about Heidi."

"Heidi! What does Heidi have to do with anything?" He seemed more angry than surprised. It was the first time I had seen him show anger. "Goddamn it! Why does that asshole want to meddle in my life! I loath people who meddle." He crushed his cigarette under the heel of his shoe, then picked up the misshapen butt, laid it in his palm and closed his fingers around it in a fist. "I have to get some air. See you later," he said.

"Wait. I don't really know that it's about her. It's just that he always seems so upset when you're out that you might be with her. That Saturday night when you caught us in the shed he joked about Heidi seeing his ass and finding him appealing." I knew that I was going too far but I wouldn't stop myself. I was choosing to ingratiate myself with Harlan at Ron's expense. But then who were all these people anyway but strangers I had been thrown together with in the course of working my way towards the good life. Considerations of taste and temperament were never a factor in the assignment of roommates. I was always aware that ours would be short-lived friendships at best—summer accommodations if you will—and that if either attachment were to survive Labor Day I hoped it would be with Harlan. Ron was just the kind of person that I was trying to grow away from. For him there would be the traditional end of summer mountain goodbye, a firm handshake and the emphatic farewell: "Have a good life!"

"So Ron has a girlfriend, Viveca or Veronica . . ."

"Vivian."

"and he's screwing Martha, and he's hungry for Heidi too, and he's concerned about my integrity?" He raised his eyebrows and sighed. "I sincerely doubt that Heidi could ever be interested in Ron." He shook his head and drew another cigarette from his pack of Lucky Strikes. Still on the lookout for that perfect smoke I asked if I could have one and he tossed it to me.

"I'm surprised Ron has any women interested in him at all. He seems to be so gruff and critical with everyone."

"Martha seems crazy about him. I don't know anything about Vivian, but Martha really likes him and he's not gruff with her." At that moment I realized that this conversation could open up the opportunity to talk with Harlan about his style and his effect upon women. The way he behaved with them was very different from the way the rest of us did and women loved him for it. "Of course he's not at all as smooth as you are, you're really something to see. So tell me, how do you do it?" I asked him, "How do you get all of those girls and women to act that way?" And then, with my head lowered so that I was practically speaking into my shirt pocket, I added, "and can you teach me how to do that." He seemed surprised by my question and he stared at me for a full minute before answering.

"Just be yourself Jack, that's the secret. Don't try too hard, don't try to be something that you're not. Be natural, that's the best advice I can give you. Just be yourself." That disappointed me. I was hoping he'd help me to be like him, not like myself. Being myself had accomplished almost nothing for me with girls. "What's wrong? Did I say something wrong?"

"No. Well . . . I don't know, it's just that you have some moves that really seem to get women interested."

Harlan emptied his laundry bag and began rolling his socks into little balls which he then lined up in neat rows in one of his drawers. He put the last pair down, came and sat down next to me on Ron's bunk, put his arm over my shoulder and exhaled loudly through his nose.

"I don't understand why you can't get this. Believe me, there are no tricks, no moves, no lines. That kind of deceit is a trap and you re the one most likely to get caught in it. Once you're caught in that trap the word gets out and no one will ever trust you again. Why can't you just relax and be yourself?" I was positive that he wasn't telling me everything. I'd watched him with different women and girls and he was not the same with each one of them. Harlan watched me as I thought this through, and though his face had been completely impassive I could feel him studying me, his eyes so piercing I felt as though I was being psychologically biopsied.

"I understand what your problem is," he said. "You're so focused on what you're going to say and how you're coming across that you are unable to pay attention to the girl you're with. Your own fears and desires are throbbing away in your mind like Gene Krupa on a hot drum solo and the girl only exists there like a living centerfold. I'll tell you the secret, Jack, it's simple. Listen."

I waited, listening for him to reveal the secret, but he said nothing else. "Is this a Zen trick?" I asked, "Is this the sound of one hand clapping?" I teased, exhausting my repertoire of Zen related information. Harlan squeezed my shoulder, laughed, and stood up.

"God you're wonderful in your egocentrism, Jack. I meant listen to the girl and hear what she feels, what she needs and desires. In typical Melvin fashion you thought I meant that you should listen to me and then I'd give up my secrets. My God do you have a lot to learn." I felt chastened and embarrassed, but also impressed that Harlan was teaching me something even my brothers had never spoken of. "Listening means using your eyes, your nose, your intuition. Your ears are the least of what you need when you listen well. Consider the human animal, Jack, an ape in velvet, a creature down from the trees only recently. Yes, he uses words, sentences, whole paragraphs, but these are communicative fine tuning, the least of what conveys meaning." He lunged forward suddenly, his jaw set, his face only inches from mine sending a fright through me and causing me to squirm away in retreat. "I didn't say anything did I? No, but you were frightened of me instantly; you who are fascinated by me, admiring of me, you who knows I would never harm you, but instinctively, reflexively, you recoiled from me. Not one word but the message was totally clear. Now there are other messages you must learn if you wish to please women and, in turn, have them please you." This was a different Harlan, one that I had not seen before. He was expansive and intense, excited by what he was telling me, like a great teacher, I thought, and it was his excitement, the pure joy of such intellectual display that convinced me Harlan must indeed be a Harvard product. "First you learn to watch. You saw me come at you and without having to think about it you moved away from me. Most gestures are more subtle. Does she smile when you approach? Does she cock her head quizzically? Saucily? With her jaw jutting out at you? Or does she bow her head slightly and avert her eyes, and then wear just the suggestion of a smile."

"What if she scowls?" Harlan turned, cocked his left eyebrow and tightened his mouth. "Sorry," I said, advancing rapidly in my understanding of non-verbal communication.

"Is she wearing perfume? Is she wearing the more alluring scent of the body's nervous tension, the gamy smell of the body in a state of anticipation? Has she just eaten strawberries, drank champagne, consumed chocolate? Look for the traces at the corners of her mouth and with a soft smile and a gentle hand, wipe the residue away with a clean handkerchief, not like this," he said, pulling a white cloth from his back pocket and unfurling it with a flourish, "but like this." And after refolding the handkerchief, he opened it only in part, refolded it into a small square, and dabbed at the corner of my mouth while smiling solicitously. "Watch her hands, her gestures, her very fingers. Do they tremble? Are her nails bitten off and jagged, or are they like talons, leaning over the edges of her fingertips? Are they polished, and is the polish clear, or red or pink? Do her hands look soft, or are they worn with work and detergent, rough and tired. Feel sympathetic to her if they are work worn, don't be repelled. She is repelled by them, but if you seem tender about the very thing that makes her most self-conscious she will adore you." He paced the room as he dilated on the process of observation, his arms flying through the air as if cutting swaths through the empty space. "What is her posture like? Does she stand straight, presenting her breasts with pride, or does she hunch her shoulders and stoop a little because her breasts are too big and embarrassing, or too small and embarrassing. Let me tell you, Jack, if you think men are self-conscious about the size of their penis, you've seen nothing until you've watched a room full of naked women studying each other's breasts." I was stunned. Had Harlan actually done that? Had he seen a room filled with naked women? I almost fainted at the thought. While others might have envied Superman or Batman, Plastic Man was the superhero of my dreams. Many times I had envisioned myself as an inconspicuous curtain hanging at the window in a room filled with naked women, and Harlan was telling me that he had actually done better than that. He looked over at me, narrowed his eyes and frowned. "Enough. I can't expect you to absorb all of this in one sitting. Besides, there is more than I could ever impart to you or anyone else in just one sitting. Anyway, is it clearer to you when I say there are no moves, is it Jack?"

"Thanks, Harlan. Yes, it's definitely much clearer. Can I ask you something?" I hesitated, concerned that I might be going too far but then, as he opened the door to leave I asked anyway. "Did you really see a room full of naked women?"

3.

It was a Friday night and husbands were arriving for the weekend. Sammy never joked about his guests but many of the rest of us in the dining room enjoyed a laugh at the expense of a buffoon, a sad sack or a mystery guest. A mystery guest was usually a husband who had deposited his family on the previous

Sunday and left without joining them for dinner. Ron always speculated they left hastily because they were screwing around in the city, Ivan thought they were racing back to a poker game, and I, the naïf, thought they were eager to get a jump on the coming work week so they could get ahead and leave earlier on the coming Friday to stay with their families for their final week of vacation. So, when Milly Goldfine told me her husband would be arriving that night and she wanted me to know a few things about him I figured this was my weekly mystery guest. She said her husband, Stan, was a war veteran who had been badly injured at Normandy. She didn't wish to go into the details but he'd had a fusion of the bones in his neck because of an explosion that nearly tore his head off. He didn't have many special needs but he did require being seated on her left side because the fusion permitted him to turn his head only to the right. Did I have any questions?

Mrs. Goldfine recounted all this in matter-of-fact conversational tones that must have evolved over years of the multiple tellings of the story. She stared at me through expressionless eyes awaiting my questions.

"No, I can't think of any," I said, "I'm sorry."

"Sorry? Sorry you don't have any questions or sorry he was wounded?" Her expression had not changed and she stood perfectly still in front of me, her hands hanging calmly at her sides.

"Both, I guess," I said.

"You guess? Well the one thing my husband does not need or request is pity. Just make him comfortable on my left and that will be sufficient, okay?" She forced a strained smile. I nodded vigorously, feeling my face flush with embarrassment. Only later did I realize that this meeting had been her opportunity to vent some small share of her bitterness.

Stan Goldfine arrived in the dining room promptly at seven that evening. He came alone and went directly to Sammy. I could tell who he was because he seemed to have no neck at all. It was as though his head had been screwed into his shoulders like a light bulb. Sammy laughed at something he said and slapping the man on the back led him over to me.

"Melvin, this is Mr. Stanley Goldfine, *Captain* Stanley Goldfine, the hero of Normandy. This is my busboy Melvin White."

"Nice to meet you Mel," he said extending his hand. "Are you Jerry White's brother?"

"Yes I am, sir, and Steve's too of course."

"Of course. Mildred has told you about the seating arrangements?"

"Yes, sir."

"Good. I won't be any bother once that's taken care of. And you don't have to call me sir, Stan is fine." I nodded, and smiled, and never called him anything the remainder of his stay. For the rest of that first night I tried not to stare at the war hero when in his vicinity. That a man's body could be so mangled and still survive was difficult to grasp. And at Normandy! A tenuous beachhead with only medics in attendance, not even a field hospital, and all of them under intense, relentless gunfire from the Germans; this was a miracle.

In a matter of days I had grown accustomed to Stan Goldfine's disfigurement and ceased to feel discomforted by it. "The Captain", as he was called by his table mates with Sammy's encouragement, became the darling of his table a charming raconteur and joke teller. He even abided Mrs. Moss, the woman seated to his left towards whom he could not turn, a woman suffused with the malodorous stench of stale body odor, as though some dreadful anxiety that dwelled within her exuded evil humors through her pores saturating her clothing leaving no escape or refuge from its presence. Moss seemed an especially fitting name for her because, in addition to her horribly snaggled teeth, as if that were not bad enough, her dentition seemed coated with a mossy covering that gave her smile an unpleasantness I heard others at the table remark upon when she was not present. Sammy, to his credit, never said a negative word about her, or for that matter, anyone,—with the exception of Abe Melman.

"Jesus, Sammy, what's wrong with that Moss woman doesn't her room come with a bath?"

"Be nice, Melvin, she's a European. They rarely bathe, at least not in the United States. Who knows, maybe they got frightened on the crossing and keep away from water after that, I don't know, but she's not the first one to need a hot shower."

Milly Goldfine seemed to soften as the week went on. She was a moderately attractive woman but she seemed to work at disguising any aspect of her allure. She wore dresses that seemed too large and billowed around her figure, baggy Bermuda shorts that made her legs appear stilt-like, and skirted bathing suits with broad spandex bands across the pelvis that you saw only when the skirt floated up in the swimming pool. Harlan and I were changing after the dinner meal when I asked if he had happened to notice the Goldfines at my tables. He smiled a knowing smile.

"What's the smile for?"

"You mean 'the hero of Normandy' and his wife? She's some looker when you get past the pinched quality of her personality and the awful wardrobe." By the time we had this conversation I was aware of Harlan's eye for the ladies and less convinced of his claim to be the unwilling object of female attention.

"At first she seemed to be pissed off all the time and I didn't think of her as all that attractive but over the week I see she has a pretty face and a nice figure that she hides. Do you think she's still upset about his wounds?"

"I know Sammy calls him 'the hero of Normandy' but that's not the case."

"He got his injury during the invasion. It was a horrible blood bath, a slaughter from what I've read, why do you think that's not his story? I mean I wouldn't have the nerve to ask him. You just don't talk about things like that. And Sammy does call him 'the hero of Normandy'."

"Sammy has a tendency to dramatize, don't you think? He likes to feel important and other peoples' importance is one way for him to do that."

"Maybe, but when he introduced the captain as 'the hero of Normandy', Captain Goldfine didn't object."

"Object? Who would object? There were so many skirmishes, so many battles, hey–they were all heroes, but the hero of Normandy? Not likely."

"I don't know why you won't let him take some credit. He was there, he was seriously wounded, he came back in pieces."

"Yes he was there, and yes he was wounded but that may be like the exam questions you get, you know, 'true, true and unrelated' that's all I'm saying. Millie, Mrs. G., would tell you it has something to do with that. Hey, look at the time I've to get Heidi. See you later." He was gone.

He had called her Millie, not his usual way to refer to guests he didn't know. I wondered . . .

4.

I think I will never forget that fourth week of July 1956. It's beginning marked the one month anniversary of my working in the dining room at Braverman's, an achievement of no special significance in itself, but one I took pride in for several reasons—for one, surviving the hardship of being Sammy's busboy. My guests' tips that Sunday were remarkably generous, just as Sammy had had assured they would be, and brought me more than twice what one would have expected a busboy to earn for a week's work. Things were proceeding in their usual monotonous, predictable way and then, bewilderingly, Thursday of that week everything seemed to come apart on a grand scale. We awoke to the news that there had been a terrible accident at sea. Radios were blaring in rooms up and down the hallway and it seemed to me Ron had his on extra-loud. The Italian ocean liner Andrea Doria and the Swedish liner Stockholm had collided in a dense fog forty-five miles south of Nantucket Island. There were many casualties reported but the fifty-two deaths that resulted had not yet been counted in the early morning hours of July 26th. I experienced a strange sense of alarm in response to this news, as though it was an omen of some sort. Imagining what those passengers were enduring was shocking to me. Hours before they had been toasting each other with champagne and luxuriating in the fantasies of their glamorous trans-Atlantic cruise and then suddenly, a grinding crash had tipped their vessel into the dark waters of the sea. I remarked on this peculiar reaction to Ron and Harlan but neither offered anything about it save their own surprise. Why the accident should have affected me so strongly was curious. The only person I knew who had ever even gone on a cruise was my aunt Ceil of "the using bastards." She went on Caribbean cruises in the winter and to the Concord hotel in the summer, her radar for unavailable married men being equally flawless on land and sea. It being July she was at the Concord so it could not have been concern for her that was discomfiting me. At breakfast some waiters and busboys talked about the fact that there were no guarantees of safety in life and that you could just as easily die falling in your bathtub as in a sports car and at least the sports car might get you laid. I felt no sense of relief from their philosophizing. Ron sat down nearby and shoved a Life Magazine in front of me. It was opened to "A Look At The World's Week," a pictorial section of the magazine, and one of the features was about fleets of tourists filling the sea out of New York harbor. The photograph showed a number of ships streaming towards the camera but not the Andrea Doria.

"So?"

"The biggest rush of transatlantic travelers in 25 years. That means the last time was just before Pearl Harbor. Maybe this is the bad sign, the omen you were talking about." He pursed his lips and narrowed his eyes.

"I don't think I'm feeling spooked because of that. What does that have to do with anything anyway?" He shrugged and took his magazine and coffee to a different table. I lit a Kent regular and poured a glass of cold milk.

"What are you doing, you want to get sick?" Ivan Goldman asked. "That's a combination guaranteed to give you cramps."

"Bad breath yes, cramps I don't know." The unrelenting feeling of apprehension was unsettling. I crushed the pack of Kents and threw it into the garbage bin. This definitely was not going to be my brand.

"Let's go to work everybody, come on," Sammy called out. I hauled myself out of the chair, gathered four pitchers from their shelf and started filling them with tap water.

"Why so somber, sullen and saturnine Melvin?"

"I don't know Sammy, it's nothing." I was torn. I wanted to tell him how I was feeling but doubted he could be of help.

"Smile Melvin. It will make you feel better to smile. And if you're really unhappy about something or someone you can smile and also say 'asshole' at the same time. Did you know that?" His face was right next to mine. "Try it. Smile and say 'asshole'." I forced a smile and said asshole. Aware that the smile never wavered and my lips never moved, I laughed. I tried it again and laughed even harder afterwards as though I had just mastered a magic trick that looked impossible but was actually ridiculously easy to perform.

"I told you, didn't I?" Sammy beamed.

"Unbelievable, Sammy."

Throughout breakfast I smiled agreeably at everyone. The talk at every table was about the cruise ship's collision.

"Whaadaya talkin' about! They do that for the insurance, it was no accident. More coffee over here, Melvin." I poured Dr. Jake Wasserman his coffee and leaned in towards the table.

"Well, actually, Life magazine says it's been the busiest year in the cruise ship industry in twenty five years. I don't think that they'd risk lives with a full ship."

"Who cares what you think, kid."

"Jake! That's no way to talk. He didn't mean it, Melvin, he's just upset about something else." Sammy had never accepted my being Jack. He insisted upon calling me Melvin even after I'd introduced myself to my guests as Jack. I'd no sooner go into the kitchen for something than he'd begin explaining to them that Jack was not really my name, Melvin was, and for some meshuginah reason I was calling myself Jack. He told them he thought that it began after I hit my head on something in the kitchen and he was making it his business to bring me back to my senses. He said he hoped they would help out by calling me Melvin, not Jack.

"Apologize to Melvin, Jake."

"Apologize to a busboy? Are you nuts Miriam?"

"Quite all right," I said, playing at being David Niven, smiling and saying asshole under my breath. Heidi, alerted by Dr. Jake's stentorian tone circled the tables in our vicinity and approached us. She smiled at me and rolled her eyes to show she understood what I was dealing with. Laying a hand on his shoulder she leaned into the group.

"Good morning everyone, how's breakfast today?" They all smiled and gushed for the lovely Heidi, as much in appreciation for her presence as for the interruption of Dr. Jake's rant.

"I thought I heard some quarreling at this table." She curled her lower lip and waved a finger at the group to show them they had been naughty. "Now it is such a beautiful day, the pool is waiting, Bernie A has a "Simon Says" scheduled in a little while and you should all be thinking about enjoying your vacation, not arguing about cruises. Here you take a row boat on a lake, not an ocean liner, so what is there to be upset about?" The wives laughed to show their affection and Heidi threw them a kiss while going to a nearby table, winking at me as she passed.

"If they were making money hand over fist there'd be no accident, believe me," Dr. Jake resumed, his tone lowered, his spirit chastened. "You should hit your head again Melvin, maybe it'd knock some sense into you." The incident with Dr. Jake was annoying but not out of the range of the expectable in the work of a busboy. After he'd stuffed himself with enough herring to feed a large family of minks Dr.Jake, "the people's podiatrist," felt some embarrassment for his behavior and stuffed a five dollar bill into my shirt pocket.

"Don't take it personally; I was hungry," he said, patting me on the back as he left.

Work did nothing to distract me from my discomfort. I was not much inclined to premonitions or other mystical modes and I didn't really believe that the Andrea Doria's accident presaged anything of relevance to my life, but still there was the unrelenting sense of foreboding. Then the thought arrived without effort; Columbia did not accept me. I cleaned up the station quickly, sorted my silverware into the drawer of the serving stand, swept the floor, and inverted my water pitchers on a towel atop the stand. Then I raced back to the waiters' quarters for the mail, but it hadn't been delivered and still that feeling of dread clutched at my core. I went to the payphone and called Malcolm seeking the comforting sound of my best friend's familiar voice.

"I can't talk," he said when they got him to the phone, "all hell is breaking loose here. Dean Martin just broke up his partnership with Jerry Lewis, and listen to this,—it's about where Jerry wanted to open their new movie. Jerry wants it to open here at Brown's Hotel and Dean wants it in a big city. You know what the movie's called?—'Pardners!' Can you believe that? 'Pardners.' Gotta go." This news added to my upset. It seemed that nothing could be counted on to be as you were led to expect it would be. Martin and Lewis were a team. Teams were marriages of the sort in which divorce was not an option, or so I wanted to think. The Marx brothers, the Ritz brothers, Laurel and Hardy, Abbot and Costello—these guys just went on and on. I argued with myself that I was wrong, that I had no reason to be certain that I had been rejected but it did nothing to relieve my distress. It was then that I began learning an important lesson: there are times when even bad news is better than no news. With no information the mind is apt to wander off into the dark corners of the most frightening imaginings, though in this particular case there weren't that many possibilities: YES . . . NO. Still, knowing which one confronted me would allow for either grieving or celebration and the release to move on to another challenge.

Ron came into the staff quarters carrying the waiters' mail. "There's a manila envelope for you," he said, at the table where the mail was usually dropped and spread out.

"If you don't mind, I'd like to look at it by myself." I was convinced it was bad news, even though there were still some vestiges of hope buried in my pile of negative expectations. But they say bad things come in threes and I already had heard two.

"I'm going to know sooner or later so what difference does it make? Let me stay with you. Maybe I'll introduce you to Diana later and then she could be either your winner's medal or your consolation prize." I said nothing. "Okay, either way I promise you you'll meet her later today, what do you say?"

Of all people I did not want Ron there when I read the letter. He had mocked my ambition and he would not comfort me if my worst expectations were realized. Nor for that matter, would he celebrate my success were I to be awarded admission. Harlan might understand, but he was off somewhere and wouldn't be available again until after lunch was served and cleaned up.

"I'd rather do this alone Ron. I'd just feel better opening the letter in privacy."

"Diana, Di-AANNA," he crooned. "She could play Marilyn Monroe to your Arthur Miller—hey, did you know they just got married? I heard it on the radio. The president of the debating society gets to screw the head cheerleader. Unbelievable! There's even hope for you, Melvin. So come on, let's see what the letter says."

"No!" I took the envelope and walked out of the quarters. I shook the manila envelope and it seemed to contain very little. I shook the envelope several times as though I might divine the contents by its heft, but I was no more informed for the effort. A letter of rejection would be fairly thin, but then maybe the letter of acceptance would be no thicker; the full orientation packet might come under separate cover rather than with the congratulatory note. Sammy saw me walking away from the building and hurried over to me.

"Is that the letter from Columbia?" he asked eagerly, his eyes wide, his jaw agape.

"I want to open this up alone, Sammy, if you don't mind." His shoulders slumped, but then he straightened them and smiled.

"You're pessimism craves palliation and pellucid perspective my young friend. Learn now, Melvin, that hope is the staff of life as much if not more than bread. All month long you have been waiting for that missive you are holding in your hand and all month you've been hopeful and excited. Now that it is here you look like the end of the world has come. Is there an atomic bomb in that envelope? A packet of plague germs? So what if you don't get into Columbia, you'll find something else to hope for and that will keep you going. It's what keeps us all going. That's what hope is for. Hope is to life what gasoline is to the automobile's engine, it's what keeps things running and moving. Open the letter." The manila envelope had a fastener on the back which when opened allowed the letter from Columbia to slide out. My mother had either forgotten to moisten the glue or wanted me to have the answer as quickly as possible. I shook the letter just once, as though that might shake out any bad news, and then ripped the edge of the envelope from top to bottom. The letter was brief and kind, an obvious rejection from its first words which reminded me of the college's high degree of desirability and the quality of the thousands of applicants competing for the 750 places in the Freshman class. I did not cry or feel punched in the stomach. I felt defeated and I knew it would take some getting used to.

"It's a rejection Sammy." Sammy grasped my shoulder in his hand and gave it a squeeze.

"There are worse things believe me, much worse. I'm sorry." Then he left me standing in the parking lot. Alone, the sick feelings of loss and hurt began to overtake me quickly. My nose became stuffy and tears came to my eyes but I wouldn't let them flow. It would take some time to get over this. Sammy was right, eventually there would be something else to hope for but just what that would be was beyond perceiving at that moment.

Several days later, out of the blue, Ron said he would introduce me to Diana that afternoon if I was up to it. It occurred to me that Sammy must have said something to him about the letter of rejection because he was unusually soft spoken. I was surprised and somewhat excited by his offer. Diana had already become a regular subject for discussion in the dining room during set up. Everyone was interested in her but no one had been able to get her to go out with him. Ron wanted me to appreciate how lucky I was to be the one she was willing to meet. I couldn't tell if this was a generous act to distract me from my bad news or a ploy to establish an indebtedness to him.

"You've never seen her have you? She's a real knockout. I don't want to waste your time describing her so just believe me when I say you won t be disappointed." If this was true, why wasn't Ron filling up her dance card, I thought but didn't ask.

"Thanks Ron, I really appreciate this. Does she live here on the grounds somewhere?"

"After lunch, Mel, drop it for now. And if you want me to go through with this, drop the Jack shit too, okay? If you want to be Jack go back to Rosie, Diana's expecting a Mel."

I was much calmer at lunch than I had been during dinner the night I was to meet Rosie. Perhaps this was evidence of a growing maturity. Bernie Abramowitz went from table to table trying to cheer the sad, encourage the disheartened, and kibbitz with every man, woman and child in the dining room.

"Bingo this afternoon in the recreation hall. You card players come too, I'll give you a Bingo card like you wouldn't believe!" he babbled, a desperate smile stretched across his face, perspiration, like a strand of fresh water pearls, beading over his upper lip. The big card players, men who were easily identified by the smell of cigar smoke that followed them wherever they went even when their cigars didn't, stared contemptuously at Bernie but said nothing. Sammy shooed him away from our station while rolling his eyes and mugging for the benefit of the elect at his tables who grinned with the knowing appreciation of insiders. After lunch Ron brought me to Diana.

She lived a little more than a mile down the road and across the state highway that separated the hotel from its little lake. Ron was unwilling to use his car for what he considered to be short distances so we walked through the misty rain.

"When she asks you where you go to school tell her you don't. Say that you're signing up with the Marines after Labor Day. Signing up, not joining, hear me?"

"Is that why she's not sleeping with you? Did you tell her you were a Joe College?" I was feeling excited and willing to take risks, like provoking Ron.

"That's one reason. Listen, this Marine business is not something that everybody knows. It would be a mistake to let it get out. If a whole platoon of waiters turns up as Marine recruits your chance of keeping a hold on her is probably zero, understand? This is something that she told me one night when she was very drunk and very sad. She almost threw herself in front of my car back there on the road last August and I kind of helped her through her crisis. It was with some musician from Swan Lake, a piano player I think. You know the horn player-heart breaker is such a cliche that at first I almost didn't understand why she was so upset. Love is love I guess. Anyway, she's a little strange but stay with it and see where she wants to take you."

There was music playing as we neared the porch that stretched around her house in an uninterrupted band like the brim of a hat.

"Blueberry Hill", I said to Ron, who frowned at my excess; since we all knew the song, naming it was unnecessary.

"Diana? Diana are you in there? It's me, Ron, I brought somebody to meet you." There was a loud crash of glass breaking and a girl called out "shit!" in exasperation. Then the door to the house opened up and a tall, thin girl with an olive complexion and long, shiny black hair came out onto the porch.

"Jesus, you scared the shit out of me just then Ron." Her arms had the wiry sinews of an athlete and her small breasts looked as round and hard as Macintosh apples. She seemed to emit an intense and immediate sense of excitement, a tension beyond the fervid sexual urgency that attractive women evoke in men. I knew immediately that I wanted to be with her, maybe forever.

"Diana this is Mel, the fella I was telling you about." She studied me impassively, her face revealing nothing of what she was thinking. She looked me over, up and down, and then fixed her eyes on mine and locked in like a gunner on a target.

"You're going to be a Marine?" she asked, without either irony or disbelief. I had the good sense to just nod my head very slowly and keep my eyes stuck fast to hers. She smiled. "My father was a Marine, is a Marine," she quickly corrected herself. She continued in a soft and velvety voice. "My father says you only say was when a Marine is dead." Then I smiled. Her telephone rang and she went back inside to answer it.

"What do you think?" Ron asked.

"Thank you, thank you, thank you. She's unbelievable."

"I have to go," she said reappearing in the doorway. "I'll look for you Mel, Mel, right?" I nodded again. "I'll find you, don't worry, we'll see each other soon." She smiled at Ron, winked, then waved and shut the door to her house.

"Incredible! Unbelievable! God, I don't know what to say. She's the sexiest girl I've ever seen, she's . . ."

"Shut up. She's not deaf and she knows what she puts out. Get your mind off of her for a minute, damn it, and put it to work for me." He had stopped in the road to glower at me. The misty rain coated his eyeglasses with little droplets that aggregated and then ran down the lenses in thin rivulets. "O.K. I need you to help me make some calls, write some letters, contact the New York press." Seeing my perplexity he snorted and said, "About Judge Crater, shmuck, has Diana fried your brains already? We have to get them up here. Hey, I bring you to Diana and now you owe me, okay?" I nodded in agreement.

Chapter Five

Sundays always began the same way. Anticipating our tips made us edgy. We'd all come to understand there was absolutely no way to know what to expect from people. That a guest might have been especially friendly or personable in no way assured you a good tip. This was as true for those to whom you had been accommodating and to whose peculiar idiosyncrasies you were finely tuned as it was for the gruff and irascible. The meanest bastard might surprise you with an act of astonishing generosity. Despite this knowledge some of the staff persisted in figuring their take over coffee before the dining room opened for breakfast. Toting up their expected tips, some with pads and pencils, some staring up at the fluorescent lights suspended from the ceiling, their jaws slightly agape as they did the arithmetic in their heads, this group of dining room staff resembled the habitues of a betting parlor during the racing season.

Usually, the tips had already been decided by the Friday preceding the weekend but were not handed out until the coffee had been served and the farewells and goodbyes exchanged between the guests who were leaving and those who were staying on. After the Lion's Convention the Braverman regulars at Sammy's station arrived and I learned that, unlike the other busboys, I could rely on them in most cases for a generous gratuity. Once in a great while one of the embittered victims of Sammy's snubbing would simply leave without tipping—"stiffing" was what we called that—but Sammy always made it up to me. When he found me cursing into the silverware drawer in my side-stand one of the first Sundays there he put his hand on my back and said, in a voice trembling with a travesty of outrage, "Which malignant, mountebank, miser has mocked and mistreated my meticulous minion?" He must have had that alliteration memorized for the occasion. I couldn't believe he was capable of stringing that necklace of words together spontaneously.

"Mr. Klein just walked. He made no effort to even say goodbye. He was busting my balls all week, he and that silly wife of his, and nothing that I did was ever good eno . . ." Before I could finish my rant Sammy tucked a ten dollar bill into my shirt pocket.

"Leave off the lamenting. Anytime you get stiffed just come to me and I'll make it up for you."

"Sammy, that's very nice but it's not fair for you . . ."

"Melvin! I'll decide what is and isn't fair. It's no problem for me to give you a few dollars when a guest wants to punish you. I can see that you're a nice boy, not rude or snotty, so you don't deserve to be treated that way. I'll take care of you. That's all there is to it, end of story."

It was hard not to like Sammy when he treated me that way. My take that Sunday with twenty of my thirty-two guests leaving, twelve of them two weekers, should have been about ninety dollars. I'll spare you the math. Just remember the going rate in those days for a busboy was three dollars per person per week. In fact I took in a little over a hundred dollars with another thirty-six still in the bank for the dozen two week guests still at my station.

But not everyone in the dining room was as lucky as I. Waiters who found themselves receiving empty envelopes, or a fist full of crumpled ones intermixed with strips of newspaper, would curse and shout to inform the entire dining room staff of their misfortune. One time Ivan Goldman, the immense and nimble All American basketball player, vaulted out of the dining room still clutching the envelope containing the green Monopoly money he had been given by a miserly guest who imagined that he was penalizing Ivan for his disappointing service. There must have been twenty waiters and busboys pressed against the bay window at my station watching when, with one hand, Ivan plucked a white-washed stone the size of a volley ball from the row of stones lining the driveway, held it out in front of him next to the windshield of the guest's car, and said, I swear he did, "Stand and Deliver!" I bet the cheers from the dining room staff were audible even inside the locked car. Ivan had a twenty dollar bill slipped through a narrow opening at the top of the driver's side window. Then, after replacing the stone carefully in its row Ivan ran alongside the car as it left, dodging and weaving, feinting and stopping, as though he might hurl himself in its path at any moment. I doubt if that family ever returned to Braverman's again.

The farewell handshakes completed, the crumpled currency that had been pressed into my palm sorted and arranged by denomination, I sat down at one of my tables and lit up an L&M King.

"How'd you make out?" Ivan Goldman asked, sitting down next to me.

"Good, good. How about you?"

"Oh yeah, good. Melvin, can I ask you something?"

"Sure, what can I do for you?"

"That army guy with the funny neck, 'The Captain' Sammy keeps calling him, was he easy to get along with? I mean, was he bitter, did he bust your balls?"

"Not at all, he was fine, why?"

"I don't know, it's creepy to see someone busted up like that. I played with a guy at Kansas who broke his neck in a game. He was a great rebound man, jumped like a kangaroo, but he got hit coming off the boards one day and landed upside down on his head and broke his neck. He never played again and he was mad as hell whenever you'd talk to him, bitter and mean. So, I just wondered, you know, was that soldier like that." Harlan came up from the back of the dining room and joined us cigarette in hand.

"No, Stan was a good guy, friendly, funny, a gem."

"You talking about 'The Captain', Jack?" Harlan said.

"Yes." Harlan snickered.

"What is it with you, Harlan? Any time I mention his name it's like you find him amusing. Don't you feel any respect or sympathy for this guy? He almost got killed winning the war. Maybe it means less to you because you wouldn't have ended up in a death camp like the rest of us Jews." I disliked the mocking tones he used whenever he discussed Stanley Goldfine, 'the hero of Normandy,' my hero of Normandy.

"Now that's uncalled for. It's got nothing to do with his fighting in the war but then neither does his injury." He tamped out his cigarette in the saucer I was using for an ashtray and smiled. "Now here's what really happened." He sat forward in his chair and became more serious. "I don't for a minute want to minimize or dismiss the enormous risk and horror of that invasion and beachhead. It was hell from what I've heard, but . . ." and then his smile returned, he lit a Lucky Strike and relaxed against the chair's backrest, "having survived that bloodbath and re-grouped with his unit, he and a few buddies decided to have some fun the night before they were to move in-land and battle the Nazis in France. One of them was a medic who had access to an ambulance—you know after the beach was secured all kinds of equipment started arriving—so they commandeered the ambulance and took off for a place where they heard there were some girls eager to show their gratitude to the Yankee liberators. It was while they were driving into this little town that they hit a land mine planted by the Germans as they were fleeing. The two other guys in the vehicle were killed but Captain Stan—who was only a lieutenant at the time—survived." He stopped to take a deep draw on his cigarette and exhaled a smoke ring through pursed lips. "So, when I seem a little amused when Sammy insists on calling him 'the hero of Normandy' understand it's because, in a way, it is humorous. I mean it's one thing to get caught cheating on your wife, but who would ever imagine you could get blown into the sky doing it?"

"How do you know this is true, who told you this?" I couldn't believe it was true; I didn't want to believe it was true.

"Millie Goldfine told me. Now you know why she's so pinched. She's screwed. She could never leave a war hero, she'd be outcast from her family, her friends, everyone. You see how admiring and sympathetic people are when they hear where he received his injuries; no one would forgive her if she left him.

And she can never tell the truth of what happened because they both would be laughingstocks. She's screwed."

"How did you get her to tell you this? Why did she pick you?" Ivan sounded wary.

"Women like talking to me," Harlan said with a shrug, "I listen and they talk, it's that simple."

"I bet you do more than listen," Ivan said in a lascivious tone.

"Bet all you want but that's a losing bet. Ask Jack here, women just come to me, it's nothing I do, and I'm perfectly happy with Heidi. I don't need any land mines in my life." Ivan snorted. It sounded more like disbelief than laughter. Harlan looked at me and raised his eyebrows.

"Jack?" he said.

"It's true, Ivan, women do flock to our friend Harlan. I've seen it a bunch of times. He's the honey that draws flies, or is it his fly that draws honeys," I said, pointing at his crotch, weary of his self-proclaimed innocence, more doubtful now that it really was true.

"Jack!" Harlan said, as if injured by my joke, "some friend you are," and he walked back to his part of the dining room.

"Why did she tell him, Mel, ask yourself that, why would the woman give up her secret to him, if she stands to lose so much, why tell a stranger?"

"Maybe that's the only person you can tell, a stranger. There's no harm done that way, she gets it off her chest and leaves it in the mountains. I don't know. I hate to think that's what really happened. I'm still a little bit shocked."

"Yeah, I don't know that I believe it either. I like to think there are real heroes too. "

I looked at the back of the dining room where Harlan was laughing with his busboy. Did all these women just come to him uninvited, or was there something he did to encourage them?

2.

To relieve myself of my obsession with Harlan I sometimes resorted to pondering the question of Abe Melman's presence in the hotel dining room. His proximity made it clear that he had experienced some form of personal tragedy, one that had inscribed visible signs of pain into his face. He was a loner, almost a recluse, and he had chosen work as a waiter because it gave him a good income without the complications of co-workers who would inquire into his personal affairs or witness his comings and goings. You didn't even need a social security number to work in the hotels because your paycheck was next to nothing after the deductions for room and board were taken off the top so, if it was the government you were hiding from, this was the place to be. Private though he was, he left the door to his room open often so that we could see his law degree from New York University and his bachelor's degree from City College. The walls were otherwise bare, no pictures, no photographs, no newspaper clippings, not even a calendar. Ron interpreted this as Abe's giving us a cautionary lesson.

"He hangs them there to tell us that he did something so terrible he can never hope to return to a conventional life. He doesn't even have to say what it was that he did, he just makes it clear that he is outcast. Maybe that's why we haven't asked him what he's doing here point blank, it's just too terrifying to know the whole story of his exile from middle class society."

Indeed, like a character in one of Aesop's fables, Abe Melman's life seemed to bear the weight of the moral consequences of a mistaken choice. But what was his mistake? I was beginning to appreciate Sammy's relentless disparaging of him. He was a nerve- wracking puzzle, an enigmatic but no less intensely felt object lesson whose very ambiguity and mystery screamed out at all of us: BEWARE! THIS COULD BE YOU. But how? What misstep could send you plummeting downhill to end up flat on your ass like Abe? It was most likely a criminal act, I thought. A fall this steep had to be the consequence of a crime. But what crime? Abe did not seem capable of violence and when provoked by Sammy he seemed even more leaden and immobilized, surely not someone capable of being physically dangerous. And that failure to react, to stick up for himself and lash back at Sammy could be infuriating and make you want to hurt him too. It was unseemly for a man to be so pathetically passive and for me, this man in particular, as old as my father, better educated than my father, yet unquestionably an utter failure. The great promise of education had been broken in Abe's case. He just didn't belong in this place.

Nor was I alone in trying to figure out what Abe was doing at Braverman's. Ron and Ivan Goldman and I sat around one humid afternoon discussing it and on that day was born the "What's With Abe?" game, a game Ron and I would play, but only twice in the course of that summer.

"He's in hiding, that's all there is to it," Ivan said. "Look, you come here, you make a few thousand dollars, you don't have to give anyone your social security number or file a withholding tax, you're anonymous." Ivan chopped at the air with his huge right hand to emphasize each of his points. "I don't know what he did, but it probably was something illegal having to do with his being a lawyer. He's trying to stay out of jail."

"No, I don't think so," Ron objected, "that just doesn't feel right. Why would he hang his law degree in his room and leave it in plain view if he was trying to be inconspicuous? No, it's about a lost love, a broken heart or a broken promise. It wrecked him." Ron sounded sad just imagining the scenario.

"Well I think he did something that disgraced him, either with a woman he was working for as a lawyer or just with a woman. Look, short of murdering someone how long will your conscience punish you like this for?" No one had suggested murder. I looked over at Ron knowing that I couldn't refer to Lenny's story of a shooting but wondering if it could be true after all, and if Abe might have been party to it.

"Murder's too wild," Ivan said. "Does Abe look like someone who could do something like that? He's much more likely an embezzler or a cash skimmer kind of crook."

"Yeah, you're right," I said, again looking at Ron, trying to convey my suspicion with facial contortions and grimaces.

"Well, I'm gonna shoot some foul shots," Ivan said, "I can't take all this sitting around, it makes me nuts."

"In this heat?" we both said.

"Heat, shmeat, it's all in the touch. Heat don't bother me." When he left I closed the door and beckoned to Ron to come closer. "Do you think Abe could have had something to do with this Crater shooting that Lenny was talking about?" I whispered.

"Oh, so now you're interested in Lenny's story?" He jutted his jaw and arched an eyebrow. "Maybe, there's always a possibility. But you said yourself Abe doesn't seem the kind of man who'd be violent. I can't figure it out." He turned the radio on, the same kind of temporizing diversion that lighting a cigarette usually provided, but when "Why Do Fools Fall in Love" was what he reaped for his effort Ron snapped the radio off, grumbling something about Frank Sinatra, Tony Bennett and Vic Damone. Left unchecked Ron would be likely to launch into a polemic about slum music and the decline of the romantic love song. I intervened immediately.

"But not at all seriously, folks, why is he here?" I ventured, attempting to get Ron to play. "Really, this is a question of some magnitude, Ronald. For me it comes right after 'what became of the dinosaurs?'" Ron craned his neck and looked up at me and a smile slowly appeared on his face.

"So you want to figure Abe out? Okay. We'll play 'What's With Abe?' Give me a minute. But then you have to be prepared to play 'Who's Harlan Hawthorne?' at some time. I know that you're smitten with that fraud, but I'll find out who he is with you or without you." That was a gratuitous remark so I let it pass unchallenged. "So, what's with Abe," he mused. Reaching under the bed and pulling out a Camel Ron lit up. "What's with Abe, what's with Abe, GOT IT!" He shifted in his bed. "Abraham Melman, lawyer extrordinaire, was hired by a woman to represent her in a lawsuit. This was not a difficult case. Her landlord had promised to give her a new refrigerator and a new stove when she moved in to her rent controlled apartment and now, five years and two leases later, nothing had been done. The woman was unmarried and this surprised Abe because she was very beautiful. For him beauty was the only qualification required for a woman to be eligible for marriage and her being single made him feel he had to protect her. And it made him angry at the landlord for taking

advantage of an unprotected woman. Abe had a promising career, everybody told him that, and he had opened his office at
the bottom of Manhattan near City Hall expecting to prosper because of that location. The woman, let's call her Linda, took the
subway down to Abe's office and came all dressed up for their
meetings. Abe began to think that she did this just for him, not
understanding that she dressed up for the people on the street
and the people on the train the way that women do."

"Come on, you mean women dress up just for strangers?"
I said in protest, incredulous.

"You didn't know that? Well neither did Abe and that's
where the trouble began. He started thinking about Linda day
and night. He talked to her in his mind, explaining what it felt
like to shave in the morning, how his coffee tasted, everything.
He included her in his life as though she was really a part of it.
Sometimes what you wish for can feel so close, so much a reality you forget that it is only a dream. He took her into his bed at
night and soon he was jacking off with her in mind. His obsession with her, and there's no other way to describe it, this obsession became so real to him that he began to believe she was
as eager for him as he was for her and that she wanted him to
show her a sign of his interest. She's a dignified and good person, he thought, so her signs will be subtle. One day, while giving her a pen to sign her complaint he tried to touch her fingers,
but he fumbled the pen and it dropped on his desk spraying ink
on the sleeve of her white blouse. She was very upset about the
stain but tried to be polite to Abe; after all it was an accident.
Flustered half out of his mind, Abe said that he could take care
of the ink blot if she would just slip out of her blouse and let him
rush it to a dry cleaner he knew on Chambers Street. He handed
her his raincoat to show that he had nothing up his sleeve, only
the most respectable of intentions. Linda hesitated. 'Please, it's
the least that I can do to make it up to you,' he begged, but still
she refused. 'The longer that you wait, the harder it will be to remove the ink stain,' he insisted, and standing close to her,
smelling her perfume, he reached for the button at the neck of
her blouse. 'Back off, jerk,' Linda said, and she gave him a shove.

Abe took this to mean that she wanted to touch him but was disguising her interest as a rejection. You should understand, Mel, that women do that almost as much as they dress up for strangers. Anyway, this is when all hell broke loose. Abe grabbed Linda, pulled her close against him and tried to kiss her on the mouth. She struggled and that excited Abe more so he put his hand on her boob and squeezed telling her how much he loved her. Linda, who had once been Sophie Tucker's assistant and knew how to handle guys when they got too pushy, jammed her knee up into Abe's balls doubling him over and putting out his fire. The next day Abe got a call from another lawyer who said that he and Linda would see to it that Abe was disbarred and disgraced. The lawyer hung up the phone without waiting for Abe to say anything.

Panicked by the threat, already feeling disgraced, Abe knew that he had to get out of town. He called his cousin, Ben Braverman, and asked if he could put him up for a few days. A few days became a few weeks, and then a few months, and the only way that Abe could make it up to Ben was to work in the hotel and that's what Abe Melman is doing in the mountains."

"Good story, bad guess. Abe doesn't care about women as far as I can tell. He doesn't seem to care about anyone."

'Well, then you come up with a better story. But it has to he funny. I hate thinking about what might have actually happened to land him here in the borscht belt."

3.

Sammy had one or two guests who stayed for the season. This meant these people had money because The Hotel Braverman was not cheap. It also meant that I would have to keep alert to one of the infamous season guest tipping tricks I learned about in Fleischmans, the practice of advancing the day you tip by one day each week. For example, if at the end of the first week you tipped the staff on Sunday, the next week you would tip on Monday and the week after that on Tuesday and so on. In this way, over the course of eight weeks you successfully finesse one week of tips for your waiter and busboy. It would seem peculiar, to say the least, that one who could spend so much for a vacation in a resort hotel would still aspire to screw two college kids out of what is now called "chump change" but, not only are the rich not like you and me, they rarely are generous for generosity's sake. Usually they expect some recognition or social compensation for their largesse. Some poor working slob, as my father would refer to the average working man, is much more likely to want to treat a busboy fairly, even ingratiate himself with him, than to stiff him.

Solly Schwartz was one of Sammy's regulars and he seemed to me to have the potential to be trouble. Every morning Schwartz would be waiting just outside the curtained French doors to the dining room, pacing back and forth, checking his watch, peering at Stuart Stein through a gap in the curtains, impatient but always smiling. I could not imagine what it was that he envisioned to be waiting for him but whatever it was seemed to animate him with an attitude of buoyant expectation. A large part of it was appetite, to be sure, but there was something besides food on his mind. He always entered the dining room with the demeanor of a family's favored child who expected an acknowledgement of his specialness with every appearance. Stuart Stein opened the French doors promptly at 7:15 and Schwartz would dash through, eyes wide, smile wider, and skitter down the center aisle as fast as a silverfish, spewing greetings to the bleary-eyed staff still setting their tables. No one bothered to respond.

"Good morning Melvin, what have we got today?" he asked, rubbing his palms together gleefully.

"The clap, I hope," I muttered into my shoulder.

"What was that you said?" he asked, still eager. "Flapjacks?"

A glass of grapefruit juice, a standing order for breakfast, was already at his place and he lunged for it as though it might try to escape him if he didn't trap it. He lifted the glass of juice from the table and held it up to the light scrutinizing the color and observing the bottom for sediment as though it were a glass of Chateau Margaux. Then, clutching the glass in his fingertips, he raised it to his lips suddenly, inverted it, and emptied the juice in a single gulp.

"Ahhh," he said with contentment. What a schmuck, I thought. "So, what's with these flapjacks Melvin, something special?"

"I was just kidding Mr. Schwartz. Why would a hotel known for its Jewish cooking want to make flapjacks?" His face sank. You'd have thought I'd just told him his kitten had died.

"Ohhh," he lamented. "To tell you the truth Melvin I was getting a little tired of herring in cream sauce. The onions give me gas."

"How about some eggs? Scrambled, fried, poached, hard medium or soft boiled, raw . . ."

"What are you a wiseguy?" he said irately. Stuart Stein's ears pricked up like a deer's at the snap of a twig and he started towards us. Seeing this, Sammy cut him off in the aisle and put a hand on Schwartz's shoulder.

"Solly he's only a kid kidding around, come on, relax. Over here Melvin, please." He put his arm over my shoulder and led me to the serving stand where he pretended to search the silverware drawer. "Apologize to him. Say you're sorry and look like you mean it. Do it!" he spat.

"Mr. Schwartz I was only kidding around with you. I apologize if I offended you. That was certainly not my intention." I chose to look remorseful. I was learning to lie in so many different ways; I thought, this must be what they mean when they say "grow up". The other guests trickled in slowly and Schwartz kept an eye on me to see if I was treating other people the way I had treated him. He stayed longer than usual and seemed to be in a sulk. Sammy wearied of trying to kid him out of his mood but I persisted in dancing attendance on his water goblet and coffee cup, refilling each one after every sip. I was not going to hide or cringe. I was smiling broadly much of the time and hating every second of contact. Then I tried a different tack.

"Mrs. Schwartz didn't make it to breakfast this morning, is she unwell?" I asked, in the tone and vocabulary that might suggest that Schwartz was the Duke of Marlborough.

"She's a little under the weather Melvin. Tell you what! Make me a tray for her and bring it back to the room this morning and we'll be all squared away, all even-Steven." His mood was revived.

"What would you like, tea and toast and jam?"

"No no no no no. Two bagels, a big square of cream cheese, some lox, some onions and tomatoes, a fruit cup, coffee, sweet rolls and if there are any eclairs left over from last night bring two of those." His request made it sound like the weather she was under was usually somewhere over Miami Beach. After cleaning up I told Stuart Stein what Solly Schwartz had requested and he called their room to verify it. Good old Sandy, always the trusting soul. I loaded the tray with all that Schwartz had asked for, certain he was likely to be the one to devour most of it, and mounted the stairs from the main lobby to the second floor where the Schwartzes were staying when a terrible commotion erupted at the front desk.

"I want that cleaning girl here right now! I want her room searched, her house searched if necessary and don't give me any crap about her honesty, she stole my bracelet, goddammit!" The enraged woman had command not only of Belle's attention but of everyone's within earshot. I remained frozen on the staircase. Belle said something that was inaudible to me but the protesting woman reacted immediately, her sun-tanned cheeks darkening with the flush of her anger. She was a pretty woman even in her rage.

"That bracelet had rubies and pearls, for chrissakes, it's a very valuable piece of jewelry. Of course she took it, who else would have easy access to my suite?" Mrs. Braverman emerged from the office behind the front desk and speaking softly to her, guided the irate guest from the public area and into the private room. I turned to continue up the stairs to the second floor and Diana, a cloud of cigarette smoke engulfing her as she exhaled, raced up the stairs after me.

"Where have you been?" she demanded.

"Working, where else would I be?" I answered defensively.

"Not just this morning. Where were you last night? I thought you were interested in seeing me." Her face was pained and it appeared that she might cry. I lowered the tray to the floor to free my hands and approached her.

"I thought you said you'd find me. I didn't want to crowd you. I really want to see you Diana. I'm glad you came here." I tried to take her in my arms but she shrank from me.

"No, not here." Her eyes widened and her mouth fell open. "I want to be with you so much," she said. And then she fled down the back stairs.

Flushed, my heart pounding, I lifted the breakfast tray and knocked on the Schwartzes door.

"Must be pretty heavy Melvin, you're all perspired. Here, let me take it. Your breakfast is here Mildred," he called out as he shut the door in my face. I muttered your welcome under my breath and raced to the rear stairway but she was already gone.

Back in the dining room cleaning up my station Diana was all that I could think about. She had seemed genuinely distressed that I wasn't searching for her, pursuing her, craving her with more ardor. Imagine how that felt. No, don't imagine, I'll tell you how it felt: thrilling and dizzying as if in a delirium. The dining room was almost deserted and that was a relief because there was no one I wanted to talk to. All of my thoughts were focused on Diana and that evinced intense feelings of desire and expectation. I sorted the silver quickly, determined to go find her when my work was done. I had no sooner reached this conclusion than she appeared at the bay window with that pained expression of thwarted desire distorting her face. I dashed from the dining room but when I arrived outside the bay window she was nowhere to be seen. Now what the hell was I supposed to do? It was almost eleven o'clock and I would have to be back in the kitchen in half an hour. It was very likely that she was still somewhere on the grounds but where? We were barred from wearing our waiter's outfits in the hotel lobby and the canteen, a combination snack bar and convenience store where we bought our sodas and cigarettes, and they seemed the likely places to search for her. I looked at my watch again, as though maybe time had agreed to stand still for me, but it hadn't. We all do that don't we? When we're in a state of confusion we check our watch repeatedly as if some answer will appear on its face, as if time *will* tell. I took out my pack of Raleighs and lit up to think over where to go next. The morning's mail likely would be waiting at the mail drop in the waiters' quarters and maybe there'd be a letter from Columbia saying they'd changed their decision, but at that moment it was only Diana's acceptance that mattered to me. I extinguished my cigarette, went back into the dining room, lit another Raleigh, then went out again this time leaving through the kitchen. When he saw me Rudy waved a chicken neck at me and laughed his brutish laugh.

Just beyond the kitchen the rear stairway of the hotel exited on to a sandy, rock strewn, barren stretch of ground barely able to support the few forlorn weeds that struggled to survive there. The chambermaids were the ones who used these stairs most often but it was also known that band members, tennis pros and the occasional mountain rat, the sobriquet of choice for a member of the dining room staff, crept up to visit women guests in their rooms by this route. Perhaps it was that traffic that had worn the topsoil into dust. Someone who had been lurking outside the kitchen disappeared inside the doorway to the stairs as I left the kitchen and I hurried after her. The door was ajar and when I stepped out of the sunlight into the darkened entryway my eyes seemed still to be filled with the brilliance of the day rendering me totally blind in the dark stairwell.

"Diana?" I called out. There was a rustle of activity nearby. "Are you in here Diana? It's me, Mel."

"Up on the landing. Come up here Mel." Out of the darkness above me came Diana's voice. I groped my way to the banister and started to mount the stairs when a body brushed past me and fled towards the door. Damn it! I thought, she's crazy. But then all at once she grabbed me from behind and kissed me, a furiously passionate and exhausting kiss, a kiss like no kiss ever known, a remarkable, unforgettable kiss, a soul freeing make-me-immortal kiss.

4.

I can still feel the nauseating misery of that night. I had thought of nothing but her throughout that day. Her mysterious appearances and disappearances of the previous day had made Diana thrilling and exciting to me. I didn't know what to expect from her, but it was as if she was capable of conjuring fantastic magic. Her brooding quality and her intense and dramatic emotional contortions suggested a churning eroticism I had no experience with and the very idea of it excited and terrified me. We had kissed just the day before on the stairway at the rear of the main building. It was the most passionate kiss a girl had ever given to me. She was taut, muscular, pressing into me with her mouth and pelvis one minute, and then suddenly limp, spent, weak and crumpled the next. "Stop, not here,—tomorrow night. I'll meet you at the lake." She was breathless and so was I. Can you imagine how this felt? What a drama! Had I done that? I had kissed a girl to the point where she had swooned and gasped for air! Amazing. I couldn't quite believe it, frankly, but I wanted to so much that suspending disbelief would never again be as easy. Ron had been right when he said Diana was something special and it was all I could do not to run wildly to the waiters' quarters to tell him what she had just done. Telling Ron what had happened would not have been bragging, it would have been making it more real for me.

So, I had been in excellent spirits all day immune to the usual hectorings of Sammy and the guests at my station, nonplussed by the chattering of the sous chefs, counting minutes and hours and waiting for the night. When the last guest left I piled the coffee cups and dessert dishes into my box, hoisted it up to my shoulder and brought it into the kitchen exchanging it for a clean and empty tray to be used to collect and remove the glassware. While I had been feeling very excited and enthusiastic all day, as the time for my meeting with Diana came closer I began to feel a nervous anxiety, a sense of apprehension. The glasses on my tray were stacked close together and when I hoisted this load and balanced it on my fingertips, a busboy conceit, the glassware clinked and jingled like an ill-tuned carillon.

"Melvin must have a date," Ivan Goldman said to the assembly of waiters and busboys. "You'll never get her brassiere open with those hands if they don't stop trembling, Melvin." I looked at him, wanting to glare indignantly, but I could feel my eyes were wide, not narrow, and fear had raised my eyebrows almost to my hairline. Ivan saw the panic in my face and came over to me. He put one of his gorilla-long arms over my shoulder, stooped down and in a soft voice said, "Do you need a rubber?" I hadn't considered that. It was in fact beyond my wildest dreams that Diana would ever make love to me, let alone on our first date.

"Yeah, good idea," I said. My mouth was so dry I could barely get the words out. Ivan squeezed my shoulder, fumbled in his pocket and came up with a foil wrapped condom, the outline of its elliptical roll clearly visible through the wrapper.

"I thought you'd need this one day. I've been carrying it around with me for weeks waiting for you to ask." He squeezed my shoulder again and walked back to his station. I looked up and scanned the dining room furtively, but no one seemed to be paying attention, not even Ron. Did Ivan really mean that? At that moment I felt completely helpless. I wanted to believe what he had said to me, but this was a rough and cynical bunch. One of their most common games was to say something in very sincere tones to a waiter or busboy, and as soon as he accepted them at their word, they ridiculed and mocked him for his gullibility. I was already too filled with anxiety to risk being the butt of a nasty joke. I tossed the condom into the air, caught it behind my back in my left hand, picked up the tray of glasses, this time balancing it on my palm instead of my fingers, and walked into the kitchen. If my mouth had not been so dry I would have whistled.

Back in my room I laid out my clothing for the date with Diana. Ron came back while I was studying the effect my plaid shirt would have with my khaki pants.

"Do you have anything in black besides your work pants?"

"What's wrong with these pants?"

"They're ordinary Joe College, Ivy League issue pants. Does Diana look like someone you'd expect to find at Bryn Mawr?" Neither of us really knew what to expect to find at Bryn Mawr, but the spelling and sound of the name were so exotic to two Bronx boys we spoke of it as if it were a Martian station on earth. Diana, the dark and sensual, the erotic, feral child of the earth, was a familiar creature, even if familiar only from dreams.

"So what do you want me to do?" I was irritated and impatient, and without another pair of pants. Ron was shorter than I and stocky in the bargain so I could not expect to borrow anything from him.

"Okay, you can't do anything about the pants. Now with the shirt, leave a button open one down from the neck." He stopped to think, staring at me with a frown on his face that told me he wasn't at all satisfied with what I had given him to work with. I could only wonder if that included my anatomy as well.

"What are you smoking now?"

"Winstons. Why?"

"Buy a pack of Camels, open it, get rid of half the cigarettes, crumple up the pack a little bit but leave enough room so you can toss a butt up from the pack and catch it in the opening where you tore off the aluminum foil. Lift the butt to your mouth and snatch it with your lips. Then flip open your Zippo lighter, light the cigarette, and snap the lighter shut. Don't offer her one. It's a Camel. Not for the ladies." It sounded fantastically right to me.

"Don't wear that Aqua Velva crap you keep on your dresser. Rub this on your chin." He handed me a pint bottle of gin.

"Come on, you're not serious. Is she impressed by alcoholics? I'd rather use nothing."

"Just trying to be helpful." Ron kept looking at me and frowning.

"What is it? What's bothering you?" All my insecurities had been called into play by his look. My nose was too big, my ears stuck out too much, my arms were too thin, my feet too large. I was a latter day Ichabod Crane trying to be Cary Grant.

"You look fine. Your looks aren't the problem. With women, unlike men, looks aren't that important. Strength, that is what they want. Strength and a sense of danger. Not real danger, not pain, but a feeling of risk, a feeling that you might just go out of control, like a horse. That's why girls like riding horses so much. They like the feeling that they have control of a powerful animal, and they know that if they let up for a second, the animal will carry them away. Is there an animal inside you Mel?" Yeah, a chicken, I thought.

"Well . . ."

"Forget it. Don't be too eager and don't talk too much. Let her come for you. Don't chase after her."

"Sounds like a prizefight," I said.

"That's one way to look at it. But actually it's more like a duel where you spar with words."

"Ron, you're full of shit," I said, hoping I was right.

"Fine. Think that if you like. Just don't chew her ear off about your college applications and your life as a busboy. Remember that you're supposed to be joining the Marines after the summer and find something interesting to say." And with a brief gesture of salute he left me standing in the room alone.

I bought the pack of Camels, tore off one corner of aluminum wrapper, emptied out some of the cigarettes, crumpled the pack a bit, and started practicing the flip. The first few times the cigarette shot out of the pack like a missile and landed at my feet. I had gotten the wrist action right, but it was the timing of the squeeze that caught the cigarette in the mouth of the pack that was off. I was beginning to perspire. I decided to give it a few more tries and if that wasn't enough I'd figure out something else to do. The last thing I wanted was to hit her in the eye with a cigarette because I was trying to look cool. On about the fourth try I got the timing. I did it a half-dozen more times to be sure and then headed for the lake.

The air was cool and had a smoky smell, probably a fireplace in use in one of the cottages across the water. The dew had already dampened the ground making the grass slippery as I descended the hill to my meeting with Diana. I was shivering, more from my own anxiety than the damp, when Diana appeared from around the boathouse. Even in the dim light of the quarter moon she was a wonder to see with eyes luminous against her olive complexion that seemed all the more mysterious and sensual at night. That slightly strained and contorted emotional quality I associated with her was there, but now, in the darkness beside the lake, it didn't seem so exotic. It made me uncertain of what she expected from our meeting and I wondered if she had come, not to take me into her arms again, but to tell me it had all been a mistake; a terrible mistake.

"Hi," I said, and dug into my shirt pocket for the pack of Camels. She stood still, brooding, seeming almost to be suffering, and I resisted the impulse to go to her and touch her. I flipped the cigarette into position, lifted it from the mouth of the pack with my lips, and then flicked open my Zippo lighter to light up.

"I can't stay," she said in a breathy voice as I pressed down on the gritty wheel of the lighter and sent a burst of fire into the air. I sucked in the smoke, heavy and abrasive in my chest, flipped the lighter closed, and said nothing. I had forgotten how strong Camels were and I couldn't tell if the dizziness I was feeling was from the cigarette or from the announcement Diana had made.

"Did you hear me? I can't stay." Irritated, she looked away but didn't leave. I looked down at the red ember of my cigarette, its glow dimming under the accumulating ash, and felt a tingling in my forehead like a dull electric current, while nausea took up residence in my stomach.

"Gee Diana, I was hoping . . ." I started to feel faint and dropped my cigarette on the ground so I could stoop over and get some blood to my brain.

"What are you doing?" she demanded, while I remained pitched forward fumbling with the cigarette, which had soaked up enough water from the grass to extinguish itself.

"I'll be with you in a minute." My nausea had become intense and I had soaked my clothes with a cold, clammy sweat.

"I forgot I already had a date for tonight. I'm sorry. Another time maybe. Are you all right?"

"Fine," I said remaining bent in half, afraid that if I stood up I'd pass out right at her feet. "You go on, we'll set something up later. Go ahead, meet your date."

"I'm sorry," she said. "Are you sure you're okay?"

"Yeah, terrific. It's just my back goes out every now and then. I'll be okay, don't worry, this has happened to me before, it'll let up in a minute," I lied, "go on." I wished she'd leave. My intestines were churning like the propeller on a motor boat and the nausea, like a fist wrapped around my stomach, was squeezing harder and harder and I felt that something was going to explode out of me, one end or the other or both simultaneously if I had to stand there for even one more second. But I could tell

that Diana wasn't ready to leave. It was as if all at once I had become weird enough to be interesting to her. I pitched over on to
the dew drenched grass and lay on my side. As soon as I went
down the nausea eased, and my head began to clear. Diana knelt
down beside me and stroked my brow. Her hand felt very warm.
"You're all perspired."

"When the pain lets up I'll be fine. It's an old hockey injury."
Where the hell did that come from, I wondered. What I knew
about hockey wouldn't fill the space on a puck. It's Harlan, I
thought, Harlan has gotten through to me. Harlan has changed
me. "Really, don't worry about me I've survived this before, really, go." Suddenly, she turned away abruptly, as if she had been
slapped in the face, rose quickly, and was gone. Another of her
dramas. Another mystery. But all I could feel was a shameful and
humiliated misery. I lay there for several more minutes with no
place to go and no one waiting for me, at least not just then.
Later, Ron and Ivan, and God only knew who else would, like the
cast of a Broadway show on opening night, be waiting eagerly for
my review of the evening's adventure—though in this instance
they were the critics and I the player.

Exhausted by my cowardly performance I remained supine
on the ground, staring into the star filled sky where the quarter
moon had moved directly over the lake. I had allowed my nerves
to sabotage me and I was disgusted with myself. The theme
music from the movie "Picnic" calmly coasted over the water
from one of the cottages in the bungalow colony, the one with
the fire burning in the fireplace it seemed.

"Harlan!" a voice cried out from across the lake all at
once, shrill and indignant, and then laughter, the delighted, excited abundance of a woman's jubilant laughter, followed by
the leaky steam pipe hiss of someone trying to quiet her. I sat
up all senses focused and alert, listening, watching the house
with the light from the fireplace flickering in the windows, shadows dancing on the walls of the room. Two silhouettes passed
in front of the windows and then a lamp was lit in the house.
They were too far away for me to see their faces and within minutes I began to doubt that I had heard Harlan's name called

out. The music stopped but within a minute "Picnic" was playing again. Someone had left the armature on the record player
turned to the side so the record would keep replaying until they
grew bored with it or just stopped hearing it. I watched the couple move about in the living room, watched them come together and dance, swaying slowly to the dreamy music. That
looking gave me a strange feeling of power over them, as
though I might will their actions and control their movements.
Lying on the moist grass across the lake, hidden in darkness, I
willed them to undress. They stopped dancing but remained in
the dancer's embrace. My heart began to pound. Undress, I
urged. They parted and one of them left the center of the room.
The music stopped and the light dimmed, the flickering of the
fire once again shifting the shadows in the room. I began to
wonder how close I might get without being detected, and
while this thought both excited and disgusted me it did not
deter me from weighing the options available to cross the lake.
It was chilly and the water would feel cold, too cold for such a
long swim. The rowboats and canoes were locked in the
boathouse and breaking the lock would compound my sense of
guilt. It seemed it would be impossible to cross the lake and
with a sense of relief, assuring myself I was not a total coward,
I rose from the grass and walked down to the dock. From the
edge of the wooden platform the cabin seemed closer than it
had been from the grass and swimming across might not be so
impossible after all. Kneeling down to test the water with my
fingers, aware all the while that this was a hollow, empty display for no one's benefit—even I wasn't fooled—there was no
way that I'd swim across the lake to peer into those windows, I
scooped at the water and began to move it aside as if I might
part the waters of the lake and walk across its muddy bottom.
My scooping had caused enough agitation under the dock for
the bow of the little skiff used by the waterfront counselor to
come bobbing out from underneath me. This was an unconsid-
ered option, as if sent there to test me. Was I a coward, or a
moral degenerate? There was no longer room for self-deceit.
Not going across would be about fear, not righteousness. The

oars lay inside the rowboat and it was easy enough to get in-side and push off from the dock into the cold and still waters of the lake.

The movement of the air across my damp clothes and clammy flesh sent chills through me, and rowing gently so as not to make any noise did nothing to warm my body. My back was to the cabin and when the skiff came close to the other shore I turned the boat around to land it stern first and park in the reeds. Wading through the shallow water, still torn about what to do, I shuddered as much from my apprehension as from the cold. But now it was about seeing if it was Harlan who was here, not about voyeurism. Just as I was securing the tether to the branch of a fallen tree at the water's edge a car's engine started and head-lights were turned on illuminating the shoreline and the skiff in a brilliant and blinding white light.

"Okay Harlan honey, I'll see you tomorrow night. Thanks for the pastries." I heard Harlan say goodnight, and as his car pulled away the woman called out after him "I love you" in a tone that urged him not to forget that fact.

When the door to the cabin closed I unfastened the rope and climbed back into the skiff where I remained quietly trying to understand what I had just witnessed. Who was this woman? Why would Harlan want to be with someone who seemed so much older when in Heidi he had everything imaginable that anyone could want There didn't appear to be anything especially sexy about her, and to top it all off, something in the way she spoke, her enunciations and rhythms, suggested that she prob-ably wasn't even Jewish. So much for the sex with Jewesses hy-pothesis. Back at the dock I threw the bow line around a post and pulled the skiff close to its mooring. After securing the boat I stayed down at the waterfront to avoid the postmortem Ron would conduct in our room. Harlan's mysterious liaison had rat-tled me and I didn't want to betray my knowledge of that any-more than I wanted to be interrogated about my own romantic misadventure. So here was another secret to harbor. The Judge Crater story was something I'd thought of telling Harlan about but I was so unsettled by what I'd seen that night I couldn't think clearly. I was filled to the brim with information and needed to spill some of it somewhere. Malcolm was a good friend but not likely to keep the Crater secret if he could harvest some laughs by planting it with the band at Brown's, and my brothers would laugh at me for being gullible. But Harlan's secret was one I would not decant.

5.

"So how did it go?" I had barely opened my eyes and Ron's face was hovering at the edge of my bunk. I looked past him to Harlan's cot and seeing that he was not in the room I said, "It didn't go."

"It didn't go? What the hell does that mean? Did you pull another Rosie?" It was clear to him that if I hadn't slept with Diana it had to have been my fault. She was a sure thing.

"I never got to pull anything. She said she forgot she had a date with someone else last night and she was sorry. She came down to the dock just to tell me that. It was . . . what is she a tease or something? I mean one day she's grabbing me on the back stairs and telling me I'm not chasing her hard enough and the next she's irritated and impatient because we have a meeting set up."

"I told you she's something special, you misplayed her. There was no meeting, no other date, you just fucked up."

"How can you say that—you weren't even there? She came to tell me she had forgotten she had another date. It was the first thing she said to me, she didn't even say hello." Still, I was afraid he was right. I'd been so nervous she'd probably smelled my fear from her cabin.

"I didn't have to be there, I know you. If you were going to meet Harlan you'd have shown some excitement and some charm, but for a girl like Diana you behave like you've just been asked to cut off your dick."

I sat up in my bed, furious. "That's complete bullshit, how can you say that."

"Easy, I told you, I know you." He sank down on his own bunk, its tired springs creaking with complaint. "I don't know what to do with you. If you can't make it with Rosie or Diana there's no chance that I'll get you laid this summer. You're hope-less, Mel, completely hopeless."

I rolled over on to my side and stared at the wall. What if he was right? What if I went home still a virgin? What if I never found a girl who would want me to make love to her and I lived my whole life celibate and chaste, like a monk? I didn't really be-lieve that it would come to that but it felt oddly consoling to wal-low in self-pity. I pulled my blanket over my neck and curled up in the fetal position.

"That's right, play with yourself. That's the only action you're going to get this summer."

"Fuck you."

"No thanks, I don't want you either."

"It really wasn't my fault, Ron, she came to say she forgot she had another date. There was no time for anything to happen."

"You never touched her?"

"No."

"Never?" The kiss on the back stairs, the kiss that had left me completely breathless must have left her completely unim-pressed. "No, never."

"Then it's worse than I thought."

"I don't care what you think," I said, lowering myself from the upper bunk and grabbing at my towel. "I'm sick and tired of you and your opinions." And I stormed off to the shower won-dering where the girl of my wet dreams could be found. But Ron wasn't through with me. Just as I turned the shower on he came around the corner of the stall, his towel draped over his shoul-der. Shaking his head and frowning, he said, "Do you see how pa-thetic you are? Even those lumpy cottage cheese daughters you make fun of probably wouldn't want you. You're going to need a lot more work, a lot more. And the first thing we have to do is cure your fagitis."

"What are you talking about, fagitis?" I soaped my body with a bar of Lava soap, its medicinal smell confirming my manliness.

"Fagitis, as in infected with fag germs, as in in love with Harlan Hawthorne." He stood opposite me grinning, daring me to act. I stared back, dourly, knowing I didn't have the courage to start a fight with him, knowing that he could say or do whatever he pleased, knowing that he had the upper hand and that I was left to defend myself with sarcasm and feeble ironies. "Fuck you."

"That's brilliant! You'll win every debate you get into with crisp arguments like that." He wound his towel into a ropey strip and flicked it at my legs.

"Here we go, when the chips are down for Ron Alter, might makes right."

"Might makes right when you've got the might, Melvin. If you want to be right build up some might. You didn't seem to mind my might with those two townie assholes. There are the intellectual, work it out peacefully types, and there are the kick-ass get it done types. The Jews were negotiating with the goddamn British for a home in Palestine and getting nowhere. Then the Stern Gang blew up the King David Hotel and suddenly there was progress, suddenly it was understood that this was not a bunch of cringing, bearded, hand wringing old Jews, this was a tougher breed of new Jews. When the might is on your side you don't complain, it's only when it's directed at you that 'justice,'" he said the word justice with mockery and contempt, "is suddenly the critical issue." Dropping his towel he walked into the shower and I backed away fearing he had come to rough me up, but laying a hand on my shoulder he said, "I want you to be tough, Mel. I want parents to think, 'here comes Melvin White, lock up our daughters,' that's what I want. This Harlan guy is a fake and you refuse to see it's true and that makes me mad. And I think that's why Diana ditched you, she didn't feel you could be a man with her because you're still too much a boy." And then he turned the hot water up and left the shower. His words stung much more than the hot needles of water.

6.

After breakfast in an effort to overcome my sense of humiliation and defeat I went out to walk the grounds of the hotel. Movement alone, purposeless activity, has a soothing effect for me. Rather than dwelling on the cause of the pain my mind is thrust away from myself and into the landscape, into the billowy clouds that change their shape even as you study them; a portrait of Lincoln is transformed into a grazing sheep before your watchful eyes and the bruised and deflated self becomes a poet or a songwriter in your ever aspiring heart. While wandering past the pool and flower gardens towards the tennis courts where the snow white costumes of the players drew my attention, I heard a woman call out, "Good shot, Harlan!" and saw that it was he who was trotting back towards his doubles partner. The players across the net were what the Europeans delicately refer to as "women of a certain age," their sobriquet for the middle-aged, but Harlan's partner was an attractive and youthful woman in her early thirties. When he saw me, Harlan waved his racquet in salute.

"Hi, Jack, want to play a few sets with us?" I had never revealed that I couldn't even if I'd wanted to and merely waved back at him and shook my head no.

"Come on, give it a try, it'll do you some good," he persisted. The three women looked up at me with blank expressions as if in a contest to see whose indifference could outdo that of the others. "Thanks, but no thanks," I said, always the crowd pleaser. Harlan shrugged and tossed two white tennis balls across the net to the other players who chased after them as they went bouncing past, each squealing joyfully, her racquet extended at arm's length as she rumbled and blundered after the skittering balls. Harlan smiled and turning to his partner I saw that he winked at her. She cocked her head, smiled, and lifting the hem at the front of her tennis skirt with the tips of her fingers, waggled her hips in a seductive dance. During this provocative instant the large diamond on the fourth finger of her left hand blazed brilliantly at me. She was a married woman. My heart jumped in confusion; feelings of envy and of outrage tumbled incoherently through my mind.

"Come on you two, last set," Harlan called over his shoulder as he stared into his partner's eyes and ran his tongue across the rim of his upper lip.

I slipped away from the court and went down to the coffee shop. Inside I studied all the different brands of cigarettes, filtered and unfiltered, king size and regular, plain or mentholated that lined the wall behind the cash register. They were all the same price. Despite all that the manufacturers did to distinguish themselves from one another, their different sizes and shapes, their unique packaging and advertising slogans, they each cost the same twenty-five cents. Yet people defended their favorite brand with the same fervor they defended their favorite baseball team or automobile insisting on the special virtues and superiority of their choice. I had yet to find my brand. Thinking of the woman on the tennis court with Harlan, that sexy woman who made no pretense of disguising her appetite for him, I thought that maybe Harlan hadn't made his choice yet either. That maybe, in spite of all of her good looks and charm, Heidi just wasn't the one he'd choose; she just wasn't his brand.

Chapter Six

Sunday afternoon after the gala steak dinner meal was served, my wad of crumpled bills sorted and arranged by their denominations, farewell handshakes exchanged and the dirty dishes stacked in my bus box, I sat down and stared out the bay window at the crowd at the swimming pool. With little more than a month left to the summer season I had almost $700 set aside for tuition and personal expenses like cigarettes, movie tickets and train fares. While I felt this was an accomplishment, nonetheless it dwelt within a climate of sadness. This beautiful summer had been spent working seven days a week every week with no relief and while there had been some good times and some fun there had been no romance or passion. I lit a Marlboro and rocked back on the rear legs of my chair. Kids frolicked in the pool splashing water into the air where the larger droplets hung briefly glittering like jewels. My sadness seemed to deepen. All of this effort for the future, a distant future, a promise—a fantasy. Right then I suddenly understood that the price youth must sometimes pay for this promised future is youth itself.

One of the cocoa oil-basted beauties strolled lazily towards the refreshment stand at the near end of the pool, confident in her allure, cognizant of the many eyes assessing her and wearing a smile that suggested she was amused by her private thoughts. She could not see me as I puffed away behind the bay window and watched her with longing. What if Rosie and Diana are the only girls I get to try with this summer, I thought feeling sorry for myself, what if those failures are all I'll have to launch me into my college years. I crushed my cigarette in a saucer and said, "No!" aloud, startling Ron's busboy, Stan, who was under one of his tables picking up the pieces of a broken dish.

"Are you okay, Mel?" he asked, his concern evident in his face. I nodded briskly to reassure him. "Good. Guys begin to crack up and go nuts around this time of summer. They go out and get drunk and crack up their cars or jump into the lake with all their clothes on or just start screaming. I thought that's what you were doing. Screaming I mean. Did you scream just before?"

"No. I was saying 'no' out loud, that's all. I'm okay, I'm not cracking up, I'm just pissed that there are no girls around."

"Oh, you want girls. Well, there are plenty of girls around but not for the mountain rats. Come back as a tennis pro next year and then you'll have all the girls you want."

"Great idea." Jerk, I thought. I'd have to spend a few years learning to play the game before I could get a job teaching it and by that time I'd have laid somebody so why bother? Just then, magically, Heidi Braverman came through the swinging kitchen door and pointed at me.

"There you are. I think I may have good news for you."

"Good news?"

"Yes. One of my friends is probably going to break off with her date soon and I think you two might be right for each other."

"Who is she, what's her name?"

"Not so fast, Jack, not so fast, I said I *may* have good news for you, I *think* she's breaking up with her friend, I'm just waiting to see."

"Oh great, this is just a tease, Jack, in case you're not miserable enough already."

"It is not a tease, I think it is probably going to happen. You just never know, that's all." Worried that I might fall from her good graces I quickly shifted into obsequiousness.

"I'm sorry, I'm really grateful that you are even thinking about me and girls in the same context. That really is very generous and considerate of you. Really." Had I been convincing? Should I have groveled just a little bit more?

"Don't be silly, Jack, you're such a nice guy there's no reason you two shouldn't work out together, it's just a question of time. You'll see." She patted my cheek. "Your guests really love you, I hear only good things from them and you know what a tough jury they are."

"I didn't know I was on trial. And thanks for keeping me in mind for your friend." Thank God.

All that week while waiting for Heidi to tell me if I was set up with the girl she had told me about, Sammy talked of nothing but the anticipated arrival of Bernstein. Bernstein was his friend of the week, the person who embodied one of the riotous or hilarious memories Sammy often regaled us with. This made me apprehensive because the friend of the week wasn't always as enthusiastic or breathless with laughter as Sammy imagined he would be and the resulting disappointment was painful to witness. Sammy's mental gallery of guests past was a kind of private resort he retreated to regularly to refresh himself; here were his school ties, his sense of connection and continuity. In that private retreat he husbanded the jokes and the gibes, all of the pratfalls and seltzer sprays of the old comedic exchange, keeping them vital and then imbuing them with new life. Bernstein, Sammy seemed to think, was going to invigorate him with an infusion of love supersaturated with nostalgia.

"Bernstein! Bernstein will get a big kick out of you, Melvin," Sammy said as we set up for the dinner meal on Wednesday night. By then Sammy usually had recovered from any disappointment of the previous week and was gearing up for his next reunion. "He loved your brother Jerry like a member of his own family. He'll have elaborate expectations of the execution of your employment." I envisioned Sammy picking over the "e's" in his dictionaries.

"Did I ever tell you about the time me and Bernstein had Milton Berle in stitches? I thought he'd bust a gut. It was a riot, I'm telling you." I could only pray that Bernstein felt the same way. "We were tummeling right here in the dining room during lunch, a little loud but nothing so terrible, when Berle walked in with a cigar in his hand. Bernstein ran right up to him and swiped the cigar from him and began to do a Groucho Marx imitation, 'say the secret word and you win a ganse . . .' " at which point Sammy reeled off a punchline which, like those that ended so many jokes told in the Catskills, went completely past me because I neither spoke nor understood Yiddish.

"Can you beat that? A riot! It was a riot!"

"Yeah," I said, smiling and nodding.

Filled with anticipation and good cheer Sammy suddenly turned on Artie, pronounced "Ahdee" in New Yorkese, Ivan's busboy. "Come over here shithead,—you don't mind if I call you by your first name do you?—what the hell is this?" He pointed to a mop left leaning against Ivan and Artie's serving stand.

"Sorry Sammy," Artie Goldstein said remorsefully grabbing the mop's handle and hoping to escape into the kitchen.

"Stop! Sorry is already too late. We open in five minutes you putz. Who would even want to walk in here with that smelly rag exuding evil effluvia in their face!?" I was right, he had been at the "e's". "Now get that schmatte out of here and if it ever happens again I'll give you sorry." As Artie skulked off Sammy couldn't resist tossing a verbal grenade his way. "And better you should forget that Suzie Feldstein because she is never going to give you the time of day." I looked at Ron whose gritted teeth made his jaw muscles bulge and shook my head. There was nothing to be gained from protesting; energy would be better spent on incantations to assure that Bernstein would indeed be happy to see Sammy and to relive their old good times.

At one of my tables of eight that same week there were only six people dining. Two of the husbands were weekenders and their chairs sat empty from Monday morning until Friday night. The couples had arrived together in separate cars but the men returned to the city in only one leaving the other for their wives to share. On Friday afternoon the husbands would meet in mid-town and crawl back to Braverman's along the trafficked gauntlet of Route 17 to rejoin their families.

Paula Hirsch and Stella Meyers were the weekday widows at that table. They were good friends and they were friendly to the others sharing meals with them. I cannot tell you how old they were. At the time I was incapable of accurately judging the age of anyone over twenty-five but I would venture these two women were in their thirties or forties. Stella Meyers was a sweet faced woman who hauled fifty unappealing extra pounds on her frame which might have caused her to be erased from memory had it not been for her close relationship to Paula Hirsch. Mrs. Hirsch's appearance combined the sublime and the ridiculous; she had a face that could stop a clock but a figure that could stop your heart. Her body was so exquisite in form that you had to struggle to keep your eyes from it. What's more she was well aware of her allure and dressed in tight fitting pedal pushers and scoop-necked tops that always revealed an ample crevasse of cleavage. She festooned her body with gold bangles and chains and her fingers sparkled with jeweled rings. She wore make-up day and night, mascara and cheek blush at breakfast, that plus false eyelashes at dinner, and she was lavish in her flirtatiousness. "Darling, would you mind doing something special for me?" she'd say, taking my hand and stroking my palm with her thumb. "Would you please go into the kitchen and see if there are any black olives that I could have with my whitefish, would you sweet?" The other women at the table glared at her through narrowed eyes while their husbands looked at one another and smiled knowingly. Sammy, who made it known to his staff that he disapproved of her "cuckolding coquettishness" and threatened to fire any waiter or busboy who lingered near her after hours, arched an eyebrow at me and frowned. By staring into her face, one I thought capable of damping down even the great Chicago fire, my own fires were cooled and my role of obliging servant made all the easier.

Thursday morning of that week Paula Hirsch and Stella Meyers arrived at their table with Mrs. Hirsch in a state of agitation. They clearly had been in deep conversation before arriving and Stella was comforting a distraught Paula.

"You'll find it I'm sure, don't worry, honey. These things always turn up when you least expect them to."

"But I've looked everywhere, every drawer, every closet. Bernie will be so upset. It was a gift for our fifteenth wedding anniversary and he was so proud of himself for buying it for me because it was so expensive. What am I going to do?" she wailed. Stella rubbed her back and tsked-tsked.

"After breakfast we'll go back to your room together and I'll go through everything again myself. Don't worry, we'll find that bracelet."

As the other guests arrived at their table they offered their concern for the anguished Paula whose mascara ran down her cheeks in dark rivulets.

"I never should have . . ." She broke off in mid-sentence and stared at the table.

"Did you check under the bed? You know those catches are very iffy even on expensive jewelry. It might have fallen off you as you were undressing and just gotten kicked under the bed. You'd be amazed at what you find there sometimes." Mrs. Hirsch wore a strained smile that seemed to beg the fates for mercy.

"I can't eat, I'm too upset. Melvin, be a dear and just pour me some coffee." She looked up at me and then scanned the dining room with the frightened look of a hunted fugitive. I got the coffee pot and started to pour. "That waiter in the back, do you know him?" She nodded in Harlan's direction.

"Harlan? We're roommates. He's a great guy."

"Is he?" she said in the wan voice of one who might have a crush on him like so many other women did while passing through the resort hotel.

"Yes, he's my best friend here," I added gratuitously.

"That's nice," she said abruptly and with a series of rapid sips she finished her coffee, rose, leaned forward steeply to allow her breasts to spill outward towards gravity's irresistible force, and blew me a goodbye kiss.

"I'll bet jewelry isn't the only thing they'll find under her bed," Solly Stein offered sardonically after she and Stella Hirsch had left. "The way she dresses it's almost like she's not wearing any clothes at all." Mrs. Stein whispered something to him and he frowned. Spying me watching them he raised his hand in the air and said, "How about another glass of grapefruit juice, a big one, Melvin."

The guests filed in for dinner at seven P.M. and dispersed throughout the dining room. There were always late stragglers but by seven-fifteen everyone was eating his melon or drinking her cold juice and thinking of the soup and the salad. I had just unloaded a tray of salads at my serving stand when Sammy let out a loud whoop that silenced everyone in the dining room. And there at the room's entrance, one hand on Sandy Stein's lectern, the other resting akimbo on his hip, stood an enormous man with facial features of equally egregious proportions. Thick lips the color of calf's liver, a long, wide nose ending in a hooked bulb, and large, close set eyes that were slightly crossed to boot. His wavy, oily hair, parted just above his left ear, was swept across his pate to cover his baldness but rather than lying flat it crossed in an arc, like a ramp, revealing the sun-spotted skin beneath. A smile stretched his mouth sideways making deep lines in his cheeks.

"Bernstein!" Sammy hollered joyously. "Bernstein, you son of a gun!" Daintily, nimbly, Bernstein danced down the room's center aisle on tiptoes carrying his bloat as lightly as if he were a float in the Macy's Thanksgiving Day parade. He was as graceful and poised as Zero Mostel and I thought that at any second he might burst into song. Intercepting him with a hug Sammy found himself suddenly in the tango position, Bernstein's immense face pressed cheek to cheek against his. Titters of laughter sprang up around the dining room, though some seemed less than appreciative of this display.

"DUM dum dum dum. . . . , ba da de da da, DUM," he crooned in a resonant basso profundo, guiding Sammy to our serving stand where Bernstein released him and roared with laughter.. "You should see the look on your face Sammy boy, it's priceless, priceless." Sammy beamed. "And who is this?" he said approaching me.

"Bernstein I want you to meet my busboy, Melvin White." Bernstein narrowed his eyes and stared intently at me.

"Yes, yes, he's definitely Jerry White's little brother. And Steve? How is Steve doing?"

"Jerry and Steve are both fine sir," I said respectfully.

"Sir!?? The name is Bernstein, not mister Bernstein, and certainly not sir. Glad to meet you," he said seizing my hand and pumping it vigorously. "So, how do you like working for Sammy? You do all the work and he does all the shmoozing, right?" he said, looking at Sammy whose face was still aglow with delight. "Don't answer that. He'll give you a luch in kup. . . ." and continued on for another minute in Yiddish. Sammy took Bernstein by the arm and led him to his seat at the window table where he introduced him to the other guests. I cleared the melon rinds and the empty juice glasses from the tables and began to serve the salads. Bernstein's table suddenly exploded with laughter and when I looked over to see why there was Sammy off of his feet and cradled like a baby in Bernstein's arms. "Melvin, have you got room in that bus box for this drek?"

Bernstein's overwhelming presence so dominated everyone's attention for the next two days that concern for Paula Hirsch's missing jewelry vanished like the jewelry itself, while Sammy's unalloyed joy in Bernstein's company had him on the verge of grateful tears all weekend long.

2.

"Hi." Heidi was wearing her artsy leotards and polo shirt outfit. "Almost done? I want to show you something."

I'd be lying to you if I didn't admit that at eighteen everything a girl said to me was automatically taken as a double entendre, and I felt myself flush. If she saw it Heidi ignored my hopeful expectancy and began folding my napkins while I finished sweeping the floor.

"You like to read don't you?"

"Sure," I said. Harlan must have told her that. I had brought several books with me that summer and they were stacked up on my dresser. There was Dostoyevski's "The Idiot" which I mistakenly had imagined might be a comic novel just from the title, a Modern Library edition of William Faulkner's "As I Lay Dying" and "The Sound and the Fury"—another idiot book and J.D. Salinger's "The Catcher in the Rye" which I had read annually since the age of thirteen and would continue to read for many years after, that novel serving as a kind of plumb line which I used to measure my ascent from adolescence.

"My parents have this amazing library in our house and I thought you might want to take a look at it. You could borrow some of the books if you like, some of the ones that aren't valuable that is." I was quite stunned. It never would have occurred to me that the Bravermans could have a library let alone an "amazing" library. I had thought them a pre-literate people who signed their names with X's, all of them except Heidi, the adoptee.

"Sure, that'd be great, but I have to shower and change if I'm going to come up to your house."

"You don't have to do that," she said putting her hand on my arm. "They're away in Monticello now and this will only take a few minutes. Besides, you're cute in your bow tie."

The Bravermans' residence was at the edge of the property, a sprawling ranch style house with rhododendron bushes pressed up against its corners and a dense row of pink and white impatiens stretching the length of the house. In the front yard was a vegetable garden with tomato plants inside a perimeter of golden marigolds, and some peppers, string beans, and lettuce in nearby rows. We entered through the kitchen where Heidi had two tall glasses of lemonade already in wait and after handing one to me she said, "Bring your drink to the library there's someone I want you to get to know better."

"But I haven't washed up," I protested, hating the fact that I had been tricked, misled by her promise of good books.

"I wanted to get you here and I didn't want to make you feel nervous in advance. Come." And she took my hand and led me through the doorway. It was indeed a library, a room of generous proportions filled with oak bookcases rising from the floor almost to the ceiling and every shelf filled with a neatly arranged row of books. There were shelves of non- fiction, shelves of fiction with sets of complete works—Twain, Dickens, Shakespeare, the Greek Tragedies—leather bound sets, William Faulkner novels with their original dust jackets, encyclopedias, everything you could imagine. I was awed.

"Surprised?" she asked with some amusement. My jaw must have gaped. Shocked would have been the better word.

"Your parents read all these books?"

"My mother mostly. There's a new writer she likes very much. Have you ever heard of Saul Bellow?" I shook my head no. "She thinks he's going to be a great one. She knew that Faulkner was great the first time she read his work. All of these books are replacements of the one's she's read," she said waving her hand across the row of Faulkner's novels. "She wanted to have them without their bindings broken or their pages stained in any way." Reacting to my obvious puzzlement she said, "My mother is a tea drinker like no tea drinker you've ever known." It was then that I noticed the girl that Heidi had brought me to meet. She had been sitting quietly near the door where we had entered the room and when we had walked past her to the shelves of books my attention had been focused on the prodigiousness of the collection. Heidi saw me nod and smile in the direction of the girl and herself smiled. "Jack I want you to meet Sarah Charnoff, Sarah this is Jack." The girl rose and approached me and I met her with my right hand extended.

"Hello, I've heard so little about you," I said sarcastically, my face turned towards Heidi, "but I'm happy to meet you." I was nervous, but I was happy. A petite and pretty girl, she seemed completely at ease, open and comfortable. Like Heidi, she wore her dark brunette hair in a long ponytail and when she spoke to me she looked directly at me with hazel colored eyes that seemed to glint with green when she was amused.

"Well I've heard a few things about you so we're not complete strangers. Have you heard from Columbia yet?"

"No," I lied easily, "I've still got about one week left to pray. You wouldn't have an extra set of phylacteries with you by any chance, would you?" I ventured, hoping that she wasn't so orthodox or observant as to be offended by my Jewish joke. She laughed and I exhaled. We sipped our lemonade and browsed amongst the books, chatting agreeably, saying nothing that I can remember from this distance of time, but I do remember how immediately taken I was by Sarah. She became beautiful to me quickly, and her voice, already possessing the timbre of a woman's voice, not a remnant of girlishness left behind in it, seemed as if always poised to dance on the edge of laughter.

When we were returning to the hotel grounds I said, "You walk like a dancer," gambling that if she was a dancer she'd be pleased I'd noticed and if she wasn't she'd be flattered that I'd mistaken her for one.

"I've taken dance but I'm not a dancer," she said. I was still in that youthful phase during which I constructed imaginary conversations believing it possible to anticipate every possible answer to any question I might pose and then have a witty rejoinder prepared for every response making me sound like the new Oscar Wilde. I hadn't anticipated Sarah's reply. "Well, you walk like one," I fumbled. "You know, with your toes pointed out." She smiled and flipped an errant lock of hair off of her forehead, then ran her ponytail through the loop of her opposed right thumb and index finger, a nervous preening gesture, and then tossed her head again. "So," I persisted awkwardly, "are you part of the social staff or something?" She was quite short, little more than five feet tall, but so pretty I didn't mind stooping over a little to be closer to her face.

"No, I'm a counselor in the day camp with Heidi. I do art work and drama with the kids. I love kids. Kids just are as they are, no tricks, no guile. Working with them is so exciting."

"If only their parents were as innocent. 'Sweetie you wouldn't mind giving me a few of those cherry Danish to take back for little Norman would you?' wink, wink. Little Norman probably never got to see one of them."

"It's barely August, Jack, are you so cynical already?"

"Cynical or realistic? Anyway, you know how guys are. If a flock of birds lands in a field surrounded by girls, the girls would gape and ooh and aah at them. Land the flock in the same field but this time surround it with boys and it becomes a contest to see who can be the first one to hit a bird with a stone. So, need any stones thrown at anyone?"

"You're funny. Well, it was nice meeting you. I have to get back to work." She hesitated there in the path, smiling at me, and then extended her hand.

"Sarah can I see you tonight? Would you want to go down to the show or have a drink or something?"

"Sure, I'll meet you there, near the stamper, O.K?"

We touched hands, a touch more than a shake, and parted. I was happy. This was not a vertiginous delirium or an erotic frenzy, this was just happy. She was, mundane and banal as these words still seem, a nice girl and I, awash in aspirations and pretensions, was only a nice boy.

3.

After working dinner I showered and went through my clothes to select an outfit for my date with Sarah. I chose a shirt with the fine blue and green plaid pattern of the Black Watch and a pair of khaki pants to be worn with my penny loafers, no pennies inserted. A nervous anticipation began to churn as I walked down the covered walkway to the casino, the hotel's entertainment center where the Nick Henry band played dance music four nights a week. It was a Tuesday night, the night that Louisa and Alfredo Catalan put on their Latin dancing show with rumbas, sambas, mambos and cha-chas in quick succession. After performing what Nick Henry referred to as their "nimble numbers" they invaded the audience to cajole, coerce and even kidnap wary guests to come up on to the stage and learn these dances publicly. Since the risk of being chosen was shared equally by the guests, there was a good natured spirit to the evening and no one was allowed to feel humiliated for his ineptness. Louisa and Alfredo, a brother and sister team often mistaken for husband and wife, born Louise and Myron Kaplan—would you have taken mambo lessons from a man named Myron?—genially teased and tickled their subjects through the rhythmic footwork of the Latin dances. The members of the hotel staff were never selected for public instruction and it was clear to me that were I to end up feeling humiliated that night with Sarah it most likely would be by my own doing.

At the end of the covered walkway leading to the recreation hall guests showed their room keys to a member of the social staff who stamped the back of their right hand with an invisible ink that fluoresced when held under the beam of a special lamp. There was a different stamp for each night of the week and a different design series for each hotel in the region. It was the owners' way of restricting access to their shows and keeping out gatecrashers. Sarah was already waiting for me by the little table the stamper used for his inkpad and guest list. She had perched herself on the edge of the table and was laughing with the tennis pro who had the stamping duty that night. She seemed so comfortable and at ease with herself that my own self- consciousness felt amplified in comparison, but when she looked up and saw me approaching she blushed. In that instant of her reaction my apprehension dissolved in the bath of color that had rushed to her face.

"Hi," I said, sliding my hands into the pockets of my khakis.

"Hi. Do you know Dick?" she asked, looking from me to Dick Hersh the tennis pro. We nodded and smiled and said the usual things that people who have no interest in one another say when they've been introduced, and then I looked at Sarah and said, "Are you ready?"

"For the cha-cha or the mambo?" Dick Hersh stamped the backs of the hands of several guests who had come down the walkway but he was clearly more focused on watching Sarah than on his stamping duties and I wanted to get her away from his scrutiny.

"No, let's go over to the lake and take a walk."

"That sounds much better," she said with relief, and saying goodnight to Hersh we left.

"So, how did you end up at Braverman's?"

"I met Heidi at school, Performing Arts."

"Really! Well, since you're not a dancer you must be an actress."

"Well, that's what I hope I am."

"I've done some acting too. I played the title role in 'Harvey' last spring. I was a big success."

"Very funny. Just don't go making yourself invisible tonight." We walked down the path that led to the highway separating the hotel from the lake and then crossed the tarmac to the sandy path leading to the beach.

"Heidi says you're friends with Malcolm Golden. He's a terrific piano player."

"Yeah, we've known each other since the fourth grade. I used to help him carry his instrument to practice."

"You're full of jokes aren't you," she said, "do you ever get serious about anything?" I stopped in my path and looked at her. "I have to tell you something. I lied to you about Columbia, I didn't get in. The letter came just a week ago. I'm still reeling a little." It hadn't been my intention to tell Sarah the truth about my rejection so quickly but there was something so genuine about her nature, a quality so free of pretense and falseness I couldn't allow that lie to remain occupying any space between us. I didn't want the lie to contaminate our relationship.

"I'm sorry. You must be very disappointed. What will you do now?"

"I'll probably register at The Heights. I really don't want to go there because my brother Steve went there and it seems I've been in his trail for as long as I can remember. Columbia would have been all my own." Suddenly I was telling Sarah personal things one usually holds back at the start of a new relationship. A stranger in a bar is more likely to have intimate revelations bared to him by another than is a new friend on a sandy path to a country lake.

"I'm an only child so I haven't experienced feelings like that myself but I think it would be worth it just to have a sister or a brother."

"My brothers are so much older that sometimes I feel like I am an only child except the snow is always full of their tracks." Sarah looked confused. "That means there's no place I can go where they haven't already been first. That's one reason why

Columbia was so important. Then there's the education of course." We both laughed. "So, an only child. I bet you had lots of imaginary friends for company."

"Aren't you smart!" she said, giving me a gentle shove, as if to say 'get out of here, how did you know?' "In fact I only had one imaginary friend. Her name was Alice because my mother used to read to me from Lewis Carroll all the time. Alice was my most trusted friend," she said dreamily. At the lake's edge I searched the sand for flat stones that might skip across the water. I side-armed the first one I found and it hit the lake's shimmering surface and immediately sank to the bottom.

"Let me try," Sarah said, lifting a stone from the ground. She zipped it like a bullet and it skipped four times before sinking. "Not bad, eh? Sandy Koufax is my cousin. He's taught me a few things about throwing." In 1956 Koufax was five years away from beginning the brilliant career he is celebrated for, but a Jew in professional baseball was still something approaching the miraculous. There was Hank Greenberg and then there was Sandy Koufax.

"You're kidding me!"

"I certainly am not kidding you. Do you think Sandy came into this world without a family?"

"Well, I'd really like to meet the rest of your family someday."

I don't remember much more of what else happened that night. Today, everywhere you go you will see people with camcorders busily recording everything in their field of vision but nothing in their field of dreams. Those recordings are pictures, they are not memories. To make a memory you must mix experience with some of your older memories and expectations, then knead in some of your feelings and longings, add a generous portion of fantasy and desire, and then allow the mixture to simmer gently in the deeper and invisible recesses of your mind, turning it over, recalling it and retelling it to yourself from time to time as a way of tasting it and then, after a while, you have a memory, hearty as a good cassoulet and just as nourishing—if it is a happy one. Even after all these years I sometimes feast on memories of that sweet Sarah.

4.

The wolf, the natural enemy and killer of deer, had already been replaced by the automobile in the woodlands of the northeastern United States by the summer of 1956. The carcass of a dead deer lying alongside the narrow state roads of Sullivan County though not an uncommon sight always made my stomach knot and my heart sink. There lay innocence slaughtered.

"Look! There's Bambi's mother. Sonofabitch hunters!" Ron was in a raucous if heartless mood. "Gather ye rosebuds, Melvin, that could just as easily have been you," he said as we drove towards Liberty for the meeting he had set up with a newspaper reporter.

"And how can you compare me to a deer? I may be nimble but I'm not stupid."

"Smitten, not stupid. You're dead in your tracks in Harlan's headlights, my boy. You trust someone who would just as soon run you down as brake for you when he has no more use for you."

"In your twisted opinion no one should trust anyone else."

"You're looking at trust there on the side of the highway. That poor dumb animal trusted some buck or some other deer to lead her across this road, and there she is, BANG!! you're dead." He shouted so suddenly and startlingly I jumped in my seat.

"Jesus, Ron, get a hold of yourself."

"*You* are the one who needs to get a hold of himself. What that deer is telling you is that life is short, that you can be snuffed out in a second. BANG!! There is no yesterday, there is no tomorrow, there is only now, there is only a Martha at this hotel for me, there is only what you can see, smell and touch. You are lucky to have Sarah today but don't count on tomorrow."

"Do you know something I don't know?"

"Are you kidding? I know a ton that you don't know, but nothing about Sarah, don't worry. No, what I mean is, well look at Judge Crater, for example. He came up here to play poker, drink some Canadian whiskey and maybe get laid. Probably in his mind he was like a king, a big man with power and money, the two most potent aphrodisiacs there are. I doubt that he even carried a gun or hired a bodyguard and then, BANG!! into the well."

"What if he's not in the well; what if there is a body down there but it's somebody else's?"

"Don't be ridiculous. The judge died from what that poor, dumb deer died from: yearning. The deer was yearning for water or for some particular blade of grass, allowed herself to be distracted by her yearning, lost control of the moment, the now, and BANG!! she was gone."

"Will you please stop that *bang* nonsense you're making me deaf."

"But that's the truth, that's what makes it so hard for you to listen to it. Crater came with his own set of yearnings, lost control of the moment, and then lost his life."

"If that's what you want to believe go right ahead."

"It's not just what I want to believe it's the truth. Lenny has no reason to make up something as crazy as this, so it has to be the truth."

"I like the way you think, Ron, crazy ideas are so crazy they must be true. You'll really go far with that kind of analytic approach. Maybe you should skip law school and consider another field where that might be more accepted, one like psychiatry or journalism." I was still dubious about Lenny's tale.

"Melvin, don't piss me off. I let you in on this because I had to tell somebody and you were the one I chose because I thought you could keep it just between the two of us and also be more serious. When we talk to the reporter in Liberty if you're gonna make wisecracks I'd just as soon you wait in the car. As it is it'll be hard enough to convince him this is not some trick or crazy joke." He accelerated into the next curve in the road.

Every television station Ron had called in New York City had thought he was just another crank. Only once was he actually put through to a newsman and that wasn't John Cameron Swayze or Mike Wallace either, and the guy he spoke with thought he was talking to a lunatic. "In a well? In the Catskills? He never went there in his life, lame brain!" And then the phone crashed down on its cradle. Furious but undefeated, Ron set his sights on more modest goals. That was why he was determined to talk to this reporter even if he was only working for a local tabloid.

"Sorry. What do you think this reporter can do anyway? Maybe he'll talk to Lenny and get the same story from him that you got or maybe Lenny won't want to talk to him at all. I don't see what a reporter on The Liberty Sentinel is going to accomplish for you."

"Sometimes I forget what a kid you are. You have to get into the real world and play there, not just in your mind. This is the difference between playing poker with your friends on somebody's kitchen table and playing poker at Las Vegas."

"The Liberty Sentinel is the Las Vegas of newspapers?" I said with undiluted sarcasm. Shaking his head, steaming but low key, Ron said, "One more of those and you'll be keeping company with Bambi's mommy back down the highway."

"I'm here aren't I? I just don't want you to get your hopes up too high, that's all." Day by day I was less intimidated by Ron's belligerence. I had finally come to understand that while he had a pretty ferocious bite he was much more likely to bark at me and chew me out than he was to chew me up.

"Well, let me do the talking. You're there just to verify what I tell the reporter." This was his way of conciliating.

When we got to the newspaper's office, a small wood frame building with a liquor store at street level and The Liberty Sentinel on the floor above, Ron looked discouraged.

"I never noticed the paper was in this building before. Not very much of a newspaper is it. Where's the printing plant?"

"Hey, what's the difference, let's just get to the reporter and see what he has to say. If he prints the story we can mail it to the New York papers and the TV stations and take it from there." "Boy, suddenly you're Sol Hurok, Mr. Producer. I'll take care of what happens next, okay?" He stared at me for a minute. "I can't figure you out. One minute you're making fun of me and the next you're an eager beaver." He shook his head. "Let's just go in."

We climbed the worn, uncarpeted wooden stairs to the office of the newspaper and entered through a door with the logo of the paper stenciled on its frosted glass window. There were a couple of desks, a wall of files, and only one person in the room, a man in shirt sleeves about fifty years old who was standing at the window that looked out over the street.

"There's more people here in the month of August than in all the other months of the year combined. Even July doesn't seem to be nearly as busy a time the way August does. Must be the vacation month of choice for your city businesses." He had remained standing with his back to us while delivering his observations, but even at a distance the harsh, frowsy smell of his body odor reached us. I looked at Ron who shrugged and approached the man.

"Excuse me, are you Bill Freeman?"

"That's me."

"I'm Ronald Alter, Mr. Freeman, I spoke to you a couple of days ago about a story you might be interes . . ."

"The judge Crater guy, yeah, I remember your call. God, the judge must be gone twenty, thirty years now."

"Twenty-six years this month," Ron said quickly, proudly, like a contestant on a quiz show.

"Yeah, that sounds about right. So what's the story you want to tell me about him," he said, turning and facing us.

"We think we know where his body is. We think we can prove that he's buried on the grounds of a hotel nearby. Interested?" A horn blew on the street followed by the screech of brakes and the sound of metal crunching. The reporter turned back to the window and leaned forward.

"Now that sounds interesting," he said, craning his neck to see the street below. "Nah, just a couple of vacationers crunching fenders. They get so busy looking at the shops instead of the street you'd think they were on Fifth Avenue." He left the window and pointed at me.

"You his friend?"

"Yes."

"Do you believe the story he's telling me about the judge? No, that's not fair, why do you believe his story about the judge?"

"Well . . ." Surprised by his question I groped for an answer; "I think it could be true. He did disappear so some kind of foul play is possible and . . ." He interrupted my explanation with an easy, conversational tone, nothing angry or impatient.

"Who says foul play? Who says he didn't just run off with one of his girlfriends?" He raised both his hands and rubbed them through his hair, a ferocious storm of body odor raged out from his underarms as he rubbed his fingers through his oily hair. "I mean why do we always suppose that there was some kind of nasty mess rather than somebody just wanting to give it all up and get away? You boys are too young now but some day you'll understand that a man can just come to a place in his life where all he wants to do is put on his hat and coat and walk away. I think the judge came to that point." He turned to Ron and stared at him long enough to make Ron fidget. "You work at Braverman 's don't you? Lenny told you his story about judge Crater and the night he got shot gambling at the poker table, didn't he." While Ron's face turned red his lips pressed into each other bleaching the color from them. "Yeah, I see that he did. And you thought you were the first person he'd told this story to." He shook his head sorrowfully. "Poor Lenny, it's the only thing he's got to give to anybody who's nice to him and that only happens once or so every three, four years. I asked Mr. Braverman if there was an old well on the grounds and he laughed at me. 'Why build a new well sitting on this water table when it's all I can do to keep the basement of my house dry in a draught?' I think he made good sense."

"But there is an old well," Ron said eagerly, "I've found the place where it was. Maybe Ben Braverman doesn't want any prying by a reporter. That could bring in the police."

"Maybe, and maybe not. But this is a small town. When things happen it's hard to keep them a secret. Even the judge's making a trip up here to gamble would have been something to gossip about when the winter closes in on you. Heck, by November if a man slaps his wife in Monticello people up in Swan Lake'll say they heard it happen, see what I mean? But gunshots? Murder? Not likely to have occurred." He went to his desk and picked up a copy of the newspaper. "Look at this," he said, pointing to a story on the bottom of the front page, "Ben

Brotkowski Injured in Fight. Does that name mean anything to you? Of course not, don't even try to answer, but my point is that in Liberty, New York that's news. Don't you think Judge Crater would have made the news just for showing up here? Forget about this Crater story boys, it's just not true." He laid the newspaper down and returned to the window. "Please close the door after you leave."

We left the building without speaking and as soon as we were in his car, after lighting up our cigarettes, Ron started to challenge Bill Freeman's stand. "Too neat, too glib, too 'go away and leave well enough alone.' I don't think he's telling the whole truth. Besides, did you smell that guy? He smells like someone who's a complete stranger to wells and water."

"Yeah, I was looking for a gas mask in there but what about what he said about Lenny telling this story to other people before, doesn't that bother you?"

"A little, but I'd have to talk to Lenny first. Look, even if he did tell somebody else nobody's done anything about it. As far as I'm concerned until proved otherwise, Crater is still at the bottom of that well." He flicked his cigarette out into the street and lit up another. "This really pisses me off. This is such an exciting story, such a find, why isn't anybody else interested in getting to the bottom of this?"

I couldn't resist. "You mean the bottom of the well?"

"You really are such a fucking kid. I'm sorry I ever told you."

5.

After the meeting with the malodorous reporter we returned to the hotel. There was still time for a little bit of basketball and that would help to break the tension that had been built up in Liberty, We changed and went to the basketball court to watch the guys who had come to play in the Friday night hotel league games. They were high quality players, like the All-American Ivan Goldman, and were so much better than we school yard pick-up players they wouldn't let us into their practice games. But, usually, at some point towards the end of their session, they'd let us get in line and dribble in for lay-ups while they took a break. A row of bleachers lined one side of the court and behind them was a softball field. In the mornings Bernie Abramowitz used this field for "Simon Says" calisthenics with the older guests, but in the afternoon, if we didn't use it the field stood bare because the male guests complained that it was too hot to play softball there. I was sitting in the bleachers waiting for the lay-up line to begin when I heard a woman's laughter in the field behind me. Turning to see what she was laughing at I saw Harlan doing some kind of a dance, his arms raised towards the sky closing in an arc above his head. The laughing woman was sitting on the infield grass, her legs curled underneath her, and because her back was to me I couldn't see her face but I knew she wasn't Heidi; something in the shape of her back, a fullness, told me she was older than Heidi. Harlan did a few turns and rocked from side to side in a sailor's jig kicking up dust from the parched base path. The woman roared and clapped her hands. Harlan couldn't see me through the tiers of benches and I thought of climbing to the top and hailing him but then felt uncomfortable and shrank back, as though I had caught him in the midst of some unseemly act. I watched as he sat down next to her and she leaned against him, nestling her face against his neck. He put his arm around her shoulders and held her close against himself. I felt suddenly sad, a little sick to my stomach, and, I'm ashamed to admit, hurt. The image of Harlan I had created in my imagination was that of an honest, loyal and sincere person, an Eagle Scout governed by conscience. In my infatuation I had, like all the infatuated, filled in many blank spaces with my own set of expectations, hopes and desires that allowed for the conjuring of an ideal person. He was, in my mind, all that I ever hoped to be.

"Hey, you playing or what?" Ron called out from the court. I turned away from the couple nestled together on the infield grass of the ball field, a picture of them still vivid in my mind.

"Yeah, yeah, yeah, I'm coming." I got in line and moved along until it was my turn. I was still so upset by the image of Harlan and the woman that I lost control of the ball and ended up kicking it out of bounds.

"What was that?" Ron offered with his usual tone of annoyance.

"I got distracted." I said, trotting back to the end of the line. One of the team's better players, Spider Johnson, came by and slapped me on the ass in a gesture of encouragement. No words were exchanged.

When my turn came again I dribbled to the right side of the basket but then spun around, ran backwards to the left side, feinted to my right and then tossed a hook shot over my head missing the backboard and the rim by about two feet, the ball describing a beautiful arc in empty space. Several of the good players made some catcalls at me and as I slunk away in a travesty of humiliation, my face buried in my hands like Adam in Massaccio s "Expulsion from Eden." Harlan called out from the bleachers, "Good try Jack." You could feel the tension suddenly rise on the court. None of the ballplayers liked Harlan, not one. It was as though every one of them perceived a quality of dissimilarity in him. I had known a lot of good ballplayers growing up. They had no problem playing with a frivolous and punky guy who kept a lit cigarette in his mouth on the court, or wore old, worn down loafers with crushed down backs that no longer gripped his heels so that he scuffed along the court dribbling carelessly mocking only himself.

Those guys were just as they were and didn't pretend or aspire to be other than that. Harlan, however, Harlan emanated an aura of intentionality, a sense of purpose that others seemed to construe as scheming. I resented that harsh assumption.

"Well, well, well. We are all honored to be visited by Mr. Harlan Hawthorne on this fine afternoon." Spider Johnson's Mississippi drawl made his sarcasm feel more cutting. "To what do we owe this pleasure, sir?" Ron positioned himself next to Ivan Goldman and smirked at Harlan. The other players sensing a confrontation of sorts stopped shooting and held on to their basketballs while they watched and waited.

"Why Mr. Johnson it is so very kind of you to ask. I happened into the neighborhood and thought I might visit with our Mr. White." Harlan's voice was soft but very clear, hinting in its cadences that it might tend to inflect towards a southern prosody. To me this was a dangerous choice. Still smarting from their defeat in the Civil War southerners were proud and prone to take insult, especially from Yankees, and then likely to demand what they called "satisfaction". While I had never seen a knock-down drag-out fight between waiters there had been the occasional shouting match about the usual things—girls or money. This dispute seemed more serious and I stepped forward to stand up for Harlan.

"Harlan is a good friend, Spider, I invited him to come down and take some practice with us."

"That's a goddamn lie!" Ron shouted. Without even looking at him Spider extended his long, left arm, the palm of his hand facing back to keep Ron in check, and slowly approached me.

"Well now, Jack, did you know our ladies' man was sitting out there in the ball field while we were playing, sitting out there in the ball field with one of his many lady friends? Did you know that? Do you think he was going to bring her out on the court with him or did she go back to her room to tape up her ankles before she tried a fast break. Or did she make a fast break when she saw all of us just on the other side of the bleachers? What do you think, Jack, what's your opinion on this matter?"

"Or maybe she was going to get knee pads for the other kind of games she plays with Harlan," Ivan interjected, causing some of the other players to laugh the locker room laugh.

"Uncalled for, Goldman," Spider said in reproach.

"Spider, where you get this idea of a ladies' man from is a total mystery to me. Ask Jack, he'll tell you that I'm involved with Heidi and why would I want anyone else if I have her?" Exactly the question I wanted to ask but this wasn't the time or place to inquire and before I could support his claim Spider continued.

"Well, Mr. Hawthorne, there happen to have been a few unhappy ladies I've heard about and strange as it might seem to you, each of them was unhappy about something having to do with you."

"I'm awfully sorry to hear that. You know, maybe part of their problem is that I'm just not available, have you considered that possibility?"

"Not available? Who was that I just saw on the softball field? Tell me it wasn't you, say it isn't so Harlan." Certain he had trapped Harlan in a lie Spider sounded smug.

"It was me on the field. In broad daylight in the middle of the day on the softball field talking with Heidi's sister-in-law Doris about a party for Heidi's birthday next week." There was a righteous tone in his voice now, and nothing of the south. Spider stared back at Harlan and clenched his teeth but said nothing. Harlan walked right up to Spider and standing face to face said, in a friendly and forgiving voice, "If that expression on your face is an apology I accept." and then turned and walked slowly away. Everyone was silent as he left until one of the players bounced a basketball and I almost jumped out of my shoes with surprise. Ron and Ivan muttered to each other and the All Stars, as the hotel team was known, passed balls back and forth among themselves but Spider stood alone, his teeth still clenched.

"It's true about Harlan and Heidi," I said approaching him. "They are together every night as far as I know and that was Doris Braverman on the softball field." I had no idea who that was in the grass but hoped to God it was Doris. Maybe Harlan was telling the truth after all. Maybe the woman on the tennis court was seductive but maybe Harlan wasn't seduced. But the woman at the lake cottage . . . I didn't know what to believe. Spider looked down at me from his six inch advantage and just shook his head slowly from side to side.

Chapter Seven

What confronted me then was the issue of credibility, not just Lenny's but Harlan's as well, but let's start with Lenny; to believe Lenny was to buy the Brooklyn Bridge from a sharpie in Grand Central Station but to dismiss his story out of hand was to risk being as doctrinaire as the members of the French scientific establishment who mocked the work of the great Louis Pasteur. What if he was right? What if his story was true? What if everyone dismissed it because it came from weird Lenny? It could be one of the great stories of the decade for sure, perhaps of the century. A conundrum? Maybe, but it was worth looking into. Harlan was a different matter entirely, one befogged by my adoring allegiance and need to sustain his unblemished image despite ample evidence to the contrary. During the month of July I had experienced many blows to my pride and disappointments of my expectations. Harlan's secretive womanizing was the most recent disappointment and no matter how I tried to rationalize and find innocent excuses for his behavior it was clearer all the time that was who he was. I had said nothing to him about that little hootchie-kootchie display on the tennis court or the woman I'd seen him visit across the lake but after the episode on the basketball court I decided to view him as if through different eyes. He no longer seemed to be like the abashed movie star in a throng of admiring fans, but an ardent womanizer who made good use of his sexual capital. Yet, despite that and Ron's mistrust of him, I decided I would take the Judge Crater problem to him. I knew Ron would object but I

163

thought Harlan might provide some reasonable sense of perspective on the whole matter of Judge Crater. After all, he was a Harvard man.

It was a very hot day and it was likely he'd be at the swimming pool taking the sun and reading. When I got there I saw several girls, and some women as well, who had settled near him laughing and talking loud, glancing over at him frequently trying to catch his eye, but he never once looked up from his novel. Was he teasing them? He had paid attention to so many different women in so many places, girls and women of all ages, it was hard to understand him.

"Hi, Harlan, can I talk to you for a minute?"

"Jack!" he called out my name in loud surprise as though I had just reappeared after being given up for lost in the Antarctic. "Of course, of course, should we go somewhere else?" he asked, beseeching me with his eyes to say yes.

"Well this is pretty private," I said, looking back at the suntanned beauty sprawled on the nearest chaise. She quickly averted her gaze and frowned.

"'Nuff said," and he closed his book and rose from his chair. Taking me by the elbow he led me to the concession stand facing the shallow end of the pool where young mothers cavorted with their children. For a few seconds I feared that his presence there would so distract some of them there soon might be dead babies bobbing in the water like apples in a tub at a Halloween party.

"I don't know what it is with those women. They see me with Heidi every night and still, well, what did you want to talk to me about?" This wasn't the time to confront his flirtatiousness or to inquire about the woman across the lake or his tennis partner or all the other episodes that accounted for my recent mistrust.

"Do you remember judge Crater?" Harlan turned to look at me the color draining from his face. He became unsteady on his feet and he grasped the ledge of the countertop.

"Are you OK Harlan?" I asked in alarm.

"It must be the heat. Jerry can you give me a glass of water please?" he said to the man tending the stand. "I was in the sun and I must have gotten dehydrated. That was stupid of me. Put some lemon in it if you could Jerry. Yes, of course I can remember judge Crater, judge Joseph Force Crater, who doesn't remember him? Why? Why is he on your mind now?" Harlan seemed very fidgety. He lit a cigarette, took a big mouthful of his water and then soaked the tip of his Lucky Strike by putting it back in his mouth before he had even swallowed. Then he had a coughing fit.

"You know Lenny, the handyman, the one with the misshapen face?" Harlan nodded. "Well he says that Crater is buried in an old well on the property and he took me and Ron to show us where it is."

"And you and Ron believe Lenny?" He took a drag on his Lucky and cocked his head when he looked at me, but it wasn't with his usual ironic amusement.

"Well that's why I've brought it to you. I don't know what to believe. It's possible. You said yourself that Heidi told you this place was once a roadhouse during prohibition and that's exactly what Lenny says. But he says that Heidi's father ran the place then too, not just in the last twenty years." Again Harlan seemed skeptical.

"That's ridiculous. Ben Braverman was a general contractor, in the building business," he explained, recognizing my ignorance of the term. "Ben is accused of all kinds of criminal acts. He's supposed to have once killed a dishwasher by kicking him to death in the parking lot, and now it's about how he ran this place as a roadhouse in the twenties. The next thing that you'll hear about is his being responsible for the assassination of Abraham Lincoln, for God's sake." Harlan was surprisingly strident in his defense and the mothers in the kiddy pool began to stare daggers at me. If Harlan was upset it had to be my fault because Harlan was always even tempered and composed. That's the thing about attractive people; not only are they perceived as implicitly better and more desirable than others, they also may be seen as more virtuous. It takes a very long time to relinquish assumptions like that.

"Why are you getting so upset about Ben Braverman's reputation? I was only asking what you thought about the idea that Judge Crater might be buried in an old well on the grounds."

"Well . . . I think . . . I don't know, I . . . you're right. It's just that I'm very protective of Heidi and anytime her father's name and reputation come up it's a very big deal to her." He calmed and the mothers in the wading pool went back to attending to their children. "I apologize Meh,—JACK! So, is judge Crater buried here, is that the question? I don't think so. There have been so many reports about the judge since he disappeared, what, twenty-five years ago? He's been seen in the mountains in California, in Mexico, North Africa, Paris, Canada, and all over Europe. I think he'd find a better place to go than Braverman's if he was looking to gamble or to escape from his wife."

"Who said he was trying to escape from his wife?"

"Well, that was one of stories about him, that he had a lot of showgirl girlfriends and was a big time playboy. But then the other story was that he was an upstanding lawyer and a real scholar which was why he was appointed to the State Supreme Court. Of course," and here Harlan smiled a smile that I remember vividly even today, a smile that I did not interpret correctly at the time, a smile I perceived as simply his pleasure in the ambiguities in the ways of the world, "it may be that both of those stories were true. Who says smart can't be sexy too?"

"How come you know so much about him?"

"I once did a paper at Harvard about him and Anastasia Romanov, the Russian Princess who people said had escaped execution by the Bolsheviks. Each of them disappeared but was never given up for dead so I called them 'The Revered Disappeared.' The Princess was not nearly as fascinating as the judge. She was just a teenager when she disappeared she'd barely begun to live. But the judge was already forty-one when he vanished and there were all kinds of stories about him. Anyway, I don't think he's in the well, but I'd be interested in seeing where it is."

He coaxed the ash off the edge of his cigarette, placed a fresh Lucky between his lips and used the ember of the one he had been smoking to light it. I had not seen him chain smoke before.

"I'd be glad to show you but I don't want Ron to see us. He'd be really pissed off because he believes Lenny and he's planning to get a news reporter up here from a New York City television station to get the well dug up. He says we could be famous for turning up the judge."

"You could also split the reward for finding him, five thousand dollars. Buy yourself a nice little car, an MG or an Austin Healy. But it won't happen because I don't think he's there."

"Why are you so sure he's not in that well? Nobody knows where he is."

"You're wrong, Jack, somebody knows where he is, somebody or somebodys. The judge didn't just disappear. Either he was kidnapped or he just decided to vanish, but there is someone who knows what happened." He crushed his Lucky Strike on the heel of his shoe and then GI'd his cigarette, stripping the paper down the seam and shaking the remaining tobacco shreds out on the ground to be blown away by the wind. "I also find it hard to believe that someone would go to all the trouble and expense of closing down a well and digging a new one to get rid of a body. There are miles of woods here where nobody ever goes and a lake right across the road where you could dump a body in a barrel of cement and lose it forever." He wrapped his book in his towel and stuffed it under his arm like a football. "That Lenny. What a pathetic creature he is, misshapen face, mentally defective, heavyset and clumsy, Heidi's father is very generous to keep him on here. Do you know why he does that?" I shook my head. "Because he was the only son of the family who used to own this property. It's the only world Lenny has ever known. He'd be completely lost if he was put off the grounds. Ben is not the monster everyone wants you to think he is. As far as Lenny is concerned he is at home, doesn't matter who the owner is, this is his home." We started back towards our room but after walking a few steps Harlan stopped and turned to me again. "Let's go talk to Lenny together. I'd like to hear what his story is from him."

We walked around to the back of the waiters' lodgings and then into the area where Lenny showed Ron and me the site of the old well. Harlan was quiet and I watched him as he studied the trees and inspected the grass. It seemed that there was nothing that he didn't find interesting and nothing about which he didn't know something.

"It's right over here. It's a circle of stones and Ron found some mortar when we were scratching around in the dirt." Harlan knelt over and brushed aside the tangle of weeds we had covered the ground with.

"I thought it might have been the foundation for a silo that you were shown not a well but this diameter is too small for that." He stroked his chin and looked around. "I bet there was another building near here once." He looked over to the house where the social staff and housekeepers lived and then back at the waiters' quarters. "I think it would be in this area," he said, pointing in the direction of the shack where Lenny and the other handymen and dishwashers were billeted.

"Why, what makes you think that?"

"This well is too far from the main house. You don't need to look so far for water here with a lake and a stream right on the property and reservoirs just up the road from here. The water table must be pretty high all over so a well this far from the main house would be unusual. I don't know where it was but there was a different building here. Let's get Lenny."

We were several yards away from the shack where Lenny lived when the smell of cheap wine blew into our faces and Harlan grimaced with recognition. "That's just the saddest smell, the smell of dreamless sleep and wasted lives. It's not just cheap booze, it's worse, much worse than that. It's the smell of hopelessness. The smell of down and out and nothing left to do but wait for death." Two dishwashers began to argue, their quarrel slurred and muffled by their muscatel delirium, and Harlan shook his head wearily. "Lenny; Lenny?" he called out.

"Who's that?" Lenny's voice came back suffused with the pleasure of being wanted by someone.

"It's Harlan." There was a loud crash, a shout and a string of unintelligible expletives but Lenny came outside while the fight inside grew louder.

"Hold it down in there!" Lenny called back over his shoulder. "Hi Harlan, Melvin, what can I do you for?" He laughed, part nervous laugh part happy laugh and kept his eyes fixed on Harlan. "Can you keep a secret Lenny?" Lenny nodded so vigorously I thought he'd break his neck. "Jack here told me about the well you showed him and Ron and . . ."

"Jack? I thought his name was Melvin." A look of wariness came across his face, the look of someone familiar with being baited and tricked and made mock of.

"It's both, to some he's Mel, to others he's Jack, it's a long story, don't worry about it. What I want to know, Lenny, is if there was another building around here once, a building that used that well you showed to Jack." Lenny stared at me suspiciously unable to shed his perplexity about my names.

"I never heard of somebody with two names before, Harlan." He glared at me and said, "Are you making fun of me?"

"No Lenny, no I'm not, really I'm not, ask Sammy, he'll tell you I sometimes use Jack for my name." Invoking Sammy's name seemed to reassure Lenny that he wasn't the butt of a mean joke and he relaxed.

"There was another building here once but it burned down," he said turning to Harlan. At that moment there was another crash inside the cabin behind Lenny and one of the dishwashers came stumbling down the steps holding a hand over his left eye. When he saw the three of us standing there he spat and raised his fists in a boxing stance, but when none of us reacted he turned and went back into the cabin. A month before I would have been frightened by his belligerent display but by that August I was not so easily threatened and it gave me pleasure to just stare back coldly at a man who had once seemed so menacing.

"Burned down, eh. Where exactly was it?"

"Come on Harlan I'll show you," and Lenny looked at Harlan as though his approval was the most important thing in the world to him at that moment. We followed Lenny to the infield size plot that stretched out to the side of his shack where he said, "it was right in here someplace. It was just a plain wooden building that burned to the ground. It didn't have no foundation or nothing so there was nothing left after it burned. It was just a wooden building."

"Was that where you lived when the building burned?" Harlan asked, gesturing at Lenny's shack.

"Oh yeah. That's the oldest building on the grounds," he said proudly. "I grew up in that house."

"So, that building that burned down, what was it used for? Was it a barn or a shed or something?" Looking at me Lenny grinned.

"No! That was a little gambling house." And then, smiling broadly at me, he said, "It was surrounded by cicadas." His diabolical laughter did not follow the reference this time.

"A gambling house," Harlan said in an excited voice. "What kind of gambling, roulette? Craps? Cards?"

"Poker. They only played poker in there," Lenny said, nodding his head to affirm his information, "and then it burned down. I tol . . ."

"Was that because of the judge?" Harlan asked, interrupting him brusquely. Lenny smiled and nodded again.

"Thanks Lenny I really appreciate your taking the time," and then Harlan turned and strode away briskly without a word to me. I turned to Lenny and said, "Don't say anything to Ron about this meeting, Lenny, okay?"

"Ron who?" Lenny said before bursting into hysterical laughter at his own joke. Then, after turning an imaginary key in an imaginary lock in his lips he said, "Don't worry Mel, I'll never tell. Hey! I made another poem."

Ron was in his bed reading when I returned to the room.

"You're a busy little beaver, where've you been? You don't look like you've been in the sun, though." He hadn't even looked up at me or lowered his book.

"Around."

"Around? What am I your mother? Answer my question for Christ's sake, what's all the mystery?"

"Well, if you really want to know I was talking to Lenny about the body in the well."

"I didn't give you permission to do that, what the hell do you think you're doing?"

"Hey, didn't you include me in this Crater business? What are you saying, that now it only belongs to you?"

"Look, this is my deal. I've let you in on it but I don't want you talking about it or telling anyone else about the judge. You start going to talk to Lenny and he'll tell everybody what a great friend you are. Then you'll have to account for why you are making friends with someone like Lenny and before you know it will all come out about the judge and that will be the end of our chance to make some money from this news."

"Don't get carried away, Ron. I won't do it again, I just needed to hear this again for myself because it still sounds so crazy, that's all." If he thought I'd told Harlan about his secret he'd have killed me so I prayed that Lenny wouldn't forget our deal. Spending time talking with Lenny could make you feel like you'd fallen down a rabbit hole and landed in Wonderland.

2.

When Heidi Braverman introduced me to Sarah I had assumed that she had done so at Harlan's instigation and because I was so smitten with Sarah I showered Harlan with undeserved gratitude. Harlan, for his part, never rejected or disowned responsibility for our pairing and smiled modestly when I gushed with thanks. "Really, Jack, stop it," he would protest, averting his eyes and lowering his head. But I was so grateful for Sarah it mattered less how she had come into my life than that she had come at all. There had been girls before her, girls with reputations, girls I had lusted after, girlfriends and girls like Ellen that I just enjoyed as friends but Sarah, Sarah connected me to emotional landscapes within myself I had never known existed; heights of

elation and of such expansiveness that I felt suffused with a royal
sense of grandeur. Walking through the kitchen, a bus box piled
high with the debris of the noon meal on my shoulder, I smiled
beneficently at the haggard dishwashers. They no longer frightened me; for it was as though I alone had known love and could
feel only pity for everyone else in the world who had never been
so charmed. And just as her affection could raise me to such
dizzying heights her withdrawal from my ardent cravings would
drop me to unplumbable depths of desolation and wretched-
ness. She was, in short, my first love. With Sarah the feeling that
life was elsewhere, something distant and out of reach, something to aspire to vanished. I was alive.

　　We met regularly in the evening when our work was done.
Some times Sarah would come to the dining room after the dinner meal had been served, the guests and waiters had left, and
we busboys were cleaning up our stations. She'd sit at one of my
tables while I dusted the seats of the chairs, swept the floor, and
then dried my silverware. When it was time to stack the chairs on
the tabletops so the floors could be washed and buffed, Sarah
would spend time chatting with some of the other busboys. I felt
proud of her and happy that we were seen as a loving pair. No
one made fun of me or teased her in the crass and salacious way
that we all were capable of. It was an acknowledged fact that
Sarah and I were very much in love and that our love was of the
kind that cynics and romantics alike might envy—what, after all,
is a cynic but a romantic who has experienced a painful disappointment. I felt her love's presence like a panoply of protection
from all that was harsh in the world and, like all first loves, I
would never know another like it.

　　"Ready?" I asked as she said goodnight to Stanley Nuss-
baum, Ron's busboy.

　　"Ready!" she said, standing on tiptoes and kissing my
cheek. Stan smiled and nodded at her and then at me and then
resumed sweeping the floor.

　　"What would you like to do tonight?" I said taking her hand.

　　"I definitely don't want to see the talent show at the
casino," she said, referring to the program designed to delude

guests into believing that one of them might be the next Eddie
Fisher or Sid Caesar.

"Then why don't you get your blanket and meet me down
at the dock in about half an hour. I have to shower and get
cleaned up." I pulled her close to me, pressed my body hard
against hers and then surprised her with a tender, gentle kiss.
She smiled up at me when I moved away, arched an eyebrow,
winked and pulled me close to her again.

"Just what do you have in mind, Mr. White, some mischief?"

"How could you think such a thing," I said, feigning injury. "I
have absolutely nothing but the most noble of intentions, miss."

"Oh, what a shame," she said, pushing me away and then
appropriating the injured posture for herself. Looking back over
our shoulders we smiled at each other as we parted.

Back in my room I hummed happily as I loaded fresh batteries into my portable radio and then laid out a change of
clothes. Harlan was off with Heidi and Ron, I assumed, was with
Martha but when I walked into the shower room Ron came up
behind me and grabbed hold of my arm.

"Can I talk to you for a minute?"

"Don't tell me, Lenny knows where Captain Kidd's treasure
is buried."

"I'm serious, come back to the room for a minute." He was
tense and very strained. I followed him back to our room and
when we were inside he shut the door, put his index finger across
his lips when I started to speak, and then turned his radio on.
"Sixteen Tons" by Tennessee Ernie Ford was playing and Ron
turned up the volume and motioned me to sit on his bed.

"Somebody robbed me today and I think it was Harlan," he
said. "I keep my cash hidden in a tobacco can. I empty out the
tobacco, put the rolled up cash in the bottom of the can and then
replace the tobacco."

"I've never seen you smoking a pipe," I protested.

"I don't smoke a pipe you shmuck! I keep one around to
chew on so that my can of Prince Albert looks like I might
smoke." He shook his head in frustration. "I like to keep a few
hundred dollars on hand all the time. Somebody had to search

through my things to find the money and that means it was either you or Harlan because nobody else comes into this room when we're not here." I was puzzled by Ron's decision to do such a risky thing. It was the practice for every waiter and busboy to open a savings account in a local bank and bring the weekend's tips for deposit on Monday, Tuesday the latest. No one kept large amounts of cash with him.

"Well it wasn't me who took your money."

"I know that. I'm not accusing you of robbing me. But that leaves your buddy Harlan and you know I've never trusted him."

"That leaves the entire population of Braverman's from old Ben Braverman to Lenny and all the guests in between! Why the hell do you have to blame . . ." I was becoming strident and Ron put his hand over my mouth to silence me.

"It wasn't Lenny, or Ben, or a guest, and I don't think it was anyone else from the dining room. It had to be Harlan."

"Just because that's what you want to think doesn't make it true. You've had it in for Harlan since the day he got here. It was practically the first thing you said to me when I came, 'I just don't trust him' you said, and you say it over and over." My voice again became too loud in my passionate defense of the one person I admired and wished to emulate and again Ron had to put his hand over my mouth to silence me.

"Look, I don't give a shit that you're so gaga about Harlan. Fine, be impressed by that phony's style if that's how you want to be, but be careful. He's a snake and he's dangerous and you'll end up being the one who gets hurt when you least expect it." There really was no way to know who took Ron's money. The doors to our rooms had very simple locks, the kind you don't see much anymore, the kind that had a keyhole that truly was a hole. The key to open the lock was a cumbersome piece of metal with an oval grip at one end of a two inch long shaft and a tab at the other end to trip the lock. Somebody once had suggested putting hasps on all the doors and using padlocks for security, but Sammy foresaw that some wise guy could lock half the waiters in their rooms before dinner and the plan was scuttled. These old locks were probably not too hard to pick if you really wanted to, but there was so much traffic in and out of the waiters' quarters it would have been very risky to try doing that. On the other hand we couldn't lock our doors every time we went to the bathroom, or washed out our shirts in the shower, or just went into someone else's room to talk. Anyone who was determined enough could rob you if that was what he wanted to do, and money was the one thing he could take that couldn't be identified as belonging to you. So the notion that Harlan had to be the thief held little credence for me.

"Look, I'm sorry that you were robbed but I can't believe that Harlan would do such a thing, that's all. I mean, I know him, he just isn't the type of a guy who would do that. Maybe you should give Belle your money to hold in the hotel safe."

"Sure, so when I come asking for it she can say 'what money?' God, you're still so trusting, Melvin. You'll learn."

I showered and dressed and was about to leave to meet Sarah at the waterfront when Abe Melman stopped me.

"I see that you're struggling with what Ronald told you, Melvin. It's the truth, someone here is robbing people of their money and jewelry. Harlan is one of the people that Ben Braverman suspects . . ."

"Not you too, for godsakes," I protested, but Abe held up his right hand like a traffic cop and placed his left index finger across his lips, silencing me with an emphatic "Ssshhhh!" He steered me into his room and closed the door. Motioning to the wooden chair beside his bed he took me by the arm and said, "Sit for a minute. I know you want to meet your girlfriend Sarah, a beautiful girl and such a name, but sit for a minute," he said, waving at the chair. I looked at my watch, sighed rudely, and sat down.

"I want to help you, Melvin. I know that you've been upset about so many things, the girls before Sarah, the college you wanted to go to, this Harlan character . . ."

"Help me? You're going to help me? Help yourself, Abe, please help yourself a little before you try helping me," I said, looking directly at his law degree.

"You think that because I don't practice law anymore there's something wrong with me? I'll do it again, don't worry.

This isn't the time. I have a different responsibility right now, that's all. Different but just as serious, maybe even more important. Definitely more important," he added emphatically.

"Waiting tables?" I asked, my incredulity obvious.

"Don't be foolish. And don't imagine that doing simple work makes me a simple man. Please, don't insult me." I felt a guilty chill ripple through me and hung my head. "I am your friend Melvin, believe me, I only want to help you."

"How are you going to help me Abe, explain that to me please." I held myself back from again telling him to try helping himself first.

"You think that Harlan is going to help you? You think he'll teach you how to be him? You don't want to be him, believe me."

"I never said that I wanted to be him Abe, that's your idea."

"You never had to say it, it was obvious. No offense intended, Melvin, I'm only saying what I can see with my own eyes. Harlan is someone that you admire very much, that's very plain to see, but there's something missing in him. I don't know exactly what it is but when I look at him he reminds me of those Greek statues you see in a museum, the ones that are missing an arm or a leg or a nose, you know what I mean? Beautiful but broken, some piece is always missing. I look at Harlan and I see all of his fingers and toes are still attached, but in spite of that I always feel that there is something important missing." Abe sighed and waved at the air as if shooing away a fly. "Meshuga, right? Crazy. But I can't help it, that's how I feel. So be careful Melvin, don't be so trusting so fast. Take your time, watch him do a little bit of this, and then watch him do a little bit of that, and maybe then you'll see the part that is missing." He stared at his law school diploma when he finished but his face was impassive and without expression. Perhaps he had imagined himself delivering a stellar closing argument, a reasoned and compelling prosecution, but all that I was left with were feelings of anger and shame as if I had somehow been violated by his intrusion into my world.

"I have to get going Abe, Sarah is waiting for me."

"Oiyoiyoiyoiyoi! You musn't keep Sarah waiting, Melvin, apologize to her for me, tell her it was all my fault, such a beautiful girl" He shook his head and opened the door to his room to let me out. "Remember, watch a little bit of this, a little bit of that . . ." I was out the door and out of the waiters' quarters before he could finish his mantra.

3.

After the night of the Rosie Moldar fiasco I had been reluctant to use the old shed for meetings with Sarah. Not only did the memory of that escapade continue to haunt the physical space, the knowledge that other couples might again wander in while we were inside had kept me away. The dock area, while open and exposed, was still fairly private. Guests did not choose to come to look at the lake at night and most of the rest of the staff either went down to the casino for drinks or left the hotel grounds in their cars. The problem with the waterfront was the cold and damp of the August nights. Even in late July there was the sock-soaking dew of night but by August there were nights you could see the fog of your own breath. Sarah and I had resorted to spreading out the stacked cushions employed to provide softer seats in the rowboats and creating a cushioned area the size of a wrestling mat where we wrestled nightly after our first impassioned kiss. But the August cold and damp soon was infesting the pillows with an unpleasant clamminess and not very long afterwards they began to reek of mildew. It was Sarah who finally suggested that we retreat to the shed.

I had just lit a Viceroy and stuffed the Zippo in my back pocket abrading my wrist on the buckle of the belt back there. "Have you figured out what this belt across the back of these pants is for?" I said, fingering its buckle.

"It's just a decoration," Sarah said, amused by my consternation.

"I think there should be a zipper there rather than a belt. If you're going to do something useless for decoration than it should he really useless. A belt makes you think that you should tighten it or loosen it or something." She slipped her arm through mine and laughed. We were standing on the dock at the lake searching the moonless night sky for shooting stars.

"Tell you what. If you stop smoking I'll sew a zipper on the back of your pants." Sarah had been unhappy about my smoking from the start more because of its effects upon my breath than my health. The first murmurings that cigarettes could be hazardous to your health had not had a dramatic impact on the society of smokers in nineteen fifty-six.

"Look!" I urged as several meteors burned their way through the earth's atmosphere, their light only a little brighter than that of the distant stars. "Isn't that beautiful?" But she gazed at them in silence. I crushed the cigarette under foot, turned to face her and took her in my arms. "So what happened between you and Dick Hersh, did you break up with him or did he break off with you?"

"It was a mutual decision. We were looking for different things in the relationship. Dick wanted to get serious and I didn't." I wondered if "serious" meant too sexual but didn't ask. Sarah put her arms around me and said, "You're a much nicer guy and if you think I have any regrets about Dick you're all wrong." I looked into her eyes and saw she was telling the truth. She stared up at me, smiled, and then her eyes shifted to the sky in search of shooting stars. "If you were to make a wish right now what would it be?" At that point in my life the answer would have been "Fuck the breath out of Marilyn Monroe, Bridget Bardot, and Gina Lollobrigida," having moved along from an earlier childhood trio of world peace, a million dollars, and a game of catch with Joe DiMaggio. The scent of soap and baby powder rose up from her body, Dial Soap and Johnson's Baby Powder, clean and innocent aromas admonishing me to tether my lust and think of something else to wish for, but they failed.

"Being alone with you in a more private place." Her gaze shifted back to my eyes where she seemed to search for my thoughts. Then she smiled.

"You mean it wouldn't be for world peace or a million dollars?" she teased, assuming the ubiquity of those two wishes among the earnest children of the middle class, wishes that we knew almost as well as the pledge of allegiance.

"Okay, world peace and peace and quiet with you. The million dollars can wait."

"And where is this 'peace and quiet' you're talking about?" From the direction of the storage shed behind us came a breathy sound of something in movement as though the building itself had just exhaled in exasperation. Abruptly we both turned towards the noise and our movements so startled the raccoon that was dragging a chair cushion he dropped it and quickly dashed into the nearby bushes.

"The storage shed?" she said. She took my hand and we walked off the dock to the building where Rosie and I had groped and struggled just weeks before. I inhaled Sarah's smell cleansing my mind of thoughts of that sorry night.

"What do we have here?" she said pushing open the unlocked door and I thought for sure some other hapless couple would be caught in flagrante by our intrusion, but the shed was unoccupied. "Broken chairs, torn umbrellas, moldy chaise lounges, raccoons, the usual," I said. Because it had not rained very much that summer there was only a faintly musty smell in the room. Dusty cobwebs decorated the windows and spanning the gaps between the aluminum arms of the broken chaises were bridges of gossamer.

"Nobody comes here usually," I said reassuringly.

"Nobody?" she asked with skepticism, "That's not what Heidi Braverman tells me."

"Well, usually nobody comes here. What else did Heidi tell you?" The memory of the flashlight's beam full in my face raced across my mind reviving feelings of shame and repulsion.

"Things. She and Harlan stumbled in on some hanky-panky here a while ago. She was embarrassed but also a little excited by what she saw. It wasn't quite like walking in on your parents when they're making love but it was that kind of shock." In the cool stillness of the shed I broke into a sweat. I waited for her to say that Heidi had seen me with Rosie; I waited for her reproach. "Anyway, is that what people come here for?" She seemed more curious than critical.

"Some." With a gentle hand I ran my fingers lightly down the length of her arm and her body shivered. She looked up at me and even in the darkness I could see her eyes search my face in earnest for the ineffable. Her lips parted and puckered forward inside her spare smile.

"Do they," she said, smiling more broadly and leaning forward towards me, raising her body on her toes.

"Oh yes," I said, wrapping her in my arms and kissing her. "Oh yes." And with that kiss, that forgiving kiss of hers, I felt a sudden restful peace envelope me. I held Sarah against me for a long time. Then, without speaking, we separated. I slapped the dust off the plastic covered cushion of a nearby chaise and dragged it onto the floor while she removed her cardigan sweater. We knelt on the cushion face to face and put our arms around each other. We had no need of words. Harlan was right; language is just the fine tuning of communication and our feelings were so in harmony at that moment that the pointy corners and sharp edges of words would have done violence to the delicate tissue of emotions that had begun to join us. Sarah pressed three fingers against my lips as if to insure the silence and I kissed them, then ran my tongue along their tips. With her other hand she stroked my face and then lifted my right hand to her mouth and enveloped my thumb with her lips. With my eyes closed the sensuousness of her mouth around my thumb felt all enclosing. It was as though all of my nerve endings were suddenly concentrated in that one place, as though all of me was safely protected behind her embracing lips. My left hand found her breast and came to rest there. She leaned into my touch rocking sideways and then all at once stiffened.

"Is that door locked? Is this safe?"

"I can secure that door with something, it just needs a rod in the door handles so they can't be pushed open." I found an old umbrella pole, slipped it into the semicircles of the two door handles, and rejoined Sarah on the cushion. But the mood had already been broken.

"This may be a little fast for me," she said, her eyes averted.

"I'm sorry," I said, feeling I had made a mistake and rushed ahead too quickly. I should have honored her cautioning odors.

"No. No, it's just that my feelings ran away with me. I want to do these things with you but . . . I don't know, maybe it's just that, well, if I knew we were really private and secure in here I wouldn't feel so nervous."

"Tell you what, I'll make sure there's always a rod to jam the door handles with so that no one can come in. They'll know soon enough this shed is off limits."

"And I'll have one of my kids make us a sign to post on the door, 'OCCUPADO' in bright red letters. Then I'll be teaching art and language both."

"Oy! She's teaching my little Rosalie Puerto Rican!" I whined in a mock lamentation. "But for tonight we'll have to settle for the old umbrella pole jammed through the handles to keep people out." We moved the chaise cushion under the dusty and unwashed window that admitted the night's ambient light but not the gaze of searching eyes and lay down together.

If Rosie had introduced me to the "afters" and, one might say, Diana had acquainted me with the "befores", Sarah was my collaborator in the explorations of sexual pleasure. She was no more experienced than I in the mechanics of sex though just as interested and together we groped our way towards gratification passionately if artlessly. Sometimes my passion was too ardent and Sarah would recoil and tell me that I was hurting her. Sometimes I merely readjusted what I was doing and sometimes I felt mortified and it was I who recoiled. But we made our way in that darkened shed, on that battered and moldy chaise cushion, made our way towards one another and towards a kind of tender sexuality that often eluded us in that summer of 1956. We were too eager and too frightened by the force of our own eager appetites, too often impatient for that erotic payoff that drives the species.

"Why don't you ever talk while we lie here touching?" she said.

"I'm concentrating. My hands are doing all the communicating."

"Oh yeah? What do you think I am, a Braille page?"

"Shhh, don't make me laugh." But we did. In the good times our awkwardness, my clumsiness, were happily risible. We approached tenderness often but only to find ourselves swept away from it abruptly by the engines of lust or the comedy of ineptitude.

That first time I undressed her I was breathless with excitement as though the pounding of my heart had beaten the air from my lungs. In the dim light seeping through the dusty window just above us I sat up and stared at her nakedness, and she, slyly smiling at me, trying to play the seductress, lay sprawled shamelessly upon the blanket covered cushion. And then, all at once, I could see the color flood her cheeks and she crossed her hands over her mount of Venus and turned her face to the side like a modest virgin in a classical painting.

"Stop staring," she said, "and take your clothes off." And I did, my elbow bruising her thigh as I struggled out of my sweater, my foot grazing her ear as I pulled off my pants. Cold mountain air filled the room and made us shiver as we stretched our bodies out and lay close together embracing.

"Maybe we should be under the blanket not on top of it," Sarah said, trying to pull some of it from under the edge of the chaise to cover her self.

"But then I can't see you," I said.

"If I don't get warm soon you'll be looking at a corpse. I'm freezing!"

We stood up and pulled the blanket out from under the edges of the seat cushion before lying down again and huddling under its warmth. I must say that seeing Sarah doing that little chore in a state of nakedness was absolutely thrilling. Many were the nights I lay awake in my boyhood bed imagining the nakedness of women. During my adolescence there was no act, however mundane or banal, that didn't seem intensely erotic when performed by a naked woman. Some women appreciate that power in their bodies and, like Cleopatra, can seize a kingdom with it. Sarah, however, was oblivious of the effect that simple act had had on me.

4.

About midway through August it occurred to me I had smoked about a dozen different brands of cigarettes that summer but still had not found the one that reunited me with the magical experience of the afternoon my aunt Ceil lit up in the family car while waiting for my father to join us. With her perfectly filed and polished blood red nails glistening, she picked a speck of tobacco from the tip of her tongue and said, "Melvin, my little darling, what ever you do, don't become a smoker. It's a disgusting habit." She took a drag on her un-filtered king size cigarette, I think it was a Pall Mall, and turning her head as far to the right as it would go, she blew the smoke over her shoulder into the well below the car's rear window where it swirled frantically as if desperate to escape. Her perfume, a richly fragrant floral scent, had dominated the space until she lit up, but the sweet tobacco smell seemed to me more pleasing by comparison, its atmosphere of sophistication, of mystery and, I have since realized, of sensuality—I felt it but couldn't name it then— totally undercut her cautionary preachings. I could not wait to smoke. Everybody smoked cigarettes in 1956 or so it seemed and the ones who didn't were more defensive than righteous about it. After all, smoking made a man a man and a woman seem willing. Sarah did not like my smoking, however, and I was torn between continuing my quest for the perfect smoke or uxoriously surrendering to her will. Of course she had a potent trump card to play: withholding her kiss. She never suggested withholding her body, but her kiss, the union of exterior surfaces with the interior surfaces, like a metaphor for intercourse itself and to me as preciously intimate, was what she held over my head. No matter how hard I brushed my teeth, how often I gargled with Listerene or how many peppermint Life Savers I chewed, Sarah would wrinkle her nose and turn away when I tried to kiss her. She didn't reject every kiss, don't misunderstand that; the "angle of the mouth press", the quick "nibble your lower lip", and the "lips on lips and withdraw quickly" greeting kiss were allowed; even the "opened mouth lingering kiss" was sometimes abided, but the "swallow me with your mouth and let me disappear into you" that intensely hungry, passionate and absorbing kiss was forbidden.

"The tarry smell comes right through the medicinal smell. Your breath smells like a doctor's office where the driveway's just been repaved." I switched to all the mentholated brands, one at a time, Salem, Spring, Kool, it didn't matter one bit. The menthol did not disguise my tarry breath. Quite unexpectedly, it was her greeting one day that ended the hunt.

It was one of those humid August days when the sky suddenly fills with clouds the color of charcoal and the air is so heavy and saturated with moisture you think the mere spray of your sneeze might bring down a torrent of rain. I had played some basketball and was having a Coke with Ron in the bleachers when she hailed me from the ball field. Watching her face as she approached from across the softball field, her luminous smile so warm it seemed to melt her eyebrows at their edges making them swoon over the corners of her eyes while the center of her mouth puckered itself softly inside her smile and her head reached towards me tilted slightly to the right as if poised to receive my kiss, well, what else could I do? Where her words had failed her very being triumphed and I succumbed, more to her than to her will. I loped across the field to meet her.

"Hi!" she said, reaching for my hand.

"I'm going to quit," I announced with determination.

"You're quitting your job?" she said with a worried look.

"Cigarettes. I'm quitting smoking. I can't stand not kissing you the way I want to." She beamed and hugged me.

"Got any gum?" she said with a wink, "or a mint, Listerine, 7–Up, Coke or a piece of pineapple will do." She pushed me away and then, still holding my hand, she pulled me back reeling me in to her, as if in a dance, and kissing me into an oblivion there on the pitcher's mound of the softball field.

After that kiss I didn't smoke again for a time. Our nightly rendezvous at the shed became more passionate and intense. There was no need to post a sign demanding privacy; somehow word had spread quickly that the shack was off limits to all but

Sarah and me, but just to be safe we secured the doors by plac-
ing the metal pole through the handles of the double doors.
Then we'd spread a blanket, turn on soft music, hug each other
close and begin to kiss there on the floor. In our hungry embrace
we rolled around on the blanket stroking and touching, pressing
hard against one another to the point of breathlessness, sometimes coming to a climax just from the friction of our bodies.
Then one night quite unexpectedly, just as we began to kiss she
suddenly went limp.

"Do you ever worry about the bomb?" Her question startled me. It was a question I had asked of girls in the past, my face
looking earnest and serious in the hope that the thought of that
nuclear Damocletian sword hanging over us might spur them to
gather their rosebuds with me in the back seat of my father's
black 1953 Buick Special, but now it was as though Sarah was
pointing us in the opposite direction.

"Not when I'm holding you in my arms," I said, trying to
kiss her again and recapture the mood. When she turned her
face away I rolled over on my back and said, "I mean that, Sarah,
really I do. I love you." Those words came spilling out, words
never before spoken by me, words I had always imagined as almost unutterable.

"I know you do. You're such a decent guy," she said,
stroking the side of my face. I waited for her inevitable "but" the
damning faint praise that had interrupted my efforts with so
many other girls, only it didn't come. She was simply express-
ing her feelings such as they were at that moment. We lay still,
side by side, holding hands. My mouth became dry and my
stomach churned. I could not hear her breathing and her body
was as still as sand.

"Why did you ask me that?"

"Because I think about it all the time. Because it frightens
me and I can't see the point of thinking about the future and of
love. Why bring children into a world which threatens to blow
them to pieces or incinerate them to atoms?" I said nothing while
time passed over and through us in a sickening crawl. Our palms
grew moist. "Did you ever read "Hiroshima' by John Hersey?"

"No, I've been meaning to though."

"I didn't eat or sleep for days after I read that book, it was so horrible. I can't get it out of my mind."

"Well, with that recommendation who could pass it up?" I joked, hoping to rescue her mood. I understood that sex was done for the night but pulling Sarah out of the depths was just as important to me, no, more important to me at that moment. I heard her laugh weakly. "Was that a chuckle? Did I hear a sense of humor stick in your throat? May I try for a belly laugh?"

"It's not funny," she said petulantly, but she snuggled into me her face against mine. Her cheek was wet with tears.

"So how do we do this, Sarah? How do we take any pleasure in a world that may end at any second? You know if we let it affect us like this we might as well be dead and I know that I am not dead. Let's see if Sarah is dead," and I slid my fingers along her ribs and began to tickle her. Her laughter came slowly, and then burst out in paroxysms. I stopped tickling her, cradled her in my arms, her small frame fitting neatly against me, and said, "You mustn't let yourself worry about it." Hardly a profound statement, banal in fact, but the helplessness and dread one feels at those moments can provoke one to wriggle, to try to escape the sight of the black pit that has just opened up in front of you. "Want to take a walk?" She mumbled something inaudible and twisted languidly in my embrace like a small child. "Is that a yes?"

She twisted about again and pushing me away suddenly she jumped astride me, pointed a finger in my face and said, "So what's it gonna be, Mel or Jack? Choose one so I know which guy I'm with, Mel or Jack?"

"You choose for me."

"Uh uhhh," she grunted, "it's your name, you choose," and in her straddle she began to post as if I was her mount. "Choose!"

"Not now."

"Now!" she said, posting more intensely and slapping my thigh with a crisp, stinging smack, "Choose!"

"Sarah, stop." Her posting grew more and more feverish and then she changed abruptly to a more stay-in-the-saddle

Western style of riding, her legs gripping me tightly and her pudenda rubbing back and forth against me with every stride.

"Choose, choose, choose . . ." Her voice choked, her face flushed, "chooooooossssse!" she sighed as she climaxed. Even with her eyes closed her tears found their way out and streamed down her face. I lay beneath her in silence strangely unaroused.

"Oh God, what did I do? That's terrible what just happened . . ."

"It's O.K. you didn't do anything wrong.

"Oh . . . God . . ."

"Shhhhh," I comforted, wiping the rivers of tears from her face.

"I'm so sorry."

"It's O.K. Sarah. I love you," I said, as though that would make all of her pain and shame, all of her fear and dread, all of the revulsion for the helplessness that human beings feel when faced with their piteous flailing, as though "I love you" could make all of that just go away.

Chapter Eight

Breakfast was the easiest meal to serve, the one which gave you time to talk to your guests and to kibbitz with the other waiters and busboys in the kitchen. The August mornings were chilly and I had given up cold milk for hot coffee, and a piece of stale cake. Sometimes I ate with Ron or Harlan but mostly I ate alone. I never felt especially social first thing in the morning and preferred to wade into the day the way one might wade into the cold water of a lake. There were those who might choose to dive into the cold water but I always took my time. I'd also begun smoking again with my breakfast coffee.

During the meal Mrs. Kimmelman spilled her hot water with lemon on Mr. Gold who graciously assured her he'd never walk again and Mr. Gotlieb—"one T, not two" he'd volunteer to every new person at the table—got a herring bone stuck in his throat which Mrs. Saperstein treated by having him swallow a large piece of bagel coated with cream cheese. It was an otherwise uneventful morning. Harlan collared me during the clean up.

"I can't talk to you right now but save time for me after lunch because I've got something I think you'll be interested in." I had been asking for him and Heidi to double date with Sarah and me and maybe this was what he was going to offer. I couldn't imagine what else it could be. Harlan disappeared at the morning break but was back at his tables for lunch. It was a sunny, cool, beautiful day. The people were eager to be out of doors and the meal went quickly. When it was finished and my station cleared I hurried back to the waiter's quarters to meet with Harlan and learn what he had to say.

"Get cleaned up and then meet me outside the coffee shop," he said. "It's about the judge." I was startled but before I could ask what about the judge, Harlan was gone.

He began speaking with urgency as soon as we met up. "When I was small, I am an only child you see, my father was at home most of the time . . ." Harlan paused and composed himself. "He almost never went out of the house. He would take my mother and me for rides in the country on Sundays but he never came to school programs or to parent-teacher meetings. I asked him why he didn't go out more when I was in grade school and he told me something vague about working for the government and having to stay out of the public eye and do his work in secret. 'Don't worry, I have a job, we're okay, it's just that it is a secret job and you have to keep it a secret.' he said. On my own, however, with the logic of a child, I decided that he must be sick with some strange disease and that was why he didn't go outside except in his car. This made it uncomfortable for me to hug him, afraid that I'd catch his disease, but he was not a very affectionate man so I learned to tolerate his rare hugs." I couldn't understand why Harlan was telling me this story about his father but I was thrilled to be taken into his confidence, whatever the reason. "And I never brought any friends to the house because I didn't want any of them to get sick. He was aware of their absence and one day he asked me who my friends were and why I didn't bring them home. 'Are you ashamed of them or is it me you are ashamed of Harlan.'" Harlan mimicked his father in a harsh New York accent. "'No I'm not ashamed, I just don't want them to catch your disease,' I said. He laughed very hard and then he took me by the shoulders and looked into my eyes with a great intensity. Studying me and looking at me up and down, nodding as he appraised me he said, 'I think you're old enough to understand the whole truth now. Routine, Harlan,' he said, 'routine is the spine of the average man's day. Wake up, shut off alarm, pee, wash face, brush teeth, shower and shave, get dressed. Eat the same breakfast, take the same walk or bus or train to the same job or office, then home the same way to the same wife and the same newspaper. Day after day after day. Soon the routine is not a supporting spine; soon you find your life is imprisoned, caged, and routine forms the bars of that cage. I couldn't take it any more, I had to escape.'" He flipped a Lucky Strike out of its pack and lit up. "You're looking at me and wondering how I can remember the words that he said to me all those years ago aren't you. Well, imagine if your father told you something so shocking, do you think you'd ever forget it?" The thought of telling him about my father's "engraved his name on my memory" recollection occurred to me but it seemed so trivial by comparison that instead I asked, "Is he still living, and if he is where is he?" The question seemed to freeze Harlan. His lips tensed, his shoulders sank, and the dark circles of sleepless and restless nights appeared suddenly under his eyes as though he had not slept for days. It had been an alarmingly transforming question and I worried that with this inept blunder I had trespassed into a zone too sensitive to be treated so matter-of-factly. Harlan took a drag on his cigarette, crossed his legs and, shading his eyes with his left hand pressed his fingers against his temples.

"He's not well. His lungs are very weak." He took another puff on his Lucky Strike, exhaled, coughed, and scrutinized the cigarette. "His doctor says he smokes too much but I don't believe smoking is all that dangerous. I think it's the pneumonias he gets in the winter that have hurt him." Then Harlan's demeanor abruptly changed again. His face brightened and he seemed to experience an unburdening release, as though after years of living in total darkness his vision had been miraculously restored.

"How would you like to meet him and have him tell you himself what happened back then?" All at once I realized that Harlan was talking about judge Crater; his certainty the judge was not in the well was because he was Harlan's living father. I almost fell over with the shock of the realization.

"Would he really want to do that?" The question was asked more with wonder than skepticism.

"It would give him a great lift, cheer him up. Yes, that's what we'll do. He doesn't get to tell this story very often, as you can imagine, and it would do him a world of good."

"Are you really sure the judge would do that just for me?" I snuck my assumption in inconspicuously and he didn't even blink.

"Don't you like to tell your miracle-of-the-broken-leg story? And who enjoys that story more than you do? You really do that for yourself even if you don't know that. Yes, I'm sure he'd be happy to meet you. You know, I've told him all about you, your family, your college plans. He's still asking me why I don't bring my friends around so he'll be delighted to meet you. We'll take my car."

We drove off the hotel grounds in Harlan's 1951 Buick, a low slung car that looked as much like a Hudson as a Buick, and headed down the State road that circled the lake. Although I had protested going to meet the judge in my soiled sneakers and wrinkled khakis Harlan said it would be best if we just left quickly and used the time for his father's benefit.

"It's already four o'clock. If we leave now we can visit and be back in plenty of time for dinner. If you change your clothes you'll only waste time and bring attention to us. This way if anyone should ask I can say we're just going into town for some things." My heart was racing. This would be the first famous person I'd actually get to meet and I was giddy with excitement.

"Do I call him 'judge' or just 'Mr. Crater'?"

"You'll call him Mr. Hawthorne. He's now Mr. Thomas Hawthorne." He laughed. "Do you want to know how he chose that name? When he and my mother were driving out of New York City the night that he disappeared, they drove up the West Side Highway, which leads on to the Sawmill River Parkway in Westchester. That highway connects with the Taconic Parkway at a junction called the Hawthorne Circle. My father said 'What a great name!' and he took it for himself right on the spot." As easy as spelling Melvin J-A-C-K, I thought. Harlan turned on the radio. The local D.J. was babbling excitedly about a Broadway show he had seen over the weekend in New York City. It was called "My

Fair Lady" and starred Rex Harrison and a newcomer named Julie
Andrews. The D.J. had bought the original cast album and would
be playing songs from it all day but he would begin with the song
he loved the most in the show: "On the Street Where You Live."
Since Harlan wasn't much of a baseball fan and although Mickey
Mantle was having an outstanding season I couldn't speculate
with him about whether Mantle would break Babe Ruth's homerun record that summer or keep his batting average above .350
so we listened to the music and drove on in silence. The earnest
lyrics of the love song made me think of Heidi and how sad she'd
be if she knew that Harlan had an older woman. It made me sad
too. I was so happy to have Sarah in my life I couldn't think of
any other girl.

The car pulled up at a small cabin on the far shore of the
lake and as soon as Harlan shut the engine off a pretty middle-
aged woman came out on to the porch. I recognized her face immediately; it was the woman I had watched from the bulrushes
at the shore the night of the Diana debacle.

"My mother is very worried about my father's condition. I
visit her every night to try to cheer her up. Sometimes we dance."
He laughed. "I think we danced to the 'Theme from Picnic' for an
hour one night."

"Pretty music," I commented, omitting my voyeuristic
escapade and suddenly feeling great relief about Harlan's
character.

"You're not to say anything about this to anyone, understand? Not your brothers or your friend Malcolm, no one." He
was very firm and very serious.

"Of course not."

"That's a promise?" I nodded vigorously. His mother
stepped down from the porch and approached the car on the still
finely shaped legs of a former chorus girl. Harlan left the car and
when he reached her they embraced.

"Mother, I want you to meet my friend Jack White," he said
motioning to me to join them. "Jack, this is my mother Helene
Hawthorne." I extended my hand to her but she didn't take it.

"What reason do you have for bringing this young man
here Harlan Hawthorne," she said sternly. "Your father is not well

and we are not receiving company today." She spoke with the soft and elegant cadences of someone from the south, Virginia I guessed, and she must have been pretty angry to speak so sternly to her only son.

"It's all right mother, Jack is a good friend. No need to put yourself out for him. I wanted him to meet you and dad but we can leave if you'd like," he offered in contrition. She looked back at me. "I've told Jack everything, mother. I've told him because I'm going to ask him to help me look for the ring." She looked at Harlan and then again at me.

"I am very pleased to meet you Jack," she said, extending her hand to me. "I apologize for being so rude. My husband has been ailing and that is very upsetting for me." Her eyes began to well with tears but taking a deep breath she composed herself and continued. "Please, do come inside." She scanned the area as if searching for spies in the surrounding woods, and motioned us inside.

The cabin was small. The couch and armchair were of pine and their cushions were covered in a brightly colored plaid fabric. The smell of ashes from a recent fire hung in the humid air. "I apologize for the smell," she said opening a window, "Mr. Hawthorne gets a chill at night so we always light a fire." A fit of coughing erupted in another room and then a voice called out, "Is somebody there, Helene?"

"Harlan's here, and he's brought a friend along," she answered and then lowering her voice she said, "he's not doing that well these last few days, coughing and wheezing something fierce." "I'll go say hello and ask if he's feeling up to meeting Jack. The company might cheer him up." She nodded her consent and then turned back to me. "Can I get you something cold to drink Jack? We have lemonade and Coca Cola. I despise that Pepsi stuff," she said smiling politely.

"Nothing for me, thank you ma 'am," I returned equally politely, a southern accent creeping into my voice, Harlan's words, "help me look for the ring" still ringing in my ears. On the fireplace mantle was a photograph of a man wearing a starched white collar and dark tie. His slicked back hair was parted down the middle, the part leading my eyes down to the bridge of a spade shaped nose whose pointed tip directed me to his wide mouth which curled at its corners with just the barest beginning of a smile. Looking back at Helene Hawthorne I saw the finer facial features that Harlan had inherited from her.

"Come on in here Jack," Harlan called out from the bedroom. His mother smiled, raised her eyebrows and nodded towards the other room.

The bedroom was a small, dimly lit space with curtains drawn across the windows. The smell of stale bedclothes mixed with the pungent odor of Musterole and made the air in the room feel close and unhealthy. In the large bed facing the curtained windows an old man lay under the cover of a wrinkled white sheet and a blue and white quilt. On the night table beside the bed there was a glass pitcher filled with water, an empty glass, a box of tissues and a bottle of aspirin all huddled under the broad shade of the reading lamp. The man, the judge, coughed and choked when he tried to speak to me. He was a big man filling the bed from the headboard almost to the foot. His head seemed disproportionately small for such a large body and his gaunt, pale face appeared different from the one I'd just seen in the photograph. For one thing his hair had turned gray and was much thinner than it had been in the picture, though it was still divided by a central part. And his nose was more bulbous than spade shaped. He pulled a tissue from the box, wiped his face all around with it and then spat into it crumpling it up immediately.

"It's a pleasure to meet you, Jack," he said pulling another tissue from its box and wiping his mouth. "You'll understand if I don't shake your hand. It's not TB but you don't want this muck on your hands." His false teeth clattered in his mouth as he spoke and when he breathed I could hear the air wheezing through his pipes and disrupting secretions that rumbled and gurgled in protest. Then he had another fit of coughing. He threw the soiled tissues into a pail beside his bed, quickly pulled out two more from the box and wiped and spat again.

"Are you okay dad?" Harlan asked with evident concern.

"Yeah, yeah," he said waving a hand at his son. "This is how it's been all week. I think those fires are too smoky for me. I'll just wear a sweater at night, that's all." His voice, authoritative and confident, had a harsh New York accent.

"I've been telling Jack about you and how we came to be the Hawthornes, but I thought it might cheer you up to tell him about your decision yourself, you know, how the routine got to you and you just had to break away." The old man smiled and looked over at me.

"You interested in this?" he asked cocking an eyebrow and smiling at me.

"Yes sir." He started to chuckle but that action triggered yet another fit of coughing and wheezing. Harlan hurried to his side and offered two more tissues.

"Maybe we should do this another time," I said.

"No! No, I'll feel better when I get started with this story. It'll get my juices flowing and that always dries up the cough. How much have you told him Harlan?"

"That you were a judge, a very famous judge, and about your speech to me about routine becoming a prison. I didn't get to how you decided to break free and the weekend in Maine when it all happened." The judge smiled.

"It was a very corrupt time. It's important that you understand that and not just see me as a middle-aged man running off with a showgirl because he was bored; a very corrupt time. Judgeships were for sale if you knew the right people. As a lawyer all you had to do was lay out one year of the position's salary in advance and the job was yours. The money went through the usual channels of the party into many, many pockets. I did not do that, Jack, I want you to know that. My appointment was made by Governor Franklin Delano Roosevelt, probably the only man in New York politics who didn't know the rules of the game. All he knew were his presidential ambitions and for them he groomed and courted people who were high above the political hurly burly. Robert Wagner knew, but he wanted me to get me on the court cleanly. I had been his law clerk years before. The Senator probably had other things in mind for me, but he didn't get the chance to lay them out because I was gone before the court's fall session began. At the time I was married to a woman named

Mary. We lived on Fifth Avenue near Washington Square and we had a summer cottage in Maine. In August I would take the month off and we'd go away to the cottage. By that August, in the summer of 1930, I had already laid the groundwork for my escape." The judge coughed once, cleared his throat, and poured himself a glass of water. "I had begun to stay late at work the previous December. My practice was busy and successful so it did not seem at all unreasonable for me to be at work into the evening. Then there was my political work for the Democratic Party as well. But I wasn't always at work. Some nights I'd go to a speakeasy, you must remember there was still prohibition in 1930, Jack, and meet some of the boys. There were always dancers and actresses, girls who liked to come to the bars too and that was how I found my Helene." He smiled and took a sip of water. "As soon as I met her I was in love in a way I had never known. The dull routine of my life became intolerable but I had to plot out an escape route that would let us disappear completely." He started to cough again and while Harlan slapped his father's back and tended him with tissues I thought of how the judge had divided himself in half just like the part that divided his hair. One half was the serious attorney in starched collars and expensive suits, the other, the half that lied about working late at the office, was a hard drinking fun loving friend of the theater. It was easy for me to imagine which life he came to love more. "I'm sorry Jack, but that one wasn't as bad as the last few so let me continue. I made a lot of money as a lawyer but by then practicing the law felt as bad as this chronic affliction that has laid me up in my bed. When Senator Wagner told me of his plans for me, an appointment to the State Supreme Court, I saw the way out. By leaving a trail of evidence that would suggest impropriety I could then expose the system and make myself appear to be implicated. In May, Roosevelt appointed me to the court and immediately I went into action. I withdrew money from several accounts and sold stocks and bonds adding up to the sum of $52,000, the annual salary of a supreme court justice, the amount it ordinarily would have cost for such an appointment, and I went on with my dual existence. Mary, my wife at the time, was a devout Catholic so divorce was out of the question. We'd been unable to have children and that might have allowed me to seek an annulment—the Church is always partial to those who wish to multiply—but to have suggested that to Mary would have raised other suspicions when I disappeared, so I held back. Then, in June, I called the district attorney, anonymously of course, and with my voice disguised like this," and suddenly he was a Boston Brahmin, "I informed the gentleman that one George Ewald had paid $10,000 for the honor of being appointed to the bench in one of the lower courts of The State of New York. When the D.A. requested more information I hung up." Then his voice returned to its casual and comfortable New Yorkese, his verbal equivalent of an old but treasured robe. "I didn't like Ewald and was happy to turn him in. I waited for August knowing from my contacts in his office that the D.A. was likely to act early in that month. Mary and I left for Belgrade Lakes on Friday August the first. Before we left I arranged with Helene to call me on that coming Sunday so I could tell Mary that something had come up requiring my return to New York." He cleared his throat, took a sip of water, but didn't cough. His enthusiasm, as he'd predicted, had released a drying flood of adrenalin. "When her call came that Sunday I said I had to go back to New York for business reasons. I told Mary it was nothing serious, just a few things to clear up, a few people who needed straightening out, and then I had the driver take both of us to the train station. Promising to be back the following Saturday in time for her birthday I left her on the platform of the station, waving goodbye. I never saw her again. After returning to New York I saw a few friends and did a little business at the office and some socializing at the restaurants. I went shopping at the Abercrombie and Fitch store in midtown and had them send a red canoe to Mary for her birthday. Red was about the last color I would have associated with that dour woman. It was my private joke of a sort. For the next few days I lunched at Schrafft's as usual and hung around the office waiting for the district attorney to go into action, but I was getting impatient and a little careless. I caught my finger in the door of a taxi and had to visit my doctor who was

also a friend and we had dinner at his home that night. That
calmed me down a bit. What I had come back to town for happened on my third day in the city. The district attorney announced he was going to investigate Judge George Ewald. The
alleged $10,000 bribe had shaken up the whole system. That an-
nouncement freed me and I went into action immediately. I had
my assistant, Joe Mara, cash checks on separate bank accounts
for more than $5,000 while I remained at my office and spent the
morning tearing up old files. It was to look like a panicky effort
to destroy evidence, but for me it was a joyful celebration of release. I would have thrown all the papers out of the office window, strewing them like bits of tickertape for a parade, but that
was not the tone I wanted to set. Then I stuffed papers and files
into two large briefcases and several cardboard boxes. When Joe
returned it was an effort not to laugh out loud when I saw the expression on his face. That poor bastard, he looked like he'd just
been caught with his hand down a young boy's pants. The impression that I had done something horribly wrong and was now
in a panic had been made. I had my assistant help bring all the
boxes back to my apartment on Fifth Avenue and told him I was
going swimming in Westchester County, but that was not what
my plans were. Instead of going swimming I went to a ticket
agent and bought a single ticket for a new show called 'Dancing
Partner'—I couldn't resist the irony—and arranged to have a
friend pick it up for me at the box office later that evening. Then
I had a showgirl friend of Helene's and mine, Sally Ritz, stage a
chance meeting. Sally was dating a lawyer friend of mine and she
got the lawyer to take her to Billy Haas's Steak House on West
45th Street where I would just happen to arrive at the same time
as they did. Do you see what I was doing?" I shook my head no,
already dizzy with the lurching pace and course the judge had
traveled. He laughed a hearty laugh and rubbed his hands together gleefully. "I was planting evidence and laying false trails
all over the place. The theater ticket, the story about swimming
in Westchester, acting like I was desperate in one place, hail fel-

low well met in another. Who was lying and who was telling the truth would be the question to answer when the police started to look for me and tried to piece together what had become of the missing judge Crater. I managed to be even more confounding by staying at dinner well past the curtain time of the play. When my lawyer friend asked what I was doing I simply said I was having too good a time and enjoying myself too much to leave. A while later, on cue, Sally excused herself to go to the little girl's room, but what she actually did was to call Helene and tell her that it was time to pick me up on Tenth Avenue and 46th Street as we'd prearranged. Shortly after Sally returned we all left the restaurant. I said goodnight, hailed a taxi and drove off towards the Hudson River at nine fifteen p.m. on Wednesday, August sixth 1930. No one, besides Helene, ever saw judge Joseph Force Crater again. I was free." The sick old man I had been introduced to was now gone. In his place was a revived man who sat up, motioned to Harlan to approach, and lifted a Lucky strike from the pack in his son s shirt pocket.

"Do you think that's a good idea dad?" Harlan gently challenged.

"Read your pack, my boy. 'L.S./M.F.T. Lucky Strike means fine tobacco.' This fine tobacco isn't hurting me, it's the pneumonias I've been getting in that drafty house in Newburgh." Harlan frowned. "Now, have you spoken to Jack about the ring?"

"Not yet. I thought I'd get to that on the way back to the hotel. I didn't want to overwhelm him, though just meeting you is probably an overwhelming experience in itself," he said with a chuckle. I shrugged, but neither was paying any attention to me.

"Well then, it was very nice to meet you Jack White. Harlan says you're planning to become a doctor?"

"I'm not sure about that."

"Well, what ever you do don't become a lawyer. It's a den of thievery and iniquity that they live in." He took a long drag on the Lucky and went into another fit of coughing. "Those damned pneumonias," he growled.

"I'll see you tonight dad," Harlan said with a wave. Despite the muck the Judge had warned me about I approached him and extended my hand.

"It was an honor to meet you sir," I said. He looked at my hand, smiled, and grasped it in both of his.

"The pleasure was all mine young man, my pleasure to meet you and my pleasure to recount my tortured tale of deception."

When we were back in his car Harlan lit a cigarette, inhaled deeply and let the smoke out through his nose. I looked into my pack of Salems but did not withdraw one. Harlan tossed me a Lucky. I lit up, crumpled up my pack of Salems and threw it on the floorboards. My hands were shaking.

"Now you know why I say judge Crater is not buried in that well. I have to say it again even though I know I can trust you, you must not say anything about your meeting or the fact that my father is still alive to anyone. There are still people out there who might want to find him."

"You don't have to worry about me, Harlan, my lips are sealed," I said, like a tough guy in the movies, and it was easy to do because none of the experiences I'd had that day felt real to me.

"Now, you're probably wondering about this ring we all kept referring to. Well, it's a very special ring, a ring that my father got from his father. It had been in the family for many centuries. It dates all the way back to the Crusades . . ." I must have gasped because he stopped and turned towards me to ask if I was all right.

"Yeah . . . yes, yes, fine. Boy! Are you ever full of surprises. And Ron is wondering about Harvard!" I laughed and he joined in and we must have laughed half the way back to the hotel. "Well, it's true; the ring, the Crusader, my father the judge, all of it. This ring is very unusual and my father is very sentimental about it. It's a gimmal ring, do you know what that means?"

"I know alef, bas, gimmel, dalid, but not gimmel rings," I said in a giddy voice.

"Its s not Hebrew Jack. It's a ring with a hinged part, or a ring with a hidden compartment. The ring has a picture of my great, great, God only knows how many greats there are, we're talking about almost a thousand years, grandfather. And it's somewhere here on the grounds of Braverman's."

"I don't understand. What's it doing here on the hotel grounds?"

"Remember what Lenny said about this being a road house once, a place of gaming and gambling, remember?" I nodded. "Well, this is where it gets a little touchy, Jack. My father did like to come here to gamble back during prohibition, as did many others I might add, and the night that Lenny told you about, with the gunshots and all, well . . . let's just say there were gunshots. There had been a quarrel, an argument between . . . there was a fight." He was very fidgety and a film of perspiration formed on his forehead and face. "There was a man from Chicago that night who had an incredible run of luck. He was on a streak that most poker players only dream about and he was getting cocky about it. My father had been losing most of the night and was running out of cash. And then, around midnight, he did something to spook the guy from Chicago. He took off his ring and opened the gimmaled setting of the stone to look at his ancestor's portrait. He kissed the picture and laid the opened ring on the table asking his remote grandfather for good luck. Whether it was a coincidence or not no one will ever know, but suddenly the tide turned and my father began to win. By some time after one a.m. he was dead even with Lou, the man from Chicago, who had come with a big wad of bills wrapped around an empty shotgun shell secured with a rubber band. Lou got more and more upset as his luck changed and my father kept winning. The other poker players had been cleaned out and had quit; by 2 a.m. just the two of them were left. The man from Chicago was rattled. He asked for a single winner take all hand, seven card open, five card roll 'em poker to be dealt by Ben Braverman. The betting was outrageous from the start. Before either one had more than one card open the guy from Chicago began to bet laying piles of cash in the center of the table. Every time another card was dealt Chicago Lou bet and answered every raise with 'see you and raise you' through the dealing of all four open cards. Then they each sorted through their hands, the four face up and the three face down cards, and each selected the five cards he would play. Then laying them face down in a pile they began turning them over one at a time, betting back and forth with each flip of a card. Every bet was again met with, 'I see you and raise you' until, finally, my father didn't have enough cash to meet the last bet. He had a very good hand, most of it the cards that had been hidden from view during the open part of the game, and he was sure he could win if he could meet Lou's bet. He picked up his golden piece of heritage, his Crusaders s ring, a ring that had been in his family for a thousand years, and he laid it on the pile of bills. His gimmal ring, the ring that he had worn proudly most of his adult life, this precious heirloom, was all that he had left to bet. The man from Chicago looked the ring over and refused to accept it as being of any value. Stunned, my father argued that it was in fact a rare ring, an heirloom of great value that by itself was worth many times more than the entire pile of money on the table. They went back and forth about it each one getting more heated as his turn arrived when, abruptly, the man from Chicago took the ring from the pile, scru- tinized it closely while turning it around in his fingers, and then suddenly went to the window, pushed out the screen and flung the ring deep into the woods. 'Fuck you and your goddamn ring, you lose.' he said. That was when the shooting started." Barely turning his head Harlan looked at me from the corners of his eyes. "Do I need to say anymore?"

"No," I said, but that was not what I thought. For the first time that day I had the feeling that asking me to believe this story was asking too much. There were too many fantastic acts and incidents cobbled together for me to believe they all were true. "For twenty-five years that ring has lain somewhere out there in the grass waiting for me to come here and reclaim it. And for twenty-five years my father has been without his her- itage, his patrimony. When I go out early in the morning before shaving and showering for the breakfast meal, that gimmal ring is what I've been searching for. I owe you some thanks. You showed me where the well for the old roadhouse is. The ring is somewhere in the field between that old well and the handy-men's shack. Will you help me to look for it?"

"Help you how? You mean get up early in the morning and go out looking for the ring in the weeds?"

"If you imagine you can do it any other time of day that you like and still be discreet, that would be all right with me too." He sounded sarcastic.

"You're really serious, aren't you. You're really expecting me to look for this ring." Surprise and annoyance outweighed what flattery I might have attributed to Harlan's request. He was asking for a lot and taking it for granted that I'd comply.

"Why do you think I came to Braverman's, Jack, to wait tables? You have been asking me that question one way or another all summer long and when I finally put the truth out on the table in front of you, you balk. Look," his voice was suddenly both soothing and contrite, "I did not intend for one minute that you feel taken for granted. I hoped that you, being my friend, would want to help. I came here to find the gimmal ring. It means every-thing to my father and, as you saw today, he's a very sick man, maybe a dying man, and this ring is all that he talks about to my mother. 'Do you think Harlan can find that ring Helene? Does Harlan know where to look Helene?' It's an obsession." Despite my doubts I still found myself eager to please Harlan. Raised with Ripley's "Believe it or Not," stranger things than his story had proved to be true and my disbelief began to evaporate as soon as we drove through the iron gate of the hotel entrance. "What do you want me to do?"

"I'd like you to accept the role of decoy. If we both go scratching around in the field before dawn someone will see us and his suspicions might be aroused. Then, even if they don't know why they're doing it, dishwashers and handymen will start searching the ground for an imagined treasure. I would hate it if one of them actually finds the ring before I do." He lit another Lucky when we pulled up in his parking place. "If you were to poke around elsewhere, say near the main building, no, that would be too conspicuous. Back near the Braverman's residence, yeah, that's far enough away and out of the sight of everyone," He paused, and with the fingers of his right hand gesticulating in the air, his eyes squinting, his lips moving around unvoiced words, he calculated the consequences of this proposal before turning to me and speaking. "Yes, that'll do it. You'll go foraging around the Braverman's house. I'll tell Heidi that you and I are out looking for my lost ID bracelet so if she or anyone else in her family spots you there she'll know that you are helping me and will explain it to her family."

"But you won't be there with me," I argued.

"Of course not. Heidi and I have been all over the grounds here so there are lots of places to be looking for the bracelet. It would be foolish for us both to be searching in the same place." There was a compelling logic to his argument.

"Okay, I'll help."

"Good. We'll get started with this in the morning," he said crushing his butt in the ashtray. "Want another Lucky, Jack?"

"Sure," I said, feeling conspiratorial.

"Keep the pack," he said, winking and dropping it in my lap.

We returned to our room separately with Harlan going first and I following him a few minutes later. I knew if Ron were to see me with a pack of Lucky's he'd accuse me of trying to copy Harlan so I put them back into Harlan's car and went to the snack bar to buy a pack of Chesterfield's, the third brand of short, unfiltered cigarettes. Regardless of the brand I showed up with rising early and disappearing from the room would be a sure sign that Harlan and I were up to something and Ron would never let that pass unremarked. And how would we explain it to him if it went on for too many mornings, we hadn't considered that. And with summer waning sunrise was later every morning sending us out in a dim light. I would have to bring all of this up with Harlan before we enacted his plan. Ron's suspiciousness had become worse since his money was stolen and he rarely spoke directly to Harlan; he communicated with him by thinking out loud for my benefit.

"I wonder how a guy can live with himself knowing that he's taken something valuable that doesn't belong to him, something that another person has earned and sweated for.

What do you think, Mel, could there be such a person who could feel no guilt or shame in the presence of his victim? Who, besides a Nazi, who would be capable of such behavior, I ask you?" There was nothing I could say to answer him in Harlan's presence and when we were alone he would sneer at me for suggesting that he stop asking me his hypothetical questions. Sneaking out in the morning would be the only way to get out of the room without arousing Ron's suspicion. Still, it would be risky. Ron would think it had something to do with Judge Crater, but he wouldn't have the remotest idea how close to the truth he was. I'd have to trust my ability to be stealthy, something I developed to sabotage my older, stronger brothers. Fortunately, Ron snored like a sawmill so a little bit of noise would probably never wake him.

2.

While Elvis Presley's popularity continued to grow that summer with each new song he recorded, Sarah and I remained true to the more conventional romantic music of the time like film scores, and songs with Frank Sinatra, and Sammy Davis Junior. Radio stations were playing Tennessee Ernie Ford, Johnny Cash, The Platters and, of course Elvis, as much if not more than they played "Moonglow," "Around the World in Eighty Days," "The Poor People of Paris," "Lisbon Antigua" and "Que Sera Sera." We listened to them all unaware of the change that was about to erupt through the calm surface of the mid-1950's.

The political conventions of August 1956 would be a reprise of 1952 with Adlai Stevenson and Dwight Eisenhower once again facing off, the only change being that the Democratic vice-presidential nominee would be Estes Kefauver in place of John Sparkman. The controversial Republican veep would survive efforts to dump him, go on in later years to lose one and then win two presidential elections, and ultimately be the first sitting president to resign his office in the midst of scandal; Richard Milhaus Nixon of course. But a more immediate scandal was brewing at Braverman's that summer.

"Can you keep a secret?" Sarah asked as we walked down to the old shed at the lake. We had been seeing each other on a regular basis for several weeks. We had developed a pattern of going down to the storage shed, spreading a blanket and making out after our first week together. The one thing I knew with certainty was that I was in love.

"Of course," I answered, not remarking upon the several other secrets I had yet to confide to her.

"I really shouldn't be telling you this but, well . . . I know that you're not a thief. Heidi told me that someone is robbing people at the hotel, has been all summer long."

"Yeah, I know, Sammy told us weeks ago. You know I was in the main lobby once and a woman was really giving it to Belle about a missing bracelet, but I never heard anything more about it. Mrs. Braverman took her into the office and that seemed to be the end of it."

"Not at all. Heidi says the Bravermans ended up giving her a free vacation just to keep her from making another scene, but the bracelet was never found. And they don't think it was a chambermaid who took it."

"Who do they think did?"

"This is very secret, you have to promise me . . ."

"I promised already, didn't I?" I was hurt that she challenged my sincerity: it was my long suit.

"Well, they believe that it might be Harlan."

"Jesus Christ! Not them too. Is this about somebody stealing jewelry or about him stealing their precious jewel Heidi?" I reached for her hand but she pulled it away.

"This is why I was reluctant to tell you. Harlan is perfect in your eyes. Don't you ever get the sense that he's just too perfect, too charming, too . . . too nice?"

"Oh, those are really deadly characteristics aren't they? Of course, who would trust a person who is charming and too nice, what a fool I've been."

"I'm not saying it right," she said, shaking her head, "it's not that he's too nice, it's that there's something just a little unbelievable in the niceness—I mean have you ever seen him get angry or upset?"

"Yes!" We had reached the waterfront but our quarrel had made me feel remote from her and our mood was less than amorous.

"I'm sorry I shouldn't have said anything, Mel. Wait, there's another example of what's wrong with him, didn't he tell you to call yourself Jack? Didn't that strike you as strange?" I'd felt odd when Harlan renamed me but I'd grown used to the change with time and I really had liked being called Jack.

"I hate the name Melvin, I wanted to change it. He didn't change my name I did."

"Yes, but you could have done that anytime and you didn't, you didn't until Harlan told you to do it."

"He didn't tell me. I asked him. He was just supporting what I intended to do anyway. And if you hadn't made such a fuss about it I'd still be calling myself Jack." Hearing the petulance in my voice I curled my lower lip, snuffled, and added, "so there" in the hope that lightening the mood might rescue the evening and allow for more tenderness and sensuality.

"I'm not kidding around Mel, this isn't a joke. I don't know, it's hard to find the words, there's something that's just not right, about him. I don't trust him."

"Does Heidi trust him? Who knows him better than she does?"

"Oh Mel, she's in love with him, how else could she feel?"

"So love really is blind?" I said in an acerbic tone.

"I'm afraid so," she said walking away, "and right now it looks to me like there's an epidemic of blindness."

"Come back here," I said walking briskly after her, "don't run away from me." But she continued to walk back towards the hotel. "Sarah please, please stop and talk to me."

"Talking means listening to the other person too. You get so defensive about Harlan that you start defending him before you've even heard the whole story. Doesn't that tell you something?" There was no question but that she was right. I was wrong.

"I'm sorry. I want you to like him as much as I do, I want the two of you to be friends too. It upsets me when you have negative things to say about him that's all. It's like when you've read a book or seen a movie that you really like a lot and want a friend to like it just as much as you do. You take that friend to the movie and sit watching him instead of the movie and if he doesn't laugh at the things you thought were funny, or get excited about the part that excited you, well, you feel like you've lost the thing that you had been so excited about and also that you've lost a bit of that friendship." Sarah came up to me and took my hand.

"Let's take a walk." She led me back to the lakefront and sat down on the bank. "I know that you want me to like him as much as you do but I can't. I've never told Heidi this," she said, pursing her lips and looking over the lake, "but I don't think he's loyal to her; no, I know he's not loyal to her." She closed her eyes and when she opened them again she was looking at me. "One of my kids hurt himself in camp one day and I had to take him back to his mother. I went to the pool because she was the kind of woman who was always sunbathing, but she wasn't there and no one had seen her that day. I asked the boy where he was staying and he pointed to the main building. At the front desk Belle called up to his room and Mrs. Cohen took a long time to answer. She said she wasn't feeling well and could I please just send him upstairs. He was still upset and I couldn't make him go alone so I walked him to his room. When we got there I knocked on the door and Mrs. Cohen opened it only a crack. She was wearing a thin robe, her hair was mussed and her face was all flushed and perspired. 'You must have the flu' I said sympathetically, but she just nodded at me. She reached out to David who started to cry and when she spread her arms to embrace him her robe fell open and I saw that she was completely naked. The door had come ajar behind her and I peeked over her shoulder and looked inside. There was a man's shirt draped over the back of a chair and it was a shirt I had seen Harlan wear, a brown cotton plaid that I'd seen before but only on him." Sarah looked back at me and then out over the dark waters of the lake. "I knew that Harlan was in that room, I just knew it. When David came back to camp the next day I asked him how he was feeling. He said that he was fine and that his mommy had made his boo-boo all better with a special medicine that a man had given to her just for him, but that was all he'd say. I didn't press him. Mel I know it was Harlan in her room, I just know it. I can't say anything to Heidi but I don't know what I'd do if we were to be together all four of us."

"I can see why you'd think it was Harlan but there never was a one of a kind shirt in the history of shirt manufacturing. I mean somebody else could have worn a shirt like that. Ron could have worn Harlan's shirt. I could have worn Harlan's shirt." I was becoming extravagant in my defense of Harlan.

"You mean it was you in Mrs. Cohen 's room?"

"I mean that Harlan gets accused of all kinds of things but I trust him anyway. Women flirt, with him and he flirts with them but nothing ever comes of it."

Sarah frowned and cocking her eyebrow said, "You just can't believe he's not the person you wish he'd be."

"All right. I'll tell you a secret. I'll keep your secret if you'll keep mine." She nodded. "One night when I was down at the lake I heard a woman call out Harlan's name." I told her about rowing the skiff across the lake and seeing Harlan and the woman at the cottage. "That woman turned out to he his mother, not some cheating married woman."

"You took his word for that I suppose."

"No, I took her word for that. Harlan's mother and father rent one of the cabins across the lake. Harlan's father is sick and he wanted to be near Harlan so they rented one of the cabins. He took me to meet them." I had to restrain myself from telling her about his father, about judge Crater.

"Well, I don't know. He's just so, so slick." She said the word as though it were some kind of filth. "Another thing I don't understand. You already have two older brothers why do you need another one?"

"Harlan's a friend, not a big brother," I said, feeling stung but not showing it. "Harlan is someone I like and respect someone I might get some sense of direction from." I weighed explaining to her the real extent of my admiration, the wish to get more than just direction from the person I admired and looked up to; the wish to experience the world as that person, to *become* that person, not permanently but for a discrete period of time. I had imagined that by concentrating my thoughts and attention upon that person I might consolidate all the forces that comprised my self into a small but dense body of energy and then, like a spark jumping a gap, transubstantiate my self into his self. How better to learn to be like someone you admire than to *be* that someone you admire, to dwell inside his mind and hear the thoughts as they form; to live inside his skin and experience feelings as they course through his blood and inform his every cell of the will behind his acts. Don't be alarmed, this was a telekinetic fantasy not a reality. Only a madman would believe that he has temporarily taken up residence inside of someone else's consciousness. But there were some times I felt so close to making that leap it was almost as though I was about to leave my body. Of course it never occurred; reality is ineluctable. And even then, as I listened to myself considering it, the whole notion sounded so insane to me I dared not tell Sarah. "He doesn't condescend to me, he doesn't bait me, he talks to me like he respects my intelligence and like my feelings and opinions matter for something. That's why when people criticize him I always defend him. He's been loyal to me and that's the least that I can do for him." I finished my explanation just as we reached the vicinity of the dock and shed. Sarah was still rubbing her arms to warm them.

"I'm sorry but I just think that Harlan is not who you think he is. We'll have to agree to disagree on this one Mel. Boy it's cold." She shivered. We moved closer to each other and I put my arms around her to warm her. But with that nearness the beckoning perfumes of her soap and powder released yearnings and desires in me that shrank the visible world to just her face and erased all sound save the windy rush of her breath; her touch as light as the stroke of a feather, her kiss the purest bliss, all of me, every molecule of every cell, in a state of perfect harmony with her every atom. I could have stood there with her for eternity.

"Let's go inside," she said, nodding her head towards the shed.

"You sure that you want to?" She smiled a mischievous smile and started walking backwards towards the shed, beckoning me with her curling index finger she curled towards herself again and again. At that moment I was more in love with her than ever and the feeling she loved me was strong and thrilling. It was my first experience with the intense eroticism that flows when lovers reconcile after a quarrel.

After securing the door we embraced and slowly lowered ourselves to the blanket covered chaise longue we kept under the window. Over the weeks our petting had gone from holding and touching to passionate kisses after I gave up cigarettes. There was a night or two of dry humping, as we called it, which involved my rubbing myself against her until I climaxed, but there had been no touching under the clothing, until that night. They say that the smoothest and softest skin is that of a woman's inner thigh. Sarah's skin felt like that everywhere on her body; smooth skin, smoother than silk, softer than satin and warm, alive, pliable flesh with its vital and unique texture. The chill that had driven us indoors was gone replaced now by flushed and heated flesh that wept a fine mist of perspiration. I removed my shirt, she her sweater, and our bodies touched very lightly, teasingly, before pressing together tightly. Her soft breasts spread out under the pressure of my embrace and then sprang back into their tear-shaped contours when we parted. My heart was pounding so hard I was breathless from its concussion and my excitement made muscles all over my body jerk out of my control, as though I was receiving tiny electric shocks, but stopping was unthinkable. We rolled apart only long enough to shed the rest of our clothing and then fell back into one another's arms. When we looked into each other's faces we'd smile but we never spoke. Rolling onto my back I pulled her on top of me and slipped my erection against the moisture between her legs. I wanted to look at her almost as much as I craved holding onto her, pressing her against me, running my hands over her body, over the slightly moist and warm flesh that rose and swelled into buttocks and thighs and neck and brow. She pressed her thighs together enclosing me and began to rock slowly at first, then more intensely and more eagerly, all the while staring into my eyes until our excitement drove me to release, ejaculating wildly, an ammonia like smell rising from the creamy ejaculum running down our legs. Life is never more complete than at that stunned, satiated moment after climax, one that for all its vigorous force is as insubstantial as a dream; intense, alive with power, and then gone even as you try to sustain its presence and arrest its departure.

"We should quarrel about Harlan more often," I said, "that was fantastic."

"Well, it was okay but fantastic? For you more than me."

"You're kidding, right?" I was surprised by her reaction, surprised and hurt. She just shrugged.

3.

After that night I began to look at Harlan through different eyes. Sarah had been so certain that it was Harlan with her camper's mother that I no longer could lull myself with easy assurances that he was simply the honey that drew flies. Would honey want flies in its syrup or did Harlan want his syrup in these honeys was the question. After all, the woman on the tennis court, the woman on the softball field, the women who flirted with him, these all could not have been members of an aggressive tribe of Amazons. And then I remembered the woman at the pool who wanted Harlan to teach her son to dive. Her little boy's name was David. Half the children in the camp were probably named David, a favorite name for Jewish boys, but Harlan had agreed to teach that one only after a careful appraisal of the mother's physical assets. The more I thought about it the clearer it became that he must have encouraged these women, given some indication he was interested or available or both. But why should that have mattered so much to me? Wasn't it the ambition of every healthy young man to bed as many women, scores and scores if possible, before he found that one true love he would take away with him and then live happily ever after? I was certain that it was not envy or jealousy that was propelling my feelings about Harlan's seductions and liaisons. Only a fool would begrudge a Cary Grant or a Robert Redford his amorous successes and to me Harlan was in possession of that kind of star-like charisma. It was his disloyalty, his betrayal of Heidi that had gotten to me. Sarah was right to mistrust him. That woman on the softball field was not Doris Braverman and there never was a birthday party for Heidi that week.

While this realization discomfited me it did not put me off enough to distance myself from Harlan and his plot to retrieve his father's ring. The reservations I'd had on the first hearing had been discarded, my credulity triumphing on Harlan's behalf. And why not? This whole story, his father the notorious missing judge Crater, a precious, ancient heirloom lost on the grounds of the hotel I had known for years and was now working for, Harlan's quest to retrieve the ring for his dying father, it was irresistible. It was as though I was living as a character in a great and grand novel, an observer somewhat peripheral to the main plot but always available to witness its unfolding. Who would not be enchanted by such a tale? And who would turn his back and walk away from the chance to participate in and maybe even affect the outcome of the story? It was impossible for me to even consider such a course.

And for all the suspicion about Harlan that Sarah had stirred in me, my nagging doubts about him and his seeming disloyalty, there was still a desire to win his admiration and affection with a grand and unexpected act of discovery. I wanted to find that ring. I could not yet redefine him as a bad person, a calculating and self-serving opportunist, a grifter. That sounded like Ron's and Abe's position, a sour grapes position. No, I wouldn't boast to Sarah about my loyalty but I wouldn't relinquish it either. At least not then.

4.

Harlan woke me with a gentle tug on my shoulder. Expecting his summons I was prepared to be very quiet and simply nodded to him. My clothes were balled up at the foot of the bed and I took them into the hall with me and dressed in the shower room. The snores of one sleeper, more like the ratcheting of a metal gear than the sawing of a log, disturbed the early morning stillness of the quarters.

"Do you . . ." Harlan put his hand across my mouth and shook his head sternly. Grasping me by the elbow he led me out the door and did not speak until we were well away from the building. "Loud as that snoring was it becomes like a white noise, a soft protective curtain of sound, and even a whisper can wake someone if he hears that. Now, you get over to the lawn beside Heidi's house and I'll go to the field near Lenny's. Don't slink or look suspicious, you're not doing anything wrong you're just looking for my I.D. bracelet, OK?"

"It's five fifteen, is half an hour enough time?" I was worried that Ron would wake up before six and wonder where I'd gone. He was used to seeing Harlan's bed empty at that hour but would be very interested in knowing where I'd disappeared to.

"Half an hour is fine. It's just to divert attention from what I'm doing, don't worry." We waved and separated.

The birds were chirping happily at the dawn but a pack of crows began a raucous protest as I intruded too close to their area of the grounds. Disney had convinced me that crows were the gangsters of the bird world. He caricatured them sporting battered porkpie hats and gripping cigarettes in their pointy beaks. Frowning and arching an eyebrow at them I walked onto the Braverman property and slipped around the side of the house. There were some sounds of people stirring inside and I hunched over and scurried to the side lawn. It was beginning to feel like this wasn't such a good idea after all. Why would Harlan send me here when it made much better sense for him to be the one searching the area near Heidi's house. The grass was wet and in need of a mowing and each step I took left a record of my trail. Crouching on my haunches and brushing the grass aside, I raked my fingers through the growth and hoped no one inside the house would see me, but if they did at the least it would appear as though a search was in progress. As a boy whenever I lost something in the park I would toss a heavy object, a cap pistol or a baseball, up in the air and then scour the site where it landed for the missing object hoping that serendipity had guided the landing. That had worked once or twice and wedded me to the process with an unrealistic loyalty. There was nothing heavy with me to toss in the air, nothing lost to find here, but I told myself to bring something the next time anyway. Still on my haunches I ventured further into the side garden. Harlan should be the one searching here and I should be scouring the field near the old gambling room, I thought, raking my fingers through the moist grass. After fifteen more minutes of fruitless search I heard an alarm clock go off in the house and scurried through the range of trees framing the side of the yard that abutted the main building of the hotel. That half hour had seemed to take years. My hands were green with grass stains and there were dark lines under my fingernails where the soil had embedded itself. I was supposed to be a decoy and yet I found myself thinking seriously about ways I might actually discover the missing fictitious bracelet. When I appreciated the absurdity of this it became even clearer to me how passionately I wanted to be the one to find the judge's ring. The morning charade could continue for a while but there would be times, maybe right after a meal when the dishwashers were working or at night when they were passed out drunk, when it would be possible to search that field. To find that ring and bring that prize back to Harlan and the judge would be to become a hero of a sort. No dragon slain, no battles waged but a treasure wrested from the earth, a treasure the dying judge cherished and longed for. I marched confidently back to the bunkhouse. I'd do it, damn it, whatever it might take. I'd find that goddamn gimmal ring myself.

Harlan met me as we approached the quarters from opposite directions.

"How'd it go?" he asked.

"Fine. I don't think anybody saw me. How about you, did you find anything?" Smirking and releasing a burst of air through his nose in an attenuated laugh he extended his arm and opened his hand to display a collection of rusty old "Meyer's 1890" soda bottle caps which he then flipped over his shoulder into the grass behind him.

"I know it's out there somewhere. I've just got to make more time to find it without attracting attention."

"What if we go to that field to throw a ball around after lunch. I'll throw you grounders and you throw me pop flies that I keep dropping. That way we can both poke around in the grass without looking like we're looking."

"Why choose that place for a catch when no one ever goes there? That's the kind of action that would bring attention and that's just exactly what we're trying to avoid." Recognizing my disappointment he added, "Anyway, we might pass out with all the cheap booze in the air. Let me take care of this and you keep on being a decoy at the Braverman's for a while until I think of an alternative place for you to search." He looked off into space, pressed his lips together into a narrow line and then smiled. "I know that ring is still out there somewhere, Jack, I feel it and I just know it's there. And I am going to be the one who finds it, nobody else."

"I know how strongly you feel about that," I said, not admitting my own ambition to beat him to it, "but I was thinking that it really makes more sense for you to be the decoy and me to do the search in the field." His brows pressed down on his eyes and frown lines appeared at the corners of his mouth.

"What are you talking about, didn't you hear what I said?"

"Of course I did, but look, if you're crawling around Heidi's yard," I deliberately chose to make it Heidi's yard, not the Bravermans', "it would be no big deal, while I would have a harder time explaining my reason for being there. And anyway, people are much more curious about what you do than they are about me so if I go searching in that field it won't make other people start creeping around in the grass there too." My logic seemed impeccable.

"No. That's not what I want to do. I told you how important it is for me to be the one who finds that ring. No, damn it, I'm the one who finds that ring, Jack, I am!" He was agitated and more upset than I thought reasonable, but I nodded my assent and dropped the discussion. We snuck back into our room without disturbing Ron and got ready to wash up for breakfast. I still was not sure that I'd relinquish my part in the quest. I hated the thought of being just a decoy, a dummy. But I endured it for two more mornings before it was abruptly called to a halt.

Chapter Nine

The break after lunch was usually our time to refresh our selves. There was maybe an hour or an hour and a half between breakfast and lunch and the dinner meal kept us in the dining room until dark so the mid-afternoon break was the only good opportunity for some recreation. In the first weeks I'd swim a bit and then retire to the basketball court and get in line to run in for lay-ups when the All Stars took a break or waited for them to finish practice so some of us could play a half-court game—three on three—but once Sarah came into my life I did these things less and less. A few times a week I'd go for a swim but I was usually so bone tired I'd jump into the shower after work and then rest on my bed with a book or a magazine. Sarah and I would be up late into the night talking and petting and exploring new sexual frontiers, activities we both preferred to other recreational choices. And for the past few mornings I'd been crawling around at dawn acting as a decoy in Harlan's search for his father's ring so I was even more sleep deprived than usual. Of course, I had not mentioned a word about meeting judge Crater to Ron who continued his pursuit of television journalists from New York to Boston in the hope of bringing a camera to the old well at the hotel. There were no takers and I told him that apart from writing letters to the editors of the Daily News, The Mirror, The New York Post, the Herald Tribune and the Times, I would have no more of it. In fact I had written only to the Post and the Mirror, not the other papers, and now saw no reason to do so. In fact, aware of how worried Harlan and his family were about the discovery of the judge's identity, I hoped no one would grant Ron's assertions credibility and respect. Why should they, he was wrong.

We were well into August and with an early Labor Day coming up, it would fall on September third, there wasn't much summer left to us. I was already thinking about starting school and planning trips upstate to visit Sarah at college once we were settled in and that softened the blow of having to trudge along yet again in Jerry and Steve's footsteps. The uniqueness of my first love, my Sarah, was my salvation.

I had showered and was in my underwear resting in bed reading a Life magazine when Harlan entered the room. His face was haggard and drawn and he was clearly distressed. He sat down on his bed, got up, lit a Lucky Strike, sat down again, and released a long, soughing sigh. There were tears in his eyes. "Are you all right?' I asked, startling him.

"Jesus, Jack, I didn't know you were up there." With the cigarette dangling limply from his mouth he rubbed at his eyes with his fists to clear the tears, then rose and approached me. "It's my father, he's very ill." He took a deep breath and sighed again. "I spoke with his doctor in Newburgh. He wants him in the hospital for treatment. He said there's an operation that could save his life but it would cost a lot of money, more than we have. Even if I put in all of my earnings, all of the money that was to pay for my tuition and room and board for my senior year at Harvard next year, we'd still be short. Damn it! If only I'd found that damn ring of his, it must be worth a few thousand dollars at least."

"You mean you'd sell it?"

"I mean I'd do whatever I have to do to pay for that operation." He wiped his face with his hand, walked over to his cot and stood with his back to me, his head slumped forward. The hallway became quiet as the ballplayers receded to the shower room and the sound of Harlan's breathing, the drafty sound of air rushing in and out of his nose, grew louder. His shoulders convulsed for an instant then slumped and I heard the breath of air that he inhaled ratcheting through the knot of muscle at his throat. He shook his head briskly, as if he'd just broken through the surface of a swimming pool and was ridding his face of water, then wiped at his brow with his hand. "Sorry," he said.

"That five thousand dollar reward . . ."

"Out of the question. His life would be a living hell if his true identity were known. The reporters, the gossip columnists, the potential lawsuits from Mary, it would be hell."

"I could let you borrow five, no six, six hundred dollars if you think that would help." As soon as I said it I wished I could take it back. That money was meant for college and I couldn't afford to give it away but the wish to please Harlan could still take control of me.

"How much do you have in the bank now, six hundred? A thousand? How much do you have Jack?" Suddenly his face was barely a foot away from mine, his eyes wide, his gaze intense.

"About a thousand, but I can't let you have . . . I mean I can't lend you all of that money. It's for school."

"What if I get it back to you before you need it for school? What if I promise you that your money will be in your hands the day you go to register for classes, would you trust me with your money then?"

"But if you could get it back to me that fast why would you have to borrow it in the first place?"

"This is an emergency! he shouted in his agitation. "Maybe I didn't make it clear enough to you, this is an emergency. He needs that operation soon, this week or next at the latest."

"Can't you owe the money for a while? Do you have to pay for everything before he goes to the hospital?"

"Yes." His voice softened and he looked away. "He could die in this operation, Jack. Doctors know that with a risk like that they may not get paid if the patient doesn't survive so the surgeon will want me to pay for this in advance. I have about seventeen hundred dollars. When you add it all up, the surgeon, the anesthetist, the hospital charges—he'll be there for a month or two—it'll cost four, maybe five thousand dollars. I just don't have enough." He looked up at me through eyes dark with a terrible sadness. "I shouldn't be asking you for this, I know that, but it is my *father*, do you understand? Would you do any less for yours?" He buried his face in his hands and wept. I felt a terrible helplessness and didn't know what to do. "Forget it I can't take your money, Jack, you'll need it for school. It would be great if everyone were as generous as you are but, well, that's life isn't it? It's funny when you think about it; here we are, surrounded by tens of thousands of dollars in tips that were collected three and five dollars at a time, and just one small fraction of that could save my father's life. I suppose that's what makes life such an ironic form of torture." Hearing those last words I felt guilty for not giving him my money, all of it, every penny.

Then, what he had said struck home to me. There was a small fortune stored in the local banks, the savings of the hundreds of waiters and busboys who served the guests at the mountain resort hotels. While five or six hundred dollars might be too much to ask of a person, twenty or even fifty dollars to save a man's life was certainly reasonable, maybe even possible. "What if I were to ask the guys in the dining room to donate to a fund to help pay for your father's surgery, you know, twenty or fifty dollars each. I bet even the Bravermans would be willing to donate . . ."

"I don't want the Braverman's involved in this. They already tell Heidi that I'm only interested in her for her money so don't say anything to them." He looked over his shoulder at me. "You're a good friend Jack. That's a nice thought but I don't want my father's identity revealed, it would mean the end of his privacy forever."

"Why would his name have to be anything other than Mr. Hawthorne just like you're Harlan Hawthorne." He laughed and shook his head.

"You're right! I'm so focused on his being judge Crater I forget that that's a secret only a few of us know." His smile faded again. "I don't know, I don't have that many friends in the dining room and I do seem to have some enemies. Ron, Abe, Spider and maybe even Sammy himself."

"Ron yes, Abe maybe, but not Sammy, and I don't know who else you could be thinking of when you say enemies. Let me try to do this for you. I'm sure Sarah would be glad to help too." If I was sure about anything it was that Sarah would see this as some kind of scheme on Harlan's part and definitely would not offer to help out.

"Sarah will tell Heidi and that will just bring the Bravermans into it. Don't tell Sarah. In fact I don't see how you can tell anyone without it becoming common knowledge that you're trying to raise money for my father's operation." He paused, turned away, looked back at me and turned away again. "Of course! No, that wouldn't be right."

'What were you going to say?"

"Well, and I can't see how you could do it, if . . . no forget it, it would never work."

"Goddamnit! Tell me your idea, Harlan, tell me the damned idea and let me decide if I think it can be done."

"Okay, okay, calm down Jack. Well, what if we said you needed the money for your father's operation. Hell, people would be glad to help you."

"I don't know, a lot of people here know my family, Sammy, Rudy, even the Bravermans themselves. It wouldn't take long for one of them, somebody, to call my parents or one of my brothers, I just don't see how we could get that to work."

"Yeah, yeah I see the problem." Once again his shoulders slumped as if finding the money was a weight that would crush him. Their showers over the ballplayers came back into the hallway, their boisterous commotion preceding their return up the narrow corridor. Harlan chuckled. "Boys being boys." Then, suddenly, he grew sombre. "It requires tragedy to make men of boys." His simple words landed upon me with the weight of the truth.

"Maybe that's what we need, a tragedy of some kind that people would be willing to give money for. But what could that be?"

"It's a good thought, but you're right; what could that be?" We searched each other's faces as though we might find an answer. "You know, if it was your tragedy we'd have no problem raising the money; people would gladly donate money for your problem."

"Well, as I said, there'd be no way to keep people from calling my parents or my brothers if I said my father was sick."

"No, no, I mean your problem—*you*; maybe we can get people to give money because you are the one who's got the tragic illness. The question then is how to keep it just among the waiters and busboys." He frowned and furrowed his brow with the effort of his concentration.

"I know! It wouldn't be me, it would be me who's responsible. Say I got somebody pregnant and she needed to have an abortion and . . ."

"You could afford that Jack. It might cost some money but no more than any waiter or busboy has already put away."

"But suppose there were complications, more hospital bills, more doctor bills, things like that, wouldn't that be a reason to raise the money and keep it a secret too?"

"And Sarah? You'd be willing to risk her hearing that story? I don't think you'd want that to happen. No, I'll just have to work something else out." Again this burden seemed to crush him. "Well, at least I can lend you six hundred, no, make it seven hundred. I won't need that back right away because I should still have almost another five hundred by Labor Day and that will be more than enough for expenses for the first term. I would have to keep this from my parents, but, hell, it's my hard-earned money and I'll lend it whether or not they like it." Harlan smiled at me and laid his hand over mine. Tears filled his eyes.

"I can't begin to tell you how much this means to me, Jack. I've always known you were a friend, a special guy and this really proves it. I won't let you down, I promise. I'll get the money back to you but I have to find a way to raise the rest. You give it some thought too, okay?"

"I will, Harlan, I'll think about a way maybe while I'm searching for the ring." He grinned.

2.

Sarah did not meet me at the usual time that Wednesday night. The day camp counselors had scheduled an after-dinner party for their eight to eleven year old campers, something special to give these children a taste of the social excitement that their approaching puberty and adolescence would introduce them to in the near future, but a taste of the sweet expectations only. The bitter disappointments and rejections that each might confront in the coming years were thoughtfully excluded. Then, after the children skipped happily away home, the staff would clean up and begin the first of their year-end evaluations and reviews of how the summer had gone. Sarah had been happy with her work and with the youngsters she cared for and because she was recognized to be by nature a positive and generous spirit her comments, as was expected, were devoid of either cynicism or complaint. I knew this to be the case because she had read her comments to me just a few nights before and I marveled at her ability to keep focused on the loveable attributes and humanity of everyone she worked with. I was also a little hurt by her need to focus on these comments to the exclusion of any intimacy with me.

Returning to my room around nine o'clock and thinking it likely that Sarah was still involved in her meeting I showered and lay down for a nap hoping to stir myself around ten and go to meet her. Ron and Harlan had come and gone quickly and we'd barely spoken. The tension between them was very wearing and ever since meeting Sarah I had little interest in trying to mediate their dispute. Ron was accustomed to irritating people with his abrasive personality but Harlan, familiar only with my idolatrous side, seemed almost hurt by my suddenly flagging interest.

"Have I done something to upset you, Jack? You seem different with me, distant."

"Really? No. I guess I'm just so into Sarah nothing else seems to be important to me. Did you ever feel that way with a girl? Does Heidi make you feel that way?" I saw his face set, a strange adjustment in the muscles and tone, subtle but distinct, a reaction he had whenever I tried to inquire about Heidi; it said to me "keep away from there."

"I know what you're referring to, Jack, it's just that you can't allow any woman to become an obsession. That only alienates your friends and, before you know it, it alienates the woman too. Then you're left with nothing." I was speechless. His response seemed disproportionate to what I'd said. So, I shrugged, nodded, faked a look of thoughtful surprise, cocked my head and left our room.

The noise level in the building that night was in its usual range, a few people listening to their radios tuned to the same station that was playing Elvis's "Heartbreak Hotel" which sounded less irritating to me than it did the first few times I'd heard it. Not only didn't I like Elvis's music I didn't like what it represented to me: change. There was something subversive in his music and his style, something that wanted to upend the world as I knew it, the world I was equipped to engage. Thinking about Elvis and his mutiny of the social order made me weary, though this was a disquieting idea, and I must have dozed off while considering it because later I was awakened by someone tugging on my arm.

"Hey, Jack. Jack get up or you'll miss Sarah."

"Jesus, Harlan, what time is it?" But I looked at my wristwatch before he could answer and seeing it was already 11:30 threw my legs over the edge of the bed and sat up. "Christ, it's late."

"Maybe you should just forget about going out tonight. What's one night more or less?" In a summer romance one night more is always a festival crowded with glorious hours of revelry, one night less, a wasteland.

"No, I want to see Sarah. Besides, I'll never get back to sleep now right after a nap." Harlan shrugged and walked to his bed.

"Better hurry or it will be tomorrow before you see her."

It was a clear night and the brilliance of the full moon illuminated the hotel's buildings and grounds with a brightness that seemed unnatural, as if one were walking in the artificial light of a photographer's studio. The ambience was surreal with planes of harsh light flattening out the contours of the trees and driving the shadows receding from them into a depthless darkness. The band had quit for the night, the usual noise from the hotel casino was gone and a glacial silence overhung the landscape. I felt as though I had walked into a black and white photograph and the feeling of unreality this engendered was disorienting. Walking quickly towards Sarah's dormitory I was suddenly overtaken with intense feelings of love. Imagining her twirling towards me, dancing out of the darkness, quickened my breathing and made me dizzy as though it had been I who was twirling around and around. This sudden and urgent intensity of love for her was overwhelming and why it should have felt so profound right then and there was a feeling fraught with some alarm. It was as though, somehow, I had sensed I was going to lose her. She had said nothing to suggest a change of heart, had in fact been wonderfully loving the night we fought and made up, but something was different, something I could not put into words.

The window of her room looked out onto the porch of the old building that housed the girls working at the hotel. The room was dark but a broad shaft of moonlight had penetrated the window illuminating her curled form lying atop her bed. She had fallen asleep in clothing she might have worn were she going home to New York City, a gray suit, white blouse and sheer stockings; short white gloves covered her hands. It was odd that she should be dressed in such a manner on a weeknight and I worried that she had gotten some bad news from home and would have to leave in the morning or, worse still, that for her own reasons she was leaving for good. The feeling that I could be losing her seemed to have been justified after all but I calmed myself thinking it more likely to be just another of the manifestations of her feminine mystique. She and Heidi seemed always to be trying on clothes, configuring outfits, trying out lipsticks and makeup, changing hairstyles and experimenting with eye shadow. The arrangement of a single lock of hair, insignificant to the casual male observer, could make all the difference in her mind between her feeling alluring and attractive or hopelessly dowdy and plain. I leaned forward to whisper her name through the open window and wake her but stopped when she shifted on the bed and her face was suddenly bathed in blue-white moonlight. She was so beautiful. The light had disturbed her and as her eyes slowly opened she awakened from a peaceful sleep. Then, startled by my silhouette in the window, her jaw dropped and she drew a quick, fearful breath relaxing only when she recognized me.

"You startled me," she said, stretching her arms up on either side of her head, yawning, then smiling and lowering them to her sides. "How long have you been out there?"

"Not long. Why are you so dressed up?" She curled up again, her face averted from me, and took a deep breath.

"Just trying on clothes, what time is it?" she asked sleepily.

"Midnight."

"Midnight?" she said in disbelief, "is it too late for you?"

"No, it's not that late." I looked into her room and seeing the other bed was empty I asked, "Where's Barbara?"

"I think she went to stay in Swan Lake with her boyfriend."

"Staying the whole night?"

"Yes. She's always wanted to do that and since it's already close to the end of summer I think she felt she'd take the risk of being late for work in the morning."

"Wanna take a risk yourself?" With her roommate Barbara away I hoped that maybe we could stay together for one night.

"I know what you're thinking, Mel. You're thinking that with her away you could sleep in my room with me, right?"

"Well, why not?" Sarah rolled over on her bed and stared at me.

"I don't think you should do that. I'm uncomfortable with that."

"What if I just come into your room for a while and lie on the bed with you?" It would be the first time we would hold and touch each other on a bed with clean linens rather than on a musty cushion in a dim and dusty storage shed, the first time we could be loving in a private but not deliberately hidden way. "I promise not to fall asleep." Smiling, her lips pursed, she said, "Just for one hour."

Rather than walk into the building I hoisted myself up on to her window ledge and climbed into her room. "If I knew it was that easy I'd have done this before," I said, kicking off my loafers and sitting on her bed.

"If I knew it was that easy I'd have put barbed wire on the window sill," she said giving me a little shove. I pulled her closer to me but she ducked out from under my arm.

"Let me get out of these clothes first."

"It will be my pleasure," I said, sprawling on my stomach and cupping my chin in my palms to watch her as if she were about to do a striptease just for me.

"What do you think you're doing?"

"I'm watching you get undressed."

"No you're not. Turn the other way." She was blushing.

"Come on, what's the big deal, I've seen you nak . . . undressed."

"This is different, Mel, it feels creepy. When we're petting things seem to just happen naturally but taking off my clothes in front of you, just like that, well, I don't know," She turned her back to me. I could see her discomfort, like someone caught off guard and embarrassed, but I was excited and didn't want her to turn away from me when she undressed. I got up from her bed and went to her, grasping her shoulders when I stood behind her.

"Let me help you then," I said, sliding my hand down her arm and reaching around to unbutton her jacket. She leaned in to me, her small frame suddenly seeming smaller upright than it did when we lay beside each other. I undid the three buttons of her jacket, slipped it off her shoulders and let it drop to the floor. A shiver trembled along the length of her body and, as if in sympathy, a shudder coursed down my right leg. "Now this," I said, unbuttoning her blouse at the neck with my right hand while sliding my left hand under her arm and onto her breast. The contour of her brassiere cupped her softness firmly but I could feel her nipple rise to my touch. Restraining my excitement, left unchecked I'd have torn her clothes from her body, I slowly stripped the blouse from her, and then her brassiere so that she stood there, her back to me, naked to the waist, in her skirt, stockings, and short white gloves. "Now the skirt." I unbuttoned the tab at the back and unzipped the zipper slowly, my hand trembling and almost snagging the zipper as it descended. Her skirt sank to her feet and as I pulled down her half-slip she peeled the short white gloves from her hands. My legs trembled with excited spasms that threatened to pitch me over on to the floor.

"That's enough, now what about you?" she said, turning to look me up and down. I pulled my crew neck sweater over my head and stripped off my shirt. I had stopped wearing undershirts just that summer. It looked more rugged and manly to be bare-chested under your shirt, more Dean Martin, less Jerry Lewis. I undid my trousers and when they fell to my ankles I kicked them off, my erection tenting my underpants in front of me. Sarah giggled. "Let's lie down," she said taking my hand and leading us to her bed. I was so excited I was breathless. In each other's arms we fell on the bed, our mouths searching for the entryway into the union in which boundaries disappear and a fusion occurs. The few, scant underclothes remaining came off as we rolled over and under one another with my erection gripped against her moistness, our mouths joined as if breathing life from each other. I wanted to enter her, I had to be inside her, I had to be completely one with her. I raised my body from hers and looking into her eyes I said, "Let me come inside you now." Her lips were swollen and she had a dreamy unfocused look in her eyes. She moaned. "Please, Sarah, let me make love to you." My words tore through her reverie. A look of alarm crossed her face and she suddenly came alert as if startled by a stranger in the dark.

"Don't you think we're going a little too fast?" she said in her small, tentative voice.

"I want . . ."

"No," she said more forcefully, fully awake, "not yet, Mel."

"Yes, now, don't be afraid it'll be all right," I urged.

"No!" she said and jumped up from her bed. "No, not now. No."

And all the harshness of the names I'd learned to use for my male member,—cock, prick, dick, all those stiff, assaultive and disonant consonants that batter aggressively at the soft feminine dominion of pussy and poon like weapons, like rock, like stick and pick, descended in a sudden and embarrassing cacophony to disgrace and shame me. Once again my lust had mortified me. I slumped on her bed. She was right; maybe we had been going too fast.

"Why must you insist on pushing me to do something I'm not ready to do?" She was stern.

"I'm sorry, I get carried away with you, I'm sorry."

"That is not going to happen this summer. I am not going to have intercourse with you this summer. It's not about you, it's what I promised myself before I came up here. I knew what might happen, what people do, and I didn't want this to be my summer of regret. Can you understand what I'm telling you?"

"Yes, Sarah." Yes, there'd be no consummation, just consuming desire.

"Okay." She stroked my face with her palm. "Get some sleep, you have work in a few hours."

3.

When I returned to my room Harlan and Ron were still out and the bunkhouse was fairly quiet. There would be traffic in and out of the building throughout the night and a radio might be turned on too loud at an odd hour but we were generally pretty considerate of one another and kept the noise to a minimum. My shame had begun to relent; nothing bad had actually happened I assured myself. Sarah was protecting her virginity and as much as I wanted to lose mine, it would not be with her. She hadn't sent me away or said it's over. Sarah was being true to herself and I was going to have to accept that. I was still in love with her and Sarah hadn't said "never" she'd said "not this summer" so what was I moping for?

I washed up at one of the sinks in the shower room, brushed my teeth and picked at a few pimples before returning to my room and changing for bed. The door to Abe's room had been left ajar and I tiptoed past in the hope of avoiding any contact with him. His unsolicited counsel about Harlan still irked me. I had climbed into the upper bunk and was just straightening my covers when I heard his voice.

"You in there Melvin?" Shit. He had come out of his room and across the hall as noiseless as a shadow. "Melvin?" and this time he rapped gently on the closed door.

"Yeah, who is it?" I said, pretending not to know.

"It's Abraham." To my recollection he had never used his full name before nor spoken so clearly and forcefully. It was as though the majesty of all three syllables had straightened his spine, expanded his lungs, and thickened his vocal cords.

"I'm very tired Abe, I was just falling asleep." It was a very deliberate choice not to call him Abraham. Whatever new dignity he was striving for was not my concern.

"I just want to talk to you for a minute. Let me come in." The door was closed but unlocked and he could have entered if he had insisted but I knew he was too timid to do that—at least that was what I thought. The one rule we all obeyed and strived not to violate was our right to privacy. But Abe was very determined that night and opened the door without invitation. "Only a minute and then I'll go," he said closing the door behind him. I exhaled loudly and refused to look at him staring instead at the circular marks on the ceiling made by the Spalding rubber ball Ron and I had been throwing there all summer long.

"Ben Braverman asked me to ask you what you are doing crawling around in his yard in the middle of the night."

"Looking for Harlan's I.D. bracelet." My voice did not crack but it was a struggle to get the words through my throat. I'd been seen and though I'd done nothing wrong still there was guilt. "Looking for Harlan's what? Harlan's I.D. bracelet? What are you his servant, his lackey, his his . . . his *flunky*?" Abe fumed and blustered indignantly giving me time to compose myself.

"No, I'm just his friend. Will there be anything else?" I said, using the David Niven voice trick. This was beginning to feel good. The sound of Abe's restless shifting made me look in his direction. Once again he was unfolding and refolding Harlan's blanket. "Is there?"

"Yes. You didn't listen to me when I tried to tell you that your friend has something missing. Now I know what it is. It's not something that's visible to the naked eye but to the spirit, that's already a different story. He's missing something that makes human beings different from the other animals, he's missing a conscience." Abe's voice dripped with piety.

"Finished? Because if you are I'd like you to leave so I can go to sleep."

"I'm finished for now, Melvin, but I'm not finished with you. You should only know how lucky you are that I am your friend. Ben Braverman was ready to fire you for crawling around near his house. What's the matter with you, are you meshugah? Let Harlan crawl around the Braverman's for his jewelry, but is it really his own jewelry that he is looking for? Is it?"

"Who's looking for jewelry?" Ron asked as he entered. Abe started to answer him but I interrupted not wanting this to become a dump on Harlan rally.

"Abe was just leaving, Ron. It wasn't anything important."

"Wasn't important!? He almost loses his job for creeping around the lawn at the Braverman house in the middle of the night, but it isn't important?" He got up from Harlan's bed and approached Ron. "This boy is in love, and I'm not referring to Sarah."

"Get out, Abe, you sonofabitch, get the hell out of here."

"What kind of a way is that to talk to Abe? In love with who? Who is Mel in love with?" I threw my legs over the edge of the bed to jump down but Ron grabbed me by the ankles locking me in place. "Abe, tell me who you're talking about."

"It's whom not who. I'd better go. Melvin, I'd like to be your friend, excuse me, I am your friend, you just don't know it yet." Even after Abe left Ron would not release his grip and squeezed me until it hurt.

"Who was Abe talking about? Ohhhh, not Heidi for godsakes."

"I don't know who he was talking about and no, I'm not in love with Heidi. Sarah is just fine with me, more than I ever imagined I'd have. Now let go of me." And I pulled my legs back underneath the blanket and turned to face the wall. The contest for which hurt more at that moment, Ron's bruising grip or Abe's stinging words, ended in a draw.

"What were you doing crawling around the Braverman's house at night anyway, trying to peep on old Ben and Molly?"

"Drop it Ron. Just forget it."

"What was the jewelry he was talking about? How can you expect me to just drop this? This sounds really interesting. Come on, spit it out Melvin, I'm not quitting and I'll get nasty if I have to."

"Well, that shouldn't be much of a reach for you." He punched me in the buttock and stripped off my blanket and sheet.

"You re really pissing me off wise ass, and you'd better cut it out if you know what's good for you. Now tell me what the fuck is Abe talking about!" When I turned to look at him his face was contorted with anger.

"I was looking for Harlan's I.D. bracelet, that's all. Harlan lost it last week and asked me to help him search for it, okay? Satisfied?"

"What I.D. bracelet? Harlan doesn't have an I.D. bracelet, he never wore one once all summer long. Do you think I'm an idiot?"

"When he comes back to the room, ask him if he's found his I.D. bracelet yet. See what he says."

"I'll ask him all right but don't you say a word, not one word or I'll kick your ass so . . ." Back from his evening with Heidi, Harlan returned in the middle of Ron's threat.

"Am I interrupting something?" he said as he tossed his wallet and car keys on his cot.

"No, as a matter of fact, you're right on time. So what's this about losing an I.D. bracelet?" Harlan looked at me, then at Ron, and then back at me again.

"Why did you tell him?" He frowned at no one in particular. "Yes, I lost my I.D. bracelet last week and Jack is helping me look for it. Is there anything wrong with that?"

"See!" I said triumphantly.

"You don't have an I.D. bracelet . . ."

"Will you keep it down in there you faggots!" someone called out from down the hall. Ron pulled the door open, almost tearing it from its hinges, shouted "Fuck you!" into the empty space, and then slammed the door shut. "You're up to something, you scumbag, I know you re up to something. Do you know that you almost got Melvin fired for creeping around the Braverman's house in the middle of the night . . ."

"It wasn't the middle of the night it was around dawn," I said.

"What difference does it make, dawn or the middle of the night, you had no business there and you almost got yourself fired, you putz."

"You didn't tell me you got caught, are you in trouble Jack?"

"He goddamn well is in trouble and it's because of you. And stop this goddamned Jack crap! His name is Melvin, Melvin goddammit."

"I'm not in trouble, Harlan, don't listen to him."

Teeth clenched and nostrils flared Ron came towards my bunk, rage reddening his face. "I've had it with you. I've tried to warn you about him, I've tried to teach you a few things, to get you laid, to . . . to let you in on important things that no one else knows about. His voice trailed off while he stared at me with hatred like nothing I had seen before in his eyes, a hatred even more intense than that he'd shown to Joe and Johnny, the townie thugs. "I'm finished being nice to you. I'm finished with you, finished with you and your miserable idolizing of this fake and his phony upper east-side style and moves."

Approaching the double decker Harlan looked at us and said, "Well, that's not so bad is it? To have Ron finished with you may be a bonus in the end. I wish he was finished with me is all I can say. Then his jealousy of me, for God only knows what . . ." but before he could finish Ron interrupted.

"You smarmy sonofabitch. I don't know why you came to this hotel, I don't know what you have up your sleeve, but I know that if I ever catch you doing anything that causes pain to anyone I'll smash you into little bits like a piece of cheap glass." Harlan did not flinch or avert his eyes as Ron delivered his threat. Standing only inches apart the obvious disparity in their size was stunningly clear. Harlan towered over Ron. And more striking still was the frigid, dead-eyed stare, a fearless killing look he gave back to Ron's overheated glare.

Then he said, "I'm not intimidated by you, Ronald, not in the least." I jumped between them, unthinking, and forced them apart. "Cut this out you two, just cut it out. I won't allow this fight to happen. I pushed Harlan back towards his cot knowing that Ron would have resisted me, maybe even taken a punch at me if I had grabbed hold of his shoulders. They continued to stare coldly at each other neither one blinking, neither one speaking, neither one relenting. "Let go of this, you two. There'll be no fight in here tonight and that's it." Grabbing his towel from the railing at the foot of his bed Ron stormed out of the room.

"That was very good, Jack, very brave. Ron could go berserk at any time. I wouldn't trust him if I were you. He's capable of going crazy and causing real harm."

I went back to my bunk and hoisted myself up onto my bed knowing I would say no more to either one the rest of the night. Something I had read before leaving home began repeating over and over in my mind like an annoying jingle or phrase of music that pesters you relentlessly and won't give you peace. "Nothing worth knowing can be taught." As I lay there trying to go to sleep, fully aware that I was too agitated to succeed, Oscar Wilde's words buzzed around and around in my mind persistent as a horsefly: "nothing worth knowing can be taught". It's about experience, I said to myself, it's about your own experience not someone else's, and that's what is meant when they say experience is the best teacher. That night I had kept Ron and Harlan apart and succeeding with that was so stimulating I was wide awake. "Nothing worth knowing can be taught, nothing worth knowing can be taught." Of course, choosing to force Harlan back from their confrontation made the intervention easy; I took Harlan's self-control for granted. But I was not yet willing to truly believe what my experience was trying to teach me about Harlan. Was I on the verge of coming to terms with the complexities of his character, that he was neither a good person nor a bad person but both, good and bad and often at one and the same time? At least that was what I wanted to think. Sarah, Ron and Abe were able to see him only as a bad person, a danger. They hadn't heard him discourse on life, on women, on his own family. Living under the weight of such secrecy had to have had a profound effect upon him and his mysteriousness may have been the product of nothing more forbidding than that. Still, I could not explain these facts to anyone, not even Sarah, at least not until after the summer. She was sensitive enough to understand there was more than he was revealing. She could accept that the whole story isn't always told; that sometimes we remain in the dark; sometimes we are just left to wonder.

Chapter Ten

"I'm going to go into New York for my day off," Sarah said coming up behind me in the dining room after lunch the next day.

"Oh, hi, going to visit your folks?"

"My folks and some other people." She blushed and I saw that she was suddenly very uncomfortable. "Doris, my head counselor, said her husband is driving back into New York after lunch, today, and Doris said I can leave early and get a ride with him. So I'm going now and then I won't be here for our date tonight." I could tell she was trying to hide something from me and she was doing a lousy job.

"What is it that you're not telling me? There's something else going on here, I can tell."

"Well, I didn't want to hurt your feelings but there is a boy that I've been seeing at home who's going to meet me tomorrow." For the first time since we'd started seeing each other I felt jealousy and fear gather me in their arms and squeeze. Who was this "boy" and why hadn't she said something about him before? I sorted the spoons from the forks and staring into the drawer said nothing. That was why she was trying on clothes last night; that was what the suit and gloves were about last night, I thought. "He's somebody I've been dating for about a year and he goes to college near where I'll be going. His name is Hank."

"Do you love him?" I asked in the same voice one might use to ask 'am I going to die?' because the feeling of dread was as intense, and the potential for the answer 'yes' equally devastating.

"I don't know." She looked at her wristwatch, frowned, and put a hand on my shoulder. "I have to go and change. I'll see you when I get back on Saturday. We'll be okay," she said, giving me a peck on the forehead and hurrying off. Christ! I was stunned. How could she be doing all of the physical things that we'd been doing with each other if she was in love with somebody else, somebody with a name like Hank? I felt myself choke up and looked around the dining room. Most of the staff had cleared out and only a few other busboys were around sweeping and straightening up their tables and chairs. The last thing I wanted was to begin bawling in front of everybody so I slammed my silverware drawer shut and hurried out through the kitchen.

It was hot outside. The sun was high and the dusty patch of ground behind the kitchen was bare save for the garbage bins that held the day's detritus from the dining room. I felt myself choke up with grief. She's lied to me, I thought. How could she give me her body so liberally, her breasts and her kisses and her sweet and powdered pussy for me to touch and kiss; how could she let me be with her in that way and still have someone else on her mind? I had no illusions about men being that way but her? Sarah? Men will say they don't need love to have sex with a woman and I believed that was true even if I had had no such experience personally at that time. But Sarah? Her? Slut! Whore! CUNT! my mind screamed. And just the night before when she had said no to me and my wish to enter her, when she said we were going too fast, I had held back, I had retreated and then slinked away ashamed and filled with self-loathing, for this? That was when I broke down and cried, hugging the back of the garbage bin and hiding from the world, sinking to my knees on the barren ground. And what was most humiliating to me as I thought about it huddled there in the stench of the rotting garbage amidst the swarming, buzzing flies was that it was I who was the callow and tender virgin betrayed; I who was the pathetic naif; Me!

When I composed myself I wandered off onto the hotel grounds still wearing my busboy's uniform. We were told not to go to the coffee shop or to any public space in these clothes so by just walking along the driveway I was violating no rules. And if they wanted to fire me, fine! Fuck 'em! Fuck Sarah! She'd come back from New York City all ready to sit me down and lecture me about how I should feel and how I shouldn't think. Wouldn't that be a hoot, her finding that I was already packed and gone. With my head down and my gaze fixed on the pebbled path I almost walked right into Ben Braverman but his two-toned white and brown shoes caught my eyes before I collided with him.

"Looking for something Melvin?" His voice had an amused tone.

"No, sir. Just taking a walk."

"You're not looking for something? I ask you that question because for the last few mornings I've seen you crawling around in my yard at dawn." I looked up at him through eyes wide with fear, eyes that witnessed his expression change from one of bemusement to one of concern. "Are you okay Melvin? You look like you're going to faint, come here." And he put a heavy arm over my shoulder and held me up against himself. "You know, I've known your family for a long time, your father and mother, your two brothers, so don't think that I don't care about what happens to you, but you have to be truthful with me. Are you all right?"

"Yes, yes I'm a little upset about something but I'll be okay," I said, grateful for his nonchalance but wishing he'd release me.

"Well, Melvin, I'm a little upset too. What are you looking for in my yard at the crack of dawn?" His tone had become more challenging.

"Harlan lost his I.D. bracelet somewhere so I'm helping him look for it." Suddenly the notion that this alibi was plausible seemed completely ludicrous, dangerously ignorant. "He thought that if you saw me in your yard you'd be less upset . . ." It was becoming clearer by the nanosecond that this explanation was absurd.

"Vey is meir, it's as bad as Abe says it is. You really are blind when it comes to Harlan. What is the matter with you aren't two big brothers enough for you?" That infuriated me. I wasn't going to lose both Sarah and my sense of dignity in one day.

"Wait a minute, Mr. Braverman, I didn't do anything wrong, I didn't peep on you and your family, I didn't steal anything, I didn't . . ."

"Calm down Melvin, it's not your fault. That Harlan Hawthorne cocksucker would sell you out as soon as shake your hand. He has something up his sleeve and I just haven't figured out what it is yet. He removed his arm from my shoulder but turned me to face him. "I don't want you to say anything to him about what I just said, do you hear me? If you do then the innocent crawling around in my yard will become a criminal act and the South Fallsburg police will not be kind to you, understand?" I nodded wondering if he talked to Heidi about Harlan in this way. Then startlingly, as if reading my mind, he spoke directly to that question. "My sweet Heideleh is beginning to lose some of her infatuation with this ganef. She's learned her father is not such an ignorant putz after all. I warned her right from the start. She still spends time with Harlan but she's much more cautious. You're little girlfriend Sarah told her about his fooling around with another woman, the mother of one her campers, so she's very upset that this bum Harlan would do that to her. Cheating. That's a terrible thing to do to somebody."

"Yeah, I know." What I didn't know was whether Sarah would be cheating on me that night with Hank or, if by being with me, she had been cheating on this guy Hank for the last three weeks. And why her sudden hankering for Hank? All at once a flood of images came cascading through my mind, scenes of Sarah lying naked, each breast listing a little to the side, the hand of a faceless man stroking her crotch; Sarah on her side, the columnar swell of her thigh joining with a rounded capital of buttock supporting the pediment of her back; the mischievious look on her face as she reaches down between my legs and seizes my erection in her hand. But is it me that she's grasping for in this picture?

'What is it Melvin, you look sick, are you all right?"

"Yeah. No. I think I have to go back to my room."

"Let me help you back. I'll help you and then maybe there's something you can do to help me out. Once again he draped his arm across my shoulders and started walking me back towards the waiters' quarters.

Ben was still robust and strong for a man in his sixties. He was as tall as I and stood quite erect. He had a full head of snow white hair that he trimmed short and wore unparted, large shoulders and powerful arms. There was a bulge at his waist but nothing you would call a pot belly. Looking at him and weighing the possibility I believed that he was definitely capable of doing what Ron had described to me my first day at Braverman's: angrily kicking a man to death. "So, I hear you're curious about my nephew Abe."

"Where did you hear that from?"

"Where else? From Abe! Abe is a good listener. He spends his time listening in on the conversations around him." He leaned forward and turned his face to be in front of mine. "Surprised Melvin? I run a big business here, I need to have information."

"So it's true that Abe is a member of your family. Does he eat with your family, is that why we don't see him in the kitchen at meal times?"

"True, it's all true. Want to know what isn't true?" His voice was merry with teasing. "Want to know?" he repeated, causing me to nod my head. "Promise that you'll keep this just between the two of us. I'm telling you because I want to give you an incentive to do something for me. And I'll tell you right now, if you break your promise I'll find out and then the good deed that could befall you will not be done." I stopped in my tracks and turned to him. I had had enough with secrets and mysteries and surprises dropping out of the sky on me like bird shit. Sarah's secret was the only one I wanted exposed; who will it be, me or this Hank guy?

"No offense Mr. Braverman but don't tell me any secrets and don't expect . . ." Grasping my arm with a strong hand, he held and fixed me in place. His face was stern and serious.

"Don't you talk to me that way, sonny, I can be friendly or I can be tough but either way you'll do what I want you to do." A smile spread across his lips like a cloud changing shape in the sky. "His name is not Abe, it's Bernard. He got those fahrcocteh diplomas in a junk shop. Some poor bastard named Abe Melman either died or went broke, who knows, but he is Bernard Steinberg, my nephew, my older sister's oldest son, not Abe Melman." I was more wary of this story than surprised. I no longer knew what to believe about anyone. "Very blase, Melvin. You don't believe me? It's the truth, he's my nephew. And I'll tell you something else. He is a holy man, a hidden saint. Have you ever heard of the *lamedvovniks*, the thirty-six righteous men, saints every one, one more humble than the next? No? Well, we think that Bernard is one of them. The fate of the world depends on these humble men. They have hidden powers. They alone are privileged to see the Divine Presence. In bad times they can rescue us from evil and danger. Maybe Bernard will perform a miracle for you. He thinks very highly of you but he is upset that you persist in admiring this Harlan character despite all that you've already seen and recognized about him."

I was about to tell him that I was less in thrall to Harlan and that I had begun to understand why people were wary of him but, being in a somewhat unfocused and distressed state to begin with, his deluge of strange and mystical information had left me reeling and more confused. I was so upset about Sarah that Ben Braverman's impression of me didn't mean a thing.

"So, look what I've done, I've told you two secrets! And now I'll tell you what I want you to do for me," he said, leading me into the waiters' quarters.

2.

After Ben Braverman stated his intention to entrap Harlan, withholding the details of his plan, I felt the need to get away from the hotel and all things familiar. I changed my clothes, went into the hallway of the waiters' quarters and called out to ask if anyone was going into South Fallsburgh. One of the waiters that I knew only to nod hello to, Larry Pincus, offered to give me a lift and we rode into town talking about the Yankees and the Dodgers and the likelihood that they'd have a rematch in the '56 World Series. It was just talk. At that moment I didn't give a damn about a stupid game and wondered how I ever could have been excited or distraught by anything so banal as a baseball game. When we pulled into town I said I had some errands to run and left the car with an agreement to meet back at the post office in one hour.

Alone on the street I wandered aimlessly from storefront to storefront thinking about Sarah. I knew that we would never be the same with each other again. It wouldn't matter whether she chose me or Hank, the illusion of perfect harmony, of oneness, was destroyed, lost forever with no hope of restoration. People passed around me chattering happily, laughing, complaining, arguing, but it was as though all the color had been drained from my world; life seemed as slate gray and dull as an overcast sky. There was a deep sadness, a kind of grief that had me in the disoriented state you can see on the faces of the victims of natural disasters, people who have seen a river carry away their home or an earthquake swallow up the ground beneath them. No one seemed to notice my distress. I went into the drug store to remove myself from the pedestrian traffic. I had no need to be there and did not want to shop just to take my mind off Sarah. Anyway, I knew that wouldn't work. Shopping was not something I did for relief or distraction. It was totally foreign to me. And what was there in a drugstore to buy? Beach toys, water wings and sun tan lotions by the score. Plain old Coppertone wasn't good enough for the members of the harem. Christ, I mused, it's a goddamn swimming pool, not a beach, the mountains, not the seashore, how hot do they think the sun gets in the Catskills? In my mind I was ranting, venting frustration about things other than Sarah and this Hank guy. I went to the front of the store without making a purchase, making certain the people at the counter saw I was empty-handed. With forty-five minutes left to kill before meeting Pincus back at the post office I walked out to the street trying to find distraction. Images of Sarah in the arms of faceless men intruded into every thought I enlisted to divert myself from worry; there was no refuge. I scrutinized each couple that passed by on the street and eavesdropped on their conversations. This is where we live, I thought, this is what really matters, this is what we live for: the one, the perfect other in the perfect fit. A couple with a small child passed by, the father grim, the mother with tears in her eyes, the little girl, oblivious to the tension, skipped along humming to herself. A pair of teenaged boys, heads bent close together conspiratorially, joked and laughed, and tried to bump one another into other pedestrians as they passed. A young couple holding hands, smiles lighting their faces, passed in the silence of their pleasure. Then a threesome, two men and a woman approached from the opposite direction. It seemed clear that the shorter of the two men was the woman's companion while the taller one was just a friend. He kept a slightly greater distance between himself and the woman and bent his head forward to talk across her to the other man. Always the boundaries, always those inside and those outside. How could Sarah have two of us inside her boundaries of intimacy? I wanted to feel more cosmopolitan, more sophisticated and poised in this contest, more witty and glib, beyond jealousy and hurt. Maybe Harlan could accomplish that but not Melvin, I heard myself say in my mind. No, by the time she returns she'll have made her decision and mine too and that's just how it is.

I crossed the main street of the town and kept walking distractedly along the storefronts oblivious to the wares they featured, thinking of Sarah while still trying not to, but then stopped suddenly when I saw where I was. The large plate glass window bearing the name *Freddie's* was right next to me. I peered inside through the reflection of the street behind me and saw men huddled at the long bar drinking beer in the afternoon. All at once that seemed a good idea, an act of manliness, an act of defiance. Thursday afternoon with nothing better to do than get a beer. I pushed open the door and went directly to the bar. One man looked up at me, snickered and muttered something to the man next to him who craned his neck around to look at me as I landed at the formica bar.

"What can I get you, young fella," the bartender asked.

"I'll have a Ballantine ale, please," I said quickly. I didn't like beer but years of Mel Allen and Yankee baseball on the radio had led me to try the ale at the first opportunity and its drier, almost metallic taste was not at all unpleasant. I knew a Tom Collins would have been the wrong thing to ask for, something too city, too upper class. The bartender put the can on the bar and fished a glass from the sink wiping it off with his towel. Then he placed a cardboard coaster in front of me and set the still wet glass down upon it.

"You a salesman?" he asked with a broad smile while he looked down the bar at the men huddling together. They laughed. I thought about affecting a southern accent and telling him I was a basketball player up for the summer circuit, something more than an ordinary busboy or waiter, but didn't do it.

"No," was all I said. I opened the can of ale and poured it out. "You from New York?" one of the men down the bar asked. This was beginning to feel like a bad idea. I sipped some ale, cleared my throat, and looked down the row of stools to where he was seated. "Yes."

"Where, Brooklyn, the Bronx, Manhattan?" For a minute I thought I might say Staten Island and really throw him off. No one would have considered somebody from Staten Island a serious New Yorker. "The Bronx."

"Really? Me too," he said enthusiastically. "Course I was just a boy when we came up here from 138th street but even then I was swimming in the Harlem river. Where are you from in the Bronx?"

"Creston Avenue," I lied, using my high school's street address rather than my own as though this baboon could really care and might come to look me up at home some time.

"Ever swim in the river?"

"Nope," I was getting down right folksy, sipping my ale and waiting for a chance to leave without appearing intimidated. In fact, I wasn't intimidated by them. These men were just out having a beer, not looking for trouble, not meaning to do me harm. Other than making a few snide remarks under their breath just between themselves they'd been civil. It was my fear that had made them seem menacing, my cowardice that had rendered them formidable. " . . . but I've swum in the Hudson, near the bridge." The bridge meant the George Washington

Bridge. The Tappan Zee had yet to be built. "The water there is very brackish because the ocean flows in almost all the way up to Kingston at high tide." At least that was what my father had told me driving down the West Side Highway one day. "Maybe even to Albany," I added.

"Get outta here, you serious?"

"Yeah, totally. See, if you time your swim under the bridge to the high tide, you have about an hour when the current is pretty tame and you don't get swept along one way or the other." Both men looked at me with something approaching respect. Every day in every way I was becoming a more comfortable liar. "What's the Harlem River like to swim in?"

"You know, I don't remember. I was just a kid." And he laughed himself right to the men's room. The ale and the tale made me feel good. This episode might score some points for me with Ron, having a drink in Freddie's in the middle of the afternoon and making rubes of a couple of old townies. Ready to head back to meet my ride I settled up with the bartender, left him a generous tip, nodded at the man sitting at the bar, and went out into the sun. But the heartbreak over Sarah was waiting for me as soon as I walked out to the street and saw a pretty girl holding her boyfriend's hand and raising herself on tiptoes to kiss him on the lips. It made me want to throw myself into the Hudson River.

3.

We rode back to Braverman's saying very little. I was not ready to go back to my room and see either Ron or Harlan. We parked in the staff parking lot and when Pincus asked if I wanted to get a soda with him I thanked him for the ride and said I wanted to take a swim. There was no intention to swim, just the intent to get away and be by myself. I walked down to the lake to see if the rowboat was free. The day camp was ending its afternoon and the campers were out of the water, standing on the dock and shivering, towels pulled tightly around their little bodies. They rubbed their upper arms briskly with their hands and hopped from foot to foot to get warm. I could hear teeth chattering behind blue lips as I passed.

"Are you finished with the skiff for the day?" I asked the counselor.

"Yeah. Be sure to tie it up it under the dock when you're done, Jack."

Jack. He must have known me as Sarah's date. How else would he know my name? That felt good, like my world hadn't changed, like everything would be all right. I climbed into the boat and pushed off into the lake. The cold August nights and the weakened late summer sun on its course of recession towards the equator, its autumnal equinox, had rendered the lake's waters cooler. A wind came up wafting the cold off the water and chilling my body. I coughed a deep chesty cough. Shouldn't smoke again, I thought, recalling Harlan's father and his cough, fed by the prodigious mucus factory in his chest. I let the boat drift towards the opposite shore, towards Harlan's parents' cabin. I still don't know if that was intentional or accidental and quite likely, I will never know. There was no reason to expect I'd learn anything true about Harlan from his parents but maybe I'd learn if they were who he said they were, the judge and the showgirl. Now that was a love story. Imagine walking out on a life in progress and disappearing into anonymity after such a public existence. Was it worth it? Did their love withstand the disappointments of life and feel as good as it had that long ago August. I was very tempted to ask. Imagine, me, a kid, a stranger with no right to the answers to such questions, why should he tell me anything?

I rowed up on to the beach in front of the cabin and then pulled the skiff by its bow until it was completely out of the water. No one hailed or greeted me from the stillness of the house. Not even a cough broke the silence. I banged on the front door of the cabin.

"Hello? Anybody home? It's Jack White, Harlan's friend." The silence persisted, a quiet that a theater audience might envy. There was a car in the driveway, a light burning in the hall and still no answer, but I was determined to talk to the judge—if that in fact was who he was. "Hello, hello, it's Jack White," and then, for the hell of it, I said, "not the FBI."

There was a rustle inside, footsteps approached, and the judge, Harlan's father, parted the curtains at the window next to the door, raised an index finger, and then undid the locks to let me in. The smell of cigarette smoke was still fresh in the room and a gray haze lingered in the air. Waving the now invisible smoke away he smiled and stuck out his hand.

"Come in, Jack White, come in. I was afraid it was Harlan come to lecture me about the evils of tobacco, though he's a chain smoker himself, don't you know." No wheeze, no cough, no shortness of breath. "Can I get you something to drink, a coke, a beer, a cup of coffee?"

"A drink of water would be fine," I said, wondering what had become of the cardiac patient I'd visited just days before.

"Just water? You're sure? No sodas or beer? Okay. So how has your summer been, Jack?" he asked, walking me to the kitchen where he removed a bottle of water from the refrigerator.

"Boy, you've made some recovery, judge," I said, " the last time I saw you, you were pretty sick. Weren't you supposed to get an operation of some kind? Isn't that why Harlan was trying to raise money? Wasn't that for you to have heart surgery to save your life?"

"Raise money? An operation? I don't know what you're talking about, Jack, I don't need an operation. I had pneumonia, same damn pneumonia I get every year. There's nothing wrong with my heart. Oh, Jesus, has Harlan been at it again? I can see by the look on your face that he has. Oh, Jesus." The judge shook his head. "I hoped maybe he'd make some money, meet a nice girl, reform his ways. I even thought that with a friend like you he'd see there's a better way. Oh, Jesus, you didn't give him any money I hope."

"Almost."

"Well don't," he frowned. "Don't say anything about this to his mother, Jack, Helene's the one who's really not well." He rubbed his brow to remove the film of perspiration there and paced the room. "Damn! Damn, damn, damn." I sipped my water and looked at the things around me. There were ordinary furnishings worn with use and needing repair or refreshing, not what you'd expect of people with money. Was Harlan really acting alone in his hunt for the money? Is this another set up because I'm an easy dupe, someone to be gulled? I shouldn't have come here, I thought, I am way over my head. Why trust the judge, this man, any more than I'd trust Harlan?

"Harlan has been a problem for his mother and me, you must have some awareness of this aspect of my son, Jack, surely you've seen that part of him." He approached and stood too close to me. "I have tried to make him see the right way but he's determined to remind me of the path I chose, his life is his means of reproach, his disgrace is meant for me. Sex and money are all he cares about and he insists that is what I taught him. Outrageous." He retreated to the window. "He's had everything we could give to him, love, a good home, education . . ." his voice trailed off as if into the mystery of what they had overlooked, what they had failed to provide. "You know," he said, suddenly amused, "even this damn ring story seemed to be working for a time. He seemed genuinely excited, motivated, wanting to connect with this saga, this noble family history." His eyes teared. "There is no ring, Jack, there never was. It was just a story to get him involved in something bigger than himself. I'm sorry if it's caused you any trouble. I didn't see how something so innocent could become such a problem, but then, I always underestimate my son's capacity for mischief."

"Mischief? Mischief? Judge, that's like saying a pyromaniac is someone who plays with matches. Who is he, sir, who is Harlan?"

"He is my twenty four year old only child, my son, my heir, my cross."

"Does he go to Harvard?"

"Jack, what do you want with that, what do you want, would that make him better for you if he was at school in Cambridge?" He pulled a cigarette from a pack he'd hidden under a seat cushion and lit up. "You want one?" he asked absently and again began pacing the room. "It had been my hope that this summer would be different. A nice bunch of boys, some good money, some pretty girls, the girls they love him, he's like a movie star to them. Ben said it would come together, he'd straighten out, it would all be there for him, the money, the girls, the guys."

"The guys don't like him, sir, they don't trust him. I always defended him, I thought they were too harsh, maybe envious, I don't know, none of it matters now." I became unsure of why I'd come to the house. Learning that Harlan was a grifter in a charmer's clothing was something I already knew and the judge may have been no better, maybe not the judge at all. Why show him respect?

"Jack, you have to help him, he'll listen to you, he always speaks so highly of you, of your kindness and sensitivity. Help me to help him. This may be our last chance." I shrugged.

"Don't you care? Don't you have any feelings of compassion for your friend?"

"I'm not sure he's my friend when he tries to shake me down for an operation you obviously don't need to have. And while we're at it, how do I know you're really the judge? No offense, but why should I believe that's the truth?" Holding up an index finger, the social hold button before there were hold buttons, Harlan's father left the room for a minute and then returned with a piece of paper in hand.

"Will this be enough?" He handed me the paper, a certificate from the City of New York saying he was licensed to practice the law, he being Joseph Force Crater. I'd never seen any of the city's documents and was still wary this was a valid license. Flustered, I dared to do what I had imagined only minutes before.

"So, was it worth it judge?"

"What? Was what worth it?"

"Everything." I began to lose my nerve now that the words were out. "Giving up your position, leaving your life for this?"

"Jack, that's not for you to ask. Don't be impertinent. Think how you can help your friend."

"Right now, judge, I'm the one who needs help. I have to think of myself, Harlan is your problem, you think about him." I placed the glass of water on the coffee table and let myself out.

"Please, Jack, have some mercy, he needs your help," he called out to me.

The judge had tried luring me back by strumming on the strings of guilt, but I was not the guilty one and my strings were not taut enough to make the right sound.

Chapter Eleven

With Sarah gone and Ben Braverman having confided Abe's secrets to me, if indeed they were his secrets and not some confabulation that Ben had concocted spontaneously to confound me and simultaneously amuse himself, after both these upsets, I decided to get drunk that night after work. The decision to get drunk as opposed to just drinking too much, an occurrence of drunkenness, is a morbid and pathetic circumstance. It is a plan hatched in a state of defeat, a self-inflicted wound masquerading as a flamboyant and Baroque gesture or what the English call "fuck all." I have to admit I didn't enjoy alcohol that much despite having willingly participated in all of the passage rites of my generation, the beer parties and the rye, gin and scotch clandestine tastings, so getting drunk was more a torture than a comfort but somehow that seemed the right thing to do because it was what men under stress usually resorted to in the movies. I had no idea what my father and the other men of my family did when stressed and the fact that I hated feeling drunk did nothing to deter me from this decision. It is the kind of flailing we are capable of resorting to when we've been disoriented by a shock and there is no other word to explain the effect of Sarah's announcement: I was in shock.

After dinner I went to the bar in the lounge where Julie the bartender made me a Tom Collins. He joked with me about coming alone and ordering a drink. "Alcohol won't get you laid if you don't have a girl drinking with you. Ha, ha. Ha, ha." I felt worse after the first Tom Collins. The bar filled up slowly when Talent

Night ended, Ben's mid-week effort at killing time before the weekend performers started trooping through. My presence raised the eyebrows of some and the hopes of others, the latter being the anxious parents of what I would politely call unprepossessing daughters. The carbonation had evacuated my second Tom Collins by that time and the wedge of fresh lime that Julie had perched on the lip of the glass now lay in a lifeless heap at the bottom of the drink. My head spun.

"Let me buy you a fresh drink," I heard someone say as my glass was sailed across the bar in Julie's direction.

"Thank you, but I really don't want another drink," I said, not looking at the man who had seated himself beside me at the bar.

"It's not polite to refuse a generous offer, Melvin. Even if you don't drink it be gracious and watch the bubbles fizz in the glass." He punctuated his advice with a squeeze of my shoulder which made me look up to see who this sport was. The man had a sharp featured face and a crew cut, was probably around forty years old with a trim and youthful physique. He was wearing a loose fitting sport coat, smoking a long, unfiltered cigarette and he had the coldest blue eyes I'd ever seen, cold as dry ice.

"My name is Joe," he said, extending his hand, "Joe," he repeated as if it were a hard name to learn. I shook his hand but didn't speak; he already knew my name.

"Having a good season? They say you can't find a room to rent in the Catskills anymore this summer because they're all booked."

"It's been all right," I said unenthusiastically. Who knew who this guy could be, maybe an IRS agent looking for tax cheats.

"You're a pretty quiet fella, Mel, doesn't that hurt your tips?" I thought I'd say something sarcastic, like 'let me give you a tip, pal,' but not knowing who he was, and daunted by those cold, icy eyes I said,

"It isn't personal, but I don't know you and I would prefer to be left alone tonight. I've got some things on my mind and I'm not good company." He rolled the tip of his cigarette around the base of the ashtray leaving a gray trail of ash then stared at me through narrowed eyes as he lifted the butt to his mouth and took a deep drag. The smoke came out through his nose slowly surrounding his face as if in a mist.

"Let me be clear with you, Melvin, you and I are going to do some talking tonight. You and I are having this conversation because Ben Braverman has arranged for us to meet on his behalf." My stomach flipped and then sank quickly. This was about the trap for Harlan Ben had talked to me about that afternoon. He said someone would get in touch with me. Joe was the someone. "Have I made myself clear to you?" I nodded. "Good. Let me explain to you that I am here very willingly, eagerly you might say, because this Harlan Hawthorne character is bad news, a rotten apple, a parasite, a scum bag, do I make myself clear?"

"Clear as day," I said, falling back on cliche to keep the clear word in play. He narrowed his eyes suspiciously and then relaxed.

"Look, Melvin, I understand that you're very close to this boy but you don't know him you only think that you know him. This guy is nothing but a grifter, a gigolo and a user, a cheap crook who steals money and jewelry from the women that he beds."

"You can prove this?"

"You know, it's the damnedest thing, women never want to press charges against him. He must have something special, some move or some . . ."

"He listens."

"He listens?! What the hell does that mean?" He was as confused as a gorilla that has just been handed a plastic banana.

"Women adore Harlan because he understands and cares about them, maybe too many of them, but he's not mean, and he's not a thief."

"Oh boy," Joe said, wiping his brow, "we've got a lot of talking to do, you and me, a lot of talking."

"If you don't mind I'd rather that we do that some other time." I started to leave but Joe grabbed my shoulder and held me in place despite my demurrals.

"Mr. Braverman wants this Harlan character out of his hotel, out of his daughter's life, out of town and, if necessary, out cold but under any circumstances, o-u-t, out! You cannot walk away just now, you can't because I don't want you to, because I'm not through with you, because if you walk I'll call the police and Ben B will say you were at his house in the middle of the night looking for something to steal. Up here that's all Ben has to do to get you put in jail, clear?" That word again. He gritted his teeth and dug his fingers into my shoulder with a surprisingly fierce strength. "I'm asking you if I've made myself clear!" His nostrils flared and his index finger located a nerve in my left shoulder that when pressed hurt so it caused my knees to buckle. "Yes!" I said in a shaky voice, "clear as day."

"Good." He took another king size cigarette from the packet in his shirt and lit it with the ember of the one he had been smoking. After it was afire he took a deep breath and then seemed to blow the smoke out of every portal in his head. I even thought I saw his ears participate in the venting of the smoke. "Let me tell you about your buddy Harlan. First of all, his name is not Harlan Hawthorne but it's the name he uses up here. He takes people by surprise that way, disarms them, yeah that's what he does, he disarms people by using that name. Isn't that what happened to you?"

"It isn't his name it's his style and the fact that he is very smart. And I wouldn't say that I've been disarmed," hearing the defensiveness in my voice I shifted my tone, "it's more like I've been charmed, flattered by his willingness to teach me about things." I would not tell him that I no longer idolized Harlan and it was interesting hearing this portrayal of him, one closer in every way to Sarah's perception of Harlan.

"Teach you about things," he repeated, nodding his head. "Has he taught you how to slip a ring off a woman's finger so gently she doesn't even feel it disappear, or where to step on a woman's instep at exactly the same time you slide her bracelet off her wrist so that she is distracted by the pain and more focused on the prospect of podiatry than on her jewelry, has he taught you how he does that? Or has he shown you how to peel a twenty off a roll of bills, examine it very prominently and then quickly switch a two dollar bill for it so that if he's caught it can be passed off as an honest mistake, you know, confusion over the number two. And there's more, there's always more, like the name. You give that name to a person in the Catskills and it disarms them, throws them off their pace, you know what I mean?" I didn't and I told him so. "Everybody has a rhythm, a pace, a way that he operates in new situations. It's as identifiable as a signature, a fingerprint, always the same. Just the name, Harlan Hawthorne, derails people. This gives him the chance to see its effect; does it make people wary or eager to know him, intimidated or friendly to a fault. Then he can set his traps, lay his nets, snare his marks." Joe had smoked his cigarette down to his fingers while he was talking to me and again he lit another from the ember of the shrunken butt.

"I don't think we're talking about the same guy. Maybe the guy you're talking about heard the real Harlan's name and decided to use it for himself." Joe did not burst out laughing but I knew he thought my proposition was ludicrous by the gapejawed, wide-eyed look he gave me.

"Are you stupid Melvin? Do you think for a minute that I'm stupid or something? Because if you do you're in for a big surprise. No, there is only one Harlan Hawthorne and this is him." Even though I had refused it, I took a sip of the Tom Collins on the bar. My head had the fuzzy feeling it usually got after a few drinks and I knew that to go farther would certainly make me sick to my stomach and if I got sick enough he'd have to let me leave. "Let me have a scotch on the rocks, Julie. Make it a double. So let's talk about Ben's plan." Julie brought him his drink and shifting around in his seat Joe took the drink in his hand and smiled a friendly smile at the glass before swigging a large gulp of it. "You understand that any business that deals with a lot of cash is an opportunity to skim bucks out of the register and directly into your pocket. It's a good way to keep your silent partner, Uncle Sam, silent. This is the case in bars, restaurants and gas stations, and in resort hotels. People either pay you in cash or they write you a check. If you are careful and not too greedy you can skim a few thousand dollars a summer and no one is any the wiser. That's a lot of money, a year's salary for your average clerk or secretary, the kind of people who come here for a summer vacation. But you don't deposit that cash in a bank, no, no. That would leave a record of the money for the taxman who knows very well about cash skimming, he just can't prove it most of the time. You stash the cash somewhere until you want to spend it, take a trip, buy a fur coat or a car, you know, some kind of luxury. Now," he took his scotch in hand again, finished it in a swallow and sailed the glass down the bar to Julie who nodded and reached for the scotch bottle behind him. "More ice this time please, Jules. So usually the owner of this cash business has a safe or some kind of strongbox hidden away in or near his house. This is where you come in." I took another sip of my Tom Collins. The gin taste came through the lime and my nausea increased but I sipped the drink some more. While I might recently have become disenchanted with Harlan I was not going to listen to my part in this scheme to trap him if I could avoid it. I'd sooner get what we called "the whirlies" and throw up on Joe's shoes. "Are you all right? You're turning green and sweating, uh oh, you're gonna be sick!" And he jumped up and moved away from the bar taking his suede shoes out of harm's way. I took a deep breath and put my head between my knees.

"I'll be okay, don't worry. I told you I had a lot on my mind." His face darkened as he stared at me.

"If I have to I'll stick *my* finger down your throat and get the sick over with because we are going to discuss the plan and your part in it and we're going to do that tonight." He turned to Julie. "Get that goddamn drink out of here," he said, motioning to the Tom Collins with his head. I sat up, and despite the throbbing in my head and the sickening, nauseated feeling that gripped my entire body, I tried to look focused.

"Could you give me a drink of ice water please, Julie?" Warily, Joe approached the bar. I started to giggle. The extra alcohol made him now seem less imposing and the memory of him lurching away from his stool to protect his suede shoes made his vanity appear totally absurd. My giggling abruptly plunged out of control into unstoppable laughter and this behavior was clearly irritating to him. I don't remember if it was the alcohol or the fear, hysterics or hysteria, I just couldn't stop. Julie brought the ice water down to our end of the bar but when I reached for it Joe grabbed my wrist.

"Don't make me hurt you, son." It was said in a low, cold tone as icy as his eyes and it stopped my laughter as abruptly as if it had been freeze dried. "All you have to do is tell Harlan about a sack that you saw Ben put down a chute near the storm cellar doors at the back of the house, that's all. I guarantee you that he will be very interested, full of questions and changes of plans. Suddenly he'll be the one to search the grounds near the Braverman's house, not you. I'm telling you to tell him what I told you to. There's no 'please', no 'okay?' this is something you have no choice in, something that you must do." Though my infatuation with Harlan, I can think of no other word to describe my feelings for him, had ended before this encounter, and with Sarah's surprise announcement at work in me like a poison, I still could not think of being Ben's agent. The bar had filled up with people and the nervous laughter of women was all around me. I looked at Joe for a full, soundless minute and then pitched forward and vomited. Seeing what was coming Joe skipped aside to protect his suede shoes. Then he poured the ice water over my head.

"Yeah, turning on your buddy is a disgusting thing to do, but you'll do it if you know what's good for you, Melvin."

"I'm sick."

"Bring me some coffee, Jules," he called out. "Hear me? You'll do what you're told. Now drink some coffee, it'll sober you up."

2

There is a quality of exhaustion that sets in towards the third week of August for those working in a resort hotel. The very name of the month seems to echo this state of enervation: August—exhaust. I even made jokes about it with Sammy. "Boy, I'm Augusted" or "I feel like I'm in a state of Augustian." Almost every employee has been working the entire summer without relief, no days off, two months of servicing the wants and needs of the guests assigned, the gracious and the gruff, the generous and the greedy, regardless of their nature they must be served. And by that point in the summer season everyone has a good idea of how much money will be taken away when Labor Day, the finish line in the annual summer gold rush, is reached. For me, money had ceased to be an issue after Sammy guaranteed I would never go unrewarded and my ambitions had been focused on romance and friendship, ambitions that had collided with stunning surprise when Sarah exposed Harlan's repeated betrayals of Heidi, and then what I took to be her own as well: the Hank revelation.

I was expecting Sarah's return from her meeting with Hank on Saturday afternoon. The feelings of jealousy and fear that had seized me on Thursday had not relented and the anticipation of our reunion only served to add dread to the mix. I had tried and failed to deceive myself with the bravado of detachment. I didn't want to lose her and though everything had been unalterably changed by the revelation that there was someone else in the few days she was gone I had already accepted that reality and was willing to hold on even if it meant a less than perfect love. At eighteen, in our earnestness, we imagine love to be forever.

The luncheon special that Friday was cold borscht followed by cheese blintzes both served with fresh sour cream and my guests were so happy with the meal they ate themselves into a state of torpor bordering on inebriation.

"Such a meal!" Mrs. Zuckerman announced to Sammy, her hands, as if in prayer, clasped against her large bosom, "I could plotz." But she did not collapse, even after finishing all of her own and the remains of her husband's blintzes. Seeing her wobble like a toy in the rear window well of an automobile, Sammy saw to it that she left the dining room with the assistance of one of the bell hops who, with one arm supporting her bloat, steered her clear of the lobby furniture as he led her back to her room. Mr. Zuckerman, whose constipation was spoken of as if his evacuative travails were epic in scale, had felt an urge, an interior rumbling of unusual but promising proportions, and had excitedly fled the dining room for his porcelain throne. It was basically the usual doings of a usual day.

"Sarah should be getting back by now shouldn't she." Ron knew she had gone to New York. He did not know about Hank and thought my moroseness was nothing more than pathetic longing.

"No, she should be back before dinner tomorrow."

"Don't sound so overjoyed. Mel, she'll think somebody died while she was away." I frowned and turned my back on him. I didn't see how it would be possible for me to welcome her back without seeming either wary or remote.

"How' re you doing?" Harlan had sat down at the table where I was folding the napkins for dinner. I greeted him with a nod. "You're not sure how to react to Sarah are you. Let me help you out with this." He crossed his legs, lit up a cigarette and started to blow smoke rings which I found profoundly irritating. It was as though he might next start performing card tricks while advising me on how to approach Sarah, the legerdemain infinitely more interesting to him than the counsel. "Do not seem delighted, do not be happy to see her, but don't be morose or sulky. Let her feel your strength and your dignity, like a . . . like a *prince*! Cordial but aloof, gracious yet remote, elusive." He smiled a satisfied smile and exhaled columns of smoke through his nose. "Think you can handle that?"

"That doesn't sound like me." It didn't sound like him either, not the "him" I had constructed in my admiring fantasy. It did, however, sound like the manipulative, exploitative operator that Sarah had been insisting was the real Harlan.

"Nothing sounds like anybody, Jack. You have to learn different situations call for different styles. Remember when you asked me about what I do to get women to pay attention? I told you to listen to them and by listening you learn what they want. Then you either give them that or, when you really get comfortable, you figure out how to turn that upside down, startle and disarm them, sometimes sweep them away with the unexpected." He crushed his Lucky and quickly lit another. "Sarah is probably expecting you to be either very happy to see her or very guarded and grim. By being a prince you transcend her expectations; you'll be a new Mel, a real Jack, someone she won't want to lose. Even if she's already made up her mind to stay with that

Hank fellow she'll have to retreat, rethink the choice. You'll see." He sat back, clasped his hands behind his neck, smiled, and puffed on the cigarette dangling from his mouth. He looked enormously self-satisfied and I hated him for proving Sarah so right. "You don't have very much to say today do you?"

"I don't think you'd want to hear what I have to say."

"What? You know that's not true, you know that I'm your friend and I'm interested in what you think."

"Harlan, I'm really upset about Sarah's going to see this Hank guy, so upset that I can't think straight, yet you're telling me to put on this act as though it would be no big deal to pretend being a goddamn prince!" My voice was loud when I said prince and there was a sudden silence in the dining room. With a frown on my face I looked around at the remaining waiters and busboys and then waved my hand at them as if to say, "never mind."

"You really are on edge aren't you. You know that's not going to work for you when you meet Sarah. If you can't have more control of yourself you can't have any control over the situation with her, it's that simple."

"Control? You think I can have control over her? You really are different, aren't you. Sarah has been telling me she thinks I trust you too much and this kind of talk makes me think maybe she's right."

"Sarah said that? What does she know about me that gives her the right to judge me like that?"

"It's the way you are around women."

"It's the way women are around me, Jack, and you know that's the truth, you've seen it for yourself. I don't have to do anything but show up for things to start happening."

"But you do more than just show up. Listen to the advice you were just giving me, doesn't that say you know what to do all the time? Look, I've seen you with that blonde woman on the tennis court and the woman on the softball field, the woman who wanted you to give her kid diving lessons, all the women in the kiddy pool, it's everywhere you go." The accusations the steely eyed Joe had made also came to mind but I wasn't going to list them. Nor was I prepared to warn Harlan just yet. I hadn't decided how to avoid Ben B's demand and alert Harlan without ending up in some Catskill jail.

"So? Jealous? Envious? What are you saying?"

"Well, what about Heidi, what does that say about her? Isn't she enough for you?"

"Enough? I don't understand. I'm with her every night she wants to be with me. I have never deliberately hurt or disappointed her, I . . . wait a minute. It's Sarah who's off with somebody else right now, Jack, not me. Don't you see what she was doing? She was setting it up for you to be so upset with me you wouldn't turn to me for advice when she put you in this position. Boy, that's something. Do you think this girl really cares about you or is she just trying to torture you?" I was stunned into silence by what he said. It hadn't occurred to me to scrutinize Sarah in the same way she asked me to examine Harlan. But hurt as I was I wouldn't allow myself to be positioned that way.

"I don't see it that way. Let me alone for a while please I need to think about some things." Pursing his lips, narrowing his eyes and shaking his head in assent, he slowly rose from his chair, crushed his Lucky Strike in the ashtray, said, "See you later," and left. That conversation with Harlan had Augusted me.

3.

Later that day, Ron attempted to cheer me up. I doubted that he had ever experienced the kind of threat I was feeling from someone like the durable if invisible Hank, but then he was not one to reveal himself that readily. We had just finished the lunch meal and were heading back to our room when he grabbed me by the arm.

"Come on. Mel, let's tackle something you can really handle, let's tackle the Abe Melman problem. What's with Abe? It is your turn, you know, and time is running out so give it a try. I was not particularly enthusiastic about playing. There had been such preoccupation with Sarah and with Harlan that I couldn't imagine being clever and humorous about Abe. Nor did I feel it was my right to reveal what Ben had disclosed to me about him. I shrugged, not a full-fledged denial but not a rejection of the proposal either.

When we were midway between the kitchen and the waiters' quarters. a drenching rain came down all at once, intense and loud and soaking, as if we had blundered under a waterfall. Confused, I hesitated trying to determine which shelter was nearer so I could get under cover before my shoes and trousers were soaked beyond use but Ron ran directly to our room without a second's thought. When I got there he had already stripped off his clothing and was stuffing newspaper into his shoes to absorb the water from them. I stood in the room dripping, shaking the water from my hands as it ran down my arms, trying to be a silent clown like Buster Keaton. Ron laughed.

"Get out of those wet things or I'll tell your mother," he joked "and then let's hear your story of 'What's with Abe?'" I peeled off my clothes, stuffed my shoes with newspaper, pulled on a sweatshirt and climbed up into my bunk.

"Okay, let's see. I've thought about this some, lately." Then I began. "Abe and Leah met in a small shul in the Morrisania section of the Bronx one bright, autumn morning on the first day of Rosh Hashanah. A new year, a new love, a first love for both. They began to date, if you could call the tortured silences they shared walking up and down the Grand Concourse dating, and when . . ."

"I like that 'tortured silences'. It's a nice touch," Ron said.

"Shhh! But thank you ladies and gentlemen. And when Abe went off to City College to study Shakespeare and accounting, Leah took a job in the bookkeeping department at Alexander's Department store on Fordham Road. Abe was a very serious student and he burned the midnight oil three nights a week so he could work at Feinberg's bagel bakery the other three nights for the money to pay for his books, his clothing, and the shoe repairs requisite to his long walks . . ."

"Boo!"

"Shut up! Every Friday night he saw Leah because Feinberg the bagel baker was orthodox and his business was closed for the Sabbath, so between school work and his job, Abe had only one night off, Friday night. Meanwhile, Leah was seeing a new and more glamorous side of life from inside the walls of the immense department store. On her lunch breaks she would gobble down the small sandwich her mother packed for her and then spend the rest of her time walking through the more chic women's clothing departments of the store. Seeing the cashmere sweaters, the glamorous tight fitting skirts, and the silk blouses, Leah began to feel a craving for these finer things. Three years passed. Every Friday night Leah saw Abe and every Tuesday night Abe would call to arrange a date for the following Friday. It was the rhythm of their relationship, and its steady and reliable pace had all the glamour and excitement of fingers drumming on a table top." I paused. I made most of this story up as I went along and I was not certain where I was heading just then. I leaned over the edge of my bed and looked down at Ron who was lying on his back, eyes closed, a smile on his face. Outside, the rain poured down and hissed at our windows. This was cozy.

"Go on."

"Leah had taken to wearing nylon stockings because that was how the women who shopped in Better Dresses dressed, and she began to use a darker red lipstick as well, and to wear simulated pearl earrings and a small string of simulated pearls around her neck. She didn't let Abe see her wearing the jewelry, however, because she was certain that he'd disapprove. After all, there was a depression going on and every cent counted, so spending money so frivolously . . ."

"No, no, no. Your story is all wrong," Ron interjected angrily. "Why would she get nylon stockings for God's sake, and where would she come off buying costume jewelry? Come on!" I was surprised by how seriously Ron was taking this story and how real Leah had become in such a short time.

"Okay, okay, but let me finish. This is a good one. Okay. So she took to wearing dark red lipstick and painting her nails and for a while even flirted with cutting her hair short. She ached for change, for risk, for something daring and even dangerous." I paused, timing the effect of this intermission by the sounds of Ron's twisting on his bed and then said, "Because there was a man at work who blushed whenever Leah caught him staring at her, a very fair, very blond, very Irish man . . ."

"Aha!"

" . . . and, while Richard Doyle spent many nights spilling his seed into his bathroom sink, imagining the many delights of the dark Leah's Jewish sexual mysteries . . ."

"Like whining at his touch?"

"Shhh! He pined for a deeper and purer relationship with her and would not defile her pristine person with the touch of that impure nether appendage he abused for his depraved release. The priest in the confessional was growing weary of Richard Doyle's ritual self-abuse and frustrated that the 'Hail Marys' and the 'Our Fathers' he prescribed did not deter this sheep from dreaming like a wolf . . ."

"You're starting to lose it again, Melvin, what the fuck do you know about 'Hail Marys' and 'Our Fathers?'" Ron's voice was very angry.

"In the spring of the fourth year of Abe's courtship of her, Leah became aware that Richard Doyle had begun to follow her, and while this titillated her, it also aroused a nagging and persistent anxiety. What if he approached her? What if he asked her for a date? What if, she trembled at the mere thought of it, what if he touched her. Yet, as the weeks passed, strange feelings began appearing inside her, warm and exciting feelings that she had not known before, feelings that she had never experienced with Abe. But the thought of Richard Doyle, she began calling him 'Dickie' in her fantasies, released an urgent sensation, a lava flow of longing. Abe, meanwhile, had mustered the courage to propose marriage to Leah, convinced that their weekly walks testified to his commitment and respect. It was almost summer and he would be graduating from college in just a few weeks. As they walked down the Grand Concourse that June night, the lights from Yankee Stadium illuminating the sky off to the south, Abe took Leah's hand and stopped her progress. 'Leah,' he faltered, 'Leah, you know how I . . . Leah, I . . . ' he couldn't say the words. Leah knew what he was trying to say but would offer no assistance. In fact she had begun to dread the coming of this night, the night she would have to tell him that she did not love him and could not, could never, marry him. 'Marry me' he blurted out. But before she could say anything in response, a figure came out of the shadows, a tall fair-haired man who, saying only her name, swept Leah up in his arms and ran down the street with her. And what pained Abe more than his frightened paralysis, his horrible helplessness and inaction, what tore at him that night and forever after, was that Leah never once screamed or cried out to him for help." The hissing of the rain was the only sound in the room for what felt like a long time. We both lay silent and quite still in our beds.

Then, Ron said, "You're afraid that that's what's happening with your Sarah now, aren't you. That she'll be carried away, someone else will take her away from you. Don't let that happen, Mel. Don't let it happen."

Sick with helplessness I said, "It was just a story, Ron, just a story about Abe. It could never really happen." But we both knew it very well could.

4.

In mid-August the late afternoon sun, more than halfway along its course of return to the autumn equinox, illuminates the landscape with a precision that makes each tree beckon you to scrutinize its every leaf. You look up from the field of wild asters and suddenly nature seems to say to you "Presenting the Sugar Maple," a patch of red and orange-yellow smeared on its upper leaves like a shock of white in a head of black hair reminding you that there is a change of season approaching. The leaves, a dark lustreless green, hang heavy and weary from their branches fatigued by the long season in the sun, waiting. It is my favorite time of day in my favorite time of year. How I so envied the members of the band, the camp counselors, the tennis pros and lifeguards who could relax and celebrate that special, peaceful stillness of the late summer afternoons. Being a bus-boy one rarely got to luxuriate in it for more than an hour before having to return to the kitchen. Still, at that enchanted hour on the Saturday of Sarah's return from the city and her meeting with Hank I did nothing to distract myself from the glory of the landscape. Whatever was awaiting me at our reunion, whatever changes and uncertainties might be revealed, the beauty of the hills and their turning trees and the gurgling of the water in the lake would still provide me with solace.

I had expected Sarah back around three o'clock so after a shower I went down to the lake and sat on the dock, my bare feet dangling over the water. It was four p.m. The day camp had already had its turn with the rowboats and now some hotel guests drifted around in them rowing only to keep from running aground at the shore or from colliding with one another. They bobbed idly in the late afternoon sun, the men sprawled out and asleep, one of the women tentatively dipping her fingers in the cool water, cautious and timorous, as though a school of piranha lurked in the darkness waiting to devour any flesh she bared to them. I didn't know if Sarah would come looking for me there but were she to seek me out this was the place I'd most likely be.

We had declared the lake to be ours alone only the week before. We'd come to the dock in the evening and looked over the untroubled, slowly rolling waters to the cottages on the other side and, like officious landlords, complained about the obtuse tenants' lack of appreciation for the amenities provided by the setting. There were no campfires with marshmallows toasting, no telescopes trained at the sky, no sounds of laughter or raucous conviviality. And that night, while we were pretending to be the landowners, Sarah admitted to me she had lied about Sandy Koufax being her cousin.

"I guess I was a little insecure. I thought you'd be more interested in me if I added that story about Sandy Koufax." I told her that it hadn't mattered enough to me even to bring it up again. She was perfect just as she was, with or without him, though I have to admit to some disappointment at the news. I was already imagining good seats at the World Series if the Dodgers and Yankees had another October match.

I said, "You know, in some ways I'm even more impressed with you now that you've told me Sandy isn't your cousin. You've got a hell of an arm." We laughed and cuddled and what had started out as a takeaway ended up bringing us even closer together. That's why this Hank business was so confusing and disorienting; I'd thought we were both in love. It was while I wandered in this reverie that Sarah quietly sat down next to me on the dock.

"Hi," she said softly. I felt a strong adrenaline rush rampage through me and batter at my insides.

"You're back," I said, without looking at her. All my imagined dialogues, all of the 'I say and then she says and then I say' fantastically scripted exchanges came apart and scattered like a stack of loose pages in a violent wind. I sat there feigning a stolid demeanor but inside myself the desire to plead and beg her not to leave me battled with a ferocious passion to berate her for what I took to be her betrayal and deceit.

"I'm back," she echoed in a small voice. Was this the voice of shame and remorse or the voice of the bad news to come? "Are you Okay?" she asked, her voice now registering concern. Not as stolid as I'd wished to be, I thought, but then said the words that had come to me just that morning while in the shower, words intended for lighthearted use at a hoped for more relaxed and intimate time of reunion.

"I'm fine. It only hurts when I love."

"Ohhh," she wailed softly. "I'm so sorry. I did a terrible thing to you."

"Don't tell me!" I shot back in a panic.

"No, no nothing like what you're thinking. You couldn't possibly know what I'm referring to." She put her hand on mine. "I put you through hell for no reason, well, there was a reason but I should have known better than to tell you."

"You mean you should have lied."

"Yes. No! Well, I just shouldn't have told you about Hank. I should have said I was going home and left him out of it."

"Does this mean that he's not as important to you as you were thinking he was?"

"It means you are important to me." She was writing her own script. She was avoiding my questions and giving me answers that should have made me feel reassured. But they didn't. Instead I felt mistrustful of her in the same way that I had come to feel mistrustful of Harlan. It was as though words no longer had meaning, as though the words didn't mean what they were intended to mean.

"How come what you say doesn't make me feel reassured, huh? How come?"

"I don't know. I think I'm being pretty clear. Would this make it clearer?" And she turned me around and gave me a French kiss.

"Well, that says something but I'm not sure I got all of it. Could you repeat that for me?" She kissed me again, putting her arms around me and squeezing me to her while her tongue worked its way inside and around my mouth. There was a whoop from one of the boaters on the lake, then a loud whistle and some hand clapping. We both ignored the voyeurs. But wonderful as her kiss was, delightful as her hugs and remarkable tongue work, there was still a dark climate of doubt lurking inside me, still the dank air of suspicion and mistrust. And though I wished to shake myself free of it, wished for her love to feel as it had felt only days before, I could not let go of my distrust. With just a little more than a week left to us, sadly, something precious had been lost.

"So, the usual time tonight?"

"Yeah."

"You don't seem like yourself, Mel, still mad at me about going to New York?"

"No, just a little confused, that's all." She put her arm over my shoulder and gave me a sideways hug.

"It will be all right, don't worry."

5.

The Saturday night roast beef dinner was meant to set up the guests for the big Sunday lunch steak dinner send off. Sammy was busy telling stories so once again I had to do most of the work. After dessert he pulled me aside.

"Ben wants to know if you've started to do what he wants. I don't know what he wants but you do, so have you started?"

"You mean he didn't tell you about his plan to trap Harlan?"

"Don't tell me anything, I don't want to hear it." he said, his hands raised, palms facing me as though I was a stick up man. "I'm just giving you the message. Ben knows that as headwaiter I don't want any part of anything that makes my boys trust me less. I have a reputation to protect."

"Christ. He just sent me his plan the other night, I haven't had time yet, tell him. Or just say I'll do it. I'll do it." I'd been so preoccupied with Sarah I hadn't decided what to do about Harlan.

After cleaning my station and washing up I met Sarah on the side porch of the hotel. We usually met there. After her dinner she spent time with Heidi until Harlan and I finished work. The two girls would busy themselves trying on each other's clothes and exchanging lipsticks, makeup and, I was fairly certain, intimate confidences. The waiters were done before the busboys so he and I arrived separately and Harlan and Heidi would just go off, never waiting for the double date I had tried to arrange. I also suspected that Sarah had told Heidi she'd prefer not to do that. The wariness Sarah had fostered in me, first for Harlan but then, unwittingly, for herself as well, did not alter our meeting place. When she saw me she waved but remained leaning against the railing that rimmed the porch. It was still thrilling for me to look at her, to imagine touching her, but I perceived something was wrong. At first I wondered if it was about me. The change that had occurred had made me more chary and cautious with her, but then I could see it was something coming from her. She didn't smile her little puckered smile and she began to talk as soon as I stood next to her, no greeting, no embrace, no kiss. I dreaded that she was about to tell me she'd decided to stay with Hank and was here to say good-bye.

"I know you won't like what I did but please believe me, it was for your own good." Sarah wouldn't even look at me. She fidgeted with her cuticles, pushing at them with her thumbnail. I waited anxiously for her to go on. "Harlan flirted with me tonight after he came for Heidi. We'd been playing some music while we waited for him to come and by the time he showed up Heidi was in the bathroom so we were alone. The music that was playing was a slow song and I could tell by the way he looked at me that if I were to encourage him he would make a pass at me. So, this time, because he's done it to me before, when he smiled and winked at me in a way that could be understood to mean only one thing, I smiled back. It was as though you were irrelevant, you didn't exist, your name never even came up. There was no sense that you were his friend and that I was your girlfriend. He would have met me later, gone anywhere I asked, done anything I allowed. You didn't count."

"All this from the way that he looked at you?" I said numbly.

"No, damn it. Do you want me to give you all the gory details, Mel, is that what you need?" If a painful sense of shame was hiding behind her protest I was too much on guard to notice.

"Yes, that's what I need!" Harlan's suggestion that Sarah was criticizing him to deflect attention from her own doings had remained in my thoughts. I had raised my voice and was loud enough to disturb some men who were playing pinochle at a nearby table. A gruff, "Hey!" silenced me. "Sorry," I called out. "Let's take a walk," I said softly, but inside I was in turmoil. We left the porch and walked down the hill to the area of the swimming pool. It was too cold to swim and most of the hotel's guests were at Show Night. We sat down on deck chairs, the lights inside the pool casting an eerie, rippling aquamarine light across Sarah's face.

"Give me the details, exactly what happened." Her shoulders slumped as she began.

"I didn't have to say anything to him. I moved a little closer to him and then I looked down and away from him. He put his hand on my shoulder. I shivered, not from excitement but from disgust and revulsion. Heidi was just in the next room, Mel, and Harlan, Harlan had no concerns, no scruples." I could see that she was shivering again but I feared that if I were to touch her the feelings of disgust would spill over on to me. "Heidi called out she'd be right in and Harlan put his lips near my ear and said 'midnight at my car, and you won't be sorry'."

"What did you say?"

"Go fuck yourself. Can you believe that? I never curse, but I was so furious and ashamed I said 'go fuck yourself' to him. And I knew when I brought this back to you you'd try to find some way to make it not be what it really was." The episode with Harlan now out in the open she was calmer; her arms were folded across her breasts and her hands caressed the curves of her shoulders with light, soothing strokes. I felt the same sense of sickness I'd experienced reading the rejection letter from college, a sense of terrible disappointment and loss, not the impotent rage of helplessness. I didn't know if I had any control of what was happening with Sarah and me, and part of me could not believe Harlan had actually proposed a tryst with her, but then which one was I to believe? Maybe Sarah was trying to provoke him to make a scene in front of Heidi. Neither Sarah nor Harlan was proving to be particularly monogamous or loyal. My head was spinning and I couldn't think straight. Though I had wanted to see Sarah, be with Sarah, hold Sarah, right then I didn't want her near me. In an almost preternatural way, sensing my withdrawal, she got up and walked to the edge of the pool, her arms still folded across her breasts. "I think I'd like to go back to my room now. I don't feel very well."

When we were walking back to her building she said, "You don't believe me, do you."

"Sarah, of course I believe you, it's just that, well, possibly there was some kind of misunderstanding, a tease, a joke, I don't know. I'd like to think he didn't mean to be serious."

She stopped, turned, looked intently at me and, shaking her head, she said, "You don't believe me, it's written all over your face. My God, you don't believe me. You believe that insane story about judge Crater but you don't believe me!" She hurried away towards her room and when I caught up with her she held her hand up to stop my approach and said, "Good night, Mel." and marched into her dormitory leaving me standing at the door.

No matter how I tried to excuse the behavior Sarah had described, how I weighed possible alternative explanations, not that I could come up with any, it began to be clear to me there was no way I should ever trust Harlan again. Was he capable of trying to seduce my girlfriend? Of course he was and I became sick to my stomach considering it a likelihood not just a possibility. A cold sweat broke out all over my body and the same faintness that had overwhelmed me the night with Diana overtook me. I sat down on the stairs of Heidi's porch and lowered my head to my knees. Sarah would not make up such a story; that kind of deceitfulness and maliciousness just were not in her. He must have said something, done something to make her feel so disgusted by his very presence. And as I struggled with my confusion and injured disbelief the doubts Sarah had introduced became a swinging wrecking ball aimed directly at the already shrunken remains of my idealized creation of Harlan, one that shattered the foundation supporting the once colossal image I had erected. The entire summer it was as if I had hypnotized myself into an uncritical idolatry of Harlan and I'd behaved like a worshipful attendant who saw in him only the good. To acknowledge this now was totally humiliating. At last I asked myself why it was that Harlan had no friends. Was it because he really was so self-contained and independent or was he, like Abe Melman, hiding something from the rest of us? And when Sarah told me about his attempt to put the make on her, then what would he expect me to do? Ignore it? Make excuses for him again? It was almost ten o'clock and in a tormented and angry state I returned to the waiter's quarters, tears of sadness and rage spilling from my eyes, feelings of loss and thoughts of betrayal twisting around each other inside me. I had hoped to model myself after Harlan, to learn from him, to become something like his replica. How ridiculous and pathetic that now seemed.

At the threshold of the door to the waiters' quarters I stopped. What point in going inside now? Who would I wish to see there? I went down to the bar to be alone, have a few drinks and then go to bed after everyone else was asleep. I had no desire to drink myself into drunkenness or be a maudlin barfly, it was just somewhere to go other than my room. Julie, the bartender, smirked when I sat down. "Tom Collins?" he asked in a sarcastic voice, but before I could answer Louisa, the dance instructor, sidled up to the bar and said, "No, no, we'll have two seven and sevens and make it snappy, Julie, I need a drink." Louisa was probably at least twice my age, thirty-six or seven. We had rarely spoken but acknowledged each other with smiles and friendly nods when passing around the hotel. She was very attractive and there were times, before Sarah had come into my life, that I'd daydreamed about her so it was especially peculiar for her to be joining me just as Sarah was pulling away. She sat on the bar stool next to me and patted my shoulder. She'd already been drinking before she arrived and her hair reeked of cigarette smoke.

"It's Mel, isn't it?" she asked, lighting up a Pall Mall, "I know you were sometimes called Jack but I'll call you Mel. My brother Myron has a real problem with his name but there isn't a short version like Mel. I mean what would it be, My? This is my brother, My. I'd sound like a stammerer." She laughed and took another deep drag from her cigarette. "I heard about your girlfriend problem so I thought I'd give you some company tonight." Our drinks arrived and she quickly took a large swallow of hers while I sipped at mine. "Drink up, drink up, you'll feel better. It's what's helped me through my love affairs."

"How did you hear about me and Sarah?"

"People talk, Mel, people talk. Here they talk about very few things, tans, weight, money and sex. You and Sarah were pretty obviously . . . well, you were going with each other so people talked when she went to visit her old boyfriend." The ash on her cigarette had extended a gravity defying distance from the ember and before it collapsed on the bar she tapped it into the ashtray with an elegant gesture. It was a skill she'd mastered because I'd seen her perform that trick before. It had men staring expectantly at her cigarette waiting to see if she'd miscalculate the burn time and drop ashes all over herself, but she never did. "I know this is hard to believe, but you'll survive this and get over it. First loves never last. It took me a long time to get over my first love, . . . she's your first love isn't she?" I nodded. "Yeah, mine was a Steve. A lawyer. He came up here with his wife and kids my first summer as a dance instructor. I was such a sucker for him I could kick myself from here to Canarsie. Don't you like your drink you're not drinking it. Julie, another seven and seven please. Yeah, he was a lawyer of the tall dark and handsome variety. He signed up for lessons his first day here. Said he wanted to learn everything I could teach him but it was pretty clear pretty fast he wasn't talking about dancing." She shook her head ruefully, took a puff from her smoke and then finished her drink. Her mouth was always busy; talking, drinking, smoking at any given moment. It was amazing she had time to breathe. "He wore these loafers with tassels on them. I couldn't take my eyes off his feet when I was teaching him because those tassels looked so stupid to me." I laughed, and thought about the belt on the back of my khaki pants. "What's that, I kept asking myself, how do you fall for a guy with dumb tassels on his shoes?" And she began to laugh at her own story.

"How could you fall for a guy who wears shoes with tassels," I teased, joining in with her laughter.

"That wasn't even the worst of it, that was just his shoes. He said he'd leave his wife, Judy, but not until after his mother died. She had a weak heart and wasn't long for this world but he didn't want to be the one to do her in. She'd croak if he ever left Judy because she *luuhhved* Judy even more than she *luuhhved* him, her own son. What a load of crap." Louisa downed her second drink in one long swallow and waved her glass at Julie who nodded and poured another. "Love's a killer, Mel, a real killer. I wish I could live without it"

"Well, beware of lawyers bearing tassels," I said, pushing away from the bar. I hadn't wanted company, certainly not like hers.

"Hey!" she said in a loud voice that made people turn to look at us, "You have to see the whole picture. You're just a kid, what the hell do you know about anything," she said, wagging a finger at me. The seven and sevens had transported Louisa to the nasty subbasement of intoxication. More embarrassed than angry, I blushed and started to leave. "Don't go, baby, I'm sorry. Louisa is getting the meanies, isn't she? Sit down, stay a while, come on, don't leave." "No, I really have to. Long day coming up, the regular meals and, you know, a big steak dinner." "Yeah, yeah. Go on, it's okay, you're too young for me anyway." She took another mouthful of her drink and scanned the bar. "Way too young."

I was relieved to get away. Another broken heart, I thought, as I walked back towards my room. When you add it all up, the amount of time spent hoping and searching for love and the amount of time spent pining and grieving for a lost love probably exceeds the time spent actually loving by a factor of at least three. Still, when you have it, when you are in love with someone who makes you feel loved, well, who would want to live without that?

It was still too early to go back to my room so I wandered over to the main building of the hotel and watched the guests rocking on the front porch. I recognized a pair of couples from one of my tables. They had pulled their chairs into a little semicircle and were gently rocking while exchanging pleasantries. I didn't want them to see me. I didn't want to have to make idle conversation or pretend that everything was fine. I moved quickly away to the side and into the hotel parking lot. Walking between the cars I was able to pass unnoticed through the guest parking closest to the hotel's main building. It was cold. I could see the vapors of my breath when I exhaled through my mouth. The temperature was saying the summer was almost over. The cars that had been driven only recently radiated their engines' heat through their hoods. Now, as the steel contracted back to its resting shape, it emitted sudden metallic pings. The cars made me think of people, couples, together, easy, talking and laughing or just being. They'd have gone to town or to a movie and then driven back and parked, strolled back to their cabins or rooms, comfortable, unhurried. Then, once inside and alone, they'd undress, bathe, touch, and make love. At least that's how I thought I'd do it when it'd be me taking a vacation with my wife. Wife? Right then I wasn't even sure I still had a girlfriend, why was I thinking wife? But why not? Isn't a part of one's youth spent living in the imagined future?

I kept walking farther and farther back between the cars until I reached the area reserved for the hotel staff's cars. There

were no metallic pings or warm hoods back here. Then I heard
the creak of a car's springs somewhere nearby. Standing still and
waiting I heard the creak again only now it had become a rocking and repetitive rhythm. I looked around trying to locate the
car, hoping I was not standing too near. I had no interest in in-
truding on a couple after what had happened to me in the old
shed when I was with Rosie. The rhythmic creak became more
rapid and urgent and then I saw it was Harlan's car that was rocking and swaying four or five car lengths away from where I was
standing. He must be with Heidi, I thought, and not wanting to
embarrass her, Harlan probably didn't know the meaning of that
word, I hunched down right where I was. The creaking ceased just
as I did that, as though they'd seen me duck and they had frozen.
I peeked over the fender of the car I had knelt next to and tried
to see what they were doing but the windows of the car were
fogged with the moisture of their breath. There was some laughter and the muffled sound of voices, but I couldn't discern what
was being said. Then I realized they probably didn't know I had
stumbled upon them and were very happy on their own, pleased
and content. I squatted down again thinking of how to get away
without bringing attention to myself when I heard the car door
unlatch and swing open. Like a child I squeezed my eyes closed
and ducked my head. The sound of a woman's squeal, the sound
of a slap on the metal of the car and then Harlan's laugh made
me look up. From the back I saw the long ponytail, like Heidi's,
but this girl was smoking a cigarette, something Heidi would
never do. She took a long drag and turned as she exhaled so her
face was hidden in a dense foggy cloud of moist breath and
smoke when, holding the cigarette aloft she said, "I only do this
for you." I knew that voice. I knew it as well as any face. I didn't
have to wait for the smoke to drift away or even look up to know
it was Sarah, my Sarah, who was speaking.

I heard a groan that made the marrow of my bones rumble.
The groan grew louder and stronger. Then a loud cry, a disem-
bodied sound, a single shrill and resounding word: "NOOOO!!"
assaulted the night, awoke the sleeping crows whose carping
cries of alarm startled me into the awareness that it was I whose

howl had shattered the stillness. I sank to my knees weeping and covered my face with my hands. The sound of clicking car door locks and hurried footsteps did not raise my gaze. I was helpless with sobbing. Finally, I rubbed my eyes and rose like someone lost and confused. Harlan's car, still and empty, was just a few feet away. Stumbling forward I touched its cold hood and then, abruptly, snapped the radio antenna from its base and flung it away into the darkness. Achieving no satisfaction from that impulsive act and adorned with guilt I looked up at the star filled sky and for an instant felt the terror of insignificance that had gripped me as a child on my first trip to the planetarium. We are nothing. But, then, why such pain if we are nothing? Why?

They were gone. A man approached, I didn't know who he was, maybe a guest, maybe a member of the security staff, it didn't matter. He put his face directly in front of mine and stared into my eyes. He said, "keep it down people are trying to sleep" and left. I was glad he didn't ask me if I was okay. I was definitely not okay.

In an almost stuporous state I wandered out of the parking lot. I found myself trying to deny what I had seen, arguing that it wasn't possible, that it was *impossible* because Sarah didn't trust or like Harlan and would never be alone and intimate with him. I began to retch. This whole thing was disgusting. Who was it in the cloud of smoke if not her? Who? As much as I wished to deceive myself it was useless. I knew the music of her voice, the ballet of her gestures, the costume of her falling coiffure. My heart was broken.

I went to the lake knowing I would not sleep that night, maybe never sleep again. There was no other place to go and be left alone. Surely I could not return to my room, not there with Harlan who would deny that he was in the car, deny that Sarah would ever be with him, deny, deny, deny. I walked onto the dock and stared down into the lake. The water was very still, I remember, as if poised to receive my body. A numbness shut out the cold of the late August night. Did I want to die? Did I want to be found dead in the bulrushes along the opposite shore where the stray tennis balls washed aground? Did I want to give up my life before it had even begun?

"What are you staring at?" The voice was deep and patient. "Do you think there is peace there in the water? Do you?" I looked at the man. It was Abe but an Abe I had never seen before. He seemed taller, straighter, more dignified. "Come with me, come away from the water. Come on," he gestured, beckoning me to approach him. He was so different from the man I thought I knew it made me wonder if the entire night was some kind of bizarre hallucination, a lapse into madness. "Don't talk, it's all right. I know why you are standing on the edge. Come away from there, come with me and sit down over here," he said, motioning to the lawn chairs on the grass, "I will tell you a story that maybe can help you with your disappointment," he said softly.

"Disappointment? DISAPPOINTMENT!!!?? You do not have the words for what I'm feeling. Don't think you can just . . ."

"Enough! Don't speak to me in that tone. Listen to me, don't be so arrogant." His voice was firm and authoritative again the way he had sounded when he'd first called out to me. "I told you that Harlan was missing something and now it is clear how much he is missing. He is missing loyalty, he is missing compassion and, worst of all, he is missing a conscience. A man with a conscience could not do what he has done to you and to everyone that he charms. I have known men like him, cunning men. They are jackals. I know because I have been betrayed just like you." A cascade of questions threatened to pour from my mouth but I knew there was nothing for me to do but listen. What was occurring was remarkable, a singular event that had to be respected. Abe was going to reveal his secret to me.

"Some young men can be very vulnerable, Melvin, always on the lookout for new fathers, new heroes to mold themselves after. They may not even know it themselves but it is a function of their youth. Harlan knows that and recognizing it in you he despised you for it, yes, despised you, don't look so surprised it is the truth. He saw you as weak and he detested you for that. He respects Ron. He knows Ron is strong and independent. He also knows that Ron recognizes what he is so he woos you with false confusion about Ron's mistrust and dislike. He reeled you in like a perch from the lake and you practically jumped into his net, eager to be in his company, eager to learn." I must have grimaced because, though I didn't attempt to speak, Abe raised his hand as if to stop me. "Shush, shush, let me talk. Maybe it will help you. Then you can have your turn." We settled into the dampness of the lawn chairs and sat side by side while Abe continued. "It was so many years ago and yet there are days when it feels as fresh as right now. It involved a woman and a friend, just like you, it's an old story, happens all the time, but when it is your story, well . . . I don't have to tell you. I don't even know if you can hear me right now. My ears were ringing for weeks after she . . . after it happened."

"I hear you, Abe."

"Maybe I should just talk about the best way to handle this. What happened to me happened to me. It was different. Similar but different. It was someone I trusted who took advantage. And the woman, the girl . . ." His voice trailed off. "How do you separate the lovers? How do you assign blame? When it happened to me I was furious with my friend because I thought he had seduced Es . . . seduced her. I never considered that she was as eager for excitement as he was. I was foolish. You've been around here, you see how some of the women are, they're not all so innocent as you'd like to think." He stroked his face with a cupped hand. "Excuse me, that was unnecessary. But you do need to think that maybe Sarah was just as interested as Harlan, that's all." He had been disrupted by his musings and rose from the chair to stare out over the lake. He seemed in the process of forming himself, accreting substance and taking on a new shape. Until that moment to me he had seemed little more than an apostrophe, a presence indicating an absence. It was what was missing that had engaged me and Ron and the others and now he was revealing the pain whose existence we had only imagined, and then not kindly.

"I think Sarah was probably your first love. She will always be that for you, Melvin, no one can take that from you. Even though she breaks your heart she is the lover you will never forget and the one who will make you smile when she appears in your thoughts. But for that to happen you must find it in yourself to forgive her. If you don't, you could end up like me." This was said without ruefulness or irony and it was achingly poignant.

"Forgive her? I don't understand what you're talking about, I don't know how to do that. I can't do that. I can't."

"You can't do that tonight, I know that, I wasn't expecting you to just do it. This will take time, I understand, but I wanted to plant the seed of the idea. Time is a friend in these circumstances. My doctor, Dr. Rosensteil, always talks about 'a tincture of time' as part of his treatment. I . . ."

"Abe, please don't talk anymore." He had ceased to be transfigured and abruptly, mysteriously, had reverted to his usual dull, gloomy banal self. Whatever spirit had induced the transfiguring process making him seem like a noble sage had vanished, evaporated as quickly as the steamy breath of the lovers.

"I need to be left alone now, I need to think."

"Well, as long as you don't do anything foolish . . ."

"I'm not going to kill myself if that's what you mean. I'm not going to kill anyone. I just need to be left alone for a while. Please."

Abe looked at me with large sad eyes and shook his head no. "I can't leave you alone, that's all there is to say. I won't talk anymore but I won't leave you alone with yourself, that would be wrong." He folded his arms across his chest and waited for me to react. "Right now I'm about as upset as I have ever been in my life. You can't do anything but make me more upset. Just get away from me, you hear me? Get the hell away." I turned and walked quickly towards the path to the highway resisting the urge to look to see if he was following. I broke into a trot to keep my eyes straight ahead and fled from him. He called out to me but the slap of my soles on the tarmac road laid a noisy cover over his words and, finally, he gave up.

It was very late and when I reached the state road there were no cars to be seen. A barrier of three rows of heavy metal cable lined the shoulder at the far side of the highway and I crossed over to perch on it. The image of Sarah waving her cigarette at Harlan seized me as soon as I sat on the cables and my spirit felt as though it had been bludgeoned. Rage, jealousy, disbelief, and despair swirled over me like a swollen river that had jumped its banks. It was unbelievable, what else was there to say, unbelievable that they could be lovers. And Abe said I must forgive them if I am to get over this. He must be crazy. People commit murder over things like this, they cross continents to hunt down the lovers and repay them for the pain they've inflicted. But I knew I would never kill either one of them, would not even harm them, didn't have it in me to do harm to anyone.

I was glad to be alone. I could cry and then be silent, then cry again and not have to answer to any witnesses. It was very late but still no light in the eastern sky so there were a few hours of sleep before the morning wake-up call, the sleep of others. A car came speeding down the highway heading towards town and as it passed someone yelled "Jew asshole" out the driver's side window. "Townie prick!" I yelled back, but he was already gone around a curve. Maybe I could do harm to him, I mused, as I entered the hotel's property and walked towards the recreation hall. There was no one else around. The staff and the guests were all in bed asleep. The thought of tomorrow's ordinary routine was slowly beginning to numb the pain but then the realization that I'd have to confront Harlan in the morning revived everything. The wound was still too fresh. I wanted Harlan to be asleep before I returned to my room so I went to sit on the steps of the canteen for a while. I had barely sat down when someone screamed. At first it sounded to me like a child having a nightmare but then there was another scream and it clearly was the sound of a woman's cry from somewhere outside, not from a building. I stood up to hear her better if she screamed again and scanned the area around me but saw nothing. Then, like the echo of my own eruption, there was a loud "NOOOO" coming from the area of the tree-lined entrance driveway. I looked around for a tree branch or a large stone but seeing neither broke into a run in the direction of the screams. The lawn was soaked with dew and it was slippery but I hugged the tree line and raced towards what were now the muffled sobs of the woman. As the front gates came into view I stumbled on what seemed to be the exposed root of a tree but when I looked down there was a softball bat that had been dropped there. Lifting it, feeling its heft, gave me confidence I was well armed. There was a car parked just outside the gates and two men were struggling with a girl. One man stood behind her with a hand forced over her mouth while his other arm grasped her across the shoulders from below the chin. The other man was trying to lift her legs off the ground but she kept kicking furiously and he was cursing her and punching at her calves and thighs. Staying hidden in the line of trees I stole up behind the one whose back was to me and then leapt out and swatted him on the head with the bat. He dropped his grip on the girl and fell to his knees. Without an instant of hesitation I pulled the bat back as if to take a full swing but the sane and sober part of me realized that could be lethal and I choked up before bringing the bat around. It met his head just where the ear reaches for the temple and he quickly collapsed. His friend, initially stunned by the noise of the first blow, stopped grabbing at the girl's legs and was just about to lunge at me. That was when time itself seemed to pause and things began to happen in slow motion. There was no sound, no fear, no thoughts. It was Johnny now lunging at me over the fallen body of the girl, the Johnny that Ron had beaten outside Freddie's bar. Now my implement was no longer a bat but a ramrod, something to be thrust not swung. As Johnny leapt, his arms extended to grab me, I pushed the tip of the bat into his Adam's apple and pressed hard. Choking, he fell to the ground and then began coughing. Dispassionately and methodically I stepped beside him and swatted him in the head with the meat end of the bat. Both men lay unconscious in the hotel driveway. It was time to get away from this place quickly. As I knelt down beside the whimpering Sarah I said, "Are you okay?"

She rose slowly averting her eyes and ignoring the hand I had extended to assist her. Once on her feet she staggered for a few steps before getting her balance. She'd burst into tears, gain control, then start to cry again. I stood in place and waited until she was composed. My own state was too tumultuous to trust.

"We ought to be getting out of here before they wake up. Are you okay?"

"I'm all right, just a little shook up. Thank you," she said, looking at me for the first time.

"I did what I had to." There was so much else to be said but I didn't know how to begin. We stared at each other uncomfortably but relieved to be safe.

"C'mon, let's go," I said turning back towards the hotel.

"You must hate me."

"I do not hate you, let's just get out of here I'll walk you back to your room."

We walked down the main driveway in tandem, she leading the way. Her shoulders were slumped and her feet searched the ground with small, tentative steps. Without either hate or love in my heart I watched the twitch of her buttocks, then wondered where Harlan's hands had been on and in her body feeling suddenly enraged. Sarah stopped, as though she'd sensed my change, and turned to me.

"I heard you scream, the 'no' you let out. I walked right past you in the parking lot but your face was hidden in your hands." She embraced her shoulders with her hands trying to shut out the cold. "I didn't feel I was being bad until I saw you, crumpled up like you were broken. I know I've been bad in so many ways." She shuddered. "I've lied to you, I've cheated on you, I don't know why you're even listening to me. I thought I was so cool, above it all, not doing anything to hurt you, just having some secret fun on the side, what you didn't know wouldn't hurt you and if Harlan took advantage of you, well, I'd warned you. Then, when I saw you tonight, I realized what I had done and there's probably no undoing that damage. I walked around the grounds of the hotel trying to think of what I'd say to you. Harlan said, 'deny it was you' when we parted but I'm not that good a liar, Mel, and I don't want to hurt you anymore than I already have. I was deciding whether to look for you when those two goons grabbed me and started pawing at me and trying to drag me off into their car. Thank God you came when you did."

"It was your scream."

"God, I hoped somebody would hear that. Then one of them slapped his hand over my mouth and I bit his fingers. I managed to scream once more and then he had me from behind and I couldn't move anything but my legs and the other guy kept grabbing at them, and . . ." She was agitated, crying and speaking rapidly, trying to purge herself of the terror she had felt by telling me as many of the details of her story as she could remember. "I hoped you would be around. I hoped you weren't so angry that you'd leave me to them. I knew you'd recognize my voice, I knew it." I had recognized her dread and fear and helplessness, but not her voice. Had I been like Harlan I would have smiled modestly accepting her description and attendant gratitude and, perhaps, sought to extract sexual compensation, but I was not like him. Still reeling from the night's events I said nothing. Let her think what she likes, I mused, it's not my responsibility. We arrived at her cabin in silence a short time later and she paused at the entrance.

"Mel, I'm so sorry for what I've done. I never meant to hurt you, I care deeply for you, I . . . I'm in love with you. I didn't know that until tonight but now I know, I love you. Please forgive me."

Again the tears, the convulsive sobbing, the imploring looks and beseeching hands. And I? Once again I was numb. What I had wished and waited for from her was now being offered and it had no more effect upon me than the casual glance of a stranger.

"It's late, you're safe now, go inside."

"Don't go, Mel, please don't go."

"Shhh, you'll wake everybody up. It's okay, you'll be fine," I droned in a monotone. "Go in."

She was still crying when she turned away and left me. I was stunned, there is no other way to describe my state at that moment. Any one of the events of that night would have been sufficient to provoke a turmoil of emotions but to have experienced betrayal, revelation upon revelation, violence, and a declaration of love, the so wished for declaration of love, one after the other, torrentially, demanded an intense numbing to endure such a flood. At first I thought I should not return to my room for the remaining hours of the night. Facing Harlan in such a state would be a mistake. He would read it immediately and mold it to his own purposes. As furious as I was I knew if I was to come away with any sense of pride I would have to have control of myself when the confrontation occurred. In the past, bristling with outrage and righteous indignation, I could dissolve into tears too easily when my argument was dismissed with the dispassionate, impersonal reason of my opponent. For me, all arguments were personal and the one to come with Harlan couldn't be more personal. And it would come very soon.

6.

If you've had your heart broken then you know it is a long time your pain will be with you unrelieved. You take the pieces of your shattered story and fit them together over and over again like a jigsaw puzzle hoping each time to form a new image. You want the picture to be different than the one on the cover of the puzzle box but the pieces give you only the same sadness that you know: you've lost your love; it's over. Just then, still in the grip of the shock, I did not attempt reconfiguring events in search of a prettier picture. It was too soon for that. It did not, however, require much mulling over to see Harlan as others had perceived him from the start. Smooth glided easily into slick, charming into manipulative, instructive into destructive.

But Sarah, what was I to make of her? Had I given it any thought at all in the beginning of course I would have realized it was likely a Hank was lurking somewhere at the periphery. Such a pretty girl would not be without an attachment. There was Ron right under my nose with a Vivian in the remote reaches of the Catskills but a Martha on site. Was I no more to Sarah than what Martha was to Ron? Was I her summer accommodation? And Harlan. Was all of her criticism, suspicion and distrust just a means to keep their relationship hidden and protected, a way to avoid revealing to me the depth of their passion, a passion she did not feel for me? Was her picking a fight about him tonight a way for her to spend more time with him? The curdling feelings of humiliation were sickening. I looked up at the sky. Soon it would be dawn. There was work waiting to be done, kitchen work and personal work. I walked around the main building trying to calm myself, trying to imagine the argument with Harlan and what to say to him. After a while it was clear there was nothing to be gained by postponing my meeting with Harlan. I knew what had to be said and what I had to do. I knew it was time. I was ready.

When I returned to our room Harlan was lying on his cot and smoking. He must have been waiting for me because it was not his usual practice to just lie around smoking in the early morning hours. Late as it was Ron was still out. Stripping off my sweater I said "Hi," affecting a calm demeanor while fulminating inside.

"Did you and Sarah have a good time tonight?" he asked in a matter of fact way.

"Yeah, terrific." My legs began to quaver and I had to sit down on Ron's bunk.

"You look a little pale, are you sure you're okay?" He was so cool it was as though nothing had taken place, no change, no betrayal. "I have to tell you some bad news," he said, throwing his legs off the bed and dropping his cigarette in the soda can he was using as an ashtray. He held up a pack of Luckys, offered them to me and when I shook my head he pulled one out and lit it for himself. My heart was pounding and the muscles in my chest were tight enough to choke the air out of me but I sat there silently, seething. "While I was waiting for Heidi to get dressed tonight I was talking to Sarah, the way I usually do." He sighed and mopped at some imaginary perspiration on his brow. Then he took a long drag on his cigarette. I knew where he was heading. "Sarah came up to me all of a sudden and took my hand. She said, 'You know, Harlan, you and I could be better friends.' I said that I thought we were terrific friends already." He came to sit next to me on the bunk bed. "I really hate having to tell you this, Jack, but you're my friend and I have to do what's right for you. She put her mouth right next to my ear and whispered, 'Come on, Harlan, you know what I mean, we never get to be alone just the two of us. Mel and Heidi don't have to know anything about what we do if we keep it to ourselves. I'm not Cinderella, after midnight would work just fine for me.' I was shocked, but before I could say a word she put her hand over my mouth and said,

'Midnight at your car. If you say one word to Mel I'll tell him it was your idea.' Heidi came back into the room just then and . . ."

"Bullshit!"

"Hey, I know this is hard for you to take but . . ."

"Liar! You're lying Harlan. Stop pretending it was Sarah. It's both of you." I was shaking.

"Jack, why would I make this up? Ohhh, I know, she already told you her story. She put it all off on me. Why would I do such a thing to you, Jack, why? You know Heidi and I are . . ."

"Heidi, and your tennis partner, and the woman who wanted you to teach her son to dive and any skirt on the fucking planet so why not Sarah too?"

"You flatter me Jack . . ."

"And stop calling me Jack. My name is Mel. Melvin. Like it or not that's my name. God I was so fucking stupid to listen to you. How ridiculous I must have looked to everybody."

"You're upset. Don't take it out on me because your girl-friend made a play for me. You know I wouldn't do anything to hurt you, you know that." He slammed the soda can down on the floor and got up from the bed indignantly. He folded his arms across his chest and walked to the window keeping his back to me. For a moment, insanely, I almost felt drawn back to him. "This is insulting. After all that I've tried to do to help you with girls, after letting you in on a serious family secret, you just go and . . ."

"It's just not going to work, Harlan, don't waste your breath, it's not going to work. I saw you tonight. I saw you and Sarah in the parking lot so stop lying to me." I was gaining control as we volleyed our retorts. "You know, I should probably take a swing at you and try to knock you out. I don't know if I would hit you or just set myself up for you to beat the shit out of me, either way it wouldn't change anything. Sarah and I are done and you and I are done and that's it. As Sammy would say, end of story." He turned around and slowly unfolded his arms extending them out from his sides like a choral director gathering in the attention of his singers.

"Do you honestly believe that was Sarah in my car? Haven't you ever noticed how much Heidi and Sarah look alike? It's this

Hank thing that has you unstrung, Jack, that's what's really going on. I should be upset with you, if you think about it, creeping around the parking lot and spying on me and then accusing me of screwing around with your girlfriend." He was smiling. God damn him, he was smiling. Had my pain and outrage amused him, or was he just misapplying the Hawthorne charm he used as a balm on the wounds he inflicted so selfishly.

"The fact is I caught you by accident and . . . there you go trying to blame me and make me feel guilty for something bad when it's you who's been the lying cheat."

"Watch yourself, Melvin, or you may get that drubbing you were talking about."

"What will that solve? You've already ruined everything for me, do you think a black eye will make that much difference?"

"I won't give you a black eye, it may affect your tips and I'm not out to cost you any money."

"Oh no, just to pick my pockets for your father's imaginary heart condition."

"Imaginary? You saw him yourself, was that imagi . . ."

"Cut it out! Enough of your bullshit! I spoke with him, he told me all about you. He's not dying."

Harlan approached me with sadness in his face. He shook his head, rubbed his cheek, and the next thing I knew I was on the floor struggling for air. He had hit me so hard and so fast I still can't remember seeing the punch come.

"You shouldn't have bothered my family. You had no right to go there without me. You are never to do that again." He rubbed the knuckles of his right hand. "And that's also for your brother Steve who went where he shouldn't have. I was just re-paying you in kind with Sarah for what he did to me a couple of years ago." I was too breathless to speak but my face registered my surprise. "I know, I know, I've never worked here before, the noble Whites only work here at Braverman's, but you're so provincial you can't wander off the site. Steve is a much sharper guy than you'll ever be. He found his way to my turf a few years ago and lured away a girl I was pretty serious with." His expression hardened and his tone expressed his bitterness. "I loved that girl."

"Sorry," I said reflexively. "No, not sorry. In fact I don't believe you."

"I don't give a damn what you believe and don't believe and if I were you, with your face at the level of my shoes, I'd keep the smart ass comments to myself."

But there was to be no turning back; I had gone too far for that. "If it's true, good I'm glad Steve did it, but I can't listen to your bullshit anymore, Harlan, nothing you say can be trusted."

"Ask your brother about Shelley, Rochelle at the Pines. Ask him."

"Harlan you are not listening to me. I don't believe you. You could tell me the sky is blue on a bright sunny day and if I didn't see it for myself I wouldn't believe you." I raised myself from the floor and sat on Ron's bed. "I will not talk to Steve about Shelley because I will not make a fool out of myself because of you ever again. In fact, I am going to do you a favor by way of doing myself a favor." Harlan came over and sat down next to me. I winced.

"Don't worry I won't hit you again. What kind of favor can you do for me, kiddo?" Even in a sitting position his body seemed to swagger. He reached into his shirt and pulled out his cigarettes again but this time didn't offer one to me. "Just what kind of favor can a pathetic little boy do?"

"What can I do? I can save your ass from the roughing up Ben B. has in store for you, and from the Sullivan County State troopers waiting for their turn afterward." Harlan angled his body towards mine and for the first time since knowing him he seemed nervous.

"Now *you're* bluffing. Why would Ben want to hurt me? He knows his daughter loves me and I may not be the boyfriend of his choice, but roughing me up? You'll have to come up with something better than that."

"It's only a little bit about Heidi. It's a lot about theft, stealing, burglary—you choose the word that fits best for what you do."

"That's a lot of crap, I mean that's nonsense." If only for an instant his tension had cracked open the veneer of poise revealing the street kid hidden behind, and he knew it. "What makes me the thief? Why would I take that kind of risk, Jack? My father's privacy is my most important priority and doing anything as chancy as stealing would be crazy."

"I'm telling you what I know. I'm not going to stick up for you, I don't care. It's your ass and you can put it anywhere you like. I just think you'd be doing yourself a favor to pack up and get the hell out of here."

"If you're so angry and fed up with me why would you give me this break? Why don't you let someone who actually might be able to rough me up do it? See what I mean? Why should I believe *you*? Or are you trying to get Sarah back without me around." He was cool and in control again.

"I'm doing this because it's how I came to understand things growing up, don't rat out a friend. Like you or not, if I let Ben or the police get to you when I can prevent it, I've violated some kind of code."

"Rat out a friend? I thought you just said you don't trust me and don't believe anything I say so how are we friends?"

"I know, it doesn't make sense, but it feels like the right thing to do. I can't explain it any better than that." But I tried to anyway. "It has to do with honor, do you know what that is? Yes, of course you do because you play people for believing in things like that. Oh, just get out." Letting the smoke drift out of his open mouth he studied me, his head tilted back, and then he exhaled a cloud of gray.

"Who told you about this plan?"

"Ben. And some guy named Joe." Harlan seemed to startle.

"Joe? Tough guy, salt and pepper crew cut, blue eyes?"

"Yeah, that Joe, you know him?"

"What exactly did he say?"

"Harlan, do you think you have time for this? They are very serious and they expected me to send you out there about now, have you go to the Bravermans' storm cellar where they'd grab you. So if you don't show up they'll come here looking for you. And me." I added, realizing that if Harlan didn't leave I'd have no excuse for not following Ben Braverman's instructions. Codes of camaraderie wouldn't hold any value with Ben. My loyalty was expected to be to him alone.

"Joe is an ex-cop. A city tough guy who was as much a crook as he was a cop. So Ben has him on his payroll now." He got up from the bed and went directly to the dresser we all shared. Just as he opened his drawer Ron came in.

"Make sure you're in the right drawer, Mr. Harvard. Why is everyone up so early?" Ron had suddenly realized that preparing for work was not why Harlan and I were awake and still dressed in the clothes we'd worn the night before. I wished he hadn't come back then. It would have been so much easier if Harlan had just packed up and left.

"You'd better get going, Harlan."

"Going where, what's going on?"

Harlan nodded, pulled his suitcase out from under his bed, opened the latches and spread the case across his bed, its compartments empty but for a leather toiletry kit that was tightly strapped to the bottom half of the case that had rested on the floor.

"Harlan has to get out of here for a family emergency." I said to Ron without looking at him.

While Harlan gathered his clothes from his dresser drawer, Ron walked to Harlan's bed and looked down at the leather kit.

"What's that, your stash? Is that where you hide the cash and the jewels?"

"Actually, Ron, the only thing in there is the Hope Diamond. It takes up all the space," and with that Harlan dropped his clothes on top of the kit, threw in a pair of shoes and then closed the suitcase. "Have a miserable life, Ron. Thank you, Jack." He was out the door before Ron or I could speak.

"All right, now the truth, what just happened?"

"You saw what happened, Harlan left. He quit. Isn't that what you've wanted all summer long?"

"Don't insult me Melvin, I know there's more than you're telling me and I want to hear it, the truth!" The truth was the last thing I wanted him or anyone else to hear.

"It's what I told you, he quit. It's too late to argue." I climbed up to my bunk and kicked off my shoes. "I'm going to grab some sleep. We have to be up in an hour." I turned towards the wall as the tears began to flow.

"You're not getting any sleep until you tell me what just happened here," Ron said, pulling my sheets from me and grabbing at my leg. "C'mon the truth." The truth was still too raw to tell.

"Harlan was stealing, that's why he's beating it. Ben B wanted me to help trap him and I told Harlan about that so he's gone. Okay? Enough?"

"Help trap him how, what could you do to help trap him, c'mon tell me." He was gleeful, rubbing his palms together as briskly as Solly Schwartz.

"Oh for God's sake give up, Ron, there's nothing else to tell. Ben had the idea Harlan was the thief he's been looking for and wanted me to send him someplace on the grounds where he'd get caught. I don't know why he'd be caught, what he'd be guilty of, I was just supposed to tell him to go there."

"Go where?" Ron would be Ron no matter how I tried to ward him off. He wanted the details.

"Why don't you ask your buddy Ben? It was his idea."

"But I'm asking my buddy Mel. I have a hunch Jack also left with Harlan, am I right?" If I wasn't so tired and distraught I might have acknowledged his prescience.

"Ron, Sarah and I broke up tonight. I'll tell you about it tomorrow, but PLEASE!! I need to go to sleep now." I rolled over to face the wall and again began to cry.

Ron placed his hand gently on my hip, squeezed and said, "You and Sarah broke up? Really? I'm sorry Melvin. When you're ready you can tell me what happened." I felt him sit on his bunk below me. I heard his shoes drop on the floor, felt him struggle out of his clothes and drop them as well, and then snuggle into his bedclothes. So, finally, the night ends, I thought.

But there was to be no sleep that night. No sooner was Ron quiet than the realization that Sarah was lost overpowered and engulfed me. The ache of the loss obliterated any contact with the loving feelings that had lifted me, weightless, to float through much of August. I hoped the pain would not last and would never be available for summons as more than a memory of suffering. I had sprained my ankles so often and broken enough bones to know the brain was so constructed as to protect us from the re-experiencing of such pain. We don't have to stand in the fire a second time to remember the burn. Was the broken heart subject to the same rules of protection? Sobbing into my pillow I saw her exit Harlan's car, her cigarette held aloft, over and over again, each time her smile wider, the fog and smoke no longer obscuring her joy at having been with him. Finally, the desolation drove me from my bed. Ron's snoring blanketed any noise I made while going through my dresser for a change of clothes.

Weak with grief I went into the shower and turned on the spray. The water went from cold to hot to warm as I adjusted the temperature. The sky was already gray at the window over the toilets. Another day was beginning. I thought, the judge, or whoever he was, was wrong about routine. Sure you may get up at the same time and reenact the routine ritual ablutions of the morning but that day is different: the light is different, and you are different. If you are living, not merely existing, each day alters you and makes you a little bit different, just as every tide alters the sands of a beach. In the two months at the hotel I had been changed day by day, imperceptibly on any given day but, on a signal day, an abrupt and startling event occurs and you are transformed. The night before had been such a transforming experience. I rubbed my stomach where Harlan punched me. It was still tender between the navel and the place where the rib cage parts, the solar plexus, the place boxers try to land their body blows. If not for that pain I might have tried to trick myself into believing it all had been a dream or a trick of the imagination, something to enliven a dull summer job. I know I wished it all had been a fantasy, that Harlan had never said more than hello to Sarah and that she thought he was an okay guy but just a little too slick for her taste, a pair interested in no more than the occasional courteous exchange. Then both might still be close to me. Now both were lost. The shit had found me.

Chapter Twelve

Sammy was waiting for me as soon as I arrived in the kitchen for breakfast.

"How would you like to be a waiter for your last week?"

"Working for you, Sammy, is like being a waiter all summer."

"If my query makes you queasy do not become quarrelsome and querulous because there is a quid pro quo."

"Shit," I said, in disgust, "is this really the time for one of your dictionary games?"

"It's always the time for my dictionary games, you illiterate idiot. Ben told me Harlan left early this morning. If you take Harlan's station starting at lunch I'll collect your tips for the past week from our guests and let you collect what you can of Harlan's tips. His busboy can't wait on a whole station of tables, I know that and he knows that, and if you fill in for today you can have the station for the week and then come back as a waiter next summer." He was beaming, delighted, promoting me well in advance of the age at which waiters were hired.

"No thanks, I'll stay with you." I'd had enough changes and wasn't about to inform Sammy right then that I didn't intend to be back next year.

"Melvin, don't let me down, I know Hawthorne is gone and the employment agency only has drek available, come on, be a waiter for me."

"I'm sorry, Sammy, there must be someone else you can ask, I just can't do it." A disgusted look appeared on his face, a sneer that dilated his nostrils and pulled the corners of his mouth down.

"This is how you thank me, this is how you show appreciation for everything I've done for you?"

"That's not fair, Sammy, I've never refused you before."

"I've never asked you for anything before, for godsakes, all I ever asked you to do was your job. This is the first time I ask you for a little something extra, and this is how you say thank you to me." Despite his pressure I wouldn't change my stand. "I guess that's it. Okay, I'll find someone else. And you can be a busboy again next year."

Leaving the dining room after breakfast I was accosted by Ben Braverman at the back door.

"Melvin, you didn't tell me Harlan left the hotel. Did you tell him about your meeting with Joe?"

"Never."

"Did you tell him about a chute at the side of my house?"

"No. We had a fight about Sarah and then he left."

"He left because you two fought about your girlfriend? Melvin, do you think I'm an idiot? Why would he leave over something like that? Did it have anything to do with my daughter?"

"In a way. He was getting involved with Sarah and,—listen, I'm still pretty upset about all of this and . . ." Ben grabbed my shoulders and spun me around to face him.

"You told him about the trap, admit it, don't lie to me." I looked away and nodded.

"I just wanted you to tell me the truth, Melvin. Harlan was seen trying to leave the grounds very early this morning. I figured he was going to beat it if he got wind of my plan so I had Joe on watch in the parking lot. Joe discouraged him from trying to pack it in and leave. Joe is very persuasive," he said, with a knowing smile, "and Harlan got the message, but you won't be seeing him again. And by the way, Harlan was the thief we were looking for. He had a jewelry store in his toiletry kit. Someone will come by later to collect the rest of his things." He gave my shoulders an affectionate tug then turned and walked away. It was a relief that in the end I was spared having to turn Harlan over to Ben. He had betrayed me, but I hadn't betrayed him; I hadn't violated the code.

I walked back to my room wondering about the things Harlan left behind. What were his things? There was the temptation, a strong desire to look into Harlan's dresser drawer. Who knows what's to be found there? As a child I had discovered pornographic pictures in the dresser drawers of Jerry and Steve. They were hard core black and white photos of couples engaged in sex, the men naked but for the black anklet socks they wore. Some of the men attempted to disguise themselves by drawing the outlines of eyeglass frames around their eyes, as if these pictures might fall into the hands of their friends and relatives who'd scrutinize the porn wondering, could that be Manny? Harlan probably didn't need any pictures. He didn't flip through copies of Playboy because he had women climbing all over him like grape vines on an arbor. For all of his womanizing, his seductions and betrayals, he never joined in the waiters and busboys sex talk about girls. In the end I shrugged off the impulse to search whatever he might have left behind knowing there'd be no money, or jewels, or answers to his mystery.

There was some time to kill before lunch but it was of no use to me. I was without strength or vitality. I felt as though my muscles had been detached from my bones. If I were to go to the basketball court my shots would never reach the backboard; if I went to the pool to swim I'd sink like an anchor and drown. There was nothing that appealed. It had been several weeks since I'd smoked a cigarette and even that held no temptation. It was as though grief had removed me from myself and the world of the every day. Ron was waiting for me when I entered our room. His promise to be chaste until he and Vivian were reunited had failed the test of Martha's physical allure and, like a compulsive masturbator, Ron would be guilt-ridden and self-loathing in the immediate aftermath of an episode only to be drawn back again by desire and the need to re-test his potency.

"So, what happened with you and Sarah?"

"Not now, Ron, it's just too soon, it still hurts too much to talk about."

"Is that what you and Harlan fought about last night?"

"Who said we fought?"

"Nosy Abe. He said he heard a loud thud that woke him up. When he peeked into the room you were gasping for breath on the floor and Harlan was standing over you rubbing his fist."

"Yeah, well, I wouldn't call that a fight. It was just his one punch and that wasn't about Sarah."

"That bastard. So what was it, you wanted switchies with Heidi and Mr. Cool took offense?"

"Listen! I don't want to talk about it! Let it rest. I'll tell you when I'm ready."

"Bullshit, you can tell me right now. In a few days this will matter no more to you than judge Crater did, believe me. Remember how hard you worked to help me with that?" Because of or perhaps despite his sarcasm I wouldn't reveal what I knew about the judge.

"Another bad night with Martha, Ron, is that what you're taking out on me?" Whatever warmth he'd shown when I told him Sarah and I were through had cooled. Was it his struggle to abstain from luxuriating in Martha's spectacular anatomy that had him so tense or was he just mean by nature? Either way there was no time for this now.

"Even a bad day with Martha beats no day with Sarah."

"Whatever you say." I grabbed my towel and went to the shower room to get away from him.

Immediately I began thinking of Sarah and her demeanor just hours ago. She'd said I love you. It didn't make me feel any better then and recalling it in the midst of my pain only made it worse. Was it truly over? Was I too injured to let her back in? The pain of betrayal and loss is ineffable. You know it when you feel it. It can't be described or imagined; it is a unique pain that exists apart from language. Shakespeare wrote only "howl" for Lear when he comes upon the body of his beloved Cordelia, "howl" because the pain of that grief strikes one dumb, obliterates words and leaves one to wail like a wounded animal.

Once before in a circumstance of heartbreak I learned, completely by chance, that swimming a great distance under water grants you asylum from the pain. You become aware of everything but your thoughts then, aware of your breathing, aware of your surroundings, aware of your physical experience of buoyancy, of the temperature and pressure of the water against your body, of the quality of the light around you, of anything and everything but your emotions and your thoughts. Amidst the waterworks of showers and sinks and toilets I sought to submerge myself in an interior sanctuary but my tears would not hold back and as I started to cry Ivan Goldman and Spider Johnson came into the room. Pride could not suppress my pain but it could propel me into the shower and, still in the clothes I'd worn for breakfast, I turned on the cold water and stood under the icy spray as it washed the tears from my face. Ivan and Spider left without a word. They had witnessed my madness and turned away from it just as people do in the subways or the streets of New York City, as if to acknowledge it might somehow burden them with an insufferable responsibility for me. Better just to look away and leave.

2.

I sleep walked through lunch and dinner. Sammy did not chide me for being aloof and unsociable that night. Either he saw that I was totally incapable of any kind of friendly interaction or he was punishing me with indifference, his "eye for an eye" kind of justice. "Sammy, I don't mean to disappoint you it's just that I've had so many things change in such a short time I can't take anymore changes." He shrugged and left me sitting near our side stand. The thought of Sarah was still too painful to dwell on. I had not tried to contact her and Heidi, who was completely undone by Harlan's exit, had not shown her face all day and was not available to bear messages between us. I caromed between longing and resentment whenever Sarah's face appeared in my thoughts. I was unable to make a plan, to think straight.

With Harlan gone and Ron off to see Martha yet again I had the room to myself. A visceral churning kept launching me off my bed and into the center of the room, but for what?

My restless pacing and mindless motion was like an awkward ballet performed to atonal music. Every thought felt ugly, discordant, wrong in some way. On the one hand wait for her to come to me and beg forgiveness, on the other hunt her down and make passionate love to her, let the lusty fires consume the awkward fumblings of the past and her betrayal as well, yes, even that, like a smelting furnace, so a new love might be cast from the molten remains.

By 10 o'clock I knew Sarah was not going to come looking for me. I sat on Harlan's bed contemplating what I believed were my choices. Hadn't she said she loved me? Hadn't she sobbed and pleaded with me only hours ago? Why be so fearful of meeting her, why expect her to be other than as she was? But I had a feeling Sarah would not be as I had left her early that morning. Should I trust such a feeling? Was the old cautious Melvin back in charge? What happened to the Melvin who said even bad news is better than no news? What happened was he didn't get accepted to Columbia and had become wary of that attitude. Nonetheless, I knew it would be another sleepless night if Sarah and I didn't meet.

Once again, on the path behind the waiters' quarters, I stumbled on the old well's stones. For all I knew Judge crater was down there after all but this wasn't the time to ponder that possibility. Funny how things had proceeded since Ron and Lenny marched me to this place. I would have been laughing about how the summer had evolved if Sarah and I were okay; but we were not. This was not the time for laughter.

Sarah's roommate Barbara met me on the porch of the counselors' cabin.

"Sarah is at Heidi's house. You can imagine how Heidi is feeling." It seemed as though Sarah had said nothing about our crisis to Barbara because her tone was matter of fact and chummy.

"Yeah, Harlan left early this morning. I bet he never said goodbye to Heidi."

"Oh, but he did. He even apologized to her for flirting with other women."

"Flirting! That's a laugh."

"Well, it wasn't with other women," she said, drawing quotes in the air around other women, "it was with Sarah." I stiffened. "He said he didn't mean anything by it, just being playful, but he should never have done anything like that, however innocent, with Heidi's dearest friend."

"How did you hear about this?"

"Sarah told me. She was with Heidi all morning and at lunch she asked me to cover her group so she could stay with Heidi and comfort her some more. That was when she told me."

"Is she going to sleep there tonight?"

"Maybe, she didn't say."

"Maybe I should bring her some clothes, you know, a nightgown, or pajamas or . . ."

"Heidi has plenty of pajamas, Mel, you don't have to bring her anything."

"I want to see her," I blurted out suddenly, startling us both.

"She doesn't want to see you, Mel, not yet."

"What do you mean?"

"Mel, give her some time. She was almost raped by those two bastards last night. You saved her, I know, and she's very grateful to you for that, but she can't be around anything male right now."

"Anything male? You mean roosters, and stallions, or just men?"

"Don't be hurt, it'll be okay, just give her a little time."

"That's all there is is a little time. There's only a week left to the summer," I protested in vain. Barbara shrugged and went back into the cabin.

When you come right down to it, the last thing you think at a time like this is that she's too embarrassed to face you. No, what you think is she doesn't care about you anymore and is deliberately avoiding you rather than say it to your face. I considered going to the Braverman residence and knocking on the door but it was late and Ben probably had exhausted his tolerance for my romantic travails. The late August cold enveloped me and made me shiver. Standing on the porch of the dormitory afloat in the murmurous sounds of girls preparing for bed, I wondered about my choices. Was I already forgiving Sarah for what I'd seen? Was I craving her so ardently I'd accept her on any terms? Should I simply leave and forget her, no goodbyes, no see you in the city, no expectations of anything? I didn't have to decide at that hour. It was only later that I realized it was not even my decision to make.

That night I didn't sleep at all but swam and swam in my internal refuge.

3.

Newcomers kept arriving in the driveway for the final week of summer vacation, the exhaustion of the trip evident on their faces, in their bodies, and the wilted appearance of their clothing. Bernie Abramowitz. pacing, pinching, and pumping his way through the crowd was never happier than on these occasions of welcoming. I no longer felt irritated by his displays but instead felt pity for him and gratitude in the knowledge that my life would never be anything like his. Never.

About half of my guests were holdovers who had taken the last two weeks of August for their vacations. They enjoyed the warm days and cool nights but sacrificed the extra daylight hours the July vacationers enjoyed. There were those who were philosophical about the distribution of summer's bounty and celebrated their share, but then there were others who thrived on complaint, the ones who felt they weren't getting what was coming to them. Sammy had no patience with the latter group. His regulars were celebrants happy to be in the country and content with Sammy's kibitzing. The others, well, Sammy had a way of describing them that still makes me laugh when I think of it. "Nothing is ever good enough for these trumbeniks. Not only is their glass half empty, it's dirty and there's a chip in the lip."

Sammy was still cool with me but he introduced me politely to our new guests. No regulars were among the last week's roster of new arrivals and this seemed to drive home to him the inevitability of the end of summer. It was already as good as over. We served the usual Sunday night dinner of boiled beef, stuffed chicken breasts or steamed vegetable platter, and the ice cream dessert was the hit of the meal. During the clean-up Sammy carried in a tray of glasses for me and then sat me down.

"You made a mistake, Melvin, not taking me up on my offer to make you a waiter. I hired a man from town who will fill in for Harlan and I decided to keep that station at just three tables instead of four. You could have made extra money and worked less for it, but that was your decision."

"So does that mean Ron and I won't be getting a new roommate?" Shaking his head, he frowned.

"No, there won't be anyone else staying in the room. That's what's important to you? Not the money? Not my feelings for you? Whether there's a new roommate for one week? Meshugah."

At that moment I felt an understanding and empathy for Sammy emerge from the general climate of sadness enveloping me. Here was a man with a raw, uncultivated intelligence surrounded summer after summer by boys and young men who would go on to careers in various professions, careers that would carry them away from him and Braverman's and these sagging mountains forever. Lacking the education he admired he had settled for being a character, an eccentric personality, the unforgettable drill sergeant who never graduates with the officers he's trained. His story was hidden behind a white shirt and a black bow tie, his sad clown's costume.

I asked, "Will Heidi be working in the dining room now that Harlan, I mean the thief, is gone?" Heidi was still my best route back to Sarah.

"Probably not. She is so upset I don't think she'll be working anywhere the last week of the summer. And you, you too are upset. Who ever thought Harlan would cause so much damage?" Ron, I thought, Ron did. "Well, maybe I can give her some comfort. Do you think the Bravermans would mind?" Sammy shrugged and forced a smile for me.

"Melvin, I have no answers for that question." He squeezed my arm and left me at the side stand.

I showered and changed into khakis and a navy and green plaid shirt, my Diana debacle outfit—I've never been superstitious and may actually dare the fates to try me again—tied a crew neck sweater around my waist, and set off for the Bravermans' house. Sunday night there was no show or activity at the recreation hall so Ben and his wife would likely be in. They rarely left the grounds of the hotel at night, even with their two sons gradually assuming control of the resort's operations.

The meteor showers of late August were easy to spot in the mountains when you were away from the lights of the hotel's buildings and the path to the Bravermans' residence was unlit. I saw several shooting stars but the thrill they usually gave was occluded by the dread of what might lie ahead with Sarah. The feelings of betrayal and hurt had damped the fires of the passion I imagined might rescue us from the collapse of the meaning of "us".

It was just after nine o'clock when I knocked on the Bravermans' front door. Ben answered almost immediately, a whiskey in hand.

"Melvin, what a surprise. I was expecting company, what is it you want?"

"Is Heidi here?"

"Heidi! First you tell me you're having fights with Harlan over Sarah and now you come to my house calling on Heidi? No, Heidi is not here, she's with Sarah in the arts and crafts shed. So which one do you want to see?"

"I want to see them both, but Sarah more than Heidi." I said, trying not to exclude his daughter completely while stating my more pressing mission.

"Well, you'll find them down there. Be sure to knock louder when you get there. They're both in no condition for surprises right now," he said, shutting the door without so much as a goodbye.

The day camp occupied a stretch of land along the northwest portion of the property away from the swimming pool, tennis courts and adult playgrounds. To walk there in the dark one relied upon the neatly tended wide dirt road that led from the swimming pool to the nature cabin; the art shed could be located next to the chicken coop behind the nature cabin. A small family of local raccoons had discovered the chickens and was removing them one by one for a while before Ben and his boys ambushed them and hung their tails up on the flag pole in the center of the camp. It was illegal to hunt raccoons but no one working there told the police. Ben treated his land and his animals the way an eighteenth century English Lord might, as if he was above the law. No, as if he was the law.

The shooting stars were brilliant in their course, their silence almost a surprise in the wake of the years spent imitating the whistle of descending bombs when the U.S. was at war. The chickens were asleep and the only sound was that of Sarah and Heidi talking and giggling in the distance. I hurried towards the shed, hopeful and fearful at the same time, eager to learn where we were—where I was with her and she with me, still unclear about what I was willing to forgive and whether she was even slightly interested in having to ask for my forgiveness. Though what she had done was wrong, hurtful and destructive, feeling humiliated herself by her actions could cause her to avoid me even if I did not reproach or berate her.

Upon reaching them the sounds I had mistaken for laughter grew louder. It was Heidi talking and crying, her voice breaking into a staccato that, from a distance, resembles some forms of laughter. The bitter sweetness of the approaching summer's end and its inevitable partings accompanied me into the cabin. Inside I saw Sarah with Heidi whose face bore the puffy effects of a long crying spell. I started in their direction, but Sarah shook her head vigorously and held up a single, cautioning finger. She leaned inward to say something in Heidi's ear and then came towards me. She too had been crying. Her mouth was drawn into a thin quivering line and her swollen eyes glimmered with the light reflected from her still unspilled tears.

"Don't stay here. Heidi needs to be alone with me."

"Does she know about . . . about what I know?"

"Some of it." I felt angry then. Why was she not telling me what she'd told Heidi? Was she hiding her secret still? Had she always hidden her feelings for Harlan behind her criticisms?

"That's why you don't want me here, isn't it, you're not giving him up that easily."

"I just don't want you here."

"You just don't want me, period." She said nothing but turned away and went back to Heidi who craned her neck around Sarah's body to look at me. I could tell that Sarah was speaking and when Heidi nodded her head, I left dreading that the all too familiar moment might come when Heidi would begin to laugh and I would be the butt of the joke. There was no longer any doubt; Sarah and I were over. What had given me the idea that it was my decision to either let the relationship heal or break it off? And what had become of the "I love you" she had sobbed just the other morning? The pain was new all over again and it was clear to me another night would pass without sleep. My eyes never sought the sky on the way back to my room. The moon could have fallen into the parking lot and I would have been oblivious.

I endured the last week in a state of grief. I saw Sarah around the hotel a few times, fleetingly, but we never spoke again. What was there to say? It would have been easier to repair Humpty Dumpty than to fix the "us" I thought we had been. Each night I isolated myself from all social activity by wearing a warm sweater and bringing "The Idiot" to a side porch of the hotel that supplied sufficient light to read by. I read the story with some labor until it captured my attention when I realized that I was more like Myshkin than Candide, more a good hearted young man than the total naif. Then, finishing the dinner meal and getting to my reading chair on the porch became an absorbing preoccupation. I had to see how the prince fared with this odd assembly of people, all so determinedly Russian. And when his story ended in heartbreak and tragedy I flung the book off the porch into the rhododendron bushes aligned in front and stormed away. I would be neither Myshkin nor Candide. I would refuse to be pathetic. The end of innocence is not the end of life, it is the beginning of maturity.

Chapter Thirteen

Labor Day weekend is and always has been the grand finale of the summer and so it was at Braverman's that summer of 1956. Every chair at every table in the dining room was occupied. Even Harlan's former station was filled to capacity.

"You see? There was a couple of hundred dollars you could have taken to college, my stubborn, steadfast, stalwart. The midnight supper on Sunday night often garners grateful guest gratuities." Sammy's alliterations had the urgent and frenzied quality of the final minute of a thirty minute long fireworks display.

"Let's just get through the next few days. Don't worry, I won't let you down, Sammy."

"I wanted you to have some extra money, that's all. First that college lets you down, then Sarah, at least the money might make you feel a little better." Young as I was I knew better than to believe that money, that green poultice, could relieve my pained heart.

The diners filed in soon after bringing with them an excess of ersatz gaiety. For the first time since the embarrassment of the Lion's Club weekend in June drinking glasses from the bar accumulated on the dinner tables throughout the dining room and bursts of strident laughter were everywhere, not just in the places where the young singles usually were clustered. It was going to be a long weekend. Sammy had none of his regulars at our station and while I buried myself in work he schmoozed his new clients, hoping to recruit new loyalists to his roster of returning vacationers. I was not charming or especially friendly and Sammy accounted for my peevishness by telling everyone I was having girl trouble. That seemed a completely reasonable explanation and led one man to hold forth on the necessity of the broken heart for the education and maturation of young men. It was all I could do to refrain from dropping my tray on his head.

The next morning Solly Schwartz once again skittered down the center aisle as soon as the French doors of the dining room had been parted. For eight long weeks Solly remained as eager and enthusiastic about breakfast as he'd been on the day he arrived and, while my irritation with him had not abated, I had not had another run in with him. Maybe it was because Sammy wouldn't have supported me a second time, maybe it was because the episode reminded me too much of the Diana debacle, maybe it just wasn't worth the aggravation. Each morning I filled his juice glass with grapefruit juice and left it at his place before the doors were opened. I once asked him if he would want a different juice, fresh squeezed orange juice, tomato juice, or even prune juice.

"Oh no," he said emphatically, "I like the bite of the grapefruit juice. It's a little bit bitter, like life itself," he said with a smile. I'll give you something bitter, I said to myself, but never to him. One morning in the kitchen, early in the summer, I told Ron what Solly had said.

"A little Angostura bitters in his juice, if he likes it bitter," Ron suggested. "Or you could coat the glass with salad oil so when he picks it up it drops right through his fingers."

"Right, and he'd never think I was the one who did that. No thanks."

"Yeah, but if you really dislike this guy so much the grapefruit juice is an opportunity waiting for you to take advantage of it." Ron was right but there was nothing I was willing to resort to. So, having watched the morning ritual for scores of days, I was delighted when my patience was rewarded by the very mishap I had wished for every time Solly Schwartz lifted his juice glass from the plate, inspected its contents in the light, and raised it to his lips inverting it quickly to spill the bitter contents down his gullet. This morning it was especially bitter; something had interrupted his timing. Mrs. Schwartz, who had never appeared for breakfast at such an early hour but waited until we were half an hour away from closing the dining room to make her entry, stormed in and went directly to him. Just as he inverted his glass she yelled in his ear,

"Solly, you bastard!"

The juice splashed over his face, ran down his neck, washed over the coffee colored collar of his cafe au lait polo shirt, and landed on his two-toned brown and white shoes while Solly, trying to get out of the way of the cascading grapefruit juice, skipped and jumped backwards like a berserk dancer dancing in the wrong direction in a conga line. And all of this in seconds. The broad smile on my face was the first thing Solly saw when he wiped the stinging juice from his eyes and, disguising his embarrassment with a posture of moral outrage, he pointed a finger at me and demanded, "Don't just stand there grinning, you useless idiot, get me a towel to wipe my face with." Useless idiot. Those words extinguished my smile and tightened my resolve.

"Use this if you like," I said, tossing him the stained and damp side towel I kept tucked in my belt, "I think Mrs. Schwartz had something to say to you and I'd bet we'd all like to hear it. Mrs. Schwartz?" I said, nodding in her direction. Like an actor at a loss for words a flustered Mrs. Schwartz began to resort to "business", dabbing hastily at her husband's shirt with her flimsy handkerchief.

"Melvin, you should be more polite to your guests and give my husband a clean towel or a napkin, just get him something, please."

"What happened to the 'Solly you bastard' speech?" It was suddenly quiet in the near empty dining room. The other waiters and busboys, hearing me repeat Mrs. Schwartz's words, stopped what they were doing to watch this exchange play out while the few guests present, sensing something had gone out of control, looked nervously at one another. I had just violated the social contract of the dining room; in response to a verbal attack I had attacked back.

"C'mon Mrs. S, let's all hear it, let's hear what Solly did to get you so angry."

"Melvin!" Sammy called, not so much a summons as a warning.

"No, Sammy, stay out of this. It's between me and the Schwartzes." Ivan Goldman approached.

"Cool it down, Mel, this won't get you anyplace, what do you think this will accomplish? C'mon cool off," he said, laying an arm across my shoulders.

"I want an apology, damn it, I want some respect from this snail brained little pimp."

"Melvin!!!" Sammy shouted and then grabbed my arm to pull me away from the table where the Schwartzes stood, aghast at my outburst. "Get over here now!" he said, pulling at me, but I was stronger than Sammy and, resisting him, stood my ground.

"Melvin White, just what do you think you are doing?" Sandy Stein said, quick stepping his way down the center aisle to join the fray, his index finger already poised to be wagged in my face.

"I'm doing what every waiter and busboy who's ever been degraded by some pompous shmuck wants to do, I'm getting even."

"Not in my dining room you're not, you're fired."

"Wait a minute, Sandy, don't get carried away, not on Labor Day weekend, relax, I'll handle it," Sammy said, trying to soothe the irate martinet.

"No, it's all right Sammy, I quit, it's okay, I'm done for the summer. I quit. I don't want to be here anymore."

"You can't quit, not now, and you," he said pointing at Sandy Stein, "keep out of the business of running a dining room. You're here to make seating assignments not to boss the staff."

"I say he has to go. No one has the right to talk to a guest that way."

"And I said shut up! Go back to your desk and stop meddling in my affairs. That's it, end of story. And you calm down too, Solly, you didn't have to take it out on Melvin because your hand slipped," Sammy said patting Solly Schwartz affectionately. "So, everybody okay? Everybody satisfied? Can we all make up and say it's over?"

"I'm sorry Sammy, I meant what I said. I quit. I'm leaving today, this morning, right now."

Sammy was stunned. I doubt it was the first time a waiter or busboy walked off the job in the middle of a meal, but for me to do that, me, the youngest White brother, the good boy, the eager to please Melvin, that was a shock.

"Don't do this to me, Melvin, not now, not on this weekend, please."

"I'll finish breakfast, but that's it. And you look after Schwartz because if I do he'll need a bath towel not a napkin to wipe his face with." Solly Schwartz's face turned tomato juice red, and Mrs. Schwartz thrust her head back bringing her chin up to nose level and dabbed vigorously at Solly's neck with her scarf.

I was charming and witty and pleasant with the people at my tables and avoided eye contact with the Schwartzes who tried piercing my armor with their fierce stares while they muttered angrily to each other. Their table mates, hearing the story from Mrs. Schwartz who spoke loud enough to insure I heard it too, uncertain which side to align with ate small breakfasts and left quickly, relieved to get away from all of us. Sammy wouldn't speak to me at all trusting I could do my job without instruction at such a late date and I confess to feeling only a little guilt for leaving him stuck on the big weekend of summer's end, but I was ready to go. It was clear to me then that my outburst with the Schwartzes was fueled as much by my heartbreak with Sarah and the disappointments with school and Harlan as by the irritation of Solly's style. There was a need to break free of all that had confined and defined me. My choices had let me down and all that was left on the path to the future were defaults, choices I would not have willingly made. With twelve hundred dollars in my bank account in Liberty I could choose not to go to the school Steve and Jerry had attended. That money could support me while I figured out what to do about school, maybe travel or live in Greenwich Village or learn to play jazz piano, anything I chose.

I didn't try to collect the tips owed and no one offered to settle up that morning. Maybe they thought I'd change my mind, maybe they didn't believe I'd actually quit at such a late date, but I was through and the sense of relief and power was far greater than any guilt I might have regarding Sammy. Abe came towards me as I carried in my last bus box of dirty dishes and though I held up my hand to halt his approach, he would not be refused.

"You don't have to talk to me, but I want to say something to you. After you return home you will learn something that will make you very pleased. After you are done celebrating, think about treating people, everyone without exception, with kindness. That's it, Melvin, I'm sorry you are leaving like this but I understand your decision. So many disappointments." There was nothing for me to say. Whatever the surprise he predicted awaited me, I was fed up with him, and Rudy and Lenny, with this whole lot of misbegotten circus sideshow freaks that I'd worked with for an entire summer; fed up too with Ron, and Ivan and the basketball players and the other nameless waiters and busboys from the outer boroughs of New York City. Fed up even with Sammy, a sad and harmless man. At that moment there was nothing admirable, amusing, endearing or even touching about this pathetic hodgepodge of "characters".

Back in my room I was packing my clothing into the suitcase I'd laid on Harlan's bed—for me it would be Harlan's bed forever—when Ron came in from the bathroom.

"What's this about you quitting?"

"You were there, you saw what happened, I'm done. I've got one more thing to do here and then I'm going home."

"One more thing? What, collect your tips?" For once Ron was not sneering at me. The boldness of my act had earned me his respect.

"I don't expect to collect my tips for last week. I don't give a shit about the money. This is about Diana. I can't separate my bad experience with Solly Schwartz from my bad experience with Diana. I've settled up with Solly, and now I'm going to settle up with Diana."

"Settle what? She wasn't interested in you, she walked away from your date, she . . ." his tone was infused with his loss of respect.

"She said maybe another time. Well, this is another time. I'm going to walk over to her place and see what we can work out. Who knows? Maybe we'll check into Grossinger's for the weekend."

Ron shook his head from side to side in dismissive wonderment, but I shook my head to affirm my plan and said, "What have I got to lose?"

I called Malcolm from the pay phone in the canteen before leaving the hotel.

"Would Charles and Lillian mind if I spent a few nights with you?"

"What are you talking about, you know the Browns love you."

"I quit my job and I need a place to stay until we go home. Can I stay with you?"

"Of course, Mel, just stay out of sight during the day. It's so busy here they won't notice you at night. You quit on Labor Day weekend?"

"Yeah, it's a long story, I'll tell you later. Thanks."

I had been so focused on going to Diana's house and confronting her on what I thought were her terms I had given no thought to my appearance and found myself walking down the road in my white shirt and black pants, my bow tie still clipped to my shirt collar. I pulled the bow tie free and stuffed it into my pocket, hesitating only momentarily to consider returning to my room for a change of clothes, then rejecting that choice and continuing even more vigorously towards Diana's. It was a beautiful, sunny September morning, strokes of yellow and orange color caressed the tips of the tree top leaves; the air was mild and dry.

When Diana's house came into view I felt my heart begin to race. What if she had left the area and someone else was living in the house, what if she had someone else there with her, what if she laughed when she saw me or told me to get the hell away from her, what if, what if, what if? I pinched the skin on my forearm to disrupt this craven monologue. "The good things in life you have to seek out and reach for," echoed somewhere in my mind. I knocked on Diana's front door and waited for a response.

"Who's there?" She was there.

"I'm here."

"Funny. Who the hell are *you*?"

"White collection agency."

"What? What kind of collection agency?"

"Open up, Diana, I'm here to collect a date, I mean a debt."
The door opened wide and Diana stood there, her hands on her
hips. The frown that had drawn the corners of her mouth down
slowly faded and a smile flickered into its place as she turned her
head to avert her eyes.

"How's your back?" she said, a touch sarcastic. I smiled.
When I didn't answer her she said, "Did you say 'debt' or 'date'?"

"I think I said both." She was the sexiest girl I'd ever seen.
Standing in the doorway, wearing a simple polo shirt and jeans,
she exuded a stunning, effortless sensuality that rendered me
helpless. Too bad it didn't make me speechless. "Remember?
You'd said, 'maybe another time,' so, there's no time like the present." If I could have disappeared right then I no doubt would
have, but of course I didn't, and reminding myself that nothing
worth knowing can be taught, I forgave myself with the assur-
ance I was embarking on my course of study about Diana and all
of the Dianas of the world.

"Is your back acting up again, you look funny."

If she was trying to bring us back to that pathetic night by
the lake she had to be stopped. I was determined not to suc-
cumb to fear or any impulse to hesitate or be anything less
than audacious.

"You know, it's really beautiful out here, why don't you
come out on the porch with me or let's take a walk or drive someplace peaceful."

"Don't you have to get back to the dining room now for the
lunch meal?"

"As a matter of fact I don't, I quit this morning." Her eyebrows flew up in surprise.

"You quit on the Saturday of Labor Day weekend? I don't believe you," she said motioning me into her house. "Nobody quits
on this weekend. They get fired sometimes, but nobody quits."

"Well, Diana, as you well know, we Marines are not like
everybody else." That spun her around.

"You really are going to sign up?" I nodded. "You know
when you told me that the time you came here with Ron, I
thought you were just some Joe College bullshitter lying to me.

I'm sorry, I don't know what to say, I apologize. Where did you go to enlist, Monticello?"

"If that's where the nearest recruiting office is we can go together, today."

"Do you want a drink of something, a beer or something?"

"Sure." We stood face to face in her little living room. I smiled at her. "God, you are something."

"Yeah, that's what they say."

"Uh uh, that's what I say," I said, taking her hand. She looked down at our joined hands.

"What about the Marines, changing your mind?" She pulled her hand away.

"Hey, hey, that was you talking, I never said I wasn't ready to go to Monticello."

"Just checking," she said pressing herself against me as she had on the back stairs so long before,

"I'm just checking."

"Well, a girl like you can never be too careful," I said, reaching an arm around her.

Epilogue

In those days the future lay on the horizon sparkling like a glorious fountain spilling showers of hope in crystalline light. Back then I did not realize I had already walked into the future; that the future is always now, this minute, this experience.

That last weekend Diana became my future for three days. The U.S. Marine recruiting center in Monticello was closed by the time we arrived there. Diana had insisted on making lunch and telling me about her unhappy romance that had led her into Ron's path. Had it been open, and that would not happen for several more days with the next day Sunday and Labor Day following on Monday, I could have signed up knowing that at the physical I'd be rejected for my heart murmur, a harmless cardiac whisper that disabled me not at all but which my doctor said would exclude me from the Selective Service system. With that still undisclosed to Diana, and each of us needing the comfort of another's warm body, the weekend was everything I had wished for from a woman all summer. A gentleman does not give details. Suffice it to say it was and remains unforgettable.

When I returned home there was a letter from Columbia waiting for me. They had never told me there was still one more waiting list, the list of desirable alternates should someone drop out of the freshman class before school begins, and I was first on that list. Was I still interested in joining the class? While exhilarated and rejoicing I could not help but ponder if this was Abe Melman's magic, a lamedvovnik racing to my rescue at the eleventh hour. Was this the surprise he had forecast? I will never know the answer, but out of respect for Abe, even if his real name was Bernard, from that moment I have always tried to treat everyone with kindness.